Lockett's Innocence

A Novel by

T.J. Johnston

James Lockett Novels

Volume I

Johnston, T.J.

Lockett's Innocence: a novel / by T.J. Johnston

ISBN 979-8-99919384-0-2

1. Michigan—Tennessee--History—Civil War, 1861-1865—Fiction. 2. Shiloh, Battle of, 1862—Fiction. 3. Fort Donelson, Battle of,—1862—Fiction. 4. Army of the Cumberland—Fiction. I. Title. II. Series: Johnston, T.J. James Lockett novels.

Praise for the James Lockett series

"Johnston has fashioned a story that Civil War buffs and re-enactors will relish... a promising series."

– The Grand Rapids Press

"Excels at juxtaposing military encounters and action with matters of the heart and challenges to moral and ethical beliefs."

– The Midwest Book Review

"... research into the events around which the story took place was well done... a believable character... He's someone who makes moral decisions because it is the right thing to do. Yet, they all come with a price. I found myself hoping for Lockett as each new situation developed."

– Fredricksburg Civil War Roundtable

"Remarkably accurate descriptions of how soldiers lived and fought... descriptions of combat set this series apart... One does not need to be a Civil War scholar to appreciate Johnston's work.... a thriller... readers will learn quite a lot about how the American Civil War was fought and enjoy doing it."

– Baton Rouge Civil War Roundtable

"Johnston has done his scholarly homework and Civil War buffs will appreciate these authentic details that are interwoven with poignant plots and subplots, vivid descriptions of his characters, colorful dialogue, and moral and ethical struggles… an authentic and entertaining read.

– The Epoch Times

"… truly immersive, and the pages practically turn themselves as you can't help but read one more chapter… Five Stars… Highly Recommended Award of Excellence."

–The Historical Fiction Company

The James Lockett Civil War Series in Chronological Order

Volume I

Lockett's Innocence

(Missouri, Fort Donelson, and Shiloh)

Volume II

Lockett's Betrayal

(Aftermath of Shiloh)

Volume III

Lockett's Crucible

(Perryville and Stones River)

Volume IV

Lockett and the Devil's Path

(Hoover's Gap)

Foreword

They say that the longest journey begins with the first small step. Such is the case for James Lockett. He left Kalamazoo with a simple understanding of the world and those who live in it.

He thought that his boyhood friends had no idea what they were getting themselves into or the possible horror that awaited them. But as the reader will see throughout the series, he is fooling himself. No one is more oblivious to what they are getting themselves into than Lockett himself.

While he always thought that his friends saw things in simplistic black-and-white, even Lockett had no idea how gray the world could be.

Each step of the journey is an education.

And despite it all, at his core, there are still a couple of unshakable pillars that he holds dear.

-I-
The Boys From Kalamazoo

-II-
Separate Paths To…

-III-
…Shiloh

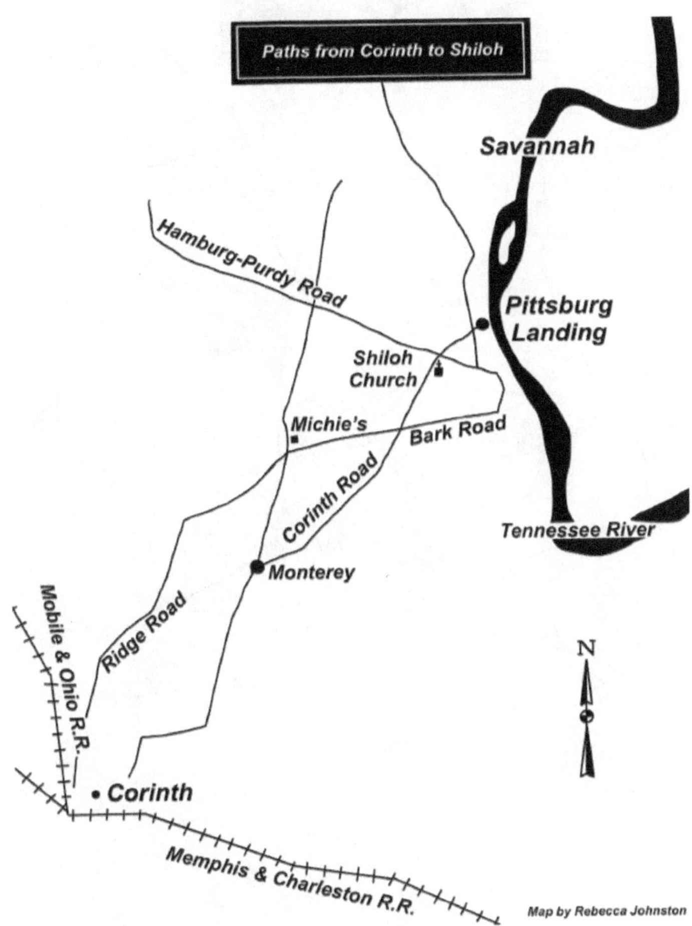
Paths from Corinth to Shiloh
Savannah
Hamburg-Purdy Road
Pittsburg
Landing
Shiloh
Church
Michie's
Bark Road
Corinth Road
Tennessee River
Monterey
Mobile & Ohio R.R.
Ridge Road
N
Corinth
Memphis & Charleston R.R.
Map by Rebecca Johnston

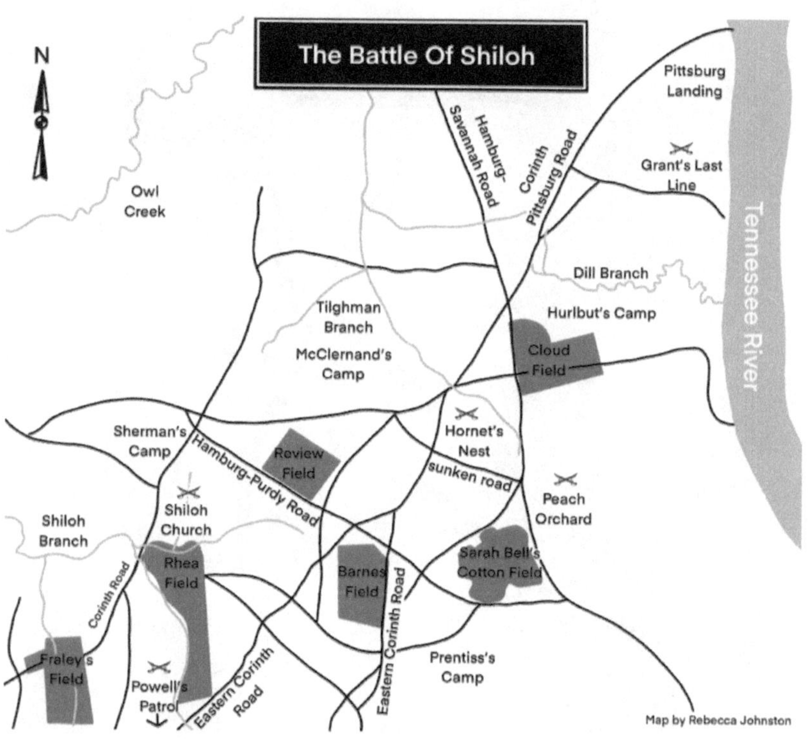
The Battle Of Shiloh
N
Owl Creek
Hamburg-Savannah Road
Corinth Pittsburg Road
Pittsburg Landing
Grant's Last Line
Tennessee River
Dill Branch
Hurlbut's Camp
Tilghman Branch
McClernand's Camp
Cloud Field
Hornet's Nest
Sherman's Camp
Hamburg-Purdy Road
Review Field
sunken road
Peach Orchard
Shiloh Branch
Shiloh Church
Rhea Field
Corinth Road
Barnes Field
Eastern Corinth Road
Sarah Bell's Cotton Field
Fraley's Field
Powell's Patrol
Eastern Corinth Road
Prentiss's Camp
Map by Rebecca Johnston

-I-

The Boys From Kalamazoo

Chapter 1

April 6, 1862

"Do I look like that right now?" he wondered to himself as he stared at his friend, James Lockett.

He knew that he wasn't as tall or as lean, and Lockett's brown hair bore no resemblance to his own red hair. But the question was not about the physical characteristics as much as it was about the stoic façade, in spite of what was about to happen.

James Lockett's youthful face stared calmly across the thicket at the terrifying mass of Confederates. His eyes narrowed momentarily as something caught his attention, exaggerating the premature crow's feet that had crept into the corners of his eyes over the past few months, but he still appeared paradoxically calm. Even the unnaturally deep furrows across his brow seemed less pronounced than usual at this moment.

Patrick McManus ran a hand across the back of his neck and through his thick red hair. He knew that he felt fear at this moment, but James showed nothing similar.

And then he saw it. Yes, there it was, ever so faintly in the tension of James's jaw muscles. A slight clench betrayed his worry, McManus realized.

Somehow, seeing the shared anxiety calmed McManus's own nerves.

Whatever was going to happen, would happen. It was largely out of their control now, much like most of the past six months had been. Oh, when they started out they were so foolish, confident even in their ability to change things, he reflected. The utter foolishness of youth!

No. No, that was not entirely fair to James, McManus reminded himself. For the rest of them, there was clearly blind oblivion for the trouble that awaited them, but James had an inkling from the beginning. He had tried to stop them from volunteering. McManus and the others had brushed that off as part of James's hard luck, overly cautious nature. Even so, there was no denying that James had been blind-sided more than once too.

So much had happened, and here they were…

James Lockett did not notice his friend's attention. His eyes were locked across the way.

The morning mist had nearly lifted when Sergeant James Lockett saw the first few heads appear across the wooded rise.

This time, they came as no surprise. They all heard the sound of 40,000 pairs of feet crashing through the forest. The steady crunch of sticks and underbrush beneath the Confederates echoed throughout the hollow. It sounded like hundreds of men being trampled upon, bones being snapped in two, but the noise was less unnerving than the fact that the earth itself seemed to tremor beneath the approach of the Confederate Army.

Lockett could swear that he felt the very ground quake, resonating up through the soles of his shoes into his feet, legs, and heart.

He stole a glance at his lifelong friend, Patrick McManus, standing shoulder to shoulder with him. They were part of a pitifully thin line of blue directly in front of the impending onslaught.

McManus's steadfast blue eyes, sunk deep into a sun-blotched Irish face, flickered back at him. As ever, he was steady, or at least appeared so. Lockett knew that they were both masking the swelling fear. Yet, the knowledge that Patrick stood next to him was oddly reassuring in spite of what was about to happen.

McManus was no longer the bull-like young man he had been when they started out just six months ago. Illness in Missouri and his own personal tragedy had seen to that, but he was still as dependable as ever.

He gave Lockett an almost imperceptible nod and turned his eyes back to the front, rifle already raised.

Across from them the enormous Confederate line reached the crest of the low wooded rise. They addressed their lines briefly, which might have given an onlooker the impression that the Rebels were hesitating, as if they had second thoughts about descending into and then out of the shallow hollow.

However, the actual impression on the soldiers in blue, the men from Peabody's Brigade, was quite the opposite. It seemed to them that the Rebels were trying to intimidate them with their sheer size, and they were doing a good job of it. A few Federals gasped at the awesome sight of so many men lined shoulder to shoulder, while others muttered prayers. The unfamiliar soldier next to Lockett took an uncertain step backward.

This was a sight that none of them had ever seen before, a sight never seen to date in the Western campaign of this War Between the States.

Two tightly packed lines of battle stretched in front of Lockett and his comrades. It was an army rumored to be 40,000 strong, and all of it seemed massed here, directly in front of Peabody's insignificant brigade of less than 3,000.

It was more men than Lockett had ever imagined.

When they had started out from Kalamazoo with 100 men… it had seemed like a lot at the time.

This Confederate line stretched out far beyond the reach of his eyes, disappearing into the branches of the thicket and the early morning gloom.

The unknown private next to Lockett took another step back, causing Lockett to turn and growl, "Steady!"

"But Sergeant…"

Lockett glared in response.

The private's eyes were as wide as saucers, but he did stop his backward shuffle.

The young private looked at the unfamiliar sergeant who had just addressed him with a menacing command that seemed strangely out of place with his physical appearance. Somewhat tall and lanky, the sergeant did seem to possess some wiry strength. He also had a grim, determined face and pale gray eyes, but the private never would have guessed that this sergeant possessed such a threatening voice. He dropped his gaze and reluctantly eased forward so that he was back to being shoulder to shoulder with the others.

Even though the soldier did not know who this sergeant was, he knew that he had been with the others who had first encountered this imposing Confederate army. Major Powell's little patrol had slowed the Confederates for an hour before being forced back to this position.

The private trembled, but he took solace in the knowledge that the sergeant next to him had already seen battle and lived to join them here.

What the private did not know was that this would be the third encounter of an already exhausting morning for James Lockett, Patrick McManus, and a few others from Major Powell's patrol. They had first laid eyes on the Confederates when their pre-dawn reconnaissance had bumped into the leading elements of this. After trading blows with skirmishers for a half hour, the patrol had been forced back by a tidal wave of Confederates.

General Grant's entire army had been caught by surprise. It was only a fluke that Major Powell's patrol had given them any warning. Were it not for that, the Union Army would literally have woken to find Rebel muskets pointed in their faces.

The Confederate line readied itself for the attack, packing itself in tightly, shoulder to shoulder. In some ways, it was a futile effort, for such cohesion would be impossible to maintain once they began marching through the heavy brush. Gaps would appear as men moved around trees and other obstacles. Still, as the Rebels stood on the rise across from them, it made for an imposing sight.

As Lockett peered down the length of his Dimick Deer Rifle, he realized that for the first time today he was getting a good look at the men who would be trying to kill him. His earlier scrapes had involved only pre-dawn silhouettes punctuated by blinding muzzle flashes and clouds of gun smoke mixed with the damp morning mist. He had only been aiming at the muzzle flashes then and shooting randomly into the smoky fog, but now Lockett could see that he was actually aiming at men, men who were not too different from himself.

That was one of the things that the last six months had taught him.

Gently, he gripped the barrel of his Dimick Deer Rifle. It was still warm.

His shooting eye sighted along the length of the octagonal barrel, knowing that the wall of mismatched gray, butternut, and homespun was within range for himself and Patrick. After all, they had started out as Sharpshooters and still carried their own Dimick Deer Rifles. The grooves inside the octagonal barrel put spin on the Minié ball, spiraling it so that it would cut through the air faster, straighter, and longer.

But the command to open fire had not yet come, and Lockett knew why. As he and Patrick had retreated from their earlier defensive position to their current one here with Peabody's men, he had realized right away that they were jumping in line with the new men from Wisconsin, and those boys all carried heavy Belgian muskets. The musket ball flying out of those smoothbore barrels would have no spin, at least no intentional spin. The range was much shorter than a Dimick, and the accuracy was similarly inferior. Who knew which way the musket ball would rattle out of the smoothbore… So they waited for the Rebels to get closer.

The tension was heavy in the air, and Lockett swore he could actually smell the fear – a noxious, vinegary scent. It was the first battle for these Wisconsin boys, the first for many in Peabody's Brigade. Even Lockett had to admit that today was his first *real* battle. The run-in with Missouri bushwhackers was no comparison to the line of battle in front of him.

"Fah-wahrd!" the command of one the Southern officers echoed across the hollow. The eerie quiet suddenly lurched into the sound of men moving again – broken underbrush, jangling canteens and cartridge boxes, and then an unnerving yip from across the way, the Rebel yell. Suddenly on the far left, the thunder and boom of cannon shattered the morning air. Most flinched at the noise that was so much deeper and louder than the sound of rifles and musketry.

BOOM! BOOM! BOOM! BOOM!

One by one, the cannon went.

His ears rang from the abuse, and he could no longer hear the unnerving sounds of the Confederate approach.

Still, he could feel the earth shake, not only from the cadence of 40,000 Rebels, more now whooping amidst the noise, but also from the Union cannon joining the fray.

It must be Hickenlooper's Ohio battery, he thought blankly.

A few Rebels fired their weapons, more out of fear and nerves than actual effect.

"Steady! Steady!" the order rang up and down the Union line.

Absurdly, Lockett realized at that moment that his precious journal was back in camp, next to his bedroll and the rest of his meager belongings. He felt a stinging sense of loss for a moment, but then he pushed aside the silly thoughts with harsh, silent words for his mental wanderings. He turned his attention back to the Rebels.

Anxiously, men gripped their rifles and muskets, their impatience growing with each step from the Confederates. To the left front of the Union line, a ghoulish yell rose up again from the Rebels, echoing in the Federals' ears. A few Rebels even raised their weapons over their heads triumphantly as they marched forward, full of defiance.

Lockett's hand tightened around the barrel to steady himself. Numbly, he aimed into the approaching wall of Confederates.

His mind screamed at him to open fire, but he resisted.

At one hundred and twenty yards, he finally heard the order reverberate down the length of their line, "*Fire!*"

The full Federal volley ripped through the air with one long, enormously brilliant flash. It blinded him for a second, and then the billowing smoke blurred his vision and stung his already reddened and irritated eyes. It was the first time that he had heard a brigade sized volley that wasn't aimed at him.

The blast tore into the Confederate line. Many of the shots were wild, slashing through the branches and leaves above the Rebels, but some of the shots smacked solidly into the advancing line, leaving men clutching chests, legs, arms, and necks as if in search of unseen protrusions. An entire section of the Confederate line broke and ran.

In the momentary stillness between cacophonies, he could faintly hear a few voices yelling, "Retreat! Run!" as they ran.

But most of the Confederates did not run. The volley had staggered them, and they seemed confused, but they did not run, rather they slowly inched backwards. The cannon continued its thunder, and then the Rebels fell back behind the low rise.

A few Union soldiers cheered, including the private next to him, but Lockett shot him a nasty glare.

The Rebels had been stunned, but they were only gathering themselves. How many times have I seen this already today, he wondered as he began to reload, and it's not even mid-morning yet!

Hickenlooper's cannon to their left roared again and then slowly began to lessen its pace. The artillery had given the Rebels second thoughts, but he knew that wasn't the last of it. There were too many Rebels and too few cannon.

"Who's to our left?" he asked the private. The man was still shaking from his first taste of battle, however abbreviated it was.

"Miller's Brigade and Hickenlooper's battery, I imagine."

The soldier, who Lockett now noticed was really just a boy, replied in a tight voice, unable to prevent the high-pitched squeak at the end of his response.

"How about to our right?" McManus asked, as he finished ramming another Minié ball home.

"Our right?" the boy asked with a puzzled look, "No one, I guess."

McManus looked at Lockett with little more than a shrug, already knowing their piecemeal defense would be no match for the long Confederate line of battle. It was only a matter of time before both flanks were overlapped. Where were General Sherman and his men?

"Best reload, friend," McManus said to the private as he slid his ramrod back down into place beneath the barrel of his Dimick, "They'll be back in a minute."

He was right. A few minutes later, the Confederates appeared at the crest of the low hollow again, and this time they meant business, Lockett thought. There was no pausing at the crest to realign. They simply came over the rise and continued advancing.

The Union fire was less directed. Rifles and muskets spat out at the Rebels well before 120 yards this time, but it did not slow them. The massive front moved toward them… 175 yards out… 150…

Lockett had already fired when they were 175 yards out, which he knew was a mistake afterward. Although, he was confident that his aim was true, his action encouraged the Wisconsin boys around him to also open fire with their Belgian muskets, and from that range, they did no damage.

He rushed to reload, working through the familiar process.

Looking up into the gray gun smoke, he saw a Confederate officer among his men, yelling something that could not be heard above the deafening din. With his gray uniform trimmed in gold braid, a broad-rimmed officer's hat, and gleaming saber, the officer cut quite a contrast to his rag-tag men. Suddenly, the Confederate officer slashed his sword downward, and Lockett knew what the order had been.

He saw the flash of hundreds of Confederate rifles and muskets.

In that split second, his mind spun faster than he ever could have imagined. The last six months exploded into his head in detail. He remembered the fateful day that he had volunteered with the others to join the Kalamazoo Sharpshooters. He remembered the life-changing experiences in Missouri fighting his own officers as much as the bushwhackers. He remembered his own odd path to a place as a sergeant in the 12th Michigan.

Six months that seemed like a lifetime, all leading him here...

Chapter 2

November 15, 1861
Kalamazoo, Michigan

"You have to promise me."

She looked at him with such earnest pleading in her eyes that he found himself speechless.

"Promise me, James!"

In all of the years that James Lockett had known her, this was the first time that he could ever remember her taking such a tone, with him or with anyone else for that matter, and because of that, he found himself utterly speechless. He stared back blankly at the small, young woman. Wisps of her thin brown hair blew freely in the cold breeze, and she tucked them back under her bonnet.

"Well, say something!" she demanded, her thin hands on her hips.

He didn't bother to hide his befuddled wonder at her request, or at the commanding way that she put it. In the ten years that he had seen her day in and day out in that one room schoolhouse, she had rarely uttered any words, and never with such force. She was as quiet and unassuming as any person that he had ever known. 'Mousy' is what most of their classmates called her, all except one.

"I… I don't know what to say," he stammered.

He looked around for some relief, but there was no one nearby. There was not another soul, just the two of them. The massing crowd was gathered at the opposite end of this Kalamazoo street. The hint of possible impropriety between the two of them standing there alone was the least of his problems though.

"Shouldn't you be asking Patrick this? I mean, he is your husband after all." He shook his head. He had never understood what his closest friend saw in her to begin with.

Maybe it was this firmer side to Martha Murphy, now McManus, that no one else had ever guessed possible? No one except Patrick perhaps?

She stood before him today like a brick wall. She wasn't going to take 'no' for an answer.

"You promise me that you won't let him sign up! I know that is what Congressman Vincent and the others want from this speech, and you know Patrick. He'll follow his friends!"

"I mean, I don't think so, Martha. I mean, I'm not signing up. I doubt most of the others will either. It's mostly talk."

"You heard Patrick yesterday, same as I did! Didn't that sound like he was intending to volunteer?"

"I, well," Lockett hesitated, knowing that there was some truth to what she said, but it had not occurred to him until now that it was anything more than boastful words. "I don't think so… I mean, he has you… and the farm. He can't volunteer." Even as he uttered the words, he realized that he was trying to convince himself more than anything else. It didn't ring true to him now that he heard the words aloud. Maybe Patrick did intend to sign up?

Martha glared sternly at him. Again, she made an impression on him that he had not thought possible before today.

"It wouldn't make sense," he managed, although his own voice sounded skeptical now.

"You're talking about an Irishman making sense? Over his heart?" she pointed out.

"Ah, but his heart is with you," Lockett countered, sounding more reassured now, "Patrick indeed loves you. There is not a doubt in the world about that."

He knew that for a fact, and the words tempered Martha's flushed cheeks, or so he wanted to believe.

"Just promise me, James. You are his oldest and dearest friend. If he'll listen to anybody, he'll listen to you!"

Lockett looked at her expectant face. He wanted to agree.

And she was right about one thing. He was Patrick's oldest friend.

Should he just utter his concurrence? After all, he doubted

that Patrick would really leave his young bride to go off and fight. It wasn't much to promise in that case, right?

But he struggled to make the commitment.

A man's word meant everything to James Lockett. The world might have its failings, and often meant nothing but unavoidable heartache, but a man always had his word. A man could always fall back on the reassurance of honoring his own promises. If nothing else, that was within a man's own control. His father had impressed that upon him in no uncertain terms before he had unexpectedly passed on, and Lockett held that lesson close to his heart.

And because of that significance, he wavered.

This was not his promise to make. As much as he wanted to reassure Martha, the choice at the end was Patrick's, and no sworn commitment from him could override the simple fact that it was Patrick's choice.

"James?" she pleaded once more. "Please, James!"

For all of the years that he had known Martha, he doubted that he had ever had such a long conversation with her, and certainly, never one with such earnest emotion. He was unaccustomed to the heart-wrought imploring.

She looked at him with moistening blue eyes, just on the edge of weeping.

"Alright, alright," he said hastily before he could stop himself.

The relief on her face was unmistakable, which only made his stumbling thoughts more jumbled as he realized what had come out of his mouth. He had not meant to agree to the promise, but there it was, out in the open now!

"I… I guess I can talk to him before it's too late."

"Thank you!" she cried with her head bobbing. "He'll listen to you! I know he will!"

"C'mon," Lockett replied, trying to keep the hint of grumbling from his voice, "We better hurry or we'll miss all of the Congressman's speech. I'm sure that there will be many lining up to volunteer afterwards."

"... our esteemed representative in Lansing, state

Congressman Charles Vincent!"

The applause erupted in the cool November air, and it struck some in the crowd that the ovation for Charles Vincent was greater than the reception Kalamazoo had given the unknown Abraham Lincoln only two short years ago.

Back then, Kalamazoo had listened attentively to Lincoln with polite, nodding heads.

But now, the talk of *action*, embodied in the refined figure of Congressman Vincent, stirred the crowd's enthusiasm. They were unleashed, unabashed! They were ready for this message!

As young Daniel Lockett watched the goings-on with devoted earnestness, he wondered if Lincoln himself would have received such a reception today, something as loud as Charles Vincent had received.

Was it the man, the message, or the mood?

And where was his older brother, James? James was a dour stick-in-the-mud, but he still expected his brother to be here today. Everyone else in Kalamazoo County was after all.

Congressman Vincent tried to wave the still cheering crowd to silence, although it was only a half-hearted attempt as he relished their welcome. The motions brought Daniel Lockett's thoughts back to his original question on Lincoln and the difference in enthusiasm.

Of course, Abraham Lincoln was the President of the entire country now, but Daniel Lockett still wondered if Lincoln could generate this type of reaction.

The country was now at war with itself, and while a wildly contagious fervor had swept through Michigan, stories of defeat out east in far off Virginia made many in this small farming and logging community bridle. They were anxious for action! For battle!

Certainly, President Lincoln would be warmly received again in this anti-slavery hotbed, Daniel thought to himself. Yet, if the President shared the stage with Congressman Vincent, the tall gaunt President would without a doubt pale in comparison to the confident and handsome Charles Vincent. It seemed that Abraham Lincoln and Charles Vincent had nothing in common other than their loyalty to the Union.

Daniel remembered Lincoln to be so unusually tall, almost all limbs, although he did not move with the awkwardness that one would assume from someone so tall and angular. In contrast, Charles Vincent was of average height, but he had an unusually long torso and when combined with his habitually puffed out chest and short legs, he gave the impression of being much shorter than he was.

Still, it was Congressman Vincent's unrelenting enthusiasm and confidence that set him apart. He was born to command the attention of a crowd of people. Oh, to be like Congressman Vincent! Daniel thought to himself excitedly.

Congressman Vincent surveyed the large crowd that had gathered in front of the courthouse. Vincent knew that there were scarcely 25,000 people in all of Kalamazoo County, and as he smiled into the sea of expectant faces, it looked like half of the county now waited for him to speak.

They clustered together on the broad dirt strip that was Main Street, spilling out onto the wood planking sidewalk on both sides of the thoroughfare, from Gibson & Brothers Dry Goods to the Burdick Hotel. A few even leaned anxiously out on the second floor balconies above the shops, saloon, and hotel.

Vincent smiled, nodding at a familiar face in the crowd before turning to the powerful ring of businessmen and town founders who stood with him on the raised platform. They too applauded him gustily.

The state congressman paused to enjoy the moment. Perhaps only U.S. Senator Charles Stuart was more popular in Kalamazoo County.

As a fit-looking man of thirty-five with thick black hair, oiled back on the sides, Vincent knew that he cut a sharp contrast to the plump mayor who had just introduced him. Square-jawed, clean-shaven, and sharply dressed in his new brown suit, Charles Vincent knew that every pair of female eyes was on him, and that was the way he liked it.

"Thank you for that nice ovation," he began, waving them to silence again, "And thank you for coming today to hear this important message..."

His booming voice allowed all but those in the very rear to hear him.

As Daniel Lockett listened, he thought to himself that even a skeptic, like his brother, would have to admit that the man knew how to address a crowd. He was sure of that.

Daniel marveled at how the congressman kept the crowd's interest, almost toying with them. He waxed and waned on the topics of unity, slavery, the Founding Fathers, and business.

And yet, they all knew the main thrust was coming, the bottom line of why they were all here.

Like steam in a covered kettle, it just kept building, and the crowd waited for its moment to give their hearty approval. And finally…

"... as many of you know, fellow Michiganders in Van Buren and Berrien counties have already taken up arms." There was a small cheer from one corner of the crowd, and Vincent paused to let it play out. "And that is why I am here before you today. This Secessionist rebellion needs to be extinguished quickly! And there is no quicker way to squash these traitorous vermin than to bring the rifles of Kalamazoo County!" A throaty cheer sounded from a separate corner of the audience. "And so I come today looking for other courageous heroes to join me in forming a company of Kalamazoo Sharpshooters! I know the spirit is there. Why, some of you already signed up before I could even start today's call to action!"

This time, the entire crowd broke into applause. Daniel Lockett looked around, and every man, woman, and child seemed to be clapping with a devotion that must have made Reverend Bailey envious.

Five months earlier, the South had fired on Fort Sumter, and President Lincoln had called for the mobilization of state militias. The initial confidence of immediate victory had been dampened by the defeat at Bull Run during the summer, but as Daniel Lockett scanned those around him, all he saw were confident faces.

From the back of the crowd, many yards behind his brother, James Lockett had a clear view of the nodding heads in front of him. Vincent's message had obviously been well-received, but with the breeze strengthening, it was hard to hear everything Congressman Vincent was saying.

Lockett turned around and looked down the other end of Main Street. Empty, it looked rather like a ghost town, which was strange given the loud periodic cheering going on in the other direction. The stillness of normally bustling Kalamazoo was strangely unreal. His mind wandered as his eyes followed the dirt strip out of town and across a low, rising, grassy hill. Behind that hill, a few miles down the road and through a strand of birch trees was the Lockett farm.

He bit his lip, already feeling guilty about being here. His place was back on the farm, toiling in the earth like he did every day, trying to scrape together a living for the family – just as he had for so many years now. If it weren't for him, he wondered how they would have survived.

He bore the burden of the family mantle after his father had died five years ago. At times, it seemed like it was a lifetime ago, and at other times, it seemed like Pa had passed on yesterday… He could still hear his father's terrible hacking cough and smell the gut-twisting, deathly stench of the room. James Lockett was sure that the terrible odor would never go away.

How many times had he awoken in the middle of the night, sitting up in bed, that smell burning like an acid in his nostrils? How many times had he pounded his chest, wondering if he too would start a mysterious hacking cough that came from nowhere, a cough that wouldn't stop, a cough that kept going so that he thought his lungs would explode from his body?

But the cough was never there, and neither was Pa anymore.

Since then, it had been up to James Lockett to take care of his mother and his three younger brothers. He loved them all, but did they really understand how much he did for them? Daniel was the closest in age, but he seemed to have nothing in common with his older brother. Daniel was always sneaking off, laughing, trying to get out of work, forever talking. Nothing ever fazed Daniel. Nothing was ever serious for the curly-haired younger brother.

Often, James spoke to himself in the dying shadows of daylight while he struggled in the field. How could it be that he and Daniel came from the same seed? When would Daniel ever understand how serious work must be? Without it, they would starve.

James knew that he himself was quiet and somber, even his reflection in the pond behind the farm was always serious-eyed, always mirroring the same unblinking determination.

But I have to be, to get them by, he thought bitterly.

"He's done," Martha McManus interrupted his thoughts, tugging on his elbow.

Pivoting, Lockett was surprised to see that Congressman Vincent had finished his oratory. With the benefit of his height, which Martha did not have, Lockett could see that parts of the crowd were dispersing, and a line of men was already forming near the table at the end of the speaking platform.

"Let's go find Patrick," she urged, towing him along for the first few steps before he caught up and walked shoulder to shoulder with her, weaving through the crowd.

To his surprise, when they reached the speaker's platform, Patrick was not in line with the others. He stood off to the side, flanked by Matthew Bauer and a few other friends. He was laughing heartily at something that one of them said, and with an inward sigh of relief, Lockett took a breath.

Clearly, Patrick had the good sense that volunteering for the army was no place for a newly married young man with a farm to run. On the other hand, it was a little unexpected that Matthew was not in line. If there was any youthful adventurer among them, it was Matthew.

"James! Martha!" McManus called out, spotting them.

"Quite the speech, eh? What do you think?" Matthew Bauer remarked excitedly, as each young man warmly shook hands with Lockett.

The youngest of the friends gave his characteristic eager

smile. With his smooth, whiskerless cheeks, Matthew Bauer looked far younger than his eighteen years. Thin boned with large hands and long limbs, he clearly had not grown into his body yet, but that had not stopped him from winning the marksmanship contest at last summer's county fair. There was no one better with a rifle in the county, and he basked in that knowledge.

"He's a good speaker," Lockett replied, knowing that he wasn't fully answering the question.

The red-haired McManus gave no reaction to his friend's reply. He had known James Lockett all his life and was accustomed to his coy, careful responses.

"What kind of answer is that? You're going to volunteer, aren't you?" Bauer said the last part with a hint of a challenge in his voice.

"That would be a terrible idea, and I don't see you in line either!" Martha McManus replied indignantly.

McManus and all those around him blinked in surprise. Other than Patrick, none had taken note that she was even there, and the fact that she said something stunned all of them. Mousy had always been as quiet as was implied by the nickname they had given her so many years ago. There was a strange silence as they all stared at her.

Finally, Matthew Bauer opened his mouth. "Not sure why you say that, Martha. Although I can tell you that I'm not in line for the simple reason that we all volunteered *before* the speech. Patrick and I were the first ones, in fact, to put our signatures on the line."

While his face was an impassive mask, Lockett trembled inside. Patrick had already volunteered? Martha was right! Dear God, what had Patrick done? Didn't any of them realize that this was not the casual parade that Congressman Vincent made it sound like. They had all seen the newspaper articles on Bull Run. They had seen the numbers of dead and wounded listed. This was surely not going to be over in a matter of weeks!

Yet, as he looked around at the others, Lockett began to wonder if he was the only one who thought that.

Martha's mouth hung open at Matthew's words. For a moment, there was a choking silence. Wide-eyed, she looked at her husband. For his part, Patrick lowered his gaze, unable to make eye contact with her.

When there was no response, she looked from him to Lockett. She said nothing, but her wide eyes implored him, 'Do something!' Lockett heard her thoughts as if they were said aloud.

But what could he do at this point? He was already too late! The damn fool had already put his promise down in writing. Patrick was going to war.

Lockett gaped back at her, searching hopelessly for some words to say, but there was utter silence amongst the entire group.

Unsure if he was more angry with himself, Patrick, or Martha for putting him in this position, Lockett yanked his gaze away. His eyes latched onto the line of men waiting to put their own signatures down. With a virtual howl, his eyes settled on Daniel's lithe frame in the middle of the line.

Startled by the sudden noise that Lockett made, the group followed his glare and quickly realized what prompted it.

"Now, James…" McManus began, but Lockett did not hear him as the older Lockett quickly stomped over to the younger brother.

Forgetting his own quandary, McManus watched his friend storm over to Daniel Lockett, comparing the two brothers as they stood side by side.

James and Daniel had always looked like different sides of the same oak leaf, one shiny and vibrant, the other dull, grayed, and weathered. It seemed that one had inherited all the seriousness, and the other all the humor, but Patrick McManus knew that this was misleading.

Despite all his grayness, James was actually good-natured and wryly humorous, as long as he wasn't thinking about the farm. James probably couldn't recall, but Patrick remembered what the elder Lockett brother had been like before his father's death. James Lockett wasn't really the limp-haired, weather-etched young face that he appeared to be. And behind those gray eyes, there was a mind that worked like the large clock above the Gibson & Bros. sign, never out of step and constantly whirling. That was James's problem, Patrick McManus thought. James was too smart for his own good. He was always thinking ahead.

Daniel Lockett on the other hand...

"Well, I'm going to volunteer. That should be pretty obvious since I am standing in this line," Daniel answered smartly to James.

"You're way too young, Daniel," James Lockett growled. He clenched a fist at his side, and it took all of his willpower not to lash out and take a swing at his carefree, younger brother. How he wanted to hit him right now! If his brother got killed, it would doom his mother. That was for certain. Daniel was the favorite, and in most ways, James could understand that without any bitterness. Daniel was handsome, lively, and quick-witted, always full of humor and optimism.

In the latter two characteristics, James knew that they were far apart.

"Well, you can't stop me, James. I'm volunteering and that's all there is to it."

The smug assuredness only irritated James Lockett all the more. This was a disaster! Not only had Patrick signed up for this insanity, so was his younger brother!

He was only one split second away from putting Daniel in a headlock and physically dragging him back to the farm where he belonged, but James Lockett stopped short of that. His coldly calculating nature burned a small hole through that emotion.

As satisfying as the headlock approach might be, it was only a temporary solution. There was nothing to stop Daniel from sneaking away in the middle of the night. James knew that he could not watch his brother's every movement; there was a farm to take care of in the meantime, and it was all his, given their mother's poor health and how young the youngest two Lockett boys were.

The farm could not take care of itself.

The line shuffled forward, moving Daniel closer to the table.

"You can't sign up, Daniel."

"You can't stop me, James."

"I already have," James Lockett answered darkly.

"What?" Daniel tilted his head at the answer. There was confusion, and for the first time, a pinprick in his certainty. "What do you mean?"

"I already have."

"What nonsense is this? What are you talking about?"

"Daniel," James Lockett said very slowly, "Someone has to take care of mother… and the farm… and your brothers." The younger brother was about to interrupt, so James Lockett plunged on more quickly.

He had not been able to honor his promise to Martha about stopping Patrick from signing up, but he could assuage some of her fears about Patrick staying safe, and at the same time, Lockett could make good on his own internal vow to keep Daniel out of the fray.

It was just one small white lie, which he could convert to a truth very shortly, without Daniel ever knowing the difference.

"You can't volunteer, Daniel, because *I already have*. It's up to you now to take care of mother and the farm."

"C'mon, Patrick," James Lockett said, "We best be getting back. Martha will be wondering where you are."

It would be dark soon, and he wanted to explain to Martha that he would watch out for Patrick.

After that, he would need to go back to the farm and talk to Daniel, who had left in a huff when it became clear to him that he could not volunteer, trapped by his older brother's pre-emptive action.

"She'll wait," McManus answered, turning back to the game of cards that he had started with Matthew Bauer and two other volunteers.

The sun was slowly sinking, but there was still plenty of activity around Main Street. Most of the volunteers still lingered. Their cocky voices carried easily across the crisp air. Some were familiar faces to Lockett, but most were not. He hadn't thought that the county was that big, but now he knew that he had been mistaken.

"You're a worrier, James," Bauer said with a smile. He looked particularly young sitting next to the thick-necked, burly McManus and the two other volunteers whose full beards made Matthew's smooth cheeks look particularly cherubic. Still, despite the obvious age difference, it didn't diffuse his confidence at all. With a pleased look, he laid a pair of aces on the crate they were using as a table.

"Again?" one of the men said disgustedly, getting up from his spot.

Though his eyes were watching the other losing hands being laid on the crate, Bauer added to Lockett, "You worry too much, James. You worry about your brothers, your farm, about Patrick, and probably a dozen things about me alone."

"Aye, there's plenty to worry about with you," McManus joked.

"Yes, but..."

"And James has to do all your worrying for you," McManus continued, "Because you were born without a worrying bone in your body."

Bauer looked up into Lockett's frowning face, knowing that he disapproved of card-playing, even the nearly stakeless version that they had just been engaged in. Lockett was about to speak when the sound of rapidly approaching hooves interrupted them. They all turned to look down the dusty street through the encroaching gloom of night.

"That looks like..." Bauer began.

"Luke?" Lockett finished with a puzzled voice.

The rider continued to urge on his mount with haste. Spotting the three of them, the rider veered in their direction, tufts of blond hair flapping in the wind beneath his hat as he pulled on the reins at the last second.

"Luke Bailey!" McManus bellowed happily, "You're back!"

"What are you doing here?" Lockett questioned in a

confused voice.

The tall, athletic Bailey dismounted and smiled broadly. Raw-boned, he was taller than both the bullish McManus and the lanky Lockett, and though the blond hair and blue eyes looked fittingly angelic for a preacher's son, he was surprisingly muscular and walked with an erect posture and confident gait.

Lockett often thought that Luke would cut an impressive figure behind the pulpit when he was done with his studies.

"You didn't think I'd let you boys go off to fight God's war without me?" Luke Bailey answered happily, shaking the extended hands.

"Welcome back, my friend," McManus laughed with a bear hug of Bailey.

"But what about your studies?"

"There will be time for that later, James. What? Not glad to see me?"

"Don't be ridiculous," Lockett said, snapping out of his confusion and shaking his hand.

They all laughed, looking more like little boys than like men on their way to war. Lockett studied the excited faces. It was a full blown epidemic. War fever had struck Kalamazoo County.

He supposed that it shouldn't surprise him. The rhetoric of Reverend Bailey and others had long since stirred up this county. He also decided that it shouldn't surprise him that Luke Bailey had left school to join the fight. Of all his friends, Luke was the most likely to join this battle. It sounded strange that the preacher's son would be the most likely to go off to war, but you only had to hear one of Reverend Bailey's sermons on the evils of slavery to know that there was nothing more central to the Bailey family's life than fighting slavery. They even aided fugitive slaves on their way to Canada, but that was a well-kept secret, lest the slavecatchers catch wind of it.

No, it was no surprise to Lockett that Luke was here to volunteer.

"Am I too late?" Bailey asked, "I was already on my way

back when I heard that Vincent was forming a company of volunteer riflemen. I hurried back as fast as old Burt would bring me."

"But you? A rifleman?" Bauer laughed, "That's a good one!"

"A good one indeed," McManus chimed in, "Have you ever picked up a gun, preacher boy?"

"Never needed to until now."

"I suppose Matthew can teach you a thing or two in a hurry," McManus chuckled, "After all those times we tried to get you to go hunting with us... Never thought I'd see the day."

"Never thought I'd see the day when we would rise up to rid this slaveholding scourge," Bailey declared with cold seriousness, "We will be God's sword."

Luke Bailey's words chilled Lockett, and he tried to brush it off.

Lockett's mother had often said that the issue of slavery was a black and white issue in the Bailey house, and she was not referring to skin color. There was a right and a wrong in the world, and Reverend Bailey left no confusion about which was which.

But '*God's sword?*' Lockett thought to himself. As he looked at the other volunteers, he guessed that some of the faces would have agreed with Luke Bailey. After all, many of them had heard the same sermons.

He could understand the sentiment towards slavery, yet for Lockett, his natural, calculating logic gave him doubt about the black-and-white of the world that Luke Bailey saw. It couldn't be that straightforward and simple.

Little did Lockett know how true those suspicions were.

Chapter 3

November 16, 1861

James Lockett shoveled the manure out of the barn. They only had one horse, but it didn't take long for it to build up. He turned around for another shovel full and saw Daniel standing in the entrance. The reddish orange hue of the dawn was framed behind him. Daniel's usually affable face was stone-like, save for the red cheeks that were caused by the morning chill. It didn't take much effort to figure out what was on his mind.

"You won't make a good soldier," Daniel blurted out.

"What?"

"I said, you won't make a good soldier. What do you know about fighting?"

"Fighting?"

"James, you know about shoveling manure and plowing the fields. What do you know about excitement and adventure? What do you know about fighting?"

"About as much as you, Daniel..."

"But," Daniel interrupted, "Your place is here."

"On the farm?" the elder Lockett finished for him, feeling his own anger rising.

"Yes, on..."

"On the farm, where I can keep this family together, Daniel? Where I can do the work of two men, because my lazy brother would rather fish down at the creek, or tease Mary Elizabeth Collins, or do anything other than work?" The words were spilling out of him faster than he could have imagined. "Is that what you're saying, Daniel? That my place is here?"

The intensity in his normally placid older brother took Daniel by surprise. While they had often argued, he had never seen his brother so charged with emotion, he had never heard his brother's true feelings come out in so naked of a form.

"Is that what you're saying, Daniel?"

Daniel gave no answer. Instead, he stood open-mouthed at his glaring brother for a moment. Then he turned and ran.

Alone in the barn, James Lockett answered his own question, "Because maybe you're right, Daniel. But how else do I protect you?"

I fear Patrick is making a terrible choice. On my way to gather him for drill, I overheard them arguing. A more shrill cry I have never heard. Martha is not well with this to put it mildly. But it is too late to change now. Patrick already signed the papers.

I should never have promised to stop him. Martha said nothing of my promise, but I can see it on her face when she looked at me.

The sound of her weeping makes me uneasy. Even when Father died, mother never cried. I suppose she did so for our benefit. She said before how guilty she feels that we must carry such a burden without a father.

But now I'm off to war. Perhaps Patrick is not the only one who makes impulsive decisions, but it was the only thing I could think of. It should work. With me gone, Daniel has to stay to take care of the farm, and he knows it.

--- the diary of James Lockett

November 18, 1861

"No, no, not like that," Matthew Bauer repeated to Luke Bailey, "Don't jerk back on the trigger so hard."

"Don't close your eyes either," Patrick McManus added unhelpfully with a laugh.

"Did I do that?" Bailey responded with embarrassment and exasperation.

"Try it again," Bauer said as soothingly as he could, "Squeeze it gently. When you jerk back like that, it goes high. It kicks high in any case and..."

It was turning out to be harder than expected to teach his friend to shoot straight.

"In your case, very high," McManus needled.

"Quiet," Bailey replied sourly, concentrating on the target. The large, hay filled sack swung lazily in the breeze as it dangled from a tree limb. "Look at it, it's moving," he complained.

McManus rolled backward in laughter. "I'll tell... them Southerners... to sit still for you... when we see'em," he laughed, struggling to get the words out between gasps.

The blond-haired preacher's son felt himself redden, and he forced himself to look down the long barrel of Matthew Bauer's Dimick Deer Rifle again, slowly going through the checklist that the others followed so routinely. He pulled the trigger, and the rifle kicked back fiercely into his shoulder. He knew he had long since bruised it, but he didn't care at this point. Though his friends were trying to teach him how to shoot without the other volunteers knowing, he knew that he was the laughingstock of the company. "What good is a rifleman who can't shoot?" he had heard one of them say.

He wished that he had learned to shoot a gun earlier, but it was the lack of improvement that irked him most.

With his eyes beginning to water from the gun smoke, he looked down at the swaying target.

"That was a better shot," Bauer said positively.

"What?"

"You were on line that time. At least I can see where this one hit the tree limb. That's a start."

"What? Where?"

The most frustrating part about this was that his aim was so bad that he hadn't even left a mark anywhere to give him a clue as to how close he was. Actually having hit something, anything, was an improvement.

"Aye," McManus said encouragingly, finally stilling his laughter, "That's a big improvement. You're just too high and a little to the right."

"I can fix that," Bailey replied, quickly reloading.

"There you are," a soft, feminine voice said from behind them.

"Martha!" McManus said in surprise, "What are you doing

here?"

They all eyed the large basket that she lugged with two hands.

"I thought everyone could use a good meal," she answered, rising on her tiptoes to kiss her husband as he took the heavy basket from her.

"Some army this will turn out to be," Bauer said, but smiling he added, "But as long as you're here, what do you have?" Despite his lithe frame, he was known for always being hungry.

"Plenty for all four of you," Martha replied. She looked around. "But where's James?"

"Off to find the latest rumors for us."

Crack!!!

Martha jumped at the sound, her already pale features blanched further.

Luke Bailey lowered his rifle and peered through the smoke. "Nothing!" he cried dejectedly.

"Time for a rest, Luke," McManus said, gently taking his wife's trembling hand.

They were partly through the meal when Lockett returned with two other volunteers, one young and one old.

They knew the younger one, Gus Jeltema, but the older one, Jeltema's Uncle George, was a stranger.

Old George VanderJagt had a thick, gnarled beard that grayed at the cheeks with isolated sprouts of gray appearing from his chin. Heavy creases lined his face above and below his eyes and around his thick nose. Much shorter than his nephew and with hunched shoulders, he gave an almost troll-like appearance.

The older man did most of the talking, in spite of the unlit, battered clay pipe that was between his teeth, and Lockett had learned a fair bit about him on the walk over. VanderJagt had a lot of opinions, but they did come from experience, not arrogance.

"There's little time to waste," VanderJagt had declared, "And there ain't a whole lot of organization here. Why, we should be practicing marching for hour upon hour, but all I see are a bunch of clueless men and boys loitering about. That will be a regret when the fighting starts, but mark my words, it will be too late by then."

"Uncle was in the army before," Gus Jeltema explained softly to Lockett.

The nephew was unusually tall and broad-shouldered, but in spite of his size, he was very quiet, like a gentle, blond giant.

VanderJagt nodded gravely. "Texas," he said simply.

"You're from Texas?" Lockett asked. The man did have an odd accent that he could not place.

"No, from Kaintuck, but that was many years ago. Moved 'round most of my life and spent a good while in Texas. Came here eight months 'go, to go into business with my brother-in-law, but it didn't work out. Don't got no head for business, unlike my poor brother-in-law. I was a terrible burden to him. Then, all this happen'd. Fig-gured it was time to go back to what I know, the only thing I know."

"What's that?"

"The army life, of course, boy. Ole army blue."

"You were fighting the Mexicans in Texas?"

"Yup, fought'em when I was even youn'er 'n you. Stayed with the army another eight years before I wen' back to Texas to try farmin'. Worse at farmin' than I am at business!" he cackled loudly.

At that point, they reached the small gathering where Lockett's friends sat on the ground, eating.

"James!" McManus greeted cheerily.

VanderJagt scowled and slowly gestured at the group on the ground.

"Like I said, most ain't got no idea what is about to happen. A picnic?"

"A man's got to eat," McManus said defensively.

"Ain't got no prob'm with that, and you should enjoy decent food while you can. God knows that you won't get much of that from the army. Mark my words on that, but time is running short. Ole Vincent says that we move out in less than a week, and you all ain't ready by any means."

"Don't know who you are, mister," Matthew Bauer answered, "But we're the best shots in this part of the state. We're more than ready."

VanderJagt snorted in amusement at the statement. He took the unlit pipe from his mouth and stifled his first words. Taking a moment to carefully select the right words, he said, "You ain't even close to being ready."

"What are you saying? You think that we are all going to get killed and sent home in pine boxes. You've never seen us shoot."

With surprising patience, VanderJagt shook his head slowly. "Like I said, you don't know the first thing. Killed, yes, but no one gets sent home in a pine box. Ain't gonna be time for that. You'll be buried out there, wherever there is, far from home. Not many get sent home in a pine box in war. You ain't a general. Thems the only ones who get sent home."

There was no sound from her, but Lockett couldn't help but notice Martha's blue eyes widen while her cheeks lost their color.

Unfazed, Bauer retorted, "I think you need to see a demonstration of our marksmanship."

"Your aim ain't half of it," VanderJagt replied, coldly serious.

The others sat stiffly, unsure if they understood what he was getting at.

"Ain't half of it? You ain't seen me shoot yet, old man. I'll take the eye out of a squirrel from 200 yards."

"T'at a fact, boy?" VanderJagt scowled.

"It is."

"A lil' contest then?"

"Contest?" Bauer answered with a sly smile, "I'm always ready for a contest."

"Gus!" VanderJagt called to the large lad with the shock of hair nearly as blond as Luke Bailey's.

It struck Lockett that the voice was louder than the rest of the old man's words and had taken on more of a commanding tone.

"My nephew, Gus Jeltema," VanderJagt explained,

"Promised my sister I'd look after 'im."

The words made Lockett flinch, and unbidden, his eyes flitted over to Patrick's wife. The words had clearly struck a similar chord with Martha because she stared right back at him.

Bauer looked up at Jeltema's pleasant Dutch boy face. But the rest of Gus Jeltema could not be confused as boyish. He was a giant with thick shoulders and long legs as wide as tree trunks.

"We're goin' have a lil' contest with Bauer here," VanderJagt continued. Taking his nephew aside, VanderJagt pulled on the man's shoulder until he was down to his uncle's height. The old man gave Matthew Bauer one last look and then whispered into his nephew's ear. He handed his nephew his own rifle and unslung his haversack as well, passing it over to the young man.

Jeltema straightened up and looked at his uncle with an uncomprehending stare and then stole a glance at Matthew Bauer. A second look at his uncle's scowling face seemed to erase the indecision, and Jeltema marched off.

"Where's he going?" Bauer asked.

VanderJagt ignored the question. "I see you already got a target out there." He pointed to the hay filled sack that Luke had been practicing on, which was about sixty yards away.

Bauer smirked, "That's easy. Too easy. Anyone can hit that, especially from this range."

"You git to prove it."

"C'mon. At least make it a challenge."

"You ain't heard what the contest is."

"What? Your nephew has to hit it too? From a hundred yards further away? What kind of contest is that? I don't need no head start."

"That's not my nephew's target," VanderJagt said darkly. "I would have Gus start out next to that sack, but I ain't sure about your aim yet… or your calm."

They all gave the older man a puzzled look.

"Would you say Gussie is about as far away from you now as that hay target is?"

Bauer nodded.

"Stop there, Gussie!" VanderJagt called out to his nephew. "That's far enough."

He nodded towards his nephew who took out a long, gleaming bayonet. With a questioning glance, Gus Jeltema hesitated, but prodded by another nod from his uncle, Jeltema fit the bayonet over the rifle.

Unaware of what was going on behind him, Matthew Bauer picked up his own rifle and began loading it, pinching a percussion cap onto the nub after he finished loading.

"You need to hit the target twice, boy," VanderJagt said. He looked at the others. "You all need to step back now."

Lockett froze in place. He wasn't sure what he was seeing, but unlike the others, he had a vague and unsettling idea of what the contest really was.

Matthew Bauer looked over his shoulder and saw the bayonet on Jeltema's rifle for the first time. "Is he already loaded?" Bauer asked with dual confusion. The real question on his mind was why put on the bayonet for a shooting contest? It would throw off the balance. It made no sense. "He's going to hit the sack from there? With a bayonet on?"

"He's not loaded, and the sack is not his target… you are. He'll stop when you've hit the target twice."

VanderJagt raised his arm, and swung it down while yelling, "Go!"

"What?"

"Hurry, boy! It's a race!"

Dazed, Bauer's movements were slow.

"You best hit that twice before he gets here," VanderJagt said calmly.

Bauer blinked in surprise and took his first shot at the target, easily hitting it.

"Hurry, boy, hurry!"

Bauer rushed to grab his powder flask, dropping it in his haste. He quickly picked it up and poured the powder down the muzzle. Next was the bullet. He looked up as he withdrew the ramrod, stuffing it all down the barrel. Jeltema was nearly upon him.

The big Dutchman pounded across the dried out November

grass like a whipped ox. Bauer could hear the panting breaths come nearer as he raised the rifle.

The nephew stabbed the ground, and the long, two-foot spike bayonet buried itself in the dirt next to Matthew Bauer.

Bauer yelped and tottered to the other side. He glared first at the nephew and then at the uncle.

"You could have killed me!" he snapped, leaping to his feet, swinging his rifle around on the older man.

Patrick McManus and Luke Bailey were frozen in place, but not Lockett. He immediately jumped between Bauer and VanderJagt, bracing himself with a firm hand in Bauer's chest. "Stop, Matthew!"

"Back up, James," old VanderJagt ordered steadily.

Lockett ignored him and used his other hand to lower Matthew's rifle so that it wasn't pointing at VanderJagt.

"I said, back up!" VanderJagt snarled.

Lockett looked over at him. Was the man insane? Was he trying to get himself killed right here?

"I'll not tell you again, Lockett!"

Lockett took his hand from Matthew Bauer's rifle barrel, but he did not stand back. Bauer kept the rifle aimed at the ground, and Lockett made sure that he was still within range to snatch at the rifle barrel if that changed.

The uneasy silence did not last long as VanderJagt stared harshly at Matthew Bauer. "Go on, boy, raise that rifle."

"Now wait!" Lockett insisted, moving a precautionary hand toward the rifle, although Matthew had not moved it.

VanderJagt shook his head angrily and stepped close to them. With both hands, VanderJagt grabbed the barrel and raised it until it was pointed square in the middle of VanderJagt's own chest.

"Pull the trigger!" he dared.

"Are you crazy?" Lockett cried.

Matthew Bauer said nothing and stared wild-eyed at the old man across from him.

"Go on! Pull the trigger!" VanderJagt urged with a deranged delight.

For a long moment, no one said a word or moved an inch.

Finally, Bauer slowly took his right hand and raised it so that it was far away from the trigger.

With that, VanderJagt ripped Bauer's rifle from his grasp and aimed it at the sky.

He pulled the trigger, but there was no crack, just the gentle clack of the hammer falling. He pulled the hammer back and did it again. Again, nothing.

He handed the weapon back to Matthew Bauer's quivering hands.

"No percussion cap. You forgot the percussion cap in your haste. Let that be a lesson, son. Fightin' is more like a race than target shooting." He turned to address his words to all of them. "What you think you know now, you'll forget once the battle starts. It's amazing how cluttered a man's mind gets in that first battle. You'll see. Mark my words."

November 19, 1861

They had all heard this morning that Captain Vincent had insisted that the old soldier, George VanderJagt, be appointed sergeant. Foregoing the normal process of having the men vote on their sergeant did not sit well with most of the volunteers, but Lockett had to admit that it made sense in this case.

While he did not care for VanderJagt's methods, the old soldier knew more about this than the rest of them put together. Although Lockett was definitely not sure about the man's stability, and frankly, did not like him very much.

In any case, the sergeant had sent for him, and there was a pricking sense of dread, like he was being called to the front of the class while the teacher held a switch in his hand.

When he arrived, he only saw a handful of men lingering in the town square and two others down by the stable. Very little seemed to be happening today. Finally, he spotted the sergeant in a heated one-way discussion with his nephew, although the sergeant drew silent as he saw Lockett approach.

He clearly didn't want Lockett, or anyone else, to hear his diatribe, but Lockett had good ears and heard enough. Again, Captain Vincent had rejected VanderJagt's request to drill the men and practice their marching. Vincent was too busy to be bothered with such trifles.

Clearly, the sergeant was bothered by this and needed to unburden himself to his nephew, but beyond that, VanderJagt was careful not to let others hear.

Now in silence, he stared at Lockett. "You heard that I sent for you?"

"Yes."

"Yes, sergeant," VanderJagt corrected.

"Yes, sergeant," Lockett repeated.

"Good, I want you to gather two men and head over to the stable behind the Burdick Hotel. Captain Vincent's lieutenants have arrived and there is some cargo that needs to be unloaded from a couple of wagons."

"Uniforms?' Lockett asked brightly. "Some of the others said that uniforms might arrive soon."

VanderJagt glared at him. "It don't matter none what it is. Now just get over there! Lieutenant Long is there. Just follow his orders.

"Yes, sir."

"Yes, sergeant," he corrected. "You use 'sir' with the officers. They're your betters. I ain't no 'sir.' I'm just a sergeant."

"Betters?"

VanderJagt gave a pained looked. "Just 'sergeant,' got it?"

"Yes, sergeant." Lockett repeated and hesitated.

"Something else, Lockett?" VanderJagt asked impatiently.

"I just had a thought. If you want Congressman Vincent to give you permission to drill us, maybe you should somehow suggest that it would make for a more impressive parade when we march out of town."

VanderJagt opened his mouth, about to skewer him for listening in and for thinking that this rabble could make any sort of parade on such short notice, but he stopped himself. On second thought, the young farmer had a point. The congressman did seem like the type to want a parade…

The sergeant nodded curtly and added, "Now go take care of those wagons." When Lockett turned around and walked away, the old soldier permitted himself a small grin.

Orrin Long smoothed his thin moustache with his forefinger. He considered this slender, manicured version on his upper lip to be more stylish and European-looking compared to the thicker, untamed facial hair that most wore around here. His sophisticated style was more fitting for his desired station in life, giving him the aristocratic air that he sought.

With undisguised disdain, he stared at the man across from him as the two of them stood behind the stables. Long had already given the three blithely ignorant soldiers their orders to unload his uncle's wagon. It would take the soldiers a good bit of time to carry the congressman's crates and trunk over to the Burdick Hotel, enough time for him to take care of some important business with this 'businessman.'

But as Orrin Long stared at the slack-jawed man across from him, he started to wonder if the man had the basic acuity to manage what was really a simple plan. "When I give you the number, you just make sure that you bid under that number… and don't forget my share of the money."

"I don't give you the bid now?"

"That would defeat the purpose of this, now, wouldn't it?" Long scowled. "Not all of the bids are in yet. They have until five o'clock this evening. Once I have received all of their bids, I will see who is the lowest. I will tell you what that lowest bid is, and then you come under it, ever so slightly under it. When I hand the bids over to the Congressman, he'll be sure to choose yours, and then the business is yours to supply his little outfit."

The man flicked a finger against thick lips. The greedy look on his face reassured Orrin Long that the plan was starting to make sense to the cretin.

"And the quality? Or the quantity counts?"

"My uncle doesn't care much about the quality. He'll just look at the price, and as for the counts, don't worry about that. I'm the one in charge of checking that. You bring me my money, and I'll make sure the count of the items equals what is on the paper, even if they actually come up short. We will both make out quite well with this…"

As Orrin Long said that, he noticed the man's gaze shift. Wheeling, he saw one of the soldiers approaching. Had the newcomer heard any of this? It was possible that he might have been within earshot.

Without a salute or any pretense, the interloper halted in front of them.

Long could smell the farm on him. There was no doubt that the tall, wiry young man was a farmer. He had a tired, but resolute face, with crow's feet already beginning to etch themselves into his otherwise youthful face. Hooded gray eyes stared back before Orrin Long finally said, "Yes, soldier? What do you want?"

"Um, well…" the soldier paused.

"It's 'sir' or 'lieutenant' to begin with," Long snapped angrily, "And spit it out!" Was the farmer's peculiar behavior because he had overheard some of the conversation?

"Oh, yes, sir," he replied sheepishly, "Still getting used to this army part…"

"This is not chit-chat, you, whatever-your-name-is. Get on with it."

"Yes, sir. My name's James, sir. Lockett…"

"I don't care to know your name," Long interrupted, "Can't you see that I'm in the middle of an important conversation here?" He paused, studying this Lockett's reaction. Did the farmer's calm stare to his last statement reveal anything?

No, there was nothing other than some embarrassment, Long decided. The dolt must not have overheard any of his plan.

"Yes, sir. Sorry, sir. It's just that one of the crates seems to be leaking, sir. I thought you might want to know."

"Leaking! By God, I'll have the hide off you and your friends! Dropped it, did you?"

"No, sir! We haven't touched this one yet. It must have just been the jostling of the roads."

"Rubbish! I packed that myself. You must be speaking of the crate with uncle's liquor and wine. I used plenty of hay."

"Honest, sir, we haven't touched that one yet. It's the last one on the wagon, up near the driver's bench."

Long turned abruptly on his heel and faced the slack-jawed businessman. "You are clear on what we talked about?"

"Yes," the merchant nodded.

"Don't be late," Long snarled before turning back to Lockett. "Now, let's go see this wagon. By God, if you were careless, you'll rue this day or my name isn't Orrin Long!"

Later that night, Orrin Long retrieved his flawlessly polished boots back from the shoeshine boy and flipped a coin into the air with the other hand. The small boy spun around, and his hand flashed high to catch the coin. With a hoarse laugh, Orrin Long gave the boy a gentle kick in the rear and sent him sprawling down the hall of the Burdick Hotel. Still laughing, he closed the door to his room and focused his attention back on the small mirror in the room.

He smoothed his thin moustache with the back of one finger and licked his lips like a hungry wolf checking his teeth in the reflection.

He had never really thought much about becoming a soldier before. When his Uncle Charles had raised the possibility of leaving the state legislature to form a company to fight in this "grand cause," Orrin Long had little choice but to eagerly nod that it was a brilliant idea.

He had little means of his own, or at least, had started that way, but as his uncle's congressional assistant, he was growing his own fortune. In the state capital, there were always plenty of opportunities.

Graft is what some called it, but Orrin Long saw it only as business opportunities. In many cases, he was convinced that by taking the money to encourage his uncle to vote a certain way, he was actually helping the state. After all, business enterprise was the true goal of the state, the only reason for doing anything.

Yet despite his last three years in Lansing, Orrin Long still had little to his name comparatively, certainly not enough money for his ambitions and aspirations. But that would soon change. As soon as he returned from this odyssey, he planned on marrying Big John Moffat's daughter. As the son-in-law of Big John Moffat, Long knew that he would never want for anything again and would have all the power that most men could ever want.

Except Orrin Long was not like most men. Simply marrying into power would not be enough to sustain him. In the heady air of the elite, he would need something else to aid him. And with that thought, he took the uniform from the rack. He was starting out as a lieutenant, but with any luck, he would be much higher by the time he finished. "A major?" he wondered aloud. Yes, that would be enough – Big John's son-in-law and a respected officer, a war hero. "Yes," he murmured in a self-assuring voice. With those credentials, the sky was the limit. Governor Orrin Long, perhaps? Yes, he smiled wolfishly.

Of course, it would be discomfiting work to lead this rabble. He had ridden past the sharpshooters' camp on his way into town. A dirty mob of ignorant farmers and loggers is what they were. He frowned, good for nothing but menial labor, probably not one brain between the hundred of them, but he had expected as much. With troops like that, they would definitely need officers like me, he thought. They would need someone to make the decisions for them.

But the thought of the present problems with the Kalamazoo farmers and loggers quickly passed from Orrin Long's head as he thought again about the future. "Governor Orrin Long," he practiced aloud, "Yes, that has a nice ring. Someday."

Captain Charles Vincent and his officers looked the part. Their bright blue uniforms were crisp and new. The gold trimmings on the shoulders sparkled in the bright November sun. It made our pitiful appearance look even more bland and unworthy.

Lieutenant Long and Lieutenant Simon were introduced as our new officers.

George VanderJagt is the sergeant now since he is the only one among us with any experience in the army.

But there is one other thing that the camp is talking about. We leave tomorrow for Chicago and eventually Benton Barracks in St. Louis to join Birge's Western Sharpshooters.

It has begun.

--- the diary of James Lockett

Chapter 4

November 20, 1861

Lockett and McManus looked at the last two cracker barrels on the train. The other barrels and crates had already been off-loaded by the others, and Lieutenant Long had long since finished confirming that all of the goods were there.

"I wonder why we just didn't bring one wagon over and load it up?" Lockett wondered aloud. "Wouldn't that have been smarter than having us all come over here and carry it piece by piece?"

"I don't know," McManus shrugged. He was just happy that they were on their way to the west later today. It was finally beginning.

Like all of the others, he could think of little else today. Only James was not wholly preoccupied with that thought.

Didn't James understand the momentous occasion? It just didn't seem right or somehow fitting. James didn't belong in this, McManus thought sadly to himself. James was his closest friend and all, but he wasn't cut out to be a soldier. Where was his spirit?

He knew why James had volunteered, or at least thought he did, and that part did seem fitting for James – to keep Daniel from getting himself into trouble.

But Daniel wanted to go off to war. James clearly did not. Wouldn't it have made more sense to let nature take its course? McManus shook his head slowly. Didn't James know better than to resist nature? Fighting the course of nature was futile.

"Crackers," Lockett remarked, unaware of his friend's wandering thoughts. He pulled the barrel closer to him, hefted it off the train car, and passed it to McManus. "Sergeant VanderJagt said that we better get used to eating this hardtack."

He lifted the second and final cracker barrel. Oddly, it felt lighter than the one he had just handed to McManus. But without giving it much more thought, they left and headed off with Lockett taking the lead.

"I wonder why we are marching to Niles and taking the train from there to Chicago? Why not just take a train from here straight to Chicago? It's the same train line."

"You're full of questions today," McManus chuckled as they walked along the planking sidewalk through town.

They each carried the cracker barrel from the bottom, which meant that they could not see where they were going, and every few seconds they would crane their heads to the side and twist a little so that they could see where they were going. "But I guess it should not surprise me. You always were more curious about things than I was."

"Just seems peculiar, Patrick. It's not a long march to Niles or anything, but it will add a couple of days, don't you think?"

"Maybe Captain Vincent thought we could use the practice marching?"

"Maybe, but that seems more like something that old VanderJagt would find as a good idea, not Captain Vincent. I mean, you should have seen what we loaded into that supply wagon today, and that was just Captain Vincent's baggage. Probably more for him in the wagons than the rest of the company combined."

"I think…"

"Whoa, you there!" a new voice cried in a warning.

Lockett twisted to the side and saw that he had nearly run over a young woman about his own age. She was taller than average with light brown hair which was mostly tied behind her head or under her bonnet, except for matching strands on either side of her face that danced cheerily in the cool November breeze. Her cheeks were flushed to a glowing red with the cool weather, and light blue eyes looked back at him with some concern.

"S-sorry," Lockett stammered. He moved to the right to clear a path, but at the same time she had moved in the same direction. He reacted by moving back to the left, but she had the same thought at the same time, meaning that he still blocked her way.

"Are we to dance now?" she asked, her tone somehow mixing a hint of imperiousness and amusement.

"I, uh, oh," Lockett managed, placing his back against the side of the building to give her maximum space on the sidewalk in order to pass by.

"Thank you," she replied, continuing on her way past him and then past McManus. Lockett did not move immediately, instead he watched her go down the walk until she turned around the corner onto Main Street.

"Who was that?" he asked once she was gone. "I thought that I knew everyone our age in this town."

"You're not serious, are you?" McManus laughed.

"What do you mean? Do you know her?"

McManus shook his head with genuine astonishment. He had never seen James have his head turned by a girl, and this was the one who caught his eye?

"James, look at what she was wearing! That is enough of a clue, even for you."

"What? What was she wearing?" Lockett paused and closed his eyes, trying to think about her attire. At first, he could not picture it, all he saw was that face, but then in his mind's eye, he saw her walking away. It was an expensive frock coat, definitely not like the quality of clothing that he and Patrick wore.

"That kind of money is rare," McManus clarified. "That was Big John Moffat's daughter, I'm sure of it." He nudged Lockett with his cracker barrel to prod him back on their way.

"One of the Moffat daughters?" Lockett mused aloud as he started back down the sidewalk. The Moffat daughters did not attend school at the one room schoolhouse. They had their own private tutor.

McManus grimaced with a shake of the head, "You'd have a better chance of being struck by lightning than you'd have with someone like her. It would probably end about the same too."

"So, when do you think *we* get uniforms?" Matthew Bauer pointedly asked Luke Bailey and Lockett as they milled about, waiting for Captain Vincent to return.

It was a motley collection of clothing that the sharpshooters wore. Only the officers had crisp blue uniforms. None of the men did, and no two men were dressed alike, although a number of them were sporting squirrel tails on their wide brimmed slouch hats. "Don't know, Matthew. We don't look much like an army, do we?"

"We're a citizen army," Luke Bailey said brightly, "Don't worry, I'm sure we'll get uniforms in Chicago."

"Hope so," Lockett replied, looking at a couple of their comrades dressed with cheap sackcoats tucked inside their trousers.

"You heard that we're going to be in Birge's Western Sharpshooters, right?" Bauer added, "Right with those boys from Van Buren and Berrien counties after all."

"Is that where they ended up?" McManus asked, "I thought they went out East."

"No, they're with Birge, and I guess he's in St. Louis."

"Wish we could get going. At this rate, the war could be over before we even get to St. Louis," Bailey sighed, "Where is our captain? I thought the army was supposed to be a punctual place."

"Maybe," Lockett shrugged with a small smile, "But none of us would know much about that, except for old VanderJagt. It would be nice if we could leave in some reasonable order. The longer we mill about here, the more likely..." He stopped in mid-sentence and leaned an ear into the breeze.

"Horses," Bauer noted.

Finally, Captain Vincent and Lieutenant Long galloped up. Curiously, the lieutenant was carrying a large bag, and shortly thereafter, the contents were distributed to the men of the Kalamazoo Sharpshooters.

"Here ya go," VanderJagt said eventually, handing Lockett a bright red handkerchief scarf.

"What am I supposed to do with this?"

"Look! I'm a bandit," Bauer joked, tying it around his face.

"Don't ask me what we're s'posed to do with this frill," VanderJagt grumbled gruffly, "God knows why we wan' to wear these."

"The women of the town took up a collection to buy them," McManus said softly from nearby.

"What?" Lockett said in surprise, "How do you know that?"

"Wives. It was supposed to be a surprise, but Martha told me. She can't keep a secret for anything."

The Kalamazoo Sharpshooters departed via an impromptu parade. Each man was surprised at the number of people who lined the dusty road to watch them march by in ragged rows of four.

They were ninety-eight strong, but it seemed like thousands. In spite of their motley attire, they marched proudly with their rifles against their shoulders. In truth, it was a shambles of a formation with men marching out of step and often not aligned shoulder-to-shoulder. Their heads turned back and forth to catch the sights, and some even waved to the crowd.

It was more like a mob moving in the same direction than an army on the march, VanderJagt thought, grinding his teeth. Some of them were more pack mules than soldiers too as they beat down the road west towards Niles. That would not last long, VanderJagt thought with vindictive pleasure.

A day's march would teach them a quick lesson. Those who carried more weight than necessary would regret it. This walking, jangling caravan of skillets, tin ware, and God knows what else, would learn soon enough.

December 6, 1861

Dear Father,

We have arrived and departed Chicago via train. We are now in St. Louis at the Benton Barracks. Have seen nothing of St. Louis, being night when we arrived. The train ride from Chicago was a blur of scenery. How flat Illinois is! Despite my excitement, I quickly fell asleep. The clickety-clack of the rails could put anyone to sleep.

We are now called Company J. I liked the Kalamazoo Sharpshooters name much better. How many stories of heroism can there be about a Company J? It lacks the vim of the Kalamazoo Sharpshooters! Next, they may take away our red scarves. I pray not!

Now that we have reached camp, I've no need for my powder horn. The army will provide paper cartridges for my Dimick.

Our spirits are high, and we are ready to teach the Rebels a lesson. Luke's improvement with your rifle has been steady. It won't be long until he is a tolerable shot, but he is still learning. He wishes me to thank you again for loaning him your Dimick. I thank you too, because I hesitate to say what he would hit with an old smoothbore! My only fear is for James. His mood is dark. He was always the cautious sort and doesn't seem to be filled with the fire of the other boys. I don't think he has what it takes to be a soldier.

Your obedient son,
Matthew

Sergeant VanderJagt drilled us into darkness today. Most of the men hate him right now, but I think most of them know now that Vincent made the right choice in making him sergeant. We are becoming very familiar with the commands and how to march. Some still don't understand though, and I truly wonder if some of them even know their left from their right. It is obvious to me that we are not performing as well as the other companies, but VanderJagt is determined to correct that. I only hope that Captain Vincent and Lieutenant Long will be as well prepared. I didn't see hide nor hair of them today. The drilling was handled by VanderJagt and Lieutenant Simon. Simon seems to know what he is doing. I was told that he was in the militia before, and that is why he is so familiar with the commands. He is a bit distant, and some of the men have taken to ridiculing him. There is no mistaking that he does look a bit like an overstuffed scarecrow, all limbs and belly, but he seems a decent fellow.

As I write this, the draft in the barracks makes my candle flicker, or perhaps it is the snoring of a hundred men. Regardless, I am too tired to write more, but I still look forward to tomorrow.

---the diary of James Lockett

December 9, 1861

"You know what one of the Ohioans in Company G told me, Matthew?" Luke Bailey asked as Bauer worked on molding his bullets and cutting his own patches.

The early pronouncement that the Army would provide paper cartridges proved to be an overstatement for now. Though promised, most of the cartridges had not arrived yet, and for now, it was up to each man to mold his own bullets and cut his own patches for his Dimick Deer Rifle. Working the plier-like device, each man molded the soft lead of the bullet.

Bauer stopped for a moment and looked into the barrel of the gun studying the long grooves that ran from the bore. Such a simple thing, he thought, the grooves would put a spin on the bullet, allowing it to cut cleaner through the air, giving it better accuracy and more distance. So simple, yet so important.

"Now, what was it you were saying?"

"I was talking to one of the Ohio boys in company G. Did you know the Western Skirmishers were General John C. Fremont's idea?"

"Fremont? Who's he? I thought our generals were Halleck and Practice."

"Prentiss," Bailey corrected, "General Prentiss. And you're right, Fremont's not our general anymore. He's out East somewhere, but he ran for President, remember?"

Bauer shrugged, "No. Never heard of him. What's your point?"

"Point? Well, I suppose, I don't really have a point, I just didn't know about that."

"Did this Ohioan tell ya that we're supposed to be used as skirmishers too?" Bauer looked back at his rifle, fingering the trigger gently. Perhaps, if he filed it down to make it even more sensitive that would further improve his accuracy?

"Skirmishers? No. What's a..."

"The advance guard, sort of. We go out in front of the main body. Feel out where the enemy is so the main body doesn't blunder into a trap."

"What main body?"

"That's my point, we don't have a main body, just skirmishers."

"That doesn't make any sense."

"Either does having no uniforms or ammunition."

"You sounded like James right there."

"Bah," Bauer replied, mildly annoyed to be compared to Lockett. He was a friend and all, but his less than enthusiastic attitude grated on him. "We'll still whup them bushwhackers out there. Jus' seems a mite disorganized, you know?"

"I know. I overheard some of the Wisconsin boys in Company A talking about how it's been a mess since they got here. They just want to get out of camp and get after the Rebels."

"At least Company A had enough food to share with us last night."

Last night, for the third time in five days, the Kalamazoo Sharpshooters had discovered that the cracker barrels and other foodstuffs were only half full. It had prompted James to remark that he thought some of them felt lighter than others when they had left Kalamazoo, Bailey reflected. The barrels had been short-changed. No doubt that was intentional with the businessmen selling them to the Army for full fare and yet delivering them incomplete.

It was a mystery how that had happened, but they were all becoming accustomed to more skepticism.

Silently, they continued working on the next bullets when Lockett and McManus returned.

"Where's the uniforms?" Bailey asked, noticing that they were empty-handed.

"Still no uniforms," McManus snorted, "The quartermaster has enough for one company, but seeing as how there's us and Company I, not to mention that G doesn't have'em yet either, he's not going to give them out to anyone."

"What?" Bailey said with a puzzled frown. "Why not give it to at least one company?"

"Welcome to the U.S. Army. That's what that

quartermaster said when James asked the same question."

"Crazy."

"Where are the rest of the uniforms? Aren't there more coming?"

"Should be, but only God knows where they are at. The Quartermaster also said that we are unexpectedly short on blankets too."

"There's thievin' going on," Lockett muttered.

"Must be," McManus agreed, "Ain't no way we can be short on nearly everything."

We thought that things would make more sense once we got to St. Louis, but we were wrong about that. Still no uniforms. It is a good thing that we brought our own rifles, or we would be walking round with sticks like some of the Ohioans.

We train, but our three month enlistment will be up before we know it. What I do then about Daniel and keeping him on the farm, I don't know. I guess I will have to re-enlist.

Still, the barracks aren't too bad, even though Luke complains about sleeping on hard boards. The bunks are in three tiers, and each barrack holds a hundred men with the officers at the end. Captain Vincent keeps other arrangements, but none of us miss him.

--- the diary of James Lockett

Dear Daniel,

As I have 10 minutes, I will spend them in consideration of your interest in our activities. Camp life is a bit boring, and most are ready to leave these barracks.

The weather has improved just as Matthew said it would. He is ever chipper, as always.

We still have no uniforms, and no one expects them soon. We look quite the hodgepodge with our country dress, bright red scarves, and floppy hats. More of the men seem to be taken by the squirrel tails in the hat, and the tails have actually begun to fetch a decent price since there are no squirrels around camp. I'm sure that you find it hard to imagine that a squirrel tail would have any value, but that is camp life.

I hope this obliges your curiosity for the moment. Please give my affections to all and keep us in your prayers. We leave soon for central Missouri to chase bushwhackers.

Your brother, James

"Ninety-nine, one hundred," Orrin Long mouthed silently. He looked up at the squat sutler with the greasy side whiskers.

"It's all there," the sutler said with a raspy voice. He held out a battered, discolored flask. "Drink to the deal?"

Orrin Long frowned at the grotesque little man and wrinkled his nose. The man's strong odor was becoming a more disgusting stench the longer he stood there.

"Suit yourself," the whiskered sutler cackled, and he took a long pull on the flask.

Orrin Long pulled three dollars from the much larger sum that he had just received. The three would be for later, for Hiram Walker and his cohorts who stood in the distance. They had loaded the army supplies into the wagon, as well as provided Orrin Long with protection. Orrin Long doubted that he had much to fear from the little sutler, but there was no trust in the selling of contraband. It was far better to project a sense of force, and that was what Hiram Walker and his brutes did.

Of course, Walker and his dull-witted cronies had no idea how little their cut was, and Orrin Long had to smile at that. The selling of the army's property to greasy little sutlers like this man was a profitable business. Virtually all profit in fact.

"Same time next week?" the sutler asked, scratching furiously at his side whiskers for a louse.

"No, we leave for Centralia soon," Orrin Long replied.

"Too bad. This could have been quite profitable for both of us."

Long grunted, turned around, and left. He stepped out of the darkened alley and joined Hiram Walker and the others. They would have to hurry. It would be dawn in a few hours. The haggling had taken longer than he expected.

Chapter 5

December 12, 1861

The Kalamazoo Sharpshooters were finally moving toward battle, Lockett thought to himself. The dust of Benton Barracks was behind them, and despite their continuing supply problems, they were headed for the war.

The other companies in Birge's Western Sharpshooters had departed four days before. In spite of their best efforts, there was no way to cram all of the men and their supplies onto that train, so it had been decided that Captain Vincent's company from Kalamazoo would wait behind in St. Louis for the next available train. It was also hoped that by then the blue uniforms would arrive.

Alas, the uniforms still had not arrived, so Lockett and the others boarded the small train in their mismatched, homespun clothes. The only things consistent in their attire were the red handkerchiefs that had been passed out upon leaving Kalamazoo.

They looked more like a rabble than anything else. Even their movements did not resemble the movements of a trained army, made even more prominent by the confusion they generated as they sorted out the baggage on the flatcar and muddled their way into the passenger cars.

As the train bounced along the track at 30 miles per hour, Lockett looked out the window and reflected that at least there was some good fortune in having been left behind by the rest of the regiment. When the bulk of the Western Sharpshooters had departed four days ago, they had crammed onto every bit of space on that train. There was not room in the passenger cars for all of them. Many of the men sat themselves down on the exposed flatcars. The cutting wind as they jolted along must have frozen those unfortunate ones half to death. At the time, he had noticed that it was the Danes from Wisconsin who were on that flatcar.

Had they been chosen because it was figured that the Wisconsin boys were hardy souls? Or had the Danes been singled out or drawn a short straw? Or had the Danes foolishly volunteered, thinking that the flatcar was better than being crammed into the passenger cars?

As the train rolled along, Lockett peered out the window at the flat terrain and cold-looking gray sky. There were not as many trees as he was accustomed to, and the flat expanses of dormant brown, winter grass went on and on. In spite of the repetitiveness, he was fascinated by the scenery. It wasn't like west Michigan. That was for certain.

For a moment, he wished that his brothers could see the sight through his eyes. They would be equally captivated by the lack of trees and flatness. In Michigan, nearly everything was tree covered, unless it was cleared. In this part of Missouri, there were patches of trees but far more open land than forest.

Frowning slightly, Lockett closed his eyes. Seeing these types of new sights was exactly why Daniel had wanted to volunteer, and he felt a twinge of guilt for what he had done to him, even if it was for Daniel's own good.

Luke Bailey dozed next to Lockett, and Lockett had half a mind to jostle him awake so that he could take in the view from the window.

Just as he decided to let him sleep, he was jolted by Hiram Walker going down the aisle, knocking him into Bailey. Unapologetically, Walker continued to the end of the car where his messmates argued over the last hand of cards.

Awake now, Bailey watched the hulking man make his way to the opposite end of the car. He did find it strange that there was such a wide range of men who had volunteered. Someone had remarked earlier that he thought Hiram Walker had joined merely for the booty of war, and while the concept was a foreign one to Lockett and Bailey, they were starting to think he was right.

Of course, Luke Bailey wanted to believe that most joined for more noble reasons. He had assumed from the beginning that most of the men had joined for the same reason as he had, to end slavery, but that was not the case. There were a handful of volunteers who were Abolitionists like himself, but there were many others who had joined for other reasons. There were some like Matthew, who had joined for the promise of adventure or for the cause of putting the Union back together. But there were also many like Patrick, who had joined without much thought, if only because his friends were doing so. In any case, James's reason was still the strangest one, to trap his brother on the farm.

It was a poor reason, and when Luke Bailey allowed himself to think about it, he had to agree with Matthew. James did not belong here, even more so than Luke himself. He was too cool, calm, and lacking in enthusiasm for this, he decided.

Sergeant VanderJagt stirred at the front of the car and made his way down the narrow aisle.

They watched him go past and out the back to the other passenger car.

"He has it in for me," Lockett said softly.

"The sergeant?" Bailey queried with some surprise, "Why do you say that?"

"Haven't you noticed that he always picks me as a 'volunteer?' Unloading wagons, demonstrating something on the drill field, how to clean a weapon properly? He always picks me."

"I had not noticed that," Bailey said with a skeptical shrug.

"Not sure what I did to him to deserve that, but that's what it is."

"Well, I'm sure it is just your imagination. He doesn't seem to be the bad sort. I think he's fair to everyone so far."

"True… I suppose he is fair, other than harping on me for each little thing. I guess we could use a few more like him. He is the only one who has been through war before."

At that point, their quiet conversation was interrupted by the locomotive's shriek from the steam whistle. It blasted three times, and they could feel a noticeable drop in speed as the train slowed.

"Are we there already?" Bailey asked.

"Can't be. I heard Captain Vincent tell the sergeant that it was a hundred and fifty miles, and that even though the train could go fifty miles an hour, it would be going much slower than that since they didn't trust the track, what with all these bushwhackers around. There is no way that we have gone that far already."

Once the train came to a stop, the reason was clear. The track up ahead had been torn apart. A good fifty yards of ties and railing were scattered down the hillside below.

The officers, along with Sergeant VanderJagt and the train engineer, had advanced on foot to examine the damage. When they returned to the area of the passenger cars, most of the men were loitering outside.

"Bushwhackers," Captain Vincent declared as they returned, "No doubt about it."

"Yes, indeed, sir," Lieutenant Long agreed.

"It's an opportunity for us to get started in this war. It will be some good practice for the men, if nothing else."

Sergeant VanderJagt stood silently at attention, unsure what the former congressman meant.

"Their trail was clear up near their handiwork. They obviously headed west after tearing up the track."

"Lots of horseshoe marks in that direction," Long agreed again.

A scolding look from his uncle drew the nephew back to silence.

"I want twenty men to go investigate these bushwhackers while the rest of the men work on repairing the track."

Since the captain was staring directly at VanderJagt as he said that, the sergeant responded, "I'll select twenty men, and we'll head off presently."

"No, Lieutenant Long can take the twenty and look for the bushwhackers. I want you to help repair the track."

As Lockett looked on, he could sense that the army veteran clearly wanted to be part of their first patrol. But VanderJagt saluted stiffly and gave a slightly delayed, "Yes, sir."

Lieutenant Long immediately began to select men from the

group loitering nearby. As Lockett watched, he could see that Long was nearly to twenty men and was about to select Patrick, when Lockett stepped in front of his old friend, making sure that he was the twentieth person selected.

He could feel Patrick staring at him from behind, but he did not turnaround and make eye contact with the red head. He had a pretty good idea that Patrick's face was turning the color of his hair, and that his brow was narrowed into a scowl.

Lieutenant Long and the selected twenty men marched two abreast down the dusty road. Their feet kicked up tendrils of dust that were caught in the cool breeze and sent twisting into the sky. The gray clouds above were starting to part and with more blue sky and sun, they could feel the temperature rise.

In the horizon, they saw nothing but more grassy prairie.

Matthew Bauer walked alongside Lockett, keeping up a constant dialogue, even if Lockett's responses were few and far between. First, he had remarked on how Missouri had been at war with itself in one way or another for nearly twenty years — from John Brown and anti-slavery Kansas Jayhawkers to the pro-slavery vigilantes. He speculated on how much blood had already been absorbed by the Missouri soil.

When Lockett's limited responses gave him the impression of disinterest, he switched topics. "Wonder how far along Luke and Patrick are with the tracks? I bet they wish they were with us."

"Probably," Lockett answered but uttered nothing more as he stared into the horizon. If there were bushwhackers out here on horseback, what were the odds of finding them on foot? They were likely to be miles away now.

"It's just good to be out of those barracks and doing something finally, right, James?" Bauer was completely undeterred by his friend's limited responses. "As flat as it is, the drifting of the snow out here must be awful, when they have snow that is."

"You think they get much snow?"

"Dunno, but I'd say it was cold enough, in the morning at least. Though I was talking to one of those boys in Company E from Edgar County, he said they don't get much snow down here, not like we're used to at least."

"That's good because we'd need to start building some shelters soon."

No one in the detachment seemed to be paying attention to anything in particular. Everyone was engaged in their own conversations, even Lieutenant Long spoke with Hiram Walker at the front.

By now, Lockett knew most of the men in the company. He had already known many before starting this journey, of course.

There was one group, however, that he did not know much about, nor care to know much about – Hiram Walker and his friends.

As he had mentioned to Luke before, Walker and his cronies were a coarse and rough sort. At best, they were men with no prospects. At worst, they were criminals on the run. They also seemed strangely eager about what Lockett considered a wild goose chase.

They marched on and on, and Lockett was beginning to wonder if they were ever going to see even a little shack to break up the monotony, but finally on the horizon, they saw two farmhouses, a pond, and a rare patch of trees.

There was a farmhouse on each side of the dusty road. The one on the right was set well off the road, back near the small copse of trees. As they neared the homes, he could see that the house on the right also had a small barn.

"Finally," Lieutenant Long said with a touch of impatience, "All right, let's see what traitors these two farmsteads have. Corporal Hollister?"

"Yessir."

"Take nine men and investigate the house on the left. The rest of us will go to the right."

As ordered, Lockett and Bauer followed Hiram Walker and his friends behind the now quickly striding Lieutenant Long. They made their way down the dusty lane to the small, but well-kept farmhouse.

Lockett looked at the long ago harvested fields and judged

them to be rather successful corn farmers, and he studied the house for any movement but saw none. Nor were there any signs that the farmers were, in Lieutenant Long's words, "traitors."

"The problem with this," Bauer remarked, accurately sharing Lockett's own thought, "Is that in Missouri, they may be Confederate, or they may be Union, but you never know."

"They're Rebel," Hiram Walker said in front of them, surprising Lockett and Bauer.

"How do you know that?"

"He can smell'em," laughed Isaac Washburn, one of Walker's messmates.

"Don't matter," Walker jeered, "They're all Rebel 'til they prove otherwise."

Lockett and Bauer glanced at each other but said nothing.

At the top of the slight knoll, near the fork, Lieutenant Long pointed at the house. One path led to the house, the other to the small barn.

Walking up to Lockett, the officer said, "You men from here, back, check the barn. Private Walker, you and the rest come with me."

"Yes, sir," Lockett said with an amateurish salute, turning toward the barn, keeping an eye on the small woods behind the barn. It was too small and too sparse to hold much of an ambush, but he still kept his eyes on it, even as he unshouldered his rifle and held it in a ready position. Without a word, the others did the same.

"Anybody see anything?" Lockett asked, as they paused at the front of the barn.

"Nothing," Sam Moss replied, and Matthew Bauer wondered how James had become the leader of their small expedition and why they were all so timid at the moment.

"This is silly," he declared, "What are you afraid of, a bunch of horses?" He jogged forward and swung open the broad barn door.

"No horses," Sam Moss said.

"No nuthin'," John Quinlan added.

The barn was mostly empty.

"That's funny," Quinlan remarked, kicking at a small pile of hay, "I see a plow, kit, and tack, but no animals? I wonder if…"

The sound of a single gunshot from the house interrupted them.

Lockett was the closest and first to react, taking off in a full sprint. His long legs immediately increased the distance from the others as he dashed toward the back door of the house.

He swung open the door and found that he was in a kitchen. In the corner, a soldier pinned a small, crying six year old boy to the floor with his foot. The boy whimpered in an odd, subdued way, and Lockett noticed a small amount of blood dripping from the side of the little boy's head, staining the child's blond hair.

Lockett looked in bewilderment at the dazed child, and then at the soldier who held his rifle in one hand and an ancient looking musket that still trickled smoke in his other hand.

"What happened?" Lockett asked, finally turning his eyes on the rest of the room.

"That boy nearly shot my foot off!" Hiram Walker stormed, tapping a hole in the wooden floor near his foot for emphasis.

"He probably can't even lift that musket…" Lockett stopped abruptly.

No longer obscured by Walker's massive body, a woman rose shakily from the floor.

"Where do you think you're goin'?" Walker snarled menacingly, grabbing her by the throat with one hand.

"What are you doing, Hiram?" Lockett questioned. His voice sounded tinny and weak, as his mind told him that he knew exactly what Hiram Walker was attempting to do. The woman stared at Lockett with pleading blue eyes.

The little boy had her blond hair, he realized, and the woman's face began to turn blue from Walker's grip on her throat. The front of her plain dress was already torn on the right side, and though she was in the midst of choking to death, she struggled to lift up the torn flap to cover herself.

"Let her go, Hiram!" Lockett cried incredulously.

"Get out of here, boyo," Hiram Walker replied without

concern, not bothering to turn his attention away from the woman's face. He was clearly enjoying the bulging of her eyes and her useless attempts for air.

"I said, '*Let her go*'," Lockett demanded in a curiously, and unexpectedly, steeled voice. A previously unknown rage fueled his veins that he did not recognize. It was reaction, not thought, that controlled him.

"What?" Walker asked with more annoyance than fear as he turned to find Lockett leveling his Dimick Deer Rifle at the larger man.

With a start, Lockett realized what he was doing. Inside, he was perplexed with what had happened. This was not calm, rational thought. But the rifle did not waver in his hand, and his face kept its hardened glare of determination.

Yet Hiram Walker did not seem fazed at all.

"I think you should re-think that, boyo," Walker said smugly.

Once he had stepped past that point of no return and aimed a weapon at Walker, Lockett expected a less confident reaction. Was the brute really that calm about having his life threatened? "Let…her… go," he repeated through a clenched jaw.

"Look around, boyo!"

From the corner of his eye, Lockett saw Isaac Washburn and Bart Randle aiming their rifles at his midsection.

"Now, why don't you be a good boy, and step outside so as's I can get down to bis'ness."

Swallowing hard, Lockett tried to think, but all that raced through him was a startling, inexplicable rage. It was a feeling that he had never felt before in such intensity, and it swelled like a blacksmith's bellow and squeezed out any other commands in his brain. His gray eyes blazed.

"I'm not going to tell you again!" he commanded in a cold voice. Even in his own ears, it sounded like someone else's voice, and he pressed the muzzle to Hiram Walker's temple.

Finally stunned, Walker muttered, "Now think what you're doing, boyo."

Lockett pressed the muzzle more firmly against Walker's temple, and his finger tightened dangerously on the trigger, just one iota of pressure away from releasing the heavy slug.

From the corner of his eye, he noticed that the other two still had their rifles trained on him, but they said nothing in their indecision.

"Private!" Lockett heard an authoritative voice say, "Drop that gun now."

He assumed that Lieutenant Long's order had been directed at Washburn and Randle, but when he turned, he could see the lieutenant standing next to them. There was no change in their weapons, and Lieutenant Long's frown was directed at him.

"Put it down, Private Lockett. Private Walker is following orders."

His jaw slackening, Lockett finally noticed that Long's own revolver was aimed at him too.

Lockett lowered his rifle more out of surprise than obedience. Then, they all heard a great commotion starting outside.

"Lieut'ant! Lieut'ant!" Sam Moss yelled, from the front door on the other side of the house. "The Rebs! They're here!" he yelled again.

"I'll be back," Walker told the woman with a back handed slap that knocked her hard to the floor.

They found Sam Moss in the front of the house, oblivious to anything else that had been occurring in the back.

"There you are! They're here, sir!"

"Who? Where?" Long asked him.

"Up the road. Cavalry, maybe ten of 'em!"

"All right, everyone outside!" Long ordered, "Into line of battle!"

Dumbly, Lockett followed Orrin Long out, not at all comfortable that he had his back to Hiram Walker as he did so. But they formed up outside the house as if nothing had happened.

"Some line of battle," Bauer grumbled, as Lockett fell into place beside his friend, "Eight men."

"Hope Perry's seen'em too," Sam Moss said excitedly from the other side of Bauer, "There they are!" He added as Corporal Perry Hollister's men left their farmhouse from across the road.

"What's wrong, James?" Bauer asked, seeing his friend's charged eyes, red face, and still clenched jaw. Thinking that it was nervousness at the prospect of their first fight, he added, "We got'em outnumbered two to one, James. We'll send'em running after one volley."

"Later," Lockett whispered, noticing Lieutenant Long coming around the side.

In the distance, down the road, the riders shifted in their saddles, as they watched the Yankees form a thin line of rifles. With some amusement, they watched the soldiers slowly come down the road.

"This is no way to fight cavalry," Bauer thought aloud as they advanced down the road, "By the time we get within range, they'll just ride off."

Exactly as predicted, as soon as the Kalamazoo Sharpshooters got anywhere close to being within range, the horsemen turned and rode away.

Lieutenant Long stopped and watched them go. He stood there for a moment, unsure what to do.

"Very well," he said finally, "Corporal, did you find anything or anybody in your house?"

"Not a thing," Perry Hollister answered, casually taking off his cap and scratching his head, "What do you wan' us to do now?"

Long said nothing while he adjusted his red scarf which had become loose in the commotion. Satisfied that he had returned it to a properly jaunty position, he turned to face the corporal. "Wait for us on the road and keep an eye out for those bushwhackers. We're almost done in our house. Private Walker, come with me. The rest of you wait here."

He turned and walked back to the farmhouse.

Lockett watched them leave with trepidation and indecision. As Long and Walker neared the house, he became more and more uncertain. What should he do? Now that the moment had passed, his brain was able to function above his anger again, and he wondered what he could do to stop what was surely about to happen. It was wishful thinking to expect any other outcome.

Obviously, I can't stop it all on my own, Lockett thought quietly. Could he rally the men against their lieutenant and Hiram Walker? If only they understood the injustice that was about to take place! But there wouldn't be time for that.

Feeling that strange anger building within again, he edged away from the others, slowly building momentum as he walked towards the house again.

"Lockett, where are you going?" Corporal Hollister asked.

But he did not answer and started to run towards the house that Long and Walker had just entered.

"Lockett, the lieutenant said to wait here!" Hollister yelled to no avail.

Stopping just short of the door, Lockett paused, strangely out of breath in spite of how brief the run had been. It was almost like he had been holding his breath. There was then the sound of crunching gravel behind him, and he whirled.

"What are you doing, James?" Matthew Bauer asked with a benign curiosity.

Lockett ignored him.

Could he muster the courage to stand up to Walker again?

As he judged the chances of that, he looked across the dormant field. Blinking twice, he squinted into the distance. Riding away at a fast gallop, with her dress streaming behind her and the small boy holding tight, he saw the shape of the woman grow smaller and smaller.

From inside the house, he could hear cursing and yelling. Hiram Walker stuck his head out the back door.

"There she goes!" he yelled angrily, "She must have hid a horse in the woods!" Upon seeing Lockett, he spat ferociously and glared before retreating back inside the house.

"Thank God," Lockett muttered softly, "Thank God,"

"What was all that about?" Bauer asked, "Where did that woman come from?"

"I'll explain later."

"What happened in there? And..." He stopped, and a look of puzzlement crossed Bauer's face.

Lockett turned to see that Matthew was looking through the

window into the kitchen. Together, they watched Hiram Walker stuff silverware into his haversack.

"What?" Bauer said in utter confusion. When Lockett said nothing, he continued, "They're stealing their silver!"

At any other time, the bewilderment in his boyish voice would have been humorous, but what they were witnessing was too disturbing for anything like that.

"I can't believe it. We have to do something, James. Get the lieutenant or something."

But Lockett put a firm hand on his shoulder to keep him in place

"Why are you..."

"Leave it, Matthew."

"But..." he stopped. His amazed eyes now saw Lieutenant Long participate in the thievery.

"We can't stop them," Lockett said in a sad voice.

"But that's probably the most valuable thing these people have. Probably heirlooms. They can't have much else. They're just farmers."

"They have one thing more valuable, Matthew, and they only barely got away with that."

Lockett slumped in the seat next to McManus. He was exhausted, more emotionally than physically.

They had marched back to the train shortly after what he and Matthew had witnessed. They said nothing of it to the others. If anyone had noticed that Matthew Bauer was unusually quiet on the quick march back to the train, they made no mention.

Upon returning to the train, Lockett was surprised to see that the track had been repaired, and that Captain Vincent impatiently waited for their return. Their leader took the news of the brief sighting of the bushwhackers and their hasty retreat with nothing more than a shrug and a derisive comment about 'bandits, bushwhackers, and highwaymen.'

After conferring with the engineer about how much time they had lost and the amount of daylight left, Captain Vincent declared that they would halt at the next train stop for the night, which greatly relieved the engineer who feared traveling in the dark of night with the potential for more torn up track.

Lockett cared little for that. All he wanted to do was rest and close his eyes, except that every time he did, he saw that mother and her little son. He wanted respite, but his own brain betrayed him with those repeating visages.

"Don't think that I don't know what you did back there, James," McManus griped.

Lockett's eyes snapped open, confusion plain on his face.

"Me?"

"Yes, back when old VanderJagt and Lieutenant Long called for volunteers." McManus stared at him with plain annoyance.

"Oh, that's what you meant," Lockett said with some relief.

"Yes. You intentionally stepped in front of me so that they would take you and not me."

"Did I?"

"You can't pretend about that! It was pretty obvious, and you're a terrible liar anyhow. You can't hide anything on that face."

"That is not true."

"Don't play poker with us."

Lockett gave no response and promised himself that he would work on displaying a less revealing mask in the future.

"Well, I don't know what you're talking about, Patrick."

"The hell you don't. It won't work, James. It's not possible. Besides, it is not necessary. I know why you did that, and you don't have to do that. It's not what you promised Martha."

"Promised Martha?"

"James, stop already. She told me all about it."

"She did?"

"Yes, she never should have asked you that in the first place, but regardless, you could not have known that I already signed up. It's not your choice. I'm a grown man, and there would have been nothing that you could have done to convince me otherwise. Even so, it was too late by then."

"But…"

"I know you well enough by now, James. I know you better than you know yourself. Honestly, I've known you every year of your life, so, yes, I know what you're thinking."

"Is that a fact?"

"Yes, it is," McManus responded indignantly, "You figure that since you could not keep that promise to my wife that you'd do the next best thing. You'd do everything that you could to keep me from harm." He paused before adding, "Tell me that I'm not right, James. I dare you!"

Lockett shrugged. There was no denying it.

"But, James, you can't make that promise, not even to yourself. We're going off to war. I do realize that, and you do too. What are you going to do, stand in front of me at every battle?"

When Lockett looked unmoved, McManus added with more urgency, "Now, be reasonable! Or least sensible!"

Lockett sighed. "I know," he replied softly.

"It's not yours to promise, no more than it is mine to promise. Only God could make a promise like that."

"Yes, but I'm going to do what I can."

"I should hope so, and I'll do the same for you, James, which you damn well know already."

Lockett's head bobbed.

"No more trying to volunteer in my stead. Right?"

Lockett nodded reluctantly.

Their second day on the train started better than the first. Perhaps it was the familiarity, but they boarded much more efficiently than they had the day before.

Their high spirits lasted well through the first hour… until there was the tell-tale steam whistle again and the slowing of the train.

With light-hearted cries of, "Again?" the sharpshooters disembarked the train.

As before, they were in the middle of nowhere. There were no structures nearby, just cold stiffened tall grasses like a sea of brown and yellow that did not so much ripple in the cool breeze as it stiffly tilted in one direction and then another. Were it not for the small copse of trees in front of the locomotive, there would have been nothing to see at all.

"Where the heck are we?" Bauer groaned, looking at the flat expanse of nothingness.

"Missouri," McManus answered with a smirk.

"Thanks, Patrick. I mean, where is the town? More track to be repaired?"

"Looks like it," Bailey joined in the conversation, staring at the dismantled track a couple hundred yards ahead of them.

Sergeant VanderJagt hopped from the car and looked around. "Ought to be setting up some pickets. Whoever did this might still be around, and they seem to know what they are doing this time."

Lockett wasn't sure what the sergeant meant by that, but he scanned the horizon and fortunately saw no one.

VanderJagt continued, "Instead, we're wandering around like a bunch of hens after the henhouse door was left open." He muttered a curse and turned in a circle. "Where's the captain? Where's Captain Vincent?"

When there was no affirmative response, he stomped off for the locomotive. Surely, the officer was already up there speaking with the train's engineer.

Lockett and the others took in the fresh, crisp air and loitered by the cars. There were no orders yet, and most did not want to stray too far. After a few minutes, Lockett succumbed to the boredom and strolled up closer to the locomotive to see what was going on.

A closer glimpse of the track ahead told him that they were not going anywhere soon. These bushwhackers were more thorough than the other ones had been. He could see what VanderJagt had spotted immediately. Rather than just ripping up the track and scattering the long iron rails down the hillside, these bushwhackers had a much more complete plan of destruction. Judging by the remnants of the bonfire near the copse of trees, the bushwhackers had placed the iron rails in the fire until the middle had glowed red. Once heated, they then proceeded to take the ends of the rails and bend the middle around the trunks of the trees. The once straight rails were now a curved and mangled mess.

They were never going to be able to use those again, and Lockett knew that they didn't carry any extra rails on the train either.

Going forward would be impossible.

"I guess we are going to have to go back," he said to no one in particular.

Except that he wasn't alone…

Turning to do an about face, he nearly walked into a small wall made up of Hiram Walker and his cohorts. Stunned that he had not heard them approach, Lockett virtually bounced off of them and took two quick steps back.

"I ain't had a chance to deal with you since yesterday, farmer boy," Walker threatened. Bart Randle and Isaac Washburn took an aggressive step towards Lockett on either side. "Nobody holds a gun to my head and gets away with it." He made a show of sliding his hand towards the hilt of the large knife in the sheath at his waist.

Lockett's Dimick was slung on his shoulder, but before his hand could move for it, Washburn's thick hand grabbed his shoulder, right on top of the sling. "You ain't gonna get a chance to use that!"

"You think that I was just gonna forget about yesterday, boyo? You made a *big* mistake crossing me."

They were alone on this side of the train, abreast of the locomotive with the rest of the company lingering on the opposite side and further back. Ahead he could see Captain Vincent and the engineer, still within shouting distance. Their gazes were captured by the torn track, but if they made a quick turn in the other direction…

However, Walker and the others were equally aware of that. Washburn and Randle dragged Lockett between the locomotive and the tender, pulling him completely out of view. Randle clamped a hand over his mouth, and Washburn twisted Lockett's arm behind his back before he knew it.

Lockett canted his body, trying to lessen the pain in his shoulder as Washburn gleefully twisted it harder.

Walker pulled the knife from his sheath. The glinting, oiled blade contrasted notably with his otherwise grubby appearance. Clearly, Walker took considerable care of the eight inch long knife.

"I'll make sure that you don't do that again, boyo."

He took a step forward but stopped when another voice from behind said, "Do what, Private Walker?"

Sergeant VanderJagt held his rifle casually by the barrel, but his stone-faced glare matched that of Hiram Walker and the others.

Walker hesitated.

Feeling Washburn's and Randle's distraction, Lockett contorted and spun free of their grasp, barely holding back on striking out at Washburn as he did so. He stood a few feet away, fists clenched.

"Do what?" VanderJagt repeated, "And I think you better put that pig sticker away."

Walker looked down at his blade, and after a second thought, he slid the knife back into the sheath.

"Ain't nuthin', sarnt," Walker said with an oddly calm tone.

"Be on your way then."

"Course, sarnt."

With a nod towards Washburn and Randle, they departed without even a second look at Lockett. VanderJagt watched them until they disappeared around the locomotive and even then waited another minute. His grip on the rifle did not change, and while seemingly at ease, Lockett could tell the man was as alert as a hawk.

"Thanks," Lockett said eventually.

VanderJagt snorted and shook his head angrily. "Thanks, eh? You want to tell me what that was all about?"

Lockett stared directly back at him. Part of him wanted to tell the grizzled sergeant what he had seen in that farmhouse, what had nearly happened, but he shook his head. Only Patrick and Matthew knew, and he would keep it that way. Sergeant VanderJagt was in no position to help him.

What options did he have? Tell Captain Vincent? The man would never believe him. This was his nephew that he was talking about. Besides, Hiram and his cronies would back

Orrin Long's version of the story, not his. It would be multiple witnesses contradicting the report of a solitary witness. No, there was nothing that could be done, even by Sergeant VanderJagt.

"No, there's nothing to tell, Sergeant."

"Walker was about to gut you with his pig sticker, and there is nothing to tell?"

"Just a disagreement. That's all."

"You ain't good at lying, Lockett," VanderJagt winced with a shake of the head, "But suit yerself."

"Just a disagreement."

"Well, disagreement or not, you better watch yerself. Walker and those other two, they're hardened men. They ain't like you and yer friends, so don't make no mistake about it."

"You don't think we're tough?" Lockett bristled. "You don't know us."

"I know you better than you think, farmer." He shook his head. "They were about to stick a knife in you. That was no joke."

"They were just trying to scare me," Lockett insisted.

"You think so, eh?"

"Of course."

"Lad, they don't think like you do. Don't make the mistake of assuming that they think about things like you do."

"I've already seen enough from them to know that's true twice over."

VanderJagt wondered what Lockett had already seen, but he didn't pry any further. Instead, he said, "Stay alert. And one more thing, you better warn your friends, especially preacher boy. If Walker has it in for you, he has it in for them too. Now, you might as well come with me. I was on my way to see what Captain Vincent and the engineer decided."

"We will have to go back, Captain! I'm not a miracle worker, just a train man. There are no rails. What do you think I could do?"

"I can see that there is no track ahead! Don't patronize me, you damn fool!"

"Then, of course, you see that the only option is to go back, Captain."

"I didn't see any rails back where we stopped last night."

"No, I mean further back than that. Maybe even back to St. Louis..."

"Impossible! I have my orders! We are supposed to report to Sturgeon!"

"I don't know what you expect me to do," the engineer gave up with exasperation.

"There is no time for going back! Go back to St. Louis? My orders already had me in Sturgeon yesterday! We're late as it is!" He left unsaid that he didn't want such a poor first impression on his new superiors in town.

"That's Missouri for you, Captain. Best get used to it. The bushwhackers play holy hell with schedules. Nothing that we…"

"You can go back," Vincent interrupted, "But we are *marching* onto Sturgeon."

The engineer took off his soot-blackened cap and ran a contemplative hand over his bald pate. "That's a long march from here," he started before pausing, "I 'pose it would be a mite shorter as the crow flies. The tracks run south before the switch near Barber's Tavern. Then we'd head west by rail. You might cut off half the distance."

"Exactly!" Vincent declared with satisfaction, although, in fact, he had forgotten the path of the track and was surprised to hear the positive news.

"P'bably a good twenty miles still, I'd wager, but that's better than the forty or so by rail."

"Sir, if I may," Sergeant VanderJagt tried to gently interject. He and Lockett had been joined by Lieutenant Long, and the three of them had silently been watching the exchange.

"You may not! I have no time for interruptions."

VanderJagt bit his tongue and contemplated another way of making his point, but he followed his well established army instinct by giving the slightest of nods and said nothing more to his commanding officer.

"Lieutenant," Vincent said, turning on his heel, "Let's go

find that map in my papers. Sergeant, get the men ready. A little march will serve them well."

The two officers and the engineer departed, leaving VanderJagt and Lockett.

VandgerJagt turned away from Lockett and towards the empty meadow. Trying to keep his voice down, he could not stop himself from muttered curses and concluding with, "Damnation!"

Turning back to Lockett, he stalked over to the youthful private.

"We can march that far in a day," Lockett said confidently.

"Can we?" VanderJagt scowled with a knowing look.

"Of course. It's not that far."

"Oh, lad," he said with resignation, "I know it is not that far, but there is the small matter of all our supplies. We have no horses. We won't be able to carry the supplies with us. It will be bedrolls and weapons only. That ain't so bad for an old-timer like me, but can you imagine our congressman without even so much as a tent? You helped load all of his kit. God help us, but I'm sure that he hasn't thought of that."

Lockett shrugged. What VanderJagt said about the congressman's baggage was true, but he said, "I'm not sure what choice we really have. We are due to arrive, aren't we?"

"Defending the captain, are you?"

"I'm just saying that I can see his position."

VanderJagt shrugged. "Perhaps yer right."

"You don't sound convinced."

"Doesn't matter whether I'm convinced. The only one that matters for convincing is the captain."

"But there's something else, isn't there? It's not just the baggage that bothers you."

VanderJagt raised one eyebrow and ran a hand through his thick, gnarled beard. "Yer perceptive and naïve at the same time… Yes, there's one other thing."

"What's that?"

"It's not just a march. There are bushwhackers out there. Somebody tore up this track. We don't know if it was a band of eight or eighty. I'm not so worried about eight, and I wouldn't normally care about eighty. Hell, we are here to fight'em, big or small, but is this green bunch ready yet?"

The old soldier's words echoed in Lockett's ears throughout the march.

Were they ready?

It had not taken long, only a few miles, to discover that some were destined to be stragglers, even without having to carry more than their own bedroll and kit. Thank God that VanderJagt had privately convinced Captain Vincent not to bring the rest of the baggage by explaining that they could make the march, but not cover twenty miles in a day if they did bring his baggage.

In spite of some straggling, spirits were high and buoyed by the frequent breaks that Captain Vincent himself required, which he publicly blamed on the straggling.

But VanderJagt's words were not far from Lockett's mind throughout the day. Few kept an eagle eye on the flank like he did, but he saw no enemy lurking, just a flat expanse. Across the crunching winter grass, they marched in bright sunshine.

It was cool, but the constant movement made it bearable; however, as the sun began to slide towards the horizon, Lockett found himself wondering about the night. They had no indication that they were close to a town.

It must have been on the minds of others also because when they finally spotted a small farmhouse in the distance, there was a brief exclamation that sounded like relief.

Tucked into one of the bigger stretches of woods that they had seen so far, there was a small, simple house which was skirted by a small creek. Smoke curled up from its chimney.

Not surprisingly, Captain Vincent directed them to change their course slightly, and they headed straight towards it.

Lockett figured that the officer would ask the farmer how close they were to town. At least, that was what he would do, if he was the captain.

"We'll make camp here tonight," Captain Vincent announced to Lockett and the others milling about after he and the officers came out from the house.

Lockett blithely thought to himself that it would not take long to 'make camp' since they had left their tents back on the train, though he knew better than to say it aloud.

"According to that Secesh family inside, we are about seven miles from town, and I don't fancy finding that in the dark. This is a good place for tonight."

And most of the men had to agree with the officer on that. The creek flowed crystal clear water, and the rare patch of forest meant that they would have plenty of wood for a fire. Many of their heads nodded appreciatively.

"Sergeant," Vincent continued, "You and Lieutenant Simon see to passing the word and posting sentries."

As VanderJagt acknowledged and saluted, Vincent continued, "My nephew and I will take up residence in that little hovel of a farmhouse for the night."

Lockett looked over his shoulder at the farmhouse. If the captain considered that a 'hovel,' then he did not want to think about what the captain would say about the humble Lockett home.

"And the family, sir?" Lieutenant Simon asked.

"They will stay in the stable. Sergeant, select a guard to post there as well. I don't want these Secesh to slip away in the night and alert any Rebels or bushwhackers to our presence. Lieutenant Long will be ushering them out presently."

Seconds later, a small procession came from the house and headed straight for the stable, only two of them bothered to look in the direction of the milling troops.

What Lockett assumed to be the father led the way. He was a small, older man with tufts of gray hair sprouting from beneath a short top hat. He moved stiffly but held his head high as he looked emotionlessly at the soldiers who watched them. He was not dressed like any farmer that Lockett had seen before, more like a townsman than a farmer with his starched, stiff white collar poking above the dyed wool of a topcoat.

Behind him was a girl not too much younger than Lockett and many of the soldiers. Like her father she moved with a proud walk and eyed the soldiers, but unlike her father, she glared at them with undisguised disgust, even youthful fury. She too wore clothing that looked out of place for a farm, and she held her long dress slightly off the ground as they quickly walked to the stable.

The last two in the line did not bother to look at the soldiers. The older woman with the streak of gray in her brown hair stared at the ground, and the last person was a young woman who looked much like the first girl, just older. Hers was the only attire that seemed familiar to the farmer in Lockett, and all of her attention was devoted to the small bundle in her arms.

"A baby?" Lockett thought aloud, "It's going to be a cold night for that little one."

"Private Lockett," VanderJagt said authoritatively. If he had heard Lockett's comment about the baby, he made no mention of it.

"Yes, sergeant?"

"You and Bauer are on guard duty at the stable. I'll send McManus and the preacher boy to relieve you in the middle of the night."

Guard duty? Lockett knew that he had heard it right, but he kept the question to himself. Again, the old sergeant had singled him out!

He could really use a full night's sleep, but he answered, "Yes, sergeant."

Once darkness fell and the wind began to pick up, Lockett changed his tune somewhat.

Part of him was thankful that old VanderJagt had singled him out for more duty. At least the small stable supplied some protection from the wind and trapped a bit of the heat from the small fire that the family carefully tended.

Matthew was probably thankful as well, Lockett thought.

Either Matthew had not seen the young girl's frown as she tramped to the barn, or he just did not care, because he spent much of the first hour trying to engage her in a conversation.

As for himself, Lockett stood away from the family that clustered around the small fire. There was a slight opening that would have been just enough for him to join them, and the thought of warming his hands over the yellow flames tempted him, but he resisted. Blowing on his cupped hands would have to do. To join them seemed too awkward to contemplate and would only add to his guilt as he glanced at the small baby in the mother's arms.

Matthew, of course, had no awareness or discomfort, Lockett thought to himself. That was clear after the first thirty minutes of failed conversation with the girl. He had gotten nothing from her other than her name, Ivy Munroe. It was beyond comical that Matthew would carry on the conversation, virtually with only himself, for thirty minutes.

But then to Lockett's amazement, when Matthew's monologue somehow drifted onto the subject of fishing and the creek outside the farm, it actually turned into a conversation. As Matthew and Ivy talked about fish, the rest of the family conversed quietly amongst themselves, although for the most part, they were as silent as Lockett.

An hour later, Lockett's wordless duty was interrupted by Lieutenant Simon.

"Everything okay in here?" the ungainly officer asked, peeking in from the outside.

Lockett stood at the entrance to the stable and looked out to the flickering campfires that dotted the land. A gust of wind blew through, making him shiver, and he looked over at the farmhouse. Lantern light blazed through the windows, and he could imagine the full warmth of the roaring fire in the hearth inside. It was a far cry from those who tried to make do outside with only a bedroll to keep the knifing chill at bay.

He guessed that some of the men were already trying to sleep, wrapped in their blankets and curling up as close to the fire as they dared. Of course, that would not be the case for him. He would be awake at least half the night until they relieved him.

"I said, is everything okay?" Simon repeated.

"Oh, sorry, sir. Yes, no problem with the family, sir. I was just thinking to myself."

"You think a lot, James. I've noticed that. You write in

that journal of yours quite a bit too. A farmer and philosopher, is that what you are? Wondering about the great workings of the universe tonight?"

"Oh, no, sir. I think I'm too practical for that," Lockett answered, not realizing that Simon was joking. "I was thinking about Sergeant VanderJagt and wondering what I did to make him so angry with me."

"Angry with you?"

"Yes, sir. He always seems to single me out, like tonight when it came to picking guard duty for this family. It's fine, of course," he hastened, realizing that he sounded like he was complaining.

Lit by the family's small fire behind Lockett, Simon's face twisted into a curious look. "You think he is singling you out for punishment, is that it?"

"Sorry, sir, no, not at all," Lockett said quickly, recognizing that he should not have said anything to anyone, but especially to an officer.

But instead of being angry, Simon gave a short, snorting chuckle. "You think he's mad at you? That's funny."

"Sir?"

"He's not singling you out… at least not in the way that you think he is."

"I don't understand, sir."

"Look, Lockett. Look out across that camp. There are some good men out there… but they are not *all* good men. I've seen you glare at Hiram Walker and Bart Randle, for example."

Lockett kept his mouth shut, prompting Simon to continue, "Sergeant VanderJagt didn't pick you for guard duty tonight to punish you. Would you rather that Hiram Walker and his messmates were left in charge of these womenfolk tonight? The daughters are rather fetching."

Lockett leaned back visibly at the comment, and his face blanched. He had not mentioned what he and Matthew had seen the day before at the other farm, except to Patrick. Had Sergeant VanderJagt or Lieutenant Simon overheard what had nearly befallen that other woman?

"I can see by your reaction that you think that would be a

dangerous idea as well. No, Lockett, he singled you out tonight because you're one that he trusts."

Lockett looked at the ground in embarrassment before uttering, "I, uh… Thank you, sir. I didn't understand that."

"As for anything else that he is assigning to you, rest assured that there is a good reason. Perhaps he sees something in you, I don't know. Now, back to your duty. I'll have McManus and Bailey relieve you later tonight."

When Lieutenant Simon departed and Lockett turned back towards the stable, he noticed the old man staring meaningfully at him. The baby stirred and gave a brief cry while his mother adjusted the swaddling around him.

"We'll be out of here at first light, sir, I'm sure," Lockett reassured, "Then you can go back to your normal life. I'm awful sorry that they turned you out of your own house."

"It's my son-in-law's house, her husband," he replied, nodding to the oldest daughter.

"I see."

"The rest of us live in town. We were just out to stay with her while her husband is…" he hesitated, "Away."

Captain Vincent's earlier condemnation of the family rang in Lockett's ears with that. Maybe they were Secesh like Vincent had said? Of course, that still did not give them the right to kick the family out of their own home. Was the husband a Confederate soldier? They could come across him on some battlefield somewhere. God in Heaven, what a mess this was!

"Do you really believe that, son? Go back to normal? There is no normal life. Not anymore. Not while y'all are here."

"You don't even look like an army!" the young girl exclaimed, suddenly jumping out of her conversation with Matthew Bauer and pointing at Lockett. "You don't even have uniforms. You ain't no different than us."

You ain't no different than us… Lockett heard the echo of her words. She was right about that.

"The uniforms are just late," Bauer chirped, as he gave Lockett a sour look for taking Ivy's attention away.

Was the old man right? Maybe tomorrow would not be a normal day, not one that they wanted to think of as normal?

Was young Ivy right? He looked down at his plain clothing. Yes, he had to admit that she had a point. Their clothing was no different than a bushwhacker's. Further, there wasn't much difference between this farm and his.

You ain't no different than us...

It was late into the night, and Lockett fought the urge to drift off. He was more accustomed to falling asleep early and waking before dawn than he was at staying awake until the moon was so high in the night sky.

Their relief must be arriving soon, he reminded himself as the temptation to close his eyes lured him again. Glancing over at Matthew, he saw that he too was heavy-lidded and struggling.

The family had long since fallen asleep, and the overwhelming quiet only added to the temptation.

Maybe he could close his eyes for just a minute, he thought to himself.

CRACKK!

Was that in a dream, he thought wildly as his eyes snapped open. Surely, that can't have been a real gunshot!

But Matthew had jumped to his feet also.

"What was that?" he exclaimed.

Lockett finally reacted and ran to the door. As he peered out, there was a flash from within the cabin and the bang of another shot. Taking off at a run for the homestead, he couldn't understand what was happening. Had some bushwhacker slipped into the house unseen? How many were there?

He covered the short distance quickly. As he yanked open the door to the house, he could feel Matthew right on his heels and together they poked their rifles into the room, still well lit by the fire in the fireplace and the candle lamp on the table.

Other than Captain Vincent and Lieutenant Long, there was no one else in the room. A tiny tendril of smoke still twisted free from the barrel of the revolver in Long's hand.

"What happened?" Bauer exclaimed.

Lockett looked dumbfounded at the bloodshot eyes of the two officers and the heavy, sluggish grins on their faces. On the table, a large, empty stone jar of liquor lolled about on its side. It took a second, but then it was obvious to him that the officers were both extremely drunk, although why the shots were fired, he could not guess.

"My nephew is an expert shot," Vincent cackled, pointing to a candle on the edge of the hearth.

Part of it was still upright, but the upper third had been cut off and laid on the stones below, with one end still flickering.

"Shot it clean off," Vincent said proudly. "Missed the first time, but true as could be on the second."

Both privates wondered what was so impressive about that in this tiny room when Captain Vincent added, "The first one was over his shoulder, backwards! Used the reflection in the window like a mirror!"

Lieutenant Simon and Sergeant VanderJagt pushed through Lockett and Bauer at that point. Lockett wasn't sure how long they had been there. Had they heard all of this?

"Like William Tell, he is!" Captain Vincent laughed. "You know who that is, right? No? Used a bow and arrow to shoot the apple off the girl's head, right? William Tell!"

"We should try that! We have a girl in the barn after all," Long slurred.

"Oh, indeed! That would be some sport!"

"They *are* Secesh after all. There'd be no harm…" Long lowered his voice and added, "Of course, the daughters are rather attractive. Perhaps another activity?"

Both privates stiffened noticeably, waiting for some sort of rebuke from the captain, but either he did not hear or did not care, because none came.

Orrin Long looked directly at Lockett at that point, which did not go unnoticed by Sergeant VanderJagt or Lieutenant Simon, though neither could figure out why.

Sergeant VanderJagt then slid to his left between Lockett and the officers. He turned away from the drunk officers and gazed sternly at the two young privates. "Yer supposed to be on guard duty. Go back to the barn at once. The lieutenant and

I will take care of this," he ordered in a firm voice.

When Lockett hesitated, VanderJagt gave a reassuring nod and closed the door behind them.

The two friends walked briskly back to the stable and their guard duty. Neither was sure what to say to the other.

"You heard that, right?" Lockett asked, pausing just a few strides from the barn.

"Yes," Bauer nodded.

In the gloomy darkness, Lockett stared solemnly at his friend. It was insanity, but they could both imagine it – not just the second threat to the 'attractive' daughters, but even the 'William Tell' comment.

It was insanity, and Captain Vincent was right there in the room!

Bauer stared back at Lockett. He didn't know what to say.

They didn't need to see the other's face to recognize the concern and shock that they each felt at this moment.

"We need to get them out of here," Lockett decided suddenly.

"The Munroes, you mean?"

"Yes, Matthew."

Bauer made no noise. He did not even nod in agreement, even though he felt the same way now that the idea was out in the open.

Lockett needed no reassurance though, and purposefully, he marched the last few steps to the side door of the barn. It was already partially open, given their haste in running over to the cabin, and he opened it fully.

"You sure about this? How?" Bauer asked, his voice higher pitched than usual.

"I'll take care of it," Lockett said resolutely.

"What happened? Is everything all right?" Ivy asked when they entered, shutting the door behind them just as a frigid blast of wind blew through.

The rest of the family was awake now, except for the baby who continued to slumber through all the commotion. The family's nervousness was plainly apparent, particularly old man Munroe's wife who stared at the ground, clutching and unclutching her hands.

Lockett supposed he could not blame them, even though they did not know the worst of it. Still, their degree of anxiety and alertness surprised him. They were all very much on edge, especially the elder daughter and the mother.

"Well?" old man Munroe asked when neither of them answered Ivy's question. "What happened?"

The two soldiers set the butts of their rifles on the ground and casually held them with one hand at the top of the muzzle, not wanting to alarm them further.

Each family member noticed the action specifically, and before Lockett could say anything to reassure them, a new voice came from the shadowed recesses of the barn, "They found my stash of corn whiskey, didn't they?"

Two men with rifles pointed at Lockett and Bauer stepped further into the light.

"Don't!" one snapped harshly, gesturing with his weapon as Bauer made the slightest movement to lift his rifle.

Chapter 6

"Who are you?" Lockett asked in a strangely natural, even unconcerned voice, causing Bauer to sneak a sidewise glance at him.

Didn't James realize the guns were pointed at them? Bauer wondered to himself.

"I think I should be asking you that, considering that you are in my barn," the taller man answered.

He was young, only slightly older than the two Michiganders. Though he pointed a rifle at them, there was no malice on his face, which was dominated by a large, hatchet-like nose protruding from his day-old stubble. Under other circumstances, Lockett would have considered it a pleasant, friendly face.

"I said, 'Don't!'" the other one snapped at Bauer as he shifted position, although all that Bauer was doing was shifting his weight to his other foot.

The second man was a shorter, thicker version of the first. His face was similarly dominated by the same large nose; however, unlike the taller one, there was no hint of geniality about him. His thick, black brow was frozen in a harsh, stabbing glare.

"Maybe you should just put that rifle on the ground so that there are no mistakes, friend," the taller one suggested.

"Hold it, Matthew," Lockett said calmly, slowly putting his off hand on Bauer's shoulder.

"What do you think you're doin', Yank?" the shorter one growled in surprise, shifting his aim over to Lockett's midsection.

"You're Mr. Munroe's son-in-law?" Lockett ignored the shorter one, turning his focus to the taller one.

"John Cameron. This is my farm you are trespassing on."

"Where did you come from?" Bauer finally spoke up.

"How did you get in here?"

"You mean past your pickets?" the shorter one sneered, "Damn fools. Wurn't hard. They had little fires keeping'em warm, and they wurn't interested in straying far from them."

Lockett winced noticeably. He had been within earshot when Sergeant VanderJagt had specifically told the sentries 'no fires,' no matter how cold it got. He didn't even want them to light their pipes, lest it give away their position. Damn fools indeed.

"Shoulda slit their throats, but my brother here wouldn't let me."

"Quiet, Lyman," John Cameron ordered, "Not in front of the lady folk."

Lyman Cameron shrugged. "Anyhow, we just slipped past them, easy as could be."

"So you are one of these bushwhackers then," Lockett commented, "Captain Vincent wasn't wrong after all."

"No," John Cameron answered evenly, "I ain't one of them."

"But you could probably call me one," Lyman Cameron answered proudly, his chest puffing out ever so slightly. "Joined up with them a few weeks back while I waited for my durn brother to make up his mind to join me in Tennessee and enlist real official like with the rest of our home and kin. I had to do something while he dithered about with his wife and babe. Only got him to agree yesterday, and lo and behold, you all show up today."

"Tennessee?"

"John and me are going to join up with General Albert Sidney Johnston and his army. The war ain't gonna be won out here in Mizzou. Got to fight in Tennessee or Virginia to win this."

"And you?" Lockett asked the taller Cameron out of curiosity.

"Like he said… I just agreed, and then today happens to reinforce that decision. Got to volunteer so that we end this nonsense."

Lockett pursed his lips. It sounded so familiar. On the

fateful day back in Kalamazoo when they had signed their papers, the same had been said multiple times.

You ain't no different than us...

Ivy's words echoed in his ears again.

Lockett shook his head slowly with a new, grim understanding. "Well," he said with a pause, "That's grand and all, but we need to get you out of here." He turned his head in the direction of old man Munroe and Ivy.

"What?" John Cameron uttered.

"What kind of Yankee trick is that?" Lyman Cameron added.

"You did say, 'we?'"

"We don't need no help!" Lyman Cameron said pridefully, bringing the rifle fully to his shoulder for emphasis.

"Don't be a fool, boy," Munroe finally spoke up. "There are a hundred men outside."

"I'm sure that you could take a few with you, having the advantage of surprise and all, but you are outnumbered, not to mention that there are women and a baby in here." Lockett's placid calm only seemed to make the younger Cameron brother even more red-faced.

"Look, we had already decided before we came back in here that we needed to get the women out of here, and right now."

"Why would you do that?" John Cameron queried, although he did not share his brother's skepticism.

"Because we can't guarantee their safety, and we don't want anything to happen to them."

Matthew looked at Ivy with that comment and blushed.

"This is some sort of trick," Lyman Cameron replied, still unconvinced.

"No," Ivy interjected with sudden confidence, "I thought I heard them say that from outside the door before they came in. I just thought it was the wind or my mind playing tricks. I did hear them say that. I'm sure of it now."

"What happened in that cabin?" Munroe asked tellingly.

"There's no time for that now," Lockett said, "We don't know how much time we really have."

"You want to let us go? Aren't you supposed to be guarding us?" Ivy's sister asked.

"Guarding you, yes… But not from our own officers," Lockett replied tightly. He glanced over his shoulder in the direction of the cabin. "Is there a place you can go, Munroe? Sorry, but I don't know how much time we have."

"There is another farm about a mile from here. It's not on the way to town, so you won't come across it tomorrow. They're friends. We could head there."

"In the dark of night?" Ivy asked worriedly.

"There might be bushwhackers out there," Bauer commented, "Sergeant VanderJagt said that they rule the night. I'll go with them."

Munroe shook his head. "Appreciate the sentiment, son, but if there are bushwhackers out there, we'll be better off without a Yankee in tow. Besides, we have the Cameron brothers now. We'll be fine."

"He's right," Lockett agreed.

"C'mon," Munroe said, helping his wife to her feet.

"Can you get past the pickets without being seen?" Lockett asked the brothers. They both smirked in response. "Then I suggest you go now. Matthew, we need to get our stories straight for what we're going to say."

Matthew muttered something under his breath before replying, "Yeah, I know. Of course, you're one of the worst damn liars, I ever did see, James, so you better let me do most of the talking."

Chapter 7

"You didn't trust me, James," VanderJagt began, stern faced, "Or trust Lieutenant Simon for that matter. I told you that we would take care of it."

It was evening, and they had finally arrived in town only a short while earlier. Unsurprisingly, there had been a delayed start to the day for the obvious reason that their commander and his next-in-command could not be roused in the morning.

Captain Vincent provided what he thought was a convincing excuse, but the entire company knew the real reason, a severe hangover.

The captain's foul mood only worsened when he learned that the Munroe family had somehow escaped during the night, in spite of specifically placing them under guard. Promising heavy punishment for the two culprits, he nonetheless bought Bauer's and Lockett's simple story that they had fallen asleep, allowing the family to slip away.

Not bothering to hide his invectives and declarations of his own men's ineptitude, Vincent had railed against his two privates. Both Lockett and Bauer accepted it stoically. Inside, neither had any regrets.

"What do you mean? Not trust you, Sergeant?" Lockett replied to VanderJagt.

"I *know* that the family didn't slip away when you fell asleep. For God's sake, I sent yer relief only an hour after I saw you in the cabin. So, yes, I can see that you didn't have trust in me to handle the captain in that state. You let them go, didn't you?"

"But, sergeant, if you heard…"

"Oh, I heard," VanderJagt interrupted. "I heard it all. William Tell and the nonsense! God in Heaven, what stupidity! Yes, I heard the same as you."

"Oh," Lockett nodded gently in response.

"And so, you decided to act? On your own? Isn't that right, Private Lockett?"

"Yes," Lockett replied softly, "I didn't see that we had much choice. I feared for the family's safety."

VanderJagt frowned. "Of course, you had a choice. You could have done nothing. That is what most men would have done." He shook his head, and his heavy features softened. He ran a hand through his thick beard. "But… but I am not surprised. That's the type of man you are. I saw it from the beginning when you thought I was crazy enough to shoot young Bauer, and that is why I have been trying to teach you more about the ways of the army. Obviously, I haven't done well enough. You'll have to bear the captain's punishments for this. Luckily for you, he doesn't know much of the army's normal punishments, like the sawhorse."

"Sawhorse?"

"Yes, you'd be made to straddle a sawhorse while holding something heavy for hours on end. By the time they let you off, you'll wish you never had any balls. You'd piss blood for a week and wouldn't walk normal for a month."

Lockett's jaw stiffened, but his face didn't change otherwise.

"But you'd still do it all over again, wouldn't you?"

"Given the alternative for the Munroe family, then yes. I couldn't take the chance."

"I figured. So, it is a good thing for you that the captain lacks that creativity or knowledge of what else could be done to you and Bauer. As it is, yer going to march around yonder tugging a railroad tie behind you for twelve hours tomorrow without water. Lucky it ain't hot this time of year, but still…"

"It was the right thing to do," Lockett said softly.

"The right thing to do would have been to let them sleep in their own house! But this is the army, Lockett. *You* don't get to decide anything. *You* follow what the chain of command says. *You* are the lowest of privates. Why, even Lieutenant Simon doesn't get much say in things, and Captain Vincent will soon find out that he doesn't get much say either."

Lockett stood stone-faced and rooted like a tree, giving no

indication of his thoughts.

"Now, that is more like it," VanderJagt chuckled, "Now, you are learning. I can't tell if you agree or disagree with what I said, but you could always argue that yer response was one of agreement if cornered. Keep practicing that mask of a face. It will come in handy for you, Lockett."

December 18, 1861

The four friends sat around, eating a dinner of salt pork and hard biscuits that had been softened up in a skillet of grease. From the first days of its formation, the company had settled into groups usually of four messmates. In most of these groups, cooking duties rotated. Tonight, it was Luke Bailey's turn.

"Not bad," McManus mumbled with a mouthful, "Not like Martha," he added after swallowing, "But a good sight better than James here."

"It tastes the same to me as yesterday," Lockett replied.

"Nah, little Mary cooks better than you," Bauer agreed, speaking of his niece, "And she's only four."

"You certainly can't blame it on your blood," McManus added, "Because your mother is one of the best cooks I know."

"And to think I went out of the way for you, my good friends."

"Hallo, boys!" Gus Jeltema called as he approached their fire with a wide smile.

"What are you so happy about, Gus?" Bailey asked.

"Uniforms," Gus said proudly, "They're here. I just saw them arrive."

"Uniforms?"

"Are you sure?"

"Or is it just enough for one more company?"

"No, enough for all of us. Saw the crates. There has to be enough for all of us."

"Uniforms," Bauer grinned, "Maybe that means we can get off guard duty and actually get out of this camp and do something useful."

December 19, 1861

"Finally!" Matthew Bauer exclaimed.

The boys from Kalamazoo County stood proudly in two rows, their new blue uniforms topped by their bright red scarves. Some of the men fiddled with their belts and cartridge box straps. Many did it more out of newness and wanting to touch the uniforms than out of actual need to adjust anything. It almost looked like some of them wanted to touch it to make sure they weren't dreaming.

Captain Vincent slowly approached, and Sergeant VanderJagt drew them to attention.

Vincent then strutted across their front with deliberate slowness. With his chest full out, he came to a halt in front of them, pausing as if reflecting upon their first 'real' orders.

"It is my great pleasure to inform you men that today will be our first real patrol into the Missouri countryside. As with the other companies of our regiment, our mission is to seek out Rebel bushwhackers who may be roaming the countryside, or to seek out information on their whereabouts. Further, we are to bring to justice those who willingly aid the Rebels and to be a show of force to dissuade others from doing so."

The words were loud and clear, spoken with a sense of righteousness. "There is no neutrality, men. The citizens of Missouri are either loyal Americans or traitors. Obviously, those who openly work against us are our enemy. Those who provide these bushwhackers and bridge burners information or aid are the enemy and must be arrested. These are General Prentiss's orders."

Captain Vincent continued, "Due to the amount of ground we have been assigned to cover, we will split the company into three detachments." Captain Vincent stepped forward closer to the ranks. "You men from here," he said, placing and arm between where Bailey and Lockett stood, "Will go with Lieutenant Long." He moved farther down the line. "You men will go with Lieutenant Simon. Those in the middle section will go with me."

Lockett's face betrayed no second thoughts, but he knew this went against the practice of the other companies. They always left in force and never divided up. To date, there had been no serious engagements, just skirmishes with small numbers of bushwhackers hiding in the woods. Still, the idea of marching around the slave state of Missouri in groups of thirty did not seem wise to him.

Dear Daniel,

I appreciate your enthusiasm, but you already know the answer. You cannot leave the farm. The family needs you too much right now. I realize that you feel like you are missing out, but that is the way it must be. Besides, you are not missing anything. Somehow, the Kalamazoo Sharpshooters always seem to miss out on the skirmishes.

I have seen enough torn up track and burned bridges to know that there are bushwhackers out here, but there is little we can do as infantry. If only half of us were mounted, we would fare much better. The bushwhackers lurk about but do not stand and fight when confronted. It is very strange, brother, but often, we even know the names of our foes and where they live. Their neighbors have told us the names. Can you imagine a fight in Kalamazoo with neighbor against neighbor? Thank the Lord no such rift has occurred between us and our neighbors like the McManuses.

Take care. I will write again soon.

Your brother, James

December 27, 1861

The dust swirled behind them, seemingly in tune with the whistling of the Kalamazoo Sharpshooters as they marched.

Lockett looked over at his friends. Good God, if Matthew's spirit was any higher, he would be floating! Though Matthew wasn't much different than most of them. Their voices were filled with the excitement of expectation.

Battle!

When Captain Vincent had first founded the company, they all expected this to come and come easily.

And for once, it seemed likely!

They had already given three hurrahs for their Captain

Vincent. "See what having a man like Captain Vincent can do," Abe Dobbins cheered, "Only he could have convinced General Prentiss to give us the honor to confront these scoundrels!"

Lockett didn't dispute the fact that the task at hand was due to the captain's work. What he would have disputed was how much of an honor it really was, and more importantly, whether the captain was the man to accomplish the task.

The day before, General Prentiss had learned of the presence of a band of bushwhackers in nearby Hallsville. According to his information, it was only a small force but still considerable enough to deem worthy of an entire company's attention. The hope was that for once, the Rebels would feel like engaging them in battle.

All of Birge's Western Sharpshooters were tired of chasing shadows who evaporated whenever confronted. The burned bridges and torn up railroad track were clear evidence that there were bushwhackers around, but…

Matthew Bauer, like most in the company, was convinced that the bushwhackers' tactics demonstrated a distinct lack of courage on their part.

Luke Bailey thought he had read in a history book about similar tactics in Spain during the Napoleonic Wars. 'Guerillas,' he called them.

Patrick McManus wasn't at all sure what gorillas had to do with this, but he was frustrated also. They were getting nowhere like this. At this rate, he would never get back to Martha whom he found himself missing more and more with each passing day.

Lockett could only shrug his shoulders. He had not expected to futilely chase men around the prairies either. Not only did the bushwhackers' horses give them a distinct advantage, but they also knew the land and the people. Often, they would strike at night, knowing that the Union troops were usually in their camps then.

But this march on Hallsville seemed like the opportunity that every Union soldier wanted – a stand-up fight. If Rebel bushwhackers controlled the entire town of Hallsville, then maybe they would be more prone to fight for the town rather than run.

However, Lockett was still troubled, because for once, General Prentiss was breaking his rule about moving in force. "Why is the general only sending one company?" he mumbled out loud, not really meaning to bring up the subject.

Unsurprised by the comment, Bauer looked at Lockett's troubled face. "It's only a small band of scum, James," he declared with some irritation, "We can handle them." He frowned in annoyance at the constantly cautious and pessimistic nature of his friend. His cherubic cheeks were flushed, and it was hard to tell it if was from the march or his annoyance.

Lockett thought Matthew looked even younger than Daniel at that moment, and the comment also reminded him of his younger brother, but his voice remained unprovoked. "All I mean is, why only one company when General Prentiss has passed orders for everything else to be done in force?"

He really didn't expect much of an answer. He really didn't want one. He hadn't meant to bring up the subject at all since it was a moot point. He was just a lowly private after all. It wasn't his decision to make.

"Maybe," McManus said thoughtfully, "Maybe the general thought a larger force would scare them off. This time he wants an actual engagement."

"Maybe." There was a certain logic if that was the case.

"It's just a small group of Secesh," Bauer interjected, "They said it would be only about fifty men."

Lockett shrugged, but it was McManus who spoke. "We haven't been here that long, Matthew, but I think by now we all know that there's a lot of cross-eyed folks in Missouri. When they see ten Rebels, it usually means that only two or three were there. But then sometimes, it works the opposite."

"Doesn't matter. We're all ready for a fight. We just need to march faster before we miss this opportunity."

"I wouldn't worry, Matthew," Lockett replied, "I have a strange feeling that for once, you will have your fight."

It was ten miles to Hallsville, and the march seemed to take forever. Lockett imagined that they should be more serious and concerned about an ambush, but the conversational pockets did not die down even with the knowledge that they were getting very close to Hallsville.

"They're goin' run away again," Abe Dobbins said with frustration. His hawk-like face wrapped itself into a fierce scowl so that the veins in his forehead popped out like a curved web from his hairline. The nostrils in his curved, beak-like nose flared slightly. "They ran away before we even caught wind of them this time."

"Too early to tell," his more mild-mannered brother, Jimmy, countered, "Why, they could be in those woods over there." He motioned toward the barren woods a quarter mile away.

"Those woods are so sparse," Abe Dobbins argued, "They couldn't hide a fox, much less some Rebels."

A few men chuckled, but then there was a cry from the front ranks of their column, "Over there!"

They all looked forward, searching for the cause of the warning. For the briefest second, they saw a man on horseback rushing away from them. He disappeared almost instantly, below a low bluff that their road would eventually wrap around.

"We won't be a surprise now," McManus observed, itching the short growth of his reddish-brown beard.

"I guess we'll see if they're still in Hallsville. If they are still there this time, it will be because they want to fight us there, not because we caught them by surprise."

Matthew Bauer stood with his rifle ready, part of one thin line of blue.

They faced a meadow that merged into a small woods. He could make out a few figures in the trees beyond them, although it was impossible to accurately judge how many. His heart was pounding, and he suspected his boyish face must be flushed to a deep red.

To his left ran the road to Hallsville, cutting through the trees. The narrow dirt strip was barricaded at the woods line by a felled tree and two wagons, behind which he could see at least five heads.

Battle! Finally!

Patrick McManus gripped his rifle with unthinking, white-knuckled strength. It was like they were playing a game, he thought, standing here, facing the enemy, neither side moving, just staring across the empty space. It was like a great lull. How long would they stand looking across at each other like this? He was suddenly reminded of what old VanderJagt had tried to impart upon them, back in that meadow where Martha brought food. Looking down, he checked that his percussion cap was still in place and wondered how fast he could reload once this started for real.

Ominously, there was no sound. No fallen leaves blowing in the absent wind; no man moving yet in the dead winter grass of the field; no commands being given since Captain Vincent had ordered them into line of battle. One good volley, the former Congressman had said, and the Rebels would scatter like frightened chipmunks. McManus continued to wait, wondering how it could be so impossibly quiet at a moment like this.

Luke Bailey toyed with his own thoughts. He couldn't see the faces across from him, and he wondered if they were as scared as he was. He couldn't imagine that they were. Anxiously, he looked down at the Dimick rifle that looked so foreign and peculiar in his hands. For a panicked second, he couldn't remember how to reload it, and he closed his eyes and swallowed the lump in his throat. "The Lord is my Shepherd..." he began silently. Before he was halfway through the 23rd Psalm, some of the anxiety passed, at least enough so that he could remember how to load the weapon again.

James Lockett looked up and down the line of blue coated, red-scarved soldiers from Kalamazoo. He himself was standing to the right of the middle of the line. Down at the left end, just across the road, stood Lieutenant Simon and Perry Hollister. Lockett's eyes moved further along the line to the left middle where Sergeant VanderJagt stood just behind the line, and he wondered for a passing moment why he was just behind the line instead of on it.

Captain Vincent had been riding up and down the line on his horse, which he had procured in town. At this moment, he stopped and was in conversation with Sergeant VanderJagt.

To his right, Lockett watched Lieutenant Long's sword flash in the weak sunlight of the overcast day. Next to him, Hiram Walker, Bart Randle, and Isaac Washburn waited.

Overall, he judged few of the faces in the Kalamazoo Sharpshooters to be showing concern. Most wore masks of uncertainty. Some were shaped into expectant stares. A few seemed to be scowling already at the Rebels.

His own face was set in a calm gaze, devoid of any clues about his thoughts. One might have said it was a blank look, except that there was something that hinted at steadiness and determination in his gray eyes.

"Sir," George VanderJagt said again to Captain Vincent, "Please come down off the horse. Yer too much of a target up there."

"Nonsense, Sergeant. I can lead the men much better from up here. Now back in line."

VanderJagt saluted appropriately, but when the captain trotted away, he shook his head in dismay. In their first battle, many would be tempted to break ranks. How irresistible the temptation would be if the captain fell in the first seconds of battle.

Squeezing in next to his nephew, Gus, VanderJagt took one last look down to their left flank. He could see Lieutenant Simon and Perry Hollister across the road, but what he was really examining was beyond them. Further to the left ran some trees that followed them all along the approach to the blocked road. George VanderJagt could see no movement in the dead woods, but he knew that was where he would put men if he were the Confederates, place them right along the unsuspecting, oblivious Union flank.

He had already asked Captain Vincent if he wanted skirmishers to approach the dead trees on the flank, only to be told that it was unnecessary – a simple, direct approach was all that was needed. The Rebels would scatter at the first shot, or so the captain had said.

"Forward!" Vincent ordered, stiffly pointing his saber toward the Rebels in their front.

Spastically, the line advanced, some sectors before others, only to slow down and allow their comrades to move up to their shoulders again. With rifles tilted ready in a ten o'clock position, they lumbered forward.

Lockett tried to measure their speed as they moved, deciding that it had to be half as fast as their normal marching pace. Painfully slow… Lurching forward so slowly in the face of the enemy made absolutely no sense to him but hurrying on without the rest of the line would do him no good either.

McManus noticed that there was still virtually no sound, just the crunch of dead grass being trampled, mixed with the jangle of men's canteens and cartridge boxes.

Earlier, while Captain Vincent had ridden behind the men, he had instructed them to stop at sixty yards for a massed volley. He had given no orders beyond that. Were they supposed to charge after that or reload and fire again? How many men would even remember the simple instruction now? McManus could feel his heart racing, and his mouth had gone strangely dry.

But they continued to slowly close on the bushwhackers, and there was no reply to their advance.

Lockett peeked at his rifle, making sure that his percussion cap was still secured to the nub. He had already double checked that while standing in line. He hoped all of them did. Satisfied, he lifted his eyes forward again and wondered if he should lock his eyes onto a particular target. But he found that impossible at the moment, and his anxious eyes scanned the entire forest before him. How many men were out there? What were they marching into?

He looked over at Matthew Bauer next to him and observed him nervously tapping the trigger guard of his Dimick. They were within 100 yards now, well within the range of the riflemen, especially those like Matthew, and he could see the impatience eating away at the young sharpshooter as they neared the small knoll in the field, which was capped by a large, rotting tree stump.

Yes, Lockett reasoned, Vincent's massed volley would have a powerful impact, but getting this close to their adversary seemed to be taking away some of the natural advantage that the riflemen possessed, their long range Dimick Deer Rifles.

Captain Vincent calmly rode behind the line with a sense of imperviousness.

They were now within eighty yards, and Vincent prepared himself to give the order to fire, but before he could, a smattering of loud cracks broke the air, followed by a number of white smoke puffs from the tree line.

Rather than one well-timed volley, the Confederate fire seemed to spread sporadically from the middle of the forest. Almost immediately there was an odd thumping sound and an abbreviated whinny from Vincent's horse. Multiple balls smacked into the proud animal. One shot slammed into the animal's skull, and yet another tore off one of the shoulder boards from Captain Vincent's uniform.

Before he could react, Vincent's horse awkwardly hit the ground, pinning the stunned captain. The men in front of Charles Vincent looked down at two of their comrades in a puzzled fashion, perplexed at the strange thumping sound.

Only when they saw two of their own on the ground did they realize it was the sound of a lead ball against flesh. With the loud crash of their captain's horse finally registering in their shocked brains, a few sharpshooters turned around in confusion.

"Don't stop, you bastards!" Sergeant VanderJagt yelled at them immediately, raising his rifle for effect, "Advance!"

Satisfied with being given a command, any command, the men faced forward and continued. Sergeant VanderJagt lingered behind them for a moment, pulling their dazed commander out from under the large horse. It was difficult work given the size of the animal and Vincent's complete lack of help.

Though he appeared unharmed physically, VanderJagt

could see that the former congressman was stunned. In fact, given the look on the man's face, VanderJagt wondered if the captain even knew where he was.

The initial sound of the enemy's weapons put the Kalamazoo line into immediate disarray. Many halted in surprise at being fired upon, a few like Lockett, McManus, and Bauer continued on, if only because that was what they had told themselves they would do. Luke Bailey hesitated and then followed after them.

The four of them reached the tree stump on the knoll and realized that they were alone. All of their comrades on their left and right had stopped marching at the sound of the gunfire. Worse yet, no command to fire had yet been given.

A couple of additional sporadic shots spit forth from the tree line. To this point, not one of the Kalamazoo Sharpshooters had used his rifle.

"We need to fire!" Lockett reacted before he could stop himself.

Bauer happily obeyed and took a bead on a figure behind a tree who seemed to be aiming at him. The kick of the rifle against his shoulder calmed him, and he found that he had been holding his breath since the first sounds of battle. Hungrily, his lungs sucked in air, and he busied himself with reloading the rifle.

McManus flopped down on one knee behind the tree stump, fired, and began reloading. Lockett did the same next to him

Only Luke Bailey hadn't fired yet, and as he stood there, he looked around with unbelieving eyes. To their right, Lieutenant Long and those men had disappeared. Only when he looked behind their position did he see them, fleeing as fast as they could.

To their left, some sharpshooters stood and fired in haphazard fashion, but he could already see three blue coated forms down in the field. Most disturbing of all, Luke saw a dozen spouts of flame come from the forest to their far left, pouring fire into the company's left flank. Corporal Hollister turned to face the new threat but too late. He dropped to his knees, both hands grasping his stomach.

"Over there!"

Lockett looked left to see what Luke was talking about.

CRACK! CRACK! CRACK! CRACK!

It was chaos all the way around. The air was full of rifle and musket pops and the zings of whizzing balls. A cheer rose up from the left, and he saw a number of men – dressed much like the Kalamazoo Sharpshooters had appeared just days ago – swarming down on them. A ball thudded audibly into the tree stump that McManus crouched behind.

"We can't stay here," McManus yelled above the din, "The whole company's given way."

A handful of Rebels came out of the woods in front of them now. Further to the left, others were already chasing those who were fleeing and those who still stood in the middle of the field.

Bailey stared agog at the Kalamazoo Sharpshooters on the left. They stood rooted like trees in the pasture. He was sure that it was because their legs were paralyzed by fear like his were.

"Patrick's right," Bauer yelled, taking aim on a particular Rebel leaving the safety of the trees. Without bothering to see if he had hit him, Bauer slid back down to a knee. He struggled to reload from this position, but he didn't dare change it.

"Run?" Lockett decried angrily.

The others looked at his smoke irritated eyes and were surprised to see an intensity and anger they were not accustomed to from him.

"Look! Even VanderJagt is waving us back. There's too many, James!" McManus cried, grabbing him by the shirt collar and pulling him back.

Realizing that Luke Bailey was still standing dazedly in his spot, McManus halted and grabbed him too. "C'mon! C'mon!"

They ran, but none of the bushwhackers seemed to notice or care about the last four Union soldiers on the right to flee. The bushwhackers were too busy rounding up prisoners from the decimated left flank. As he ran, Luke Bailey watched with bewilderment as he saw Abe Dobbins clubbed down by two Rebels. Jimmy Dobbins tried to defend his wounded brother who struggled to lift his bloody body off the ground only to be stopped by a rifle butt to the top of his head. Whether either Dobbins brother was killed there on the ground or taken prisoner, Bailey wasn't sure as he ran after the others.

Finally, Bailey and the quartet of friends reached the thin tree line behind the disaster, and they heard VanderJagt's guttural voice call out to them from nearby. "'bout time you boys made it back! Now, c'mon, we best catch up with the rest of this sorry bunch before the Secesh round up us too!"

Chapter 8

The march back was as solemn as a funeral. For all their chatter and boasting on the way to Hallsville, they had been whipped. Friends had perished, others taken prisoner. They had shown the enemy their backsides in no time at all. Their arrogance and foolishness were laid bare. Humiliation.

That was what battle was like? It all happened so rapidly that many of them could not remember the sequence. They could only recall the moments before it started and the panicked flight. A handful could still visualize isolated memories, more like blurring glances one got when staring at the ground out the window of a moving train.

A small minority remembered everything in vivid detail, like no other day in their life. Everything was captured in startling detail. Things they would never have noticed on an ordinary day were crystal clear, like which way the wind was blowing individual blades of grass, or of a lone bird flying out of the trees above the Rebels as the shooting began.

James Lockett was one of those. For him, the fateful minutes moved with a dream like slowness. How else could his eyes have taken in so much, or his brain retained such imagery or detail?

With their failure so complete and shocking, there was nothing to be said by any of them. It utterly muted the company. Not a man spoke. They moved quickly, mindful that it might not be over. Many looked over their shoulders regularly, but there was no sign of pursuit.

At the front of the ragged column, Captain Vincent limped along. There was no fiery oratory from him now, no lifting of his men's spirits. Downtrodden, his dampened spirit dragged the Kalamazoo Sharpshooters even lower. He appeared dazed and was certainly out of place walking alongside them instead of on his towering horse.

The vacuum of silence and their lack of constant boasting and bluster hung heavy. Lockett mulled how close he might have been to losing a dear friend, or to falling short on the promise that he had made to Martha McManus. He could still taste the grains of gunpowder in his mouth. No amount of spitting seemed to help. Similarly, no amount of fresh air seemed to clear the acrid smell of the white smoke from his nostrils either. He knew his face was set in a hard grimace, but he couldn't change it despite his best efforts. The knowledge that they had all crumbled so easily burned him. For all their boasting, he had expected more from them and from himself. Were they all cowards? Was he a coward too? Deep down, he had long feared that they did not understand what they were getting themselves into, but this was even worse than he would have guessed.

Now that they had experienced defeat, for there was no other word for it, would they be better prepared for the next time? It would be difficult if Captain Vincent did not step forward and rally them. The only soldier who seemed unaffected by the catastrophe was old VanderJagt. VanderJagt still wore his customary flinty-eyed, scrutinizing glare.

He doubted that the old soldier was the type to say, 'I told you so,' but he would have been fully justified in doing so.

* * *

As they returned to camp, each section of messmates settled in around their fires for the night. The men of Company J were keeping to themselves tonight, and the other companies of Birge's men were happy to leave them alone.

Already tales of their cowardice had run through the camp. Their shame was now complete, Lockett mused.

The chill of the cloudless night air made him shiver, and he reflected on how terribly quiet the fires were tonight. There was no fiddle playing or singing or tom-foolery, hardly even a conversation. It was eerie to be in such a large encampment of men and have it so subdued.

"Mind if I join you boys?" VanderJagt asked, sitting down

next to Luke Bailey, close to the fire.

There was a very long pause before the next words were spoken. All five of them were silent as they watched the small yellow flames dance in the night air.

"A lot of boys saw the elephant today," VanderJagt said slowly, "And they didn't like it."

Bailey's confused look turned from VanderJagt to the others, wondering if VanderJagt had been mysteriously wounded in the head today.

"He means that we all saw our first battle today… I think," Lockett clarified.

"Oh."

"I don't know that I'd call that shambles a battle, Lockett, but the men got their first taste of fire today, yes," VanderJagt answered.

"We weren't ready," Lockett said softly.

"You ain't never ready for the first time, not really, but you're right. This group in particular wasn't ready… But that doesn't mean it will stay that way. I saw you boys standing there today, giving it right back to the Rebs, at least for a little while. Course, that was nothing. It will get a lot worse, a lot harder, a lot more of a test of your stamina, and I ain't talking about your physical strength either. You'll see."

They looked at each other before Lockett eventually added, "If that's supposed to make us feel better…"

"Everyone panicked when Captain Vincent went down," McManus observed in a hushed voice.

"He should have rallied us," Lockett criticized.

"He was too dazed," Bauer argued.

"You're both right," VanderJagt answered, ending the debate, "But it wouldn't have mattered anyway with both flanks gone."

"Aye. Lieutenant Long was running so fast, the Secesh couldn't have got a second shot on him even if they wanted to."

"And poor Lieutenant Simon," Bailey interjected.

"He'll live," VanderJagt remarked, "But the boy won't ever look the same again."

Though quiet, most of the men liked Simon, their young

second lieutenant. When his flank had been ambushed, Lieutenant Simon had been among the first to go down, but he was fortunate. The buckshot from a buck-n-ball that had torn through his cheek in mid yell had somehow missed bone and teeth. While his face was a bloody, ragged mess, he'd live.

"What was the total count?" Lockett asked cautiously, although he had already done a calculation in his head.

"Four killed, twelve wounded, half of 'em captured, another four missing, presumed captured."

"Twenty," Bailey said quickly, "Out of ninety-eight?"

"A poor start for the famous Kalamazoo Sharpshooters," Lockett observed.

"We were outnumbered!" Bauer countered sharply, clearly taking offense.

"Don't think so," VanderJagt answered, "If we were, why didn't they pursue us and capture the whole lot of us? We were a sorry bunch by then. The reason is because they were even smaller than we were."

"Just more prepared, waiting for us."

"Exactly," VanderJagt agreed with a sour face, "Course, Captain Vincent told General Prentiss that there were three Secesh companies there, but I sure didn't see that many. The general is no fool. He'll see through that, naturally."

"I think it was less than ten men that hit the flank," McManus added.

"There you have it then."

"We were licked by a force half our size," Lockett said disparagingly.

Suddenly, Bauer leapt to his feet and charged Lockett, angrily shoving him off the log that he sat on.

Lockett sprung back to his feet, but the others were already in the middle, separating them.

"Get your hands off me!" Bauer cried angrily.

"Save it, you damn fool!" VanderJagt snapped.

"Relax, Matthew," Bailey said more gently.

Bauer clenched his fists at his side, glaring at Lockett. With a sharp turn, Bauer pivoted on his heel and headed off into a different portion of the darkened camp.

December 28, 1861

The damage from yesterday seems irreversible. Even the good news from today made us feel worse. We endured the jeers of the other companies all day, especially companies A and H after they returned. At first light today, General Prentiss left with two sharpshooter companies and all five mounted companies of the 3rd Missouri Calvary. After routing one company of Rebels in Hallsville, presumably the same one we encountered yesterday, they proceeded to Mount Zion church, having been given information that this is where the rest of the bushwhackers were. One of the mounted companies and both of our sharpshooters engaged the enemy in heated fighting, eventually driving them from the woods. I am told the fighting in the Rebel camp was hand to hand, but eventually the enemy gave way and left us on the field. General Prentiss complimented Colonel Birge and his sharpshooters on their "gallant behavior". Though this redeemed the regiment as a whole, it only increased the disgrace of our little company. Some are calling us the "yellow company."

Sadly, we also had elections to replace Perry Hollister as corporal, God rest his soul. More proof that this is a sick world, Hiram Walker and his friends bribed enough votes with liquor so that somehow Hiram Walker is our new corporal!

--- the diary of James Lockett

December 29, 1861

Hallsville did more harm than I realized. Luke shared with me today that he thinks he is a coward.

I told him that was far from true, but it was a long talk. I even reminded him of the time that Daniel fell in the Kalamazoo River when he was young and couldn't swim. Luke was the first to jump in after him, though he was not much of a swimmer himself.

Even so, I am not sure that I got through to him. All he could think of was how he froze on that field.

--- the diary of James Lockett

December 30, 1861

Hallsville seems to have changed us in ways that I never would have imagined. First, Luke tells me that he thinks he is a coward. Now this morning, Patrick tells me that he is worried about freezing to death out here in the Missouri winter. The look on Patrick's face was like nothing I'd ever seen from him. Three years ago when the crops failed, I could always count on Patrick to have a smile and try to lift my spirits. But not anymore. Anxiety does not wear natural on him. It's almost like he's had some sort of premonition but doesn't want to talk about it.

--- the diary of James Lockett

January 3, 1862

We have left our camp for town. I never thought I would look forward to sleeping in a stable so much. The temperatures have dropped drastically, and we saw our first snow. With two other companies of Western Sharpshooters, we have swamped this tiny town. The boarding house above the saloon is even more full than the livery. Captain Vincent and Lieutenant Long have occupied the house of a Secesh who joined up with Sterling Price's men.

There have been a few small skirmishes with no casualties. Since Mount Zion, there's been no major sightings, but there is still the occasional torn up track and burned bridge. I imagine this will be normal for the winter. Maybe after the thaw there will be more to do.

---the diary of James Lockett.

"I don't understand," Matthew Bauer said without a lick of compassion, "So Martha didn't write. I didn't get mail either. It's just a letter, Patrick."

"I'm sure that it was lost in the post," Lockett hastened, noting the sorrow on McManus's face. "It will probably arrive with the next batch of mail."

McManus gave a grimace and looked upward at the sky. Pessimism was not like him, and that bothered Lockett more than the fact that there had been no mail for his friend. For the second time in a row, a slew of letters for the rest of the Kalamazooans had arrived, but there was nothing for Patrick, not a single one. They both knew that Martha had promised to write frequently.

Deep down, Lockett worried. Something was not right, but he didn't dare display that to Patrick, not now. He was not himself these days. Patrick's carefree ability to let every worry slide off his back had disappeared, seemingly overnight. For a week now, he had been unnaturally grim.

In a way, Lockett wished that he himself had not received the brief letter from Daniel. At least that way, he could have been more convinced, and convincing to Patrick, that it was just a fluke of the postal system. Except that Daniel had sent a letter, and it had arrived. It had been short and uninteresting, mostly relating to the weather and the difficulty that he had in patching a leak in the roof after a winter storm and subsequent warming period.

"Something ain't right, Matthew," McManus groused softly, "Now, don't go tellin' me anything else. Martha is the type to write frequently, even if I ain't. She must be mad that I haven't sent anything lately myself."

"Well, we're about to rectify that," Bauer soothed. "I'm sure this General Store here in Sturgeon will have some paper and envelopes for you. Then you can write to your heart's content. Of course, you may want James to write it for you since he is always writing in that journal." When the good-natured teasing did not elicit the expected reaction from either of his friends, he added, "Now, the other boys tell me that this General Store is no friend to us. They swear that there is one price for the locals and another for anyone wearing a blue uniform, but...."

"It doesn't matter what the price is," McManus interrupted, "I need to write to her."

They paused in front of the small general store. It did not resemble the large, prosperous Burdick's Dry Goods in Kalamazoo, which was one of the cornerstones of the town. Even so, this store, while small, had a freshly painted sign and gave the appearance of being well run.

"I'm sure we'll find what we need here," Lockett said, just as the front door opened. To his surprise, Lieutenant Orrin Long walked out of the store.

He had been steering clear of the lieutenant as best he could since the incident in the farmhouse. This was actually the closest that he had been to the officer since that day.

Long held the door for them as the trio started inside. "You won't find anything for sale there, not for us anyway," he warned amicably.

McManus followed Bauer into the store with Lockett in the rear. As he started to pass by the officer, Long held out an arm in front of him and let the door close, separating Lockett from his two friends.

As he did so, the friendly facade fell away from Long's face like the scales from the apostle Paul's eyes. "You hold up there, Lockett."

"Yes, sir," Lockett answered slowly, watching Patrick and Matthew disappear deeper into the store.

"I have my eye on you. Don't think that I forgot about how you were slow to obey my orders before."

"Sir?" Lockett replied, his attention now fully on the young officer. He feigned a dumb look and thought that he managed it rather well.

"At the farmhouse," Long added, studying the obtuse look on the farmer and deciding that it might be real.

The two of them looked at each other, as if assessing and weighing what to do next. It was less like two bucks weighing their foe before locking antlers, and more like two men who weren't sure that they understood the other.

Though Lockett's first instinct was to avoid confrontation with the nephew of the powerful congressman, the longer he stood there, the more the bile rose in his throat.

Despite his best efforts, images of the unknown woman and her son rose to the front of his mind, and then he remembered Long in the Munroe daughter's cabin. Would he have really tried to shoot an apple off the younger sister's head just for drunken revelry? The more that he stared at the smug face, the more that he could see Orrin Long trying to do just that…

With his anger building, Lockett tried to think of something else or to change the subject, anything to slow the rage that was building in him like a slow boil.

"Were you meeting with the shopkeeper about trying to find replacements for some of the supplies that we are missing?" Lockett asked, thinking of some of the men who were still missing a second blanket, which was becoming increasingly important as the temperatures dropped.

Orrin Long's Adam's apple moved noticeably as he swallowed hard. He suddenly recalled that the first time he had seen Lockett was in Kalamazoo. Lockett had been one of the soldiers unloading Uncle Charles's things, while Long himself had been in conversations about the kickback on the bid fixing. That scheme had been about short-changing the count and quality on the cracker barrels and the crates of winter blankets.

He had not thought that the farmer was within earshot during that 'negotiation', but Lockett's query made Orrin Long second-guess that now.

Did the dirt poor farmer know something? Was he threatening him? The gall of the impudent little farmer! Didn't he know who he was talking to?

Lockett was surprised that his attempt to change the subject had left Orrin Long so speechless. He wasn't sure what to make of that when Long suddenly stuck a finger in Lockett's chest and declared, "You'll regret threatening me, farmer. I swear you will!"

And with that, Orrin Long stalked off, leaving Lockett dumbfounded about what had just happened.

When Lockett entered the store, he was surprised to learn that the shopkeeper behind the counter was none other than the elder Munroe. Matthew was trying to engage Munroe in a conversation, oblivious to the pained look on the older man's face.

When a floorboard creaked to his left, Lockett turned and found one of the locals watching the one-way conversation. He was a short, thick-set man with a long black beard. The scowl on his face left no doubt about his hostility towards the newcomers.

Then beyond the scowling local, Lockett noticed Ivy Munroe peeking out from around the corner. Making eye contact with Lockett, she motioned for him to be quiet and flicked her eyes away. Lockett picked up right away on what she meant.

She didn't want any of the soldiers to let on that they knew the Munroes, not while the scowling local was there.

Deciding that he'd better act before Matthew saw Ivy and made the Munroes even more uncomfortable, Lockett said loudly, "I believe you were here first, sir." He motioned the local man to the front. "Matthew, let this gentleman go first."

Bauer turned and realized for the first time that someone else was in the store. As soon as he had seen the elder Munroe, he had gone straight to the counter. Bauer looked blankly at the local man Lockett had referenced. There wasn't much that was gentlemanly about the scowling local, but Bauer shrugged and said, "Of course, didn't mean to jump ahead of anyone."

Grudgingly, the man approached the counter and slowly purchased chewing tobacco. He gave all three Michiganders the distinct impression that he didn't want to leave the store until they did, but with a departing grunt for Munroe, he left.

Lockett's eyes followed him through the window until he was well down the street. Bauer and McManus watched Lockett curiously, not sure what was happening.

"Thanks for your discretion," Munroe said eventually, "If I get a reputation for doing business with Yankees, I fear what could happen to my little store."

"What does that mean?" Bauer asked blankly.

"He means that they might burn it down," Lockett speculated.

Bauer gave a skeptical frown, but Munroe nodded grimly.

"Burn it down? How? Who? That man that I just let pass?"

"Maybe him, maybe someone else," Munroe replied cautiously.

Bauer was about to make a statement about arresting the

man when he noticed Ivy poking her head around the corner again.

"Ivy!" he exclaimed.

She smiled shyly and glanced at her father.

The elder Munroe took a quick look out the window and saw no one. He nodded, which elicited a smile from Ivy and only then did she approach Bauer. Immediately, they were engaged in conversation, and Lockett turned his attention back to the father.

"I knew you weren't a farmer, judging by your clothing when I first saw you. I guess this explains it. It's a nice store, Mr. Munroe."

January 7, 1862

"What are you always writin'?" Sam Moss asked Lockett as he sat in the corner of what had once been a horse stall.

"This?" Lockett asked, holding up his small, leather-bound journal. At one point, it had looked brand new, but after two months of marching and army life, it had taken on a more battered, well-used appearance.

"Yup, what is that?" Moss said, "You're always writin' in it. I thought Luke was the student. Or are you one too?"

"No," Lockett laughed softly, "I'm just a farmer."

"But he does have a way with words," McManus broke in from the other side of the stall, his hat pulled over his face as he dozed in the corner. It had been a long day, and they all felt it. In fact, that was partly what had prompted Sam Moss's question. As tired as they were, the last thing he wanted to do was pull out a book or start writing.

"I do like my reading and writing," Lockett agreed, "It was always the numbers that gave me problems."

"Could never do my figures," Moss said with some embarrassment.

"Didn't even know that you ever tried," John Quinlan quipped from across the livery.

"Shut your trap, Johnny! You know I tried!"

If there was one thing that Lockett had noticed about Samuel Moss, it was that at times he could be surprisingly sensitive about his intelligence. "This is my journal, Sam," Lockett said, diverting his attention.

"Journal?"

"He's taking our history down," McManus explained.

"Really? Am I in it?"

"What for?" Quinlan asked sourly. "We don't do nuthin' other than drill and march, look for bushwhackers…" he trailed off into a pause before adding, "And I sure don't want no one to know about how we ran at Hallsville."

There was an uncomfortable silence as they all privately acknowledged the truth of the statement. It was an embarrassment that they would never rid themselves of.

"I wouldn't really say it is a history like Patrick said. It's more of a diary, Sam," Lockett said, gently clearing his throat, "Just some of my thoughts. Though, I guess, I do write down some of the events that have happened."

"Like Hallsville?" Moss asked in a tight voice.

Though the jeering from the other companies had subsided somewhat, the memory of their failure still clung tightly to the Kalamazoo Sharpshooters. Inactivity brought on by winter only made it worse.

Lockett nodded. He was tempted to tell a white lie that he had not written much about it, but in truth, there were numerous pages on his thoughts before and after Hallsville.

January 10, 1862

"This is ridiculous. They're goin' to kill us like this. I treated my cows better back home," Private Pete O'Shea complained to Lockett.

He was a man of average height with unusually thick shoulders, strengthened by years of hard work behind the plow. With tightly curled brown hair, thick growth along his cheeks, and a hard stare, he gave many a person the wrong impression. He looked like a man ready to fight at the slightest provocation. Despite appearances though, Lockett had found him to be one of the more practical and reasonable men in Company J.

"Those of us who aren't sick yet," O'Shea continued, "Will be sick before long. An' the ones who are already sick are goin' to die if this cold spell doesn't snap."

Lockett nodded in reluctant agreement. Cocooned in his blue wool uniform with a filthy, soiled blanket wrapped around him for additional protection, he tromped slowly over the frozen, snow covered ground.

He and O'Shea seemed to be the only ones about today. He knew that the temperature had to be below zero, but it was the wind that cut him to the bone like a sharpened Bowie knife.

The warm spell of the previous week had left muddy footprints all over Sturgeon, but now in the bitter cold, those muddy footprints had been turned into rock hard, ankle-breaking traps. The wind that blew out from the northwest lashed his face, and he knew that he better get back inside the livery before frostbite did him in.

Although he wasn't sick yet, nearly one in four of the Western Sharpshooters was feverish.

"What a wasted effort this was," O'Shea continued as if unaware that the freezing temperatures had muted Lockett's tongue, "How can the regimental surgeon turn away sick men? I know he's filled up in that tiny little house." O'Shea answered himself, "But leaving sick men in this rotting livery will kill everyone. You all right, James?" O'Shea stopped, noticing that his companion hadn't made a comment yet.

"Fine, Pete, just cold. Let's hurry."

"I know, I know. It's scarcely warmer inside that livery though. The draft that blows through there... sometimes, I think it will blow the fire clean out."

Lockett grunted in reply again. O'Shea was right. For the effort they went through in getting the army stove, it seemed of little benefit. The livery was too big and too open to be sufficiently heated by the small army stove designed to heat a Sibley tent.

They entered the crowded livery, and Lockett immediately noticed the strong smell of the place. The air outside was freezing cold, but at least it was clean smelling. The livery reeked of sick men, and Lockett forced himself to block out thoughts that he would soon be sick himself if he stayed here in this environment. Making his way over to McManus's bed of hay on the frozen ground, he went down to one knee.

"How do you feel today?"

Shivering, his normally ruddy face was pale and damp with sweat. Patrick McManus still managed a feverish smile. "Better 'n Quinlan," he said, rolling his head to a side and looking at John Quinlan across the room, mumbling in a delirium.

Unable to hide the concern, Lockett's eyes followed across the room.

"He talks more now than he does when he's well," McManus joked in a weak voice, closing his eyes again, as if the effort to speak had exhausted him.

"What did Doc Curtis say?" Bailey asked, approaching with Bible in hand. He had been reading some passages to try to lift the spirits, but if it did, he could not tell. In the back of his mind, his voice kept reminding him that it was only mid-January. He couldn't imagine another two months of this.

"The doc said that he had no room, Luke," Lockett answered, "Maybe he could take a few of the most serious cases in a couple of days."

He left unsaid the rest of the doctor's words, "After the others are dead."

"What does 'serious' mean? They're all serious," Bailey snapped, "Quinlan's dying over there. He hasn't eaten in days, hasn't come out of that delirium for days. He just..."

Lockett pulled him aside before he could finish, dragging him from the corner of the stable that was now Patrick's home. "Luke," he said in a hushed voice so that even Patrick could not hear him, "They're all dying slowly, but reminding them of that isn't going to help. Understand?"

As the sleet pelted the window and the wind gave a lonesome moan, Orrin Long pondered his bad luck.

For two years now, he had ridden his uncle's coattails in the state capital, and there had been plentiful opportunities to pad his own pockets there. He had been sure in those days that he was well on his way to becoming a great and powerful man, and even richer than his uncle, who lacked some of the necessary awareness of what opportunities were out there.

When Uncle Charles told him that he was leaving the state capital and that he was going to form a volunteer infantry company, there had been momentary alarm. The Army? He would be missing out on the opportunities that the state capital could provide…

They both knew that this new tack was never kindled by any selfless action or thought. There was a clear ulterior motive. It was a way to spread his name far beyond Kalamazoo County. For larger and greater roles, the name Charles Vincent needed to reach more broadly than little Kalamazoo. What better way to demonstrate his great leadership than in this national turmoil?

Orrin Long had to admit that his first reaction was negative to the change, but then he realized that the 'business opportunities' could be just as ripe with the army as in the halls of government, perhaps more so even. On top of that, this was his opportunity too. He could make his own name with a broader group of important people. Many of these colonels and generals were titans of business or on higher pedestals within state or national governments – all the better for his own long-term ascension to these roles.

But this posting to central Missouri was the worst of luck. Not only were there few opportunities to make money in the little communities, but there was little interaction with other military leaders at this far flung outpost. How much better it would have been to be assigned to northern Virginia and closer to Washington D.C.!

He'd do anything to get to some other posting, but he had no control over that, not yet.

Adding to his sour mood, there was this seed of suspicion. He had not forgotten the oddly spoken words from the tall, loathsome farmer.

Was Private Lockett truly aware of his activities? That was what the dolt had implied in front of the General Store, but then there had been no other mention of it since that day. Did the idiot know something or not? If Lockett intended to use that information to extort something from him, then why such silence?

Was he waiting for the right moment? Orrin Long couldn't see that simpleton farmer as cunning enough to do that. Perhaps he was overreacting and reading too much into the simpleton's words?

Long walked through the conversation again in his head. He could be reading more into it than was really there…

Regardless, he owed Lockett some comeuppance for his refusal to follow orders back in the farmhouse that they had raided during the first day on the train.

Yes, Orrin Long decided, some comeuppance was long overdue, and while he was at it, he might as well do it in such a way as to dispose of Lockett as any sort of threat. Based on Lockett's past behavior at the farmstead, he had a good idea of how to handle the farmer.

January 15, 1862

Warm weather melted the snow which had swept across Missouri, and at least for the moment, there was a slight reprieve from the low temperatures. With a growing sense of curiosity, Luke Bailey and Matthew Bauer waited outside of the small house that served as the officers' lodging and headquarters in Sturgeon.

The door opened, and Lieutenant Simon came out followed by two civilians. "How are you today, Luke?" Simon asked. The wound in his cheek was healing about as well as could be expected. The pinkish, new skin folded in on itself in haphazard fashion, leaving an ugly, puckering pocket-like scar that stretched from his cheek bone to his lower jaw. The new tightness of the skin was painful and caused him to mumble, and most found it impossible not to stare.

"Fine, sir," Bailey replied, pulling himself to complete attention.

"This is Mr. Kotler and his assistant Mr. Smith..."

Bailey's eyes flashed first from the fleshy, white-haired man to his younger, cheerful looking assistant. The older man seemed to return the scrutiny with accusing eyes set behind a hooked, hawk nose and a wrinkled, heavy brow. The younger man, named Smith, had friendly brown eyes, and he smiled in acknowledgment.

"...they're from the railroad company and are here to examine the track west of town. The captain decided that since there has been no activity since Mount Zion, it would be quickest and easiest if these gentlemen were taken out by handcar. You and Bauer are to help them in whatever fashion they require."

"Yes, sir," they answered.

Minutes later, they waited outside of the saloon with Mr. Smith. Bailey guessed that Smith was about ten years older than him and about twenty years younger than Mr. Kotler. The pleasant-faced Smith had an overall well-kept appearance that the soldiers of Birge's Western Sharpshooters had lacked for some time. Though Bailey still went clean-shaven, and Bauer appeared not to shave yet, their uniforms were rumpled, soiled, and possessed a noticeable odor if they stood in a closed room for too long. The only thing clean and polished about them was their rifles, which Sergeant VanderJagt made sure they cleaned meticulously.

Looking down at his mud-caked boots and trouser cuffs, Smith grimaced. The warmer weather had temporarily turned the roads into a shallow muck that clung to everything. "Nice weather you boys are having. Be glad to get back up on the track and out of this stuff," he commented with a friendly voice, "Call me Thomas by the way."

"Nice to meet ya, Thomas," Bauer said, taking the extended hand, "Matthew Bauer."

"Luke Bailey."

"You boys don't sound like you're from around these parts," Thomas Smith said, his own accent sounding similar to theirs.

"Michigan," Bailey answered.

"The Kalamazoo Sharpshooters," Bauer added. A few weeks ago, he would have said it with a chest full of pride that bordered on arrogance, but now, he spoke in a more matter-of-fact tone.

"Ah," Smith said with a smile, "Ohio myself."

"Mr. Kotler from there too?"

"No, St. Louis. By the way, don't mind him too much. I mean, he, ah, rubs people the wrong way sometimes. He doesn't mean anything personal by it, treats everyone like that."

Bauer gave an unconcerned shrug.

"Think we can live with that for a day?"

"S'pose we'll have to."

"Just thought I'd warn you. It could be worse though. You could be me and travel with the old coot full time," he started to chuckle as the balding, fringed with white hair Kotler emerged from the saloon.

"Let's go," Kotler said gruffly, walking past them towards the train stop with a heavy-footed gait. "Hope you boys are stronger than you look," he grumbled to Bauer, "These handcars can be hard work."

"Don't worry, they're pretty easy on the flat of the prairies," Smith countered softly.

"Huh? What's that? Smith, you say something behind my back again?"

"No, sir."

"Course not, never do, do you, Smith? Always the wind playing tricks with my ears, eh?"

"Just telling our escort that the handcars aren't complicated."

"Complicated? Course not. A monkey could do it. You just pump the bar up and down. Complicated? That's the dumbest thing I ever heard. Don't you boys know anything? No, course not, right off the farm. I can smell the manure on you still."

"Actually, neither of us are farmers," Bauer replied, causing Kotler to frown, but he ignored the interruption nonetheless.

"Just hope you boys are strong enough, because I don't do the manual labor. Do you understand me?" He stopped to look Bauer straight in the eye. "Smith here may offer to spell you once in a while, but I never do. Got it?"

"Yes, sir."

"Course, you do. And Smith, they're not an escort, they're the muscle to move the handcar. Understand? The army has assured me that there is no more Secesh trash wandering around this part of Missouri since General Prentiss chased off that Colonel Dorsey and the rest of his band of thieves and murderers."

Bauer was about to say that if there were no bushwhackers, then why the reports that the track was torn up, but Bailey elbowed him gently in the ribs before he could.

They reached the small square hut that marked the Sturgeon train stop and looked at the handcar that waited for them at the switch.

"Smith, I have one thing left to take care of before we go verify the condition of this track. I'll be right back," Kotler added brusquely and waddled inside.

"Ever done this before?" Smith asked them as they walked over to the small contraption.

"Looks easy enough," Bauer said, examining it.

"It's a simple device," Smith assured, pulling himself up onto the wooden platform, "You just grab this handle and pump it up and down."

"One of us on each side?"

"I think that works best."

"How's it know which way to go?"

"What do you mean?"

"Like if we wanted to go in the other direction?"

"Oh, that's easy enough. Stop pumping and then pump in the other direction."

Bauer made an appreciative face and jumped up onto the wheeled platform. "How far we going?"

"Good question. I'm not real sure. It's up to Mr. Kotler."

"No difference, Matthew," Bailey said, looking at his rifle, "It's better than sitting around here cleaning this again."

* * *

"Because Captain Vincent ordered it so," Orrin Long replied harshly.

The question had come from Private O'Shea.

Lockett had the same question and more. Where were they

going, and why did they need to procure two wagons temporarily? But he knew better than to utter such things aloud. Strangely, even though the query had come from O'Shea, Lieutenant Long's eyes burned directly at Lockett, as if he had asked it.

"And that is all you need to know," the officer added, still glaring at Lockett like he was the only audience, but there were ten men in the group, which included Hiram Walker and his cronies.

With the officer focused on him, Lockett stiffened his posture slightly and tried to keep an impassive mask. A couple of the other soldiers gave each other furtive, sidewise glances as the moment lengthened.

When Long finally turned on his heel and ordered them to follow, Lockett allowed himself a deep breath.

"What's this all about?" O'Shea whispered to him, but Lockett only shook his head in reply and noticed Hiram Walker grinning crookedly as the column moved out.

The sense of foreboding only grew as he reflected on the fact that Patrick was still in the stable, sick, and that Luke and Matthew had been called away on some other task. He was friends with O'Shea and most of the others, but not like with his messmates.

Angrily, he forced himself to think of something else, chiding himself silently for such unnecessary apprehension. The weather was warmer today than it had been in a while, he forced the topic into the front of his mind.

But he couldn't keep his thoughts away from trying to make sense of the tingling belief that something was up.

"Good day for a long march, I 'pose," O'Shea tried to start up the conversation again. "I guess that is why we need the wagons."

"They ain't loaded though," another soldier pointed out.

Lockett scarcely heard them, and it was only a matter of seconds until O'Shea's supposition was proven wrong.

Lieutenant Long led them straight down the muddy street to the Munroe General Store and ordered all of the men inside to their surprise. Lockett followed along with the others but with a sudden surge of dread.

There was one customer in the space that was suddenly made much smaller by the presence of ten soldiers and their officer.

"Leave!" Long snapped gruffly at the middle-aged customer who conversed with Munroe across the store counter.

When the customer hesitated with a confused look, Hiram Walker grabbed him roughly by the shoulder and propelled him towards the door. Bart Randle held the door open, and Walker's two-handed shove sent the man sprawling out onto the muddy road.

"Some people jus' don't know what's good for 'em," Walker laughed.

* * *

Matthew Bauer's eyes wandered across the flat plains as they propelled the cart with a steady up and down pumping motion. Thomas Smith had been right. It wasn't that difficult once they got the speed up. When they had first begun from a standing start, he had been a little worried, but now, they easily kept up a moderate speed.

They sliced through the cool wind, but the temperature did not bother him. In fact, it was refreshing, and he felt like he was cleaning some of the stink off of him. This way is much preferred over a dip in freezing water, he thought to himself.

"You say neither of you are farmers?" Smith called from the back. While the two soldiers pumped the lever in the center of the cart, and old Kotler situated himself in the front of the cart looking for damaged track, Thomas Smith lounged near the brake lever in the rear.

"What?"

"Young Matthew here said earlier that neither of you are farmers."

"That's right. Luke is Reverend Bailey's son. He's about the most famous person in the whole county."

"Sorry. Never heard of him," Smith answered after noticing that Matthew had paused, waiting for a reply.

"He's not that famous," Bailey blushed, "Matthew's exaggerating. He's just a small country preacher."

"But he goes to Chicago to speak at the Abolitionist meetings," Bauer added.

"Prayer meetings," Bailey corrected, "And that doesn't mean that he's famous."

"So your father is one of *those* people," Kotler broke in with a condescending tone, "It's because of people like that and their Mr. Lincoln that we're in this mess."

"It's not the God-fearing abolitionists who have caused this, sir," Bailey replied calmly. "It's those who enslave God's children."

"God's children?" Kotler laughed, "How many of these children have you met in your life? How many, boy?"

"Many," he replied coolly, "There have been dozens who have stayed with us on their way to freedom."

"Freedom? Are you trying to tell me you hid slaves?"

Bailey gave no reply, but the look on his face was answer enough.

"You're a lawbreaker. You realize that? You, who claim that the South has no right to secede, and you're a lawbreaker yourself."

"I'm obeying a higher law."

With annoyance, Kotler turned back around to face the track. Smith broke the uncomfortable pause.

"What about you, Matthew? You're not a farmer either?"

"My father owns a small sawmill. Kalamazoo is a big lumber area."

"Interesting," Smith said for lack of a better reply.

Without thinking, Bauer wondered how his father was doing. He could see the old man hoisting lumber up onto the platform for cutting. He was surely missing his son's back in that task. And though Bauer did not miss that particular aspect, he did miss hearing the reassuring swirl of the creek which provided the power for his father's sawmill.

The monotony of the pumping motion and the steady click-clack as they rolled from one rail to the next only served to add to his daydreaming. Eventually their backs and shoulders began to tire. The two of them began to alternate to give the other a small rest, and Thomas Smith also obliged them by lending a hand for a brief spell. Overall, their speed was dropping, but there was no rush. The track was fully intact, and they had seen no evidence of damage.

Bored of the silence, and not caring that it might further rile his boss, Thomas Smith asked Bauer if fighting slavery was why he had volunteered.

"Slavery?" he replied in a softer voice, "Not really. Not that I think any man should be put in chains, but I never thought about it much and still don't. No, I volunteered because it seemed like more fun than loading trees into a sawmill from dawn till dusk." He took a peek at Bailey, who gave a dissatisfied frown but said nothing about his friend's reasoning.

"This does sound more exciting," Smith agreed.

"Maybe you should get it over with and volunteer yourself, Smith," Kotler interjected from the front.

"I could never be a sharpshooter," Smith said with a shake of the head, "I'm a terrible shot."

The comment struck Bauer as funny, and he laughed aloud.

"Don't worry," Bailey explained, noticing Smith's quizzical stare, "He's laughing at me, not you."

"Oh?"

"Matthew, well, he's the best shot in all of Kalamazoo County, but me... Well, I'm not so good."

"Not so good?" Bauer teased, "You couldn't hit the broad side of a barn when we started."

"And you're a sharpshooter?" Smith asked with some confusion.

"I had to volunteer somewhere."

"But he's getting better," Bauer added, stopping his laughter momentarily, "He's hitting the barn door now." He started laughing again.

Ignoring him, Smith continued, "So how has it been? It sounds like you boys had some excitement at Mount Zion Church."

Matthew Bauer stopped laughing and bit his lip. Bailey also said nothing, but they were saved from answering by

Kotler's yell.

"Whoa! Brakes, Smith, damn you!"

Immediately, they stopped pumping, and Smith applied the brake.

"Good God, took you long enough, like a deaf man today you are, Thomas," Kotler groused, "We have some torn up track ahead."

They peered over the older man's shoulder. Twenty yards ahead, the rails had been ripped from their ties. They could see some of the steel rails off next to the track, a few others were pulled even further away.

"I guess there are still some bushwhackers out here after all," Smith remarked.

"Nonsense," Kotler replied, "This track hasn't seen a soul in three weeks. It's probably been like this since then. I'm sure the Army is quite correct in their assessment that any bushwhackers have headed to safety in southern Missouri."

"Now what?" Bailey asked after another moment, "Do we fix it?"

"With just the two of you?" Kotler replied caustically.

"No spikes or other tools with us," Smith added more gently.

"Let me examine the track a little more," Kotler ordered, lowering himself down to the ground.

"What about that farmhouse?" Bauer asked, "Should we see if they've seen anything?"

They all looked to their left where he was pointing at a small farmhouse about three hundred yards away that no one had noticed earlier.

"Looks more like a shack than a house to me," Kotler said contemptuously. Even from here, the small wooden structure looked defeated by the weather. It was not clear if there was anyone still living there, or if it was abandoned like many farms owned by Confederate sympathizers in North Central Missouri.

"Might as well see what they know," Kotler declared, taking one last look at the small stretch of torn up track. Stumping off toward the house with the others in tow, he added, "Let me do the talking."

"Yes, sir," Bailey answered, trying not to laugh, and they wordlessly followed his waddling gait to the shack.

The house was in the middle of the flat farmland. A quarter mile behind the house, there was a small forest, though it would provide scant protection from the whipping wind.

"Luke," Bauer whispered, "While Kotler does all the talking, I'm going to take a quick run into the woods. Call of nature."

While the others went straight to the front door, he headed around the side of the small house. Looking at the edge of the woods, he wondered if there were any squirrels or game in the woods. Some fresh meat for dinner tonight would be a real bonus to the trip.

Kotler knocked on the door, half wondering if the decayed wood would give him a splinter. He didn't really expect anyone still lived in the derelict structure, so he was surprised when they all heard a coarse voice yell from inside.

"What are y'all knockin' for?"

The door swung open, and a dirty looking man with a short, greasy beard stopped in midsentence. With his mouth agape, his eyes flashed immediately to Bailey's blue uniform and the rifle casually resting on his shoulder.

"Sir?" Bailey said before remembering that he wasn't supposed to speak. It wouldn't have mattered since old Kotler seemed thrown by the man's appearance as well.

"What do you want?" the man asked suspiciously. His tongue curled over yellowed teeth, and he took a step back with a furtive glance to his right.

Suspicious himself now, Bailey was about to speak when Kotler recovered. "May we come in?"

"In?" the man said slowly.

"Yes, in, of course. We want to ask you some questions about the track."

"Track?"

"The railroad track in front of your farm has been torn up."

"It has?" the man responded with a slow deliberateness.

Bailey wasn't certain that the man's reply was either a

statement or a question.

"Do you know when that happened?"

"The track?"

"Yes, the track," Kotler continued with growing annoyance.

Coming around the corner of the house, Bauer rubbed his wind chapped cheeks and began to purse his lips and whistle when his eyes were drawn to another section of the forest. Stopping short, he looked at the leafless trees that had been obstructed from view by the farmhouse. It took a few seconds for it to register what he saw.

At the edge of the woods, there were tents and a small cookfire. He stared uncomprehendingly at the men in simple, winter clothing gathered around the tents, talking, unaware of the onlooker.

He could hear the booming laughter of one of the men echo across the field, and slowly, Bauer began to back up. Within the forest, he could see a half dozen horses tied to the trees.

"Bushwhackers," he whispered to himself, and he turned and sprinted back to the front of the house.

"May we come all the way in?" Kotler asked again with some annoyance.

Stepping to the side, the man answered with a crooked smile, "Of course."

Bailey looked at Smith who shrugged in reply.

"Again, Mister..."

"Cole."

"Mister Cole, did you see who ripped up my track?"

"I did. I did indeed, suh."

"Well?" Kotler said impatiently.

Lunging with surprising speed toward the crude fireplace, the man yanked an old smoothbore musket off of its pegs above the hearth. Before anyone could react, he had the musket pointed at Luke Bailey's chest.

"Don't get any ideas, Yankee!" the man snarled, causing the volunteer soldier to drop his other hand as he reached for the rifle on his shoulder. "I saw exactly who tore up your track.

It was me and the rest of the marauders!"

Just then, Matthew Bauer violently swung open the front door, causing the bushwhacker to spin to his right and fire. The crack of the musket was deafening inside of the small room. Frozen in place, Bauer stood with mouth open and looked at the door. Just below his hand, there was a new hole in the rickety wood.

Realizing that he had missed in his haste, the man named Cole stood stock still for a moment, unsure what to do. Finally, he took a step toward the new intruder blocking the doorway, but Bailey was ready this time. The resounding bang of the man's musket had brought Bailey into action. Pivoting on his heel, he thrust his rifle as hard as he could, butt first into the side of the man's head.

Cole had scarcely hit the ground before Bauer could mumble, "Bushwhackers..."

But like a magic spell, the word broke the look of dazed wonderment on everyone's faces, and he repeated it again, this time full of energy, "Bushwhackers! C'mon, there's a whole mess of 'em in the woods back there! We gotta run for it."

They scrambled out of the small, one-room shack and raced back for the handcar. The small contraption seemed miles away from them at this moment. It seemed particularly distant to old Kotler as the three younger men quickly outdistanced him.

Craning his head around, Bauer could see a few bushwhackers coming in at an unconcerned jog to see the cause of the commotion.

They suspected old Cole was drunk again and had accidentally discharged his rusty musket yet again, but then they saw the four running away, including two in blue uniforms.

Bauer could not hear what the bushwhackers were yelling to their comrades, but he could tell by their motions that the others were being directed to their horses.

"Hurry!" he hollered at Kotler.

The old man's face was bright red and contorted in pain as his tight-legged gait struggled hopelessly to keep pace with the younger men.

Bauer readied his rifle, placing a percussion cap on the firing cone, and aimed at one of the bushwhackers running after them. Ignoring Kotler as he struggled past him, he relaxed his body and focused on the running figure carrying his own weapon in his right hand. The man did not bother to shoot at the fleeing Yankees, figuring they were too far away for an accurate shot, but the distance did not stop Matthew Bauer as he squeezed the trigger.

The Dimick deer rifle gave its customary kick. Pausing for a second, he lowered the rifle and watched the man crumple as if he had just been kicked in the midsection by a mule. The rifle dropped from the man's hand, and he sagged to the ground.

Bauer hesitated, immediately conscious that he had probably just killed a man, but he reminded himself that there were many more behind him. Turning on his heel, he quickly caught and passed Kotler again before he slowed to begin reloading his rifle on the move, and the old man re-passed him.

"C'mon, Matthew!" Bailey yelled from ahead, up on the handcar. He already had his hands on the iron lever, anxiously waiting to begin the pumping motion. "Hurry!"

Behind them, a group of riders broke from the woods.

Finally, Bauer and Kotler reached the handcar. Taking Bailey's hand, Kotler was unceremoniously yanked aboard.

"Go! Go! Go!" Bauer yelled, giving the cart a slight push and leaping aboard himself.

Smith was already struggling with the first stroke by himself when the two soldiers joined him at the lever. Fired with desperation, the three of them pushed up and down with all their strength. With agonizing slowness at first, they began to move and then accelerate.

The bushwhacking riders had now closed to two hundred yards, and the cracks of two smoothbore muskets cut through the air. Neither shot was close, but they did serve to bring the gasping Kotler to his feet. His fear stoked body brushed the youngest soldier aside and took his place pumping the lever.

"Switch... Shoot'em... Rebs," he gasped to the

sharpshooter.

"Go, Matthew!" Bailey encouraged.

Bauer grabbed his rifle from the planking of the platform, and he fired, but the jolting of the cart flung the shot high and wide. Cursing, he ripped his eyes away from the closing horsemen and grabbed another paper cartridge from his cartridge box. Using his teeth to tear open the cartridge, he poured the coarse black powder down the barrel, stuffing the remnants of the paper and Minié ball in after it. In one smooth stroke, he withdrew the ramrod from underneath the barrel and stuffed it all down, replacing the ramrod. Last of all, he pinched another copper percussion cap into place. Looking up, he noticed that the riders had closed to one hundred yards, and he took aim at the one horseman waving a revolver.

He fired and began to reach into his cartridge box again without bothering to see if he had hit the man.

"Use mine! It's still loaded!" Bailey yelled to him. Sweat streamed down his blond brow, and his muscles burned as he pumped furiously.

"Faster!" Bauer urged, "They're gaining!"

Like a spurred horse, Bailey redoubled his efforts, pushing and pulling so ferociously that the two railroad men could hardly keep up. Amazed by the young soldier's strength, each of the tired railroad men tried to redouble their own efforts but with less success.

Bauer grabbed the other rifle and checked the percussion cap. Whether it had fallen off or had never been put on, he didn't care. Quickly placing another cap on the nub, he raised the rifle, noticing that the gap was holding steady now. This time, he changed his aim from the rider to the much larger target of the horse. Using patience that would later surprise him, he waited until he heard the click of a new section of rail, and while on the flat, continuous section, he fired.

Immediately, he set that rifle to the ground and began to reload his. When he looked up again, he noticed one less horseman and an increasing distance.

"Keep going!" he yelled, "We're losing them!"

Taking aim on another horse, and waiting for another

smooth section of track, he fired again. One of the riders had his hat whipped off his head by the bullet, although it did not slow him for more than a moment.

Deciding that speed was more important, Bauer put the rifle back down and joined the three pumping the handcar. Luke was even redder than before, his breaths coming in heaving, panting bursts. Smith bit his lower lip in exertion, and his nostrils flared like that of a galloping stallion. Bead after bead of sweat dripped off of old Kotler's nose. His eyes were closed as if that would save some vestige of energy that could be put into the handcar.

Despite their fatigue and exhaustion, none of the men were letting up in their efforts to outdistance the horsemen. They continued exhausting themselves, and the bushwhackers could not gain on them. Gradually over the next few miles, they pulled further and further away.

Now as much of a test of stamina as strength, they maintained their pace for miles. About four miles short of town, they watched the riders give up the chase.

"Praise the Lord!" Kotler gasped, "They've given up."

In the distance, one of the Rebel horsemen took off his hat and waved it angrily. Then the bushwhackers pulled their mounts around and were gone.

Even so, they continued pumping without let up for another mile, not willing to believe their eyes, but finally it sunk in that they were safe. Kotler dropped to his knees.

"Is that enough excitement for you, Thomas?" he gasped, laying spread-eagle on his back, looking up at the bright blue sky.

Smith and the two soldiers slowed their pumping to a leisurely level, each man trying to gather himself in his own way. Smith took his hands off of the metal rod and bent over, throwing up over the side of the handcar.

"My sentiments exactly," Kotler wheezed, sliding over a canteen that he had tied to a corner bracket at the beginning of the trip.

Bailey watched the old man with a sense of curiosity. The stress and subsequent relief had totally changed the old man's attitude. The gruff distemper that seemed permanent had changed into a voice of warmth. The dramatic change in demeanor surprised Thomas Smith even more. Gratefully, he accepted the canteen from Kotler and swished the cool water around in his mouth before spitting it out.

"Plenty exciting," he said finally after taking a gulp of the water.

"I didn't give you credit, young man," Kotler remarked, looking at Bailey, "I could see you were a strapping lad, but even so, your strength and stamina amazes me. It was the best I could do just to keep up with you. I feared I wasn't doing anything other than slowing you down."

"Oh, no," Bailey blushed, "Your help was greatly needed."

"What happened to not doing physical labor?" Smith ribbed Kotler who surprisingly took it in good nature.

"Duty called, Mr. Smith."

"And you," Smith said, looking at Bauer, "I can see why you are the best shot in all of Kalamazoo County. It's still beyond me how you plucked that rider clean from his horse while on a moving handcar and from that range!"

Bauer shrugged, not bothering to tell them that he had been aiming for the horse.

"Oh, yes, young man," Kotler agreed, "A remarkable shot, you are. Have no fear. Your officers will hear about your bravery, skill, and strength. I assure you of that."

* * *

"What's the meaning of this?" Munroe demanded, raising his voice and staring at all of the soldiers crowding into his small store.

The noise brought his wife out from the storeroom pantry and his daughter from the stairwell that led to their living quarters upstairs. Both women stared blankly at the sudden mass of blue coats in their small space.

"You can't do that to my customers," Munroe continued, "He has just as much right to be here as you do."

"That so?" Orrin Long sneered, noticing the emergence of

the womenfolk with some satisfaction.

"Of course! I insist that you…"

"Silence! You insist?" Long interrupted harshly, "You are in no position to insist anything! Secesh scum, such as yourself, should consider themselves fortunate not to be thrown in jail, or worse!"

Munroe glowered back but said nothing.

"You see?" Long wheeled to face the soldiers, "As if more proof was needed? He does not deny it."

"Deny what?" Munroe asked softly.

"That you are a Rebel! You all but admitted it to us back when Captain Vincent and I first came upon you at the farmstead."

"I don't know what you mean."

"Your kin is away fighting with Sterling Price or some set of bushwhackers, no?"

"People have kin of all sorts fighting on all sorts of sides," Munroe answered, but his tone had lost that initial fierceness. Even Lockett had to admit that Munroe didn't sound like he believed his own words.

"And the fact that you don't sell to our soldiers, except at exorbitant prices?"

"I don't know what you mean," came back the hesitant reply.

"The hell you don't," Long said, almost laughingly. "But very well then, clear up this confusion. Hmmm?"

There was silence, and Lockett watched old man Munroe with some wonder. It seemed like the old man knew what Orrin Long was getting at, although Lockett had no clue himself. Finally, Mrs. Munroe broke the stilted silence, "How?"

"Well, that is obvious," Long said, taking a small piece of paper from his inner pocket. "I have the Oath of Allegiance to the United States of America right here. Recite it here, right now in front of us, and then again later today once we have gathered all of the citizens of this town. Then we will know."

The soldiers expectantly eyed Munroe. The silence grew, and Munroe's face showed the strain. Slowly, his cheeks reddened, and the furrows in his forehead plowed deeper into the folds.

"Don't do it, Father!" Ivy cried suddenly. "Don't!"

"Quiet!" her father answered.

"This oath is an easy request," Long taunted, "It should take no seconds at all to decide. Every man here would have no trouble at all doing it in less than a second!"

"I'll take up arms against no man."

"No one is asking you to do that, old man," Long snorted.

"Take the oath, you traitor!" Hiram Walker growled menacingly, prompting Long to hold up a cautionary hand towards the corporal.

"As I was saying," Munroe continued, starting to compose himself, "I'll take up arms against no man, but an oath before God is an oath before God."

"What does that mean?" Walker asked, stepping closer to Munroe.

"It means that to lie to God is more than dishonorable," Munroe answered steadily.

"Very well," Long replied, giving a nod to Walker, "It's decided then. No oath."

With a nod, Walker drove a heavy, left-handed hook into the old man's midsection.

Doubled over and gasping for air, Long pushed Munroe to the ground with a gentle one-handed shove of disdain.

The action had caught Lockett by such surprise that he had not moved an inch. Once Long pushed the old man over, Lockett felt the urge to take a step forward. As the notion finally occurred to him, he noticed Bart Randle from the corner of his eye. Randle had his rifle at the ready, but he wasn't looking at the Munroes. He was looking straight at Lockett.

Lockett froze, as it slowly dawned on him that the entire thing had been planned out, including for the cronies to watch him! That couldn't be right, could it? The thought plagued him. Surely not?

Orrin Long glanced slyly over his shoulder, directly at Lockett.

Yes, there was no mistake about it now, Lockett decided.

That glance had sealed it.

Mrs. Munroe and Ivy stumbled over to old man Munroe, words still caught in their throats.

"By the order of the United States government, this property is now considered null and void, and property of the army that came here to protect loyal citizens from traitors like yourself. Load everything into the two wagons outside, men, including that pot belly stove in the corner. It will keep you men a sight warmer in that stable, and the Munroes have no need for it anymore since their store is closed permanently.

"You can't do that!" Mrs. Munroe finally said, as her husband continued to wheeze.

"We can, and we have."

"But we have rights!"

"True Americans have rights, not traitors," Long gloated.

"You can't!"

"Consider yourself lucky. I'd have burnt your store and house to the ground, if it was up to me!"

"You devils!" Ivy spoke up finally, after helping her father to his feet. She glared at the soldiers.

Some of the men in blue fidgeted, and Lockett noticed a couple of them cast their eyes at him in particular, and it wasn't Walker or his cronies this time.

"Do something!" Ivy implored, looking straight at Lockett.

But he froze. There was nothing that he could do, he told himself.

Tears streamed down her reddened face. Emotion made as plain as could be etched into her normally soft, youthful features.

"Do something!" Ivy Munroe's words echoed in his brain. They pounded his skull, like a large bell being rung directly on top of him. *Do something. Do something…*

The reverberations did not stop, even later that night. Deep into the night, he heard Ivy again and again. He tried to remind himself that there was nothing that he could do, but it did no good.

Chapter 9

January 22, 1862

We shiver too much to sleep, and my hand is quickly growing too cold to write much more, though the chill is less than the one that Matthew has towards me. He holds me responsible for not doing more to help the Munroes. Maybe he is right. I tried to stop Hiram and Orrin that first time when we left the train. Why didn't I do anything this time?

--- the diary of James Lockett

"It is probably for the best that we keep ourselves busy, Matthew," Luke Bailey remarked, trying to stay positive.

The two of them worked together, each carrying one end of two railroad ties, one under each arm.

"What? So we don't freeze to death?" Bauer said sourly, his breath plainly visible in the cold. "Or so that we pretend that nothing happened last week with Ivy and her family?"

Bailey meant the latter, mostly because he did not want to go over it again with Matthew or with James. The former was clearly upset, and the latter seemed almost defeated by what he had impotently witnessed.

As for himself, Luke Bailey was conflicted. The Munroes seemed like decent people, and they didn't own slaves. Why were they aiding the wrong side then? In his mind, the world was quite simple. It was all about slavery, and that should determine everything. However, he was starting to learn that there were other factors involved with how people saw things.

"I just wish that we'd been there," Bauer repeated for the tenth time today. "I could have done something, not just turned a blind eye to it like James did!"

Bailey shook his head, deciding that he would respond for the very last time, "You keep saying that, Matthew, but what could you have done? You heard James's description. And we know that those were Captain Vincent's orders. There was nothing to be done."

"Maybe I could have convinced Ivy's father to take the oath?"

"I don't think you're that persuasive."

"Well, there must have been something that I could have done, something more than James, who did nothing."

Bailey made no response as they laid the two railroad ties on the pile and headed back for two more that had been dumped into the ravine.

The prairie winds whipped their faces. Any part of exposed skin had long since been flayed red and senseless. A few men had dripping swirls of ice hanging from their beards and moustaches, but Bauer's baby-face and Bailey's patchy growth offered no protection.

"Ivy won't talk to me anymore," Bauer complained.

"I don't think I can blame her for that. Besides, why is it so important to you?"

"You wouldn't understand," Bauer replied with a dismissive wave.

"Whatever it is yer talkin' about, stop yappin' and keep workin'," Sergeant VanderJagt growled, as they passed in the other direction. He and Gus Jeltema carried four railroad ties up from the ravine. "It's damn cold out here, and the sooner we finish, the sooner we can get back to town. Short-handed as we are with so many men sick back in town, this is going to take plenty long."

Bailey nodded and slid down the sides of the ravine to fish out the next wooden tie. The only positive from Matthew's constant lamenting was that it did take their minds away from the illness back in town.

He was really worried about Patrick, whose pallor was ghostly white and seemed to have taken a turn for the worse, as had many of the others. He prayed that Patrick would look better by the time they came back from this job, but that seemed wishful.

He joined Bauer down in the ravine and looked at the haphazard piles.

The bushwhackers had dragged a hundred yards worth of wooden ties and iron rails, dumping them into this steep ravine, but at least they had not started a fire and bent the rails. Likely, they were half-frozen when they did this two nights ago and were as anxious to get back to a fire as everybody else.

Despite Sergeant VanderJagt's prodding with Matthew, the men did not need orders from anyone today. They all knew that the sooner they repaired the track, the sooner they could find a fire. With little direction, the rails and ties were gathered up, spikes broken out, and sledgehammers hoisted.

"I better check up ahead to make sure the track up there is okay," Orrin Long said to Lieutenant Simon and Sergeant VanderJagt. "I'll take these men and check ahead."

"Yes, sir," Simon answered the senior lieutenant.

"C'mon, Lockett," Long said pointedly, stalking off, "I don't have time to wait for your lollygagging today."

The directness of Lieutenant Long's address startled him. Grudgingly, Lockett handed the sledgehammer over to Sam Moss, who sagged noticeably under the weight of the long hammer.

Lockett didn't want to follow Orrin Long anywhere, but there was little more that he could do other than look over at Lieutenant Simon who shrugged and waved him to follow Lieutenant Long and the rest of the small squad.

They had not gone very far before a sinking feeling penetrated Lockett's cold-numbed brain. Like a dozen little pinpricks, he noticed who Orrin Long was leading. Hiram Walker, Isaac Washburn, Bart Randle, and himself…

But he followed on. He wanted to chastise himself for his paranoia, but he could not help it. He could not dismiss the nagging feeling that tugged on him like a cold hand on the back of his neck.

Something was not right, and he knew it. It wasn't paranoia.

He glanced down at his Dimick and checked that the percussion cap was still on the nub of his loaded rifle. He couldn't defend himself against all of them, but he could take one of them with him!

It must be the cold, he thought. The cold must be doing this. There is nothing to fear! The cold, the cold, the cold…

He had become so wrapped up in his own thoughts that he did not notice the small farmhouse with the smoke trickling from its square chimney ahead of them.

"I think it is time we warmed up a bit," Orrin Long declared, drawing no disagreement from his chilled men.

Warmth, Lockett's mind shouted happily, but his feet were slow in following. The phantom grip around his neck was still there, and he just knew that he should not follow Orrin Long and the others into the house. He could see it in the bounce of the men's strides. Washburn, Randle, Walker… There was a purposefulness and anticipation to their increasing pace. Was it just the possibility of a warm fire?

But what choice do I have? Stand here like a fool in the middle of this frozen field? Wait here like a coward? With a nervous sensation in his stomach, he forced his legs forward and prayed that his imagination was getting the better of him.

"Cold, Lockett?" Orrin Long asked suddenly, turning around with a wolfish smile on his reddened face. "A little something to warm you up?"

The image of Orrin Long's leering grin burned into his brain. Was the man toying with him? Did he sense his discomfort and want to have a little entertainment at his expense?

Lockett could live with that, he decided. He prayed that there was nothing more to it.

Yet, the half mile to the farmhouse seemed to take an eternity as his mind urgently contemplated a number of other possibilities.

The wind whistled a lonesome tune throughout. The only other sound was the soft crunch of the frozen ground.

"What do y'all want?" they heard a new voice bark at them. He was an old man, and he glared at them with suspicious eyes.

The stare did not slow Lieutenant Long, nor even draw a comment. Only when he had reached a mere foot away from the man did Orrin Long stop. Despite the cold, the wizened old man had waited coatless for them. Now, his bent frame straightened to its full height, and he looked Orrin Long in the eye, his thin arms taut against his side.

Lockett clenched and unclenched his hands, trying to get some feeling in them and shivered.

The old man did not shiver, rather he stared unflinchingly at the men in Union blue.

"We need to check this residence for evidence of aiding and abetting traitors," Lieutenant Long snarled back, "Now step aside!"

"This is my house," the old man maintained, "An' I don' want no soldiers in here."

"Soun's like he's hidin' somethin' to me," Isaac Washburn hooted from the back.

"Step aside," Long said in a distracted voice, brushing the man away from the door with no more thought than one would wave at a fly.

"Are there no laws left in this country?" the old man cried angrily, following them inside.

"Private Washburn, please detain this man in here while we search the rest of the residence." Without a glance back, Long explored deeper into the house.

With unnecessary force, Isaac Washburn shoved the old man into a small wooden chair in the corner. The old man landed on the chair and then toppled backward over it, knocking his head on the wall as he went back. Pulling himself back to his feet, he tried to stand only to be back handed by Washburn.

"Stay seated, ol' man, before you get hurt," Washburn ordered in a pleased voice.

From the front door, Lockett watched with quiet anger. Gripping the rifle as tight as he could, he made no move nor said a word, but the expression on his face communicated all the distress and indecision.

Looking at him and his obvious unease, Hiram Walker laughed, causing Lockett to impotently stare a hole through the wood floor with his gray eyes.

"Put that down!" came the high-pitched shout from another

room, followed immediately by a crash and a thud.

Everyone, old man included, rushed to the back room. From the middle of this pack, Lockett arrived just in time to see Orrin Long get up, a trickle of blood dripping from a cut in his forehead. Standing in front of him was a young, fourteen year old girl with the handle of a broken water pitcher still in her hand. Defiantly, the young girl's eyes blazed at the Union officer.

"You thief!" she said, just before a punch from Orrin Long knocked her backwards, off her feet and onto her back.

"Leave her al-," the old man began in an angry voice, but before he could finish the sentence, Isaac Washburn wrenched one of the man's arms behind his back with such force that there was an audible 'pop.' The old man gave a howl of pain that continued as Washburn pushed him to the floor.

"Grandfather!" the girl screamed, rising up off the floor with surprising resiliency. Oblivious to her own blackening and rapidly closing eye, she ran towards the old man only to be caught in Orrin Long's grasp.

"Remind you of anything?" Hiram Walker said to Lockett with a look of sick pleasure. The ice that had coated his thick beard was melting and dropping to the floor, giving Walker the look of a rabid beast.

Bart Randle leaned in, his fetid breath curled across Lockett's face as he whispered, "How ya gonna help the Secesh this time, Lockett?"

A depraved smirk split Orrin Long's face, as he touched his forehead. "I'd say she attacked an officer in the United States Army, boys. According to General Halleck, she ought to be taken back to town…" Walker and the others looked back at their officer with knowing grins of their own. "… but, I'd say that would be more trouble than its worth. She ought to take her punishment right here, the Rebel bitch."

"You bastards," Lockett uttered in a low voice.

The girl's one good eye was wide with terror and confusion. She had gentle blue eyes, but they were now filled with panic as she scanned the room. They were all animals, animals in blue… all but one… she stared at the one, the one with gray eyes, and her young, child-like face pleaded for help.

Lockett stared back, trying to disguise the apprehension and fear that he felt, all too aware that this was what Orrin Long had planned from the beginning, all too aware that he was the cause for her pain. Orrin Long had singled out this household as a way to get at Lockett.

She was so young, he thought to himself, more child than woman. Her long, straight brown hair cascaded down to the middle of her back, and her small, fairy-like features were still unblemished by wrinkles or pimples. It made the crude damage from Orrin Long's punch all the more galling and startling. The gentle features of her pale white face were overwhelmed by the rapidly blackening eye.

The look on her young face burned Lockett, scalded him from the inside like no look had ever done before. He could feel the beads of sweat on his chest even though he was ice cold. He knew right there that hers was a face he would remember for the rest of his life.

"You can't go soft on these traitors," Bart Randle growled, "And we're going to teach you the right way to do things whether you like it or not."

Walker leered, "Well, boyo? Cat got your tongue?" With a sort of glee, he circled Lockett like a predator toying with a wounded prey. "Nothing to say? No one here but us, you lily-stomached son of a bitch!" Walker barked suddenly. "You think you know better than our officers! Than General Halleck? Damn muck farmer! What do you know? You think because you is always writin' in that little book that you's smarter than the officers! Damn muck farmer! Ignorant fool! Think you got a better way to treat this trash?" He gestured wildly at the old man whose arm was still pinned behind him by Isaac Washburn and the girl caught in Orrin Long's arms. "Gonna interfere? Well? Well? No, not this time, I can see it on your face! You frightened sow! Boys, I think he's pissed hisself. Watch where you step!" He laughed uproariously. "Boyo, you're going to watch the whole thing!"

Orrin Long began to slide a hand along the girl's thigh, and she froze, mouth open but no words came. The entire room was eerily quiet, their eyes on Lockett and his inner torment and not on the girl surprisingly.

Lockett's heart was pounding like he didn't believe possible. It was thunder in his ears – resounding, vibrating his whole body. How dare they! Every fiber of his body twitched with something alien.

Rage!

God damn them for their evil! He had never felt anything like it, a searing, burning hate!

And yet, for all of the inferno within him, there was no noticeable change in his outward appearance. He didn't move in the slightest way.

"Look at him!" Isaac Washburn laughed, "I think he's shitted himself too!"

Lockett scarcely heard him. The sound of the blood rushing through his brain was louder. He burned to do something. *Do something...*

He could hear the echo of Ivy Munroe's words, and then in his mind, those words came a second time but from his own, deeper inner voice.

Do something...

Anything!

Washburn still had the grandfather's arm pinned behind him, and Bart Randle bent backwards, laughing uncontrollably, his legs spread far apart to keep his balance.

The girl squirmed futilely to break from Orrin Long's grasp, and she gave one last pleading look at Lockett. Her blue eyes were fixated in silent terror.

With a bellicose roar that startled everyone in the room, Lockett viciously kicked upwards between Bart Randle's legs.

It seemed that the room had become frozen, and only Lockett could move for the moment. The kick was perfectly placed, and Lockett wasted no motion as he swung around instantly, elbowing Isaac Washburn in the jaw. The short, violent blow sounded like a wedge going through a log, and it was impossible to tell which man hit the ground first – Bart Randle or Isaac Washburn.

It had been all on instinct. He had hardly known what he

had done, certainly had not planned it. Now, instinct ordered him to raise his rifle, and Lockett cocked back the hammer, but the spell in the room had finally broken. He had only gotten the Dimick halfway up when it was swung high, and he found himself struggling against Hiram Walker for control of the weapon.

Walker snarled, one hand on the barrel and the other near the hammer, as he tried to wrench the rifle away.

Swinging around as if they were performing some odd dance, Lockett and Walker wrestled for the weapon. The room was ominously quiet except for their panting breaths, but the glint in Walker's eye told Lockett what they were all thinking, that the larger Walker would surely pull the gun away from him.

Again, desperation and instinct answered the call. Lockett snapped his head forward violently, connecting with Walker's nose. Walker still held tight, but he was dazed, and Lockett gave a mighty tug, trying to yank the Dimick free.

CRACKKKK!

With a resounding echo, the rifle shot reverberated within the walls of the room.

The rifle was now in his hands as Walker's grasp slid from the weapon, and Lockett then realized that the trigger had pulled in trying to free it.

"Amelia!" the old man gasped, his eyes widening so that only the whites seemed to be showing.

Turning a quarter step with the still smoking rifle, Lockett saw Orrin Long let go of the ghastly mess that had been the girl. The color in Long's face rapidly drained to contrast the bluish mess on his cheek. Flecked with the girl's red blood and bluish brain matter, Orrin Long passed out, joining the girl on the floor.

With his mouth hanging open and an inaudible cry on his lips, Lockett gaped at the girl. The Minié ball fired from the point-blank range had shattered the entire top of her skull. An enormous puddle of blood spread across the floor in horrible, ever-widening circles around her head!

Feeling himself quivering, his mind flashed from the

original image of the fairy-like, brown-haired girl to the gruesome corpse that now lay on the floor. Utterly unable to reconcile the images, they snapped back and forth like a pulse.

Then a sharp blow to the back of his head ended the torture, and James Lockett hit the ground unconscious.

-II-

Separate Paths To…

Chapter 10

Lockett felt the large clump of dried blood that matted his hair on the back of his head. Were it not for the sizable lump that accompanied it, he would have assumed it was Amelia's blood.

Visages of her shattered skull and the blood – so much blood that he would have thought it impossible in one person, much less in a small waif of a girl – dominated his thoughts. He could not get the horrifying picture out of his mind.

It was his fault! If only he had left well enough alone, at least she would be alive! If he had simply done nothing… the thought drifted off.

He wanted to throw up, but he was so exhausted that he could barely sit up in the stiff-backed chair in Captain Vincent's office. It was so tempting to just close his eyes, yet when he did, the images of Amelia only became more vivid. At least with his eyes open, he could partially dull the image by watching Captain Vincent strut nervously around the tiny room.

Vincent and the other officers were discussing the situation, his future really, as if he was not in the room at all, and in a sense, he wasn't there. Try as he might, he could not focus on their words.

Amelia! Lockett could swear that he heard the grandfather's croaking final cry, and with a start, he looked around the room for the old man, but the grandfather wasn't there. It sounded so real that Lockett looked around again, certain that he must be here.

"And you say that Private Lockett shot the grandfather too?" Captain Vincent questioned.

"Yes, after Private Lockett shot the girl, the old man took Washburn's knife and came at him. Lockett picked up Private Walker's rifle from the floor and shot him," Orrin Long answered shakily.

Walker and his cronies had cleaned the girl's blood and other matter from Long's face before they exited the house, but to Orrin Long it still felt like it was there, like a second skin. "I suppose, at least, that one was self-defense," Long concluded.

None of the officers even took a glance at Lockett. Finally, the words reached Lockett through his stupor.

What? Kill the grandfather? Him?

That couldn't be true! In fact, it was hard to believe that the old man was in any condition to attempt going after anybody. Lockett was sure that the audible pop that he had heard when Washburn wrenched the old man's shoulder was the limb breaking. He was in such agony that Lockett doubted the old man could even stand by himself.

"Two dead locals?" Vincent pondered aloud. "Why, there will be a lynch mob at my door once word starts to spread! I always knew this damn private was a laggard, knew that since he fell asleep on duty and let that family slip away that night, but I never knew he was a *cowardly* laggard! She was just a young girl, you say?"

Long nodded.

"And he just shot her?"

"I believe she thought he was stealing their valuables."

"Was he?"

Long shrugged.

"That's the problem with these penniless farmers," Captain Vincent scowled, "They can't resist the temptation. You would think that giving them a uniform would somehow instill more discipline."

With his head finally starting to clear, their words were starting to reach Lockett's brain. He couldn't believe the lies being told about him, and the anger started to replace his exhaustion. He sat up straighter in his chair and gauged how far away Orrin Long was. He could reach the man in no time, but could he strangle the man to death before they pulled him off?

As if noticing his stirring, Lieutenant Simon stepped between Lockett and the other two officers. With his back to the officers, Simon faced Lockett and gave him a sympathetic look of warning. "Not now," he mouthed the words silently to Lockett.

Lockett stiffened in his chair. If nothing else, shouldn't he defend himself with words? These were lies!

Simon continued to stare at him and slowly mouthed, "Stay quiet."

Lockett blinked in confusion but obeyed nonetheless. He knew it was his word against Orrin's, an officer and the captain's nephew to boot. It wouldn't go well, he realized immediately. In fact, Hiram and his cohorts were sure to back Orrin's version of the story as well. One word against four witnesses? Who could blame Captain Vincent for siding against him?

If only the grandfather could back his version of events… And it was then that Lockett realized they had killed the old man in cold blood, to keep him from talking.

Murderers!

He could feel his hands trembling, and he clenched them together, hoping that they would stop shaking.

"And who knows about these killings so far? This farmhouse was remote, you say?" Vincent resumed his nervous pacing, and Lieutenant Simon turned his attention back to Orrin Long.

"Just Corporal Walker and the rest of those in the house with me know about it… and now Simon and yourself."

"What about the rest of our men who were out there?"

"Well, they must know something happened," Long answered slowly, "Private Jeltema, preacher boy, and a few others took turns carrying Lockett back on a makeshift stretcher. They know something happened."

"Some of them will gossip to the others, if they haven't already."

"Probably, Uncle. Probably."

"So word will get out."

"And then there are the bodies as well," Lieutenant Simon finally spoke aloud, "There are the bodies. What did you do about the bodies?"

"We just left them where they were."

"You left them?" Simon said incredulously.

"Ground's too frozen to dig a grave now," Long replied defensively, "Besides we needed to get back before dark. What would you have me do?"

Simon bit his tongue, knowing that Long was baiting him, and Simon needed to stay above the fray, at least for now. He didn't believe a word that Orrin Long had said against Lockett. He knew that there was no way that James Lockett was going to murder a young girl, no matter the circumstances.

No, Lockett was innocent, and that meant Orrin Long was lying, which wasn't hard for Simon to believe.

Unfortunately, there was no good way to debate the innocence factor. Given that, he knew where this was ultimately heading, unless he came up with a way out for Lockett. An idea was formulating in his head, but he needed Vincent's good graces to make it work.

"We will have to go back tomorrow to bury them. It's the only Christian thing to do," Vincent declared with somber righteousness. "Of course, the townspeople will find out eventually… and then there will be hell to pay. They'll ask for Lockett's head. Of course, I have no problem with that. A quick hanging is too good for the scoundrel."

He pointed over at Lockett, acknowledging his presence for the first time. "I mean, look at him. Hasn't said one word in his own defense, not that there is any defense for murdering a young girl. Disgusting!"

"Sir," Simon interjected quickly before the words stirred Lockett's tongue.

"What?" Vincent answered with some annoyance.

"I don't think we can just hand him over to the locals. He is still a soldier after all. He would fall under military justice to begin with, and…"

"And what? You want me to hang him instead? Might as well let the locals do it for me."

"I think that would set a bad precedent, and…"

"Precedent!" Vincent scoffed. "Now, you sound like the first year law student that you are, Simon."

But Simon continued, undeterred by the interruption.

"Besides precedent, it would not bode well for how people see you, sir. Back home, I mean."

"See me?"

Simon nodded agreeably. He could see that he had the politician's attention now. "Of course, this is your volunteer company, sir. Everyone here and at home knows that… they all take great pride in that." Simon paused, hoping that the last sentence would properly stroke the man's ego.

"Of course, of course, they do." Vincent replied, trying not to give a clue that he was confused where this was going.

"The people back home wouldn't want it to be known that 'Vincent's company' had committed such a treacherous event," Simon continued, swallowing the bile that he felt even as he uttered the words.

God, if this was what being a lawyer was like, perhaps it was best that he left his studies to volunteer.

"Treacherous," Vincent agreed, nodding as if in deep contemplation.

"And Lockett is popular with many of the men, and probably folks at home too. In fact, those at home who don't know Lockett are likely to think that he was just defending himself against some sort of Rebel bushwhackers. The story will get twisted around, and no one will remember that it was even a girl. They'll say it was a bushwhacker or two. Who knows?"

"Hmmm, and then?" Vincent asked.

"And then, they will be angry that you let your man be handed over to the locals. It would be best to defuse it as much as possible. They are all voters, of course."

Vincent nodded appreciatively, as it finally dawned on him. "Yes, they are all voters, now and tomorrow."

"We wouldn't want them to see Captain Vincent's company in a negative light. It would be a shame to have it rub off on you." Simon paused, actually stunned at how smoothly the distasteful words were coming out of his mouth. He reminded himself that this was for the greater good. Something horrible had happened in that house, but he was sure that Lockett was not responsible. Compounding the tragedy by condemning an innocent man would only make it worse.

"Indeed, not," Vincent paused, lowering his volume before asking, "What are you suggesting, Simon?"

"We send Lockett home, before the locals can clamor for him. You can always tell the locals that he was sent back for a military trial, if you have to."

"Send him home?" Orrin Long finally spoke up. He had been surprised to hear Simon speak so much, never mind sound so concerned about his uncle's political calculations, but now he could see the reason for it all. Simon was trying to spare Lockett the noose! "How would you send him home, Simon? By magic carpet?"

"It's two birds with one stone, sir," Simon answered, ignoring Long's belligerent tone. "We were just talking this morning about how it would be good to send the sickest men home on the train that leaves tomorrow. Their three month enlistments will be up in a few weeks, and they are in no condition to do anything useful right now…"

"Yes, yes, send them back, and they can always re-enlist after they recover," Vincent interrupted with some annoyance, "We had talked about that earlier, but what does this have to do with Lockett?"

"We discarded the idea because we couldn't spare a man to go with them, and these men are in such a bad way that they can't take care of themselves. Well, send Lockett back with them as their caretaker. Two birds with one stone."

"Basically, you're saying put him in charge!" Long argued. "That is absurd! The man should be shot, and you want to give a promotion!"

"I wouldn't call it a promotion," Simon answered, unperturbed, "But imagine, sir, how grateful those back in Kalamazoo County will be to get their loved ones back to recuperate. We all know they stand a better chance back there than in a stable in freezing Missouri."

"Ridiculous!" Long argued, but he could see from the look on his uncle's face that the politician was calculating the impact.

"It will only further lift people's opinion of you, sir,"

Simon concluded.

With a contemplative nod, Vincent added, "I do believe you are right, Simon." There was increasing certainty in his voice as he continued. "Yes, yes indeed. Not only does this reduce the tarring of my reputation with this unfortunate business, but what the voters will remember is that I cared enough about their kin to take care of them."

Inwardly, Walter Simon sighed with relief. He may not have completed his legal studies yet, but he knew that he had just saved his first innocent man from the noose.

* * *

Lockett slid to the ground next to Patrick McManus in the stable with a sigh. He was exhausted, but the sense of relief that he felt was like nothing else he had experienced before. He had been close to a hanging; he was sure of that.

Thank God for Lieutenant Simon!

The lieutenant was far more clever than he had given the man credit before.

Next to Lockett, McManus opened his rheumy eyes and handed Lockett a blanket.

"Keep it, Patrick," Lockett replied, knowing that Patrick used it in addition to his own while Lockett was gone.

"Don't make me force you to take it," McManus grumbled in a weak, hoarse voice.

He looked horrible – pale, sweaty, and shivering. If he took a deep breath, a coughing fit would ensue.

At least it wasn't the same cough as his father's, Lockett reflected, remembering the hacking cough that brought blood with it. Day by day, it had slowly smothered his father. Consumption, they called it. Wretched is what James Lockett would call it.

Patrick was sick for sure, but at least it wasn't his father's illness, and that gave Lockett some hope. Doggedly, he refused to believe that his bull-like, age-old friend would succumb to this, in spite of the fact that two of the sharpshooters already had.

"What happened?" McManus rasped. "Some strange things being said in here."

Luke Bailey and Matthew Bauer noticed Lockett's return then, and they meandered around the blanketed men on the ground of the stable. They squatted next to McManus with their blankets wrapped around their shoulders as another frigid gust rattled the thin walls of the stable.

"What happened?" they repeated in unison.

Bailey peered over Lockett's shoulder to study the clotted blood on the back of Lockett's head.

"You took a nasty whack. That's all we know for certain," Bauer said.

"And I don't believe a word that is being said," Bailey added hurriedly.

"Who's saying?" Lockett asked slowly in a dark, ominous voice.

"Hiram and the others."

"What are they saying?"

"They say that you killed a girl back there at that house."

Lockett paused before answering aloud. In his head, he immediately had to admit that the statement was true. It had been his finger on the trigger.

"They say that you shot her."

"How?"

"How?" Bauer repeated in puzzlement.

"Yes, how?"

"They said you just shot her in the head, point blank."

"Just like that?" Lockett queried carefully.

The peculiar response only added to Luke's and Matthew's confusion.

"That's not a denial," Bauer pointed out.

"Be quiet, Matthew!" Bailey snapped, "There is no way that James would shoot a girl in the head."

It was the first time that any of their voices had risen above a whisper, and it was also the first time he noticed that the entire stable was watching them.

Lockett bit his tongue and lowered his voice, certain that only Patrick, Luke, and Matthew could hear. "It wasn't like that… but that is all I can say right now."

"What does that mean?"

Inside, his heart cried out. He wanted to explain, to make sure that everyone knew there was more to the story.

But upon leaving Captain Vincent's office, he had taken a slow, cold walk with Lieutenant Simon. With no one else around, Lockett had emptied his soul, telling Simon everything he could remember – from his sense that Orrin Long had planned it from the beginning to the horrific sight of her head and all the blood and even the guilt that he felt for little Amelia.

Simon had listened politely, never uttering a word, only nodding as Lockett had gone through the tale.

At the end, he gently grasped Lockett by the shoulders, to make sure that Lockett heard him. In no uncertain terms, he implored Lockett to keep it to himself for now – the whole, tragic tale.

Captain Vincent would send him out in the morning with the sick, and Lockett could go on with his life, but if word got back to Vincent that Lockett was spreading tales, slandering Vincent's nephew, then all bets were off. Lockett's escape from the situation would be off, and Vincent would let the full weight of local justice have their way.

So Lockett swallowed his impulse, even ignoring the comment about going on with his life. How could he go on after this? He thought angrily. This would stay with him for the rest of his life. He would think about this every day, forever regretful for his reactions.

But Simon was right. The best that could be done now was follow Simon's plan. At least for now, no one could know what really happened, even his friends.

His reputation would be tarred, but he had to stay quiet, or else he would die here.

He tried to further bolster his resolve by reminding himself that if he spoke up, it was not just about him. There were the sick also, including Patrick. Someone had to get them back to a place where more care could be given, and that someone was Lockett.

It went against every fiber to stay silent, to let the world think the worst of him, but he would keep his promise to Lieutenant Simon.

Looking squarely at Patrick and then Luke and Matthew, he balled up his fists, and finally answered Matthew's question, "What does that mean? It means it wasn't like that, but that is all I can say right now. Believe me."

And with that he closed his eyes and felt a strange, torturing weariness wash over him.

He kept his eyes closed all night but to no avail. Sleep would not come. The events wound round and round in his head, all night long.

It was bizarre, he thought at one point during the night. He could remember every detail of little Amelia's face, both before and after, like no other face in his memory, even his own.

Sadly, he knew that it would be that way for the rest of his life now.

* * *

Surprisingly, the train arrived nearly on time the next day, and the entire company swung into action. Most of the ambulatory soldiers worked to quickly offload one of the two box cars and throw some hay down before they brought in their deathly ill comrades on makeshift stretchers.

A separate group of four, which included Pete O'Shea and Luke Bailey, marched Lockett towards the train. Captain Vincent had deemed it necessary that Lockett's wrists be shackled. He wanted it plain to any onlookers that the soldier was a prisoner. This was even though the town still seemed unaware of the murder. Either way, Vincent could at least claim that the culprit was hustled out of town as a prisoner to face military justice.

If that was the plan, Lockett thought, it seemed for naught. There was no crowd of townsfolk watching the goings-on, curious about the lone, shackled Federal soldier. Everyone was just going about their business, and he would have been surprised if even one person had noticed his unceremonious exit.

In a way, it relieved some of the shame that he had felt initially when the shackles clanged shut. He tried to shrug off the growing sense of injustice and keep his mouth shut. He knew that Lieutenant Simon was right; he needed to stay quiet and not provoke Captain Vincent, but it was difficult. So difficult!

"Johnny Quinlan passed on last night," Bailey said softly to him.

"What? Johnny died?"

Bailey nodded sadly. "Thought you'd want to know."

"Are we bringing his body home?"

"No."

"No? Why not?"

"I asked the same thing, but the answer was firm. The smell would be something fierce, and the rest of the boys are in bad enough shape without smelling death every second... That's what the captain said."

"But his family," Lockett answered lamely.

"Captain Vincent wouldn't pay for it any way."

"Pay for it?"

"The army is only going to pay for you all to get to St. Louis. From there, you'll have to buy tickets for yourself and the others." Bailey reached into his pocket and pulled out a leather pouch of coins. "Lieutenant Simon gave me this."

He started to put them into Lockett's pocket, causing Lockett to pull away.

"I ain't taking charity to boot," he said angrily.

"The lieutenant knows that you and the boys don't have much," Bailey defended the officer, "He's just trying to help."

"He's helped plenty," Lockett muttered grudgingly, "I'll pay for the boys."

"With what, James?"

"We get monthly pay as soldiers."

"And payroll for this month didn't come through yet, so with what would you pay? Even if you pocketed the first month's pay, it's going to take five dollars for each of you, and our monthly pay is thirteen dollars. Besides, I know that you sent most of the first month's pay home."

With a scowl, Lockett stopped pulling away from him and relented. "Fine! But you tell Simon that I'm paying him back someday."

"Of course," Bailey said with a shrug.

They slowed as ahead of them two more men on stretchers were carefully lifted up to the boxcar.

"I can't believe Johnny's dead," Lockett said softly.

"Me too," Bailey agreed in his own gentle tone. "Wil Fulgham and Billy Stokes earlier this week… We lost more men to disease than actual weapons, even with Hallsville."

"I can't help but wonder how many more will die on the way home, Luke. I'm no doctor."

"But you'll do what you can. It will give them a better chance than if they stayed here in the stable for two more months. Guaranteed, most would die that way. You'll get them home, and kin will nurse them back to health."

"I hope you're right."

Another stretcher party came along, causing Lockett and the others to wait. As they did so, Matthew Bauer came towards them. He paused and looked uneasily at the shackles on Lockett's wrists.

"What do you have, Matthew?" Lockett said after the uncomfortable delay.

"Mail," Bauer said, eager to change subjects, "After all this time of Patrick moaning about how he never got mail from home… Well, the very train that arrived this morning had mail for us, and guess who had a letter?"

"Great!" Luke replied, happy to hear some positive news for once. "That will perk Patrick right up. Won't it, James?"

Lockett nodded. He was glad to hear it too. It would be just the medicine that Patrick needed.

"He won't even need to write a reply," Bauer said brightly, "He'll be home in less than a week."

Lockett was the last one they loaded onto the boxcar. Steering him to the side, out of sight in case there were any onlookers, Lieutenant Long and Sergeant VanderJagt dismissed the others and pulled themselves into the boxcar.

"The captain says that you can unshackle him now, Sergeant," Long ordered grudgingly.

As VanderJagt stepped forward, Orrin Long and James Lockett stared wordlessly at each other. Their hard stares were mirror reflections. They had nothing in common except for the murderous glare that each gave the other.

The outcome was not what Orrin Long had hoped for. The hanging is what he wanted, not just for the pure satisfaction, but also to be sure that if Lockett really knew anything of his profit-making dealings that it would die with Lockett. The fact that Lockett would still be alive and could potentially spread tales about Orrin Long back home did trouble him, although he reminded himself that no one of any value would believe a poor, disgraced farmer like James Lockett over himself.

Lockett's hands trembled slightly as he fought to control his inner rage. He had failed so horribly with Orrin Long – a failure like he could not have imagined in his worst nightmare before enlisting. The multiple injustices would plague him forever, he thought with certainty.

It took all of his self-control not to lash out at the man, at this last chance that he would have for satisfaction, however ephemeral it would be.

VanderJagt noticed the clenched, quivering fists, but he said nothing and did not pause in the slightest as he worked the bolt key in the lock.

"Goodbye, Private," Orrin Long smirked one last time, and he turned on his heel without another word and hopped down from the boxcar.

VanderJagt removed the shackles, and Lockett massaged his wrists. The devices had only been clapped on for a short time, but he was surprised at how they had bruised and numbed his wrists so quickly. He could hardly imagine what it would be like if they had been on for any period of time.

"Sorry, lad. Truly sorry," VanderJagt said in a kind voice that Lockett would not have thought the iron-lunged sergeant capable of. "There's more to this story. I am sure of it. Don't know why yer so quiet about it, but I'm sure ya have yer reasons."

Lockett nodded and bit his lip. Shockingly, he felt a sudden urge to weep at it all, but he did not dare do that in front of the grizzled sergeant.

VanderJagt shook hands with Lockett, not caring if any bystanders saw him shaking hands with the 'prisoner.' He hopped from the train, and Lockett stared through the open boxcar door.

"Safe travels, boys!" Bauer shouted from below, and Lockett noticed that most of the company stood outside to say goodbye and wish them well. "We'll see you at home in two months after we've won this war!"

The train gave a slight lurch and ever so slowly started to roll forward.

Lockett forgot his own misery for the moment after he heard Matthew's words. He shook his head. At least Matthew was back to his old self. He had hit some depths after Hallsville, but it looked like he had already put that behind him.

The war over in two months? Some of the others probably felt the same, but what in God's name had they seen so far that made anyone think it was ending soon? They had accomplished so little here in Missouri.

Even so, as the train slowly rolled out of town, and Lockett left the Kalamazoo Sharpshooters and the war behind, he could not help but feel that he was leaving something behind that he was not supposed to. Despite how foreign it had felt from the beginning and his own sense of dread about most of it, he felt a peculiar pull to stay. He could not shake the sense that he had fallen short of his duty. There was more to do. So much more…

But there was no use grousing about it. It was done. That was plain and simple, so with one last look he pulled himself away and considered his carload of sick soldiers. There was a pile of filled canteens in the corner, but before he checked on who needed a drink, his eye caught sight of Patrick.

He looked even more pale than before, if that was possible, and there was clear distress on his face.

Worriedly, he knelt down next to his friend. He had kept his promise to Martha so far. Patrick had not been killed or maimed by enemy fire, and he'd be damned if he failed Martha now.

"Patrick, are you alright? What's wrong?"

The red head looked at him with a bloodshot, dazed look. He was facing Lockett, but his eyes seemed unable to focus on the face in front of him.

"Patrick?" Lockett said with even more concern. When there was no audible response, and the stare continued to pass through him, Lockett placed a hand on McManus's shoulder. Was he in delirium? "Patrick, can you hear me?"

McManus grunted in response.

Lockett was about to chide him for giving him a fright, when McManus added in a choking voice, "Martha."

"It's James, Patrick, not Martha."

"No!" McManus reached up with one hand and grabbed Lockett's hand that was on his shoulder, crushing it in a violent grip. With his other hand he waved crumbled paper in front of Lockett's face.

Lockett blinked and then recognized it was the letter from home that Matthew had brought onboard for Patrick.

McManus looked up at him with a tortured grimace. For a moment, the sweaty, glazed look disappeared into one of pure clarity.

"Martha's sick! Deathly sick!"

Chapter 11

January 30, 1862

Lockett waited for McManus's wobbly legs to take him down the steps of the train onto the simple wooden platform. He looked north down Main Street at familiar Kalamazoo. It hadn't changed since they had left, but it seemed much bigger to him after spending a month in tiny Sturgeon, Missouri. Even the simple dirt road of Main Street impressed him today. Twice as wide as Main Street in Sturgeon, the thoroughfare was lined with wood planking sidewalks, a luxury that he had once wished the muddy streets of Sturgeon offered.

The four story buildings that lined Main Street were another sign that the bustling town of Kalamazoo was starting to outgrow its pioneer, agrarian roots.

"When are they going to replace the old depot?" McManus wondered, joining him on the uncovered wood planking of the temporary train depot.

"No time soon, I imagine." He remembered the beautiful high-pitched roof of the Gothic structure that had burned down in 1853. In his mind's eye, he could still remember looking at the ashes of the building that had once made Kalamazoo so proud. He had never understood the reluctance to rebuild it, especially with all of the other growth in the town, but Lockett now had larger concerns. His eyes made it over to the drawn, ashen face of his friend. Darkened sags of skin beneath his eyes aged Patrick's once youthful face like Lockett would not have thought possible. "You sure you're up to the walk back to the farm?"

"I will be once we take care of the others," McManus declared resolutely, but his shuffling steps were more than a clue as to how weak he truly felt. Still, unlike some of the others, he was determined not to be carried off the train.

Their trip over the past week had not been without event.

Their first problem had been the St. Louis to Chicago leg. In spite of having purchased tickets, the conductor had not allowed them to board the passenger car. Whether it was because of their extremely ill, and likely contagious, condition, as the conductor expounded, or because he harbored a grudge against their blue uniforms, it did not matter. No amount of arguing, cajoling, or threatening would shake him from his position. The best that they could do was crowd in with the cargo of a half-filled boxcar.

Even that had required a bribe, which took a while to figure out. Lockett was so unaccustomed to the vague hints that the conductor virtually had to spell it out for him.

To Lockett's surprise, no one passed away on that bitter, cold, and swaying ride. However, the trip cost more than the generous Lieutenant Simon had guessed. Once in Chicago, they realized that even with pulling every coin they had between them, it wasn't enough to make up the difference.

Sadly, or perhaps fortuitously, that was when two of their fifteen had passed away. When a third man decided to stay in Chicago since he had family there, the problem had seemingly been solved.

But when Lockett insisted that they bring the two corpses home with them, they were still short of the funds. In the end, the Lutheran church two blocks from the train station, where they had been staying while trying to sort this out, promised to bury the men in their local cemetery.

Deciding that it was the best that he could do and that at least their families could come retrieve the bodies if they desired, Lockett and the remaining twelve continued on.

Another man died on the way from Chicago to Niles, and five others disembarked there since Niles was closer to their homes. All of which left Lockett with Patrick and four others.

Lockett directed McManus to sit on the bench inside while he directed the assistance to move the others from the train and get messages passed to their families.

The arrival of their small contingent caused a bigger stir than Lockett expected. In no time, there were more hands to help and feed the men. Generously, the owner of the Burdick had rooms prepared for each of the four while they waited for their families to arrive, and the town doctor was summoned.

Gratefully, Lockett drifted into the background, realizing for the first time how utterly exhausted he was. He slumped on the bench next to McManus and huffed a loud sigh of relief.

They were home, he told himself, but he caught himself from saying it aloud, knowing that his friend was desperate for news of his wife.

"Let's go, James," McManus said with a hint of anger, using his arms to push himself to his feet. "I told you. I'm feeling better. Just weak, that's all, but I can still walk."

Lockett nodded. He understood, and Patrick did look a little better. His fever had broken two days ago. His forehead was finally free of the small beads of sweat.

"Right. Give me that," Lockett said, pulling on McManus's knapsack.

"I can carry my own."

"Patrick," Lockett implored, unswayed, "Give me the knapsack. I won't take any arguments here."

With a look of resignation, McManus scowled and handed over the knapsack. "When I get my strength back, James Lockett, I'm going to whup you for giving me such a hard time." And they started the walk down Main Street towards their farms four miles out of town.

"When you get your strength back, I'll give you the chance. Though I don't want any complaints from you after I have you on the ground."

"Hah! Since when did you think you can whup me in a wrasslin' match, James? I must have been sick longer than I thought for you to get that idea in your head."

Lockett laughed as their boots sounded on the planking of the sidewalk.

"At least the weather isn't too bad," he answered, noticing a wagon coming down a side street towards them. Recognizing the hunched figure at the reins, Lockett waved. "Zeke!" he called out.

"Boys!" Ezekiel Wilson said in a surprised voice, "What are you two doing back?"

Twenty years their elder, both Lockett and McManus had known Ezekiel Wilson for their entire lives, which wasn't surprising considering that his farm was just down the road from theirs.

"Term of enlistment is up soon," McManus answered.

"Patrick's been sick, and I'm here to make sure that he gets back okay," Lockett added.

"You do look a mite peaked," Zeke commented, "Skinny too. Don't they feed you boys in the army?"

"He's been fighting a fever for weeks."

"Have you talked to my father or Martha lately?" McManus interrupted anxiously.

"No," Ezekiel Wilson said hesitantly, "Not lately, though I did hear that Martha was sick... Been terribly busy since all you boys left." He finished lamely, looking away.

Lockett had a terrible feeling that he wasn't telling them something, but McManus did not seem to notice.

"Oh," he said with some disappointment.

"Want a ride back?" Zeke offered, "Just have to do one more errand on the way. Won't take long, and you'll be back on the farm a lot sooner than walking."

"Be real obliged," Lockett replied, half fearful that Patrick would stubbornly turn him down to prove that he could make the walk.

"Well, get in," Zeke said, "I just need to drop off this barrel of dried apples and butter at the Moffat house."

Zeke lightly slapped the reins on the horse, and the wagon rolled along the dirt avenue, taking them into the neighborhood of large houses on the tree lined streets east of Main Street. Though more impressive in the spring when their large trees were in bloom, the houses that they rode past were still something to see, especially when compared to Missouri. Lockett had never realized before how well-off Kalamazoo County was. Besides the influential people who owned the expensive, square brick houses, the farmers in the area were more prosperous than the Missourians. Lockett imagined that it had a lot to do with the rich soil of the Celery Flats and Gun Plain, but some of it had to do with the bustling industry that had blossomed too. Furniture, barrel-making, paper, seemingly anything to do with wood could be made in Kalamazoo.

With their wrought iron fences, impressive Gothic houses, and fancy dress, families like the Upjohns, Moffats, and Burdicks had brought much to the county, he realized.

"You seem quiet," Zeke broke the silence, as his companions observed the scenery.

"Sorry, Zeke," Lockett replied, "Just never noticed how prosperous we were before."

"Not like that out west, eh?"

"Not like this."

"Well, I think everyone will be glad when this is over and everyone comes back, especially people like the Moffats."

"The Moffats? Why's that? He doesn't have any sons."

"No, but he's got plenty of businesses to run, and there's no one around here to work for him now."

Lockett frowned in confusion.

"You see, James, you boys were just the first to leave. Since then, it seems like every able-bodied male in the county has enlisted somewhere, with somebody."

"Really?"

"So many so that Governor Blair is offering our volunteers to other states to help fill their quotas for President Lincoln."

"That many?"

"The state is ablaze, James. On fire with patriotic zeal! Well, I guess, I don't need to tell you that. You were one of the first to volunteer. Why, if I was a younger man, I'd be gone myself."

"Your wife wouldn't like that."

"Probably not, but she wouldn't say nothin'. Warring is part of her blood. Her nephew just volunteered, you know?"

"That young pup?" McManus questioned.

"The county's blood is up," Zeke replied, "Reverend Bailey and all the others have stirred everyone up. I s'pose it shouldn't be a surprise. This area has always felt strongly 'bout slavery and the Union."

"I guess there's no better way to end it quick than to have everyone possible take up arms," Lockett reflected more to himself than to the others.

Zeke Wilson pulled the wagon through the short, half moon circle drive and onto the side lane entrance at the Moffat's. Though a simple square Gothic design like many of the other houses, the Moffat's house had an additional air of prosperity about it. Whether it was the perfect whitewash coating or the polish of the oil lamps, Lockett didn't know. But there was definitely a feeling that these were people who had done well.

"Say, James," Zeke said, "I don't s'pose I could convince you to help me carry this barrel of apples in?"

"So this is why you offered us a ride home? You need help with your fields probably too," Lockett joked.

Just as Lockett hopped out of the wagon, the rear door of the house opened, and Mrs. Moffat appeared.

"In the root cellar as usual, ma'am?" Zeke asked, doffing his floppy hat.

"Yes, Mr. Wilson," she replied as she was joined by a girl Lockett's age with rosy cheeks, becoming even redder in the cold.

Lockett immediately recognized her from their brief encounter before the Sharpshooters had left Kalamazoo.

"Katherine!" her mother scolded, "Get back inside, you'll freeze to death out here!"

"It's not bad today," Katherine maintained evenly, her eyes never leaving the blue uniformed soldier helping Mr. Wilson with the apples and butter.

"Don't expect sympathy from me if you get sick, my daughter." Mrs. John Moffat left it at that. Too many times she had tried to teach her eldest daughter the proper and wise way of doing things. But often the girl, who looked like her mother, acted with the stubbornness of her father. "John," Mrs. Moffat would say to her husband, "That daughter of yours is truly a Moffat. With obstinacy like that, it's amazing I can even talk to her." John Moffat, of course, always replied that she had married a stubborn man so there must be something Mrs. Moffat liked about it. To which, Louisa Moffat would always turn away with a huff.

Aware of the female audience, Lockett took the first step

down into the root cellar with the heavy barrel of apples. Blindly, he slowly felt around with his foot for the step, and then the next.

"Got it?" Zeke asked.

"Got I---!" Lockett replied, just as his foot slipped off the last step. Awkwardly, he twisted as he fell, landing straight on his back. The barrel came down full force on his chest, but instinctively he held it tight to keep it from crashing and splitting open.

"James? You okay?" Zeke asked.

With the wind knocked out of him, he could not reply that the barrel was still intact.

"James?" Zeke said again.

Still holding the barrel on top of his chest, Lockett craned his head around to the side. The bright daylight contrasted completely with the pitch black of the root cellar. Then, like an eclipse, the light above Lockett was blocked out by two more heads peering down into the root cellar.

"Are you hurt?" he heard a pleasant, womanly voice say.

Finally able to reply, he answered, "Caught the barrel, Zeke. It's okay."

Chuckling to himself, Zeke Wilson hopped down into the cellar, rolling the barrel off Lockett and righting it. "What a clod. I think I'll do the butter myself."

"Are you sure you're fine?" the heavenly voice came again.

Looking up into the light, he could only make out a shadowy shape. Oddly, with the bright light and clouds in the background, the shape seemed to glow at the edges, almost like that of an angel, or so he thought to himself. Only as he ascended the steps could he tell that it was not a messenger from heaven but the attractive Moffat daughter.

Her light brown hair was swept up and back, and she looked at him with a gentle, youthful face atop a long, slender neck. As she stepped back, he thought she moved with an almost regal bearing. Her blue eyes watched him with some concern, but there was also a hint of laughter in the tiny curves of her lips.

Realizing that he was staring at her, he stammered, "I, I,

I'm fine. Just my... Just my pride is hurt, that's all."

The tiny upward curve of amusement on her lips remained. In the silent pause that followed, Lockett was sure that he must be blushing, and he wanted to look away, or at least step back, but he found himself unable to do so. It was Katherine Moffat who finally broke the trance.

"You're one of Captain Vincent's sharpshooters," she said, pointing at the red scarf tucked tightly down inside his collar. With only a fraction of it showing, he was surprised she could recognize it.

"Yes, ma'am," he said, self-consciously brushing dirt off his creased and rumbled uniform.

She was about to ask him something when the tart tone from her mother interrupted.

"Katherine!" her mother scolded in a voice that she rarely used, "Thank you for your concern for the young man, but I want you inside right now before you catch your death out here."

She looked at her mother, about to argue again, but seeing the rare look of determination on her mother's face and having heard the serious voice, she relented for once. "Yes, mother." Turning towards the soldier, she added, "I'm glad you are not hurt. It was nice to meet you, Mister..."

"Lockett. James Lockett," he answered hurriedly, more hurriedly than he intended.

"Inside," her mother ordered again, waving her away. Hearing the door close and with Zeke Wilson finished closing up the root cellar, Mrs. Moffat added huffily, "Thank you for your assistance, Mr. Lockett. Good day."

The wagon bounced along the mildly rutted roads, and they made their way back to the farms. McManus was still looking out ahead when he said to no one in particular, "That was strange."

"What was?" Lockett asked absently, his mind still on visions of Katherine Moffat.

"I think Big John Moffat's daughter was making eyes at you."

The rest of the ride back was ominously quiet. The haunted look on his friend's face was unmistakable, so much so that Lockett began to feel the dread also. Even Zeke Wilson was quiet, leading him to believe that the old man knew more than he was letting on.

When the wagon creaked to a stop in front of the McManus farm, not a single word was said.

For a peculiar second, Lockett stayed stuck to the wagon's bench. McManus also hesitated before weakly climbing down from the wagon.

The simple farmhouse door swung open, and Patrick's father stepped forward. Seeing his son, his shoulders slumped, and he stifled a defeated sob. Lockett felt the sorrow like a physical wave, rocking him back in his seat.

He had never seen the old Irishman like that.

"She tried to hang on..." the elder McManus's voice cracked.

* * *

The small gravesite behind Patrick's house looks so empty, so out of place beneath the clump of birch trees. I fear two people were buried today. Martha is surely in the cold earth beneath those trees, but I fear that the Patrick McManus I have known since I was a boy is gone now too.

I know that gasping look of hopelessness. It is the same as when father died. I can bear that across my shoulders, but it is utterly out of place on someone like Patrick. He was always carefree. The joy of life is a part of his core, but I fear for him now.

He is hollowed out, a shell of his self.

Patrick shed no tears, but I know that look.

He dug the frozen hole where she lays. He insisted on it, despite his weakened condition. He refused to let me help. At one point, I thought he had exhausted himself so much that he was about to faint. But he finished it. From where that strength came, I do not know. I hope it did more for him than digging father's grave did for me. There was no balm in it for me.

--- the diary of James Lockett

Chapter 12

February 6, 1862

John and Lyman Cameron stared across the landward side of Fort Henry in the early morning light. 12,000 yards of trenches were dug in the Tennessee mud about four hundred yards from the fort, supported by six landward facing artillery pieces. It was silent and still, as both brothers and every other defender of the Confederate fort expected.

They knew the Yankees were coming. It was a matter of when, not if, but there had been no indication that anything was imminent from the land side of the fort. No, all indications were that when the Yankees came, it would be from the river side of the fort. They had already exchanged some tentative, teasing fire with a couple of Yankee gunboats, although the Federals were careful to test only from a great distance, and neither side had bloodied the other yet.

The massive guns on the river side of the fort were some reassurance to the brothers – far larger than normal pieces of artillery, where a 12-pound Howitzer was frightening enough. Fort Henry boasted an evil looking 10-inch Columbiad that fired a 128-pound projectile, two 42-pounders on barbette mounts, seven 32-pounders, and a single 24-inch rifled cannon.

The younger brother turned around and grinned devilishly at the foreboding, blackened pieces. "We'll give those Yankees a thrashing, John, whenever they show up. Have you ever seen such big guns?"

John Cameron tilted his head contemplatively and itched a spot on his large, hatchet nose. "Wahl, I hope so, little brother, but I imagine them gunboats mount some big guns too, and it ain't in our favor that we already abandoned Fort Heiman down yonder. I know that General Tilghman ain't too confident in holding here. I saw him last night while I was on sentry duty. He was pacing up a storm across the ramparts – probably would have been pacing laps down within the fort base, but we had a foot of water across the fort."

"Aye, it ain't the best place for a fort. Most of the time this damned place is flooded. At least it is a little better this morning."

"Be better to fight it out from Fort Donelson, if you ask me."

"Bah, we can swim."

The elder Cameron chuckled. "I ain't as worried about drowning as getting blown up. We have hundreds of rounds of ammunition sprinkled around the fort instead of in that dandy little bombproof they dug. The ammunition was supposed to go in there, but since it floods, it's out here with us. One lucky shot, and we'll all go sky high."

"Look on the bright side. Yes, the river is high, and it is flooding the fort, but the river has also flooded the swamps and creeks around here. It'll make it harder for them to attack by land."

"Not much of a bright side," John Cameron snorted.

"Wahl, if's you so gloomy about it, then why did you volunteer to stay?"

At sunrise, General Tilghman had ordered the infantry support to evacuate. Only 80 gunners and a handful of volunteers, including the Cameron brothers, remained in the fort.

"You'd already volunteered, you damn fool. So of course, I had to volunteer too. Someone has to watch your back. Though I got a feeling that at some point we'll be making a dash across that swamp with the devil on our tail."

Shortly before lunch, the Yankee boats appeared. This time, it was not just one that teased them from a distance. Seven gunboats steamed toward the fort with obvious intent.

From the packed earth rampart, John Cameron watched the first approaching gunboat with such intensity that Lieutenant Colonel Haynes let him borrow his field glasses for a quick look.

"Odd looking things, aren't they?" the officer commented.

There seemed to be two types, both painted black and ominous looking, full of malevolent intent.

"It's the iron clad ones that I am most curious about," he continued.

"Iron clad, sir?" John Cameron asked with some wonder, "How do they float?"

"They're mostly wood with iron plating bolted to the sides."

"As big as our guns are, will that matter?"

"Probably not on a direct hit," the officer shrugged, "But I guess we'll find out."

To Cameron's surprise, the lead boat was not an iron clad. It was a wooden gunboat that was curious looking in its own right. Through the field glasses, he watched it create a small wake as it chugged closer.

In the middle of her 180 feet of length, two tall, slender smokestacks stretched high into the air. The rest of the boat was covered with black painted wooden planking. To Cameron, she looked like a floating barn, or perhaps how Noah's Ark looked, except that Noah did not have four gunports on each side and twin side wheelers for propulsion that were encased with wood planking.

It gave her a solid looking appearance, but he was sure that one well placed shot from a 32-pounder would tear through the wood planking with no problem.

About a mile from the fort, the lead boat discharged her bow guns. For the next forty-five minutes the gunboats and the fort exchanged thunderous but ineffective fire. The air within the fort buffeted with concussions and filled with smoke, punctuated by showers of dirt as Federal shells impacted the earthen defenses, but no one suffered more than scratches.

The Cameron brothers carried ammunition back and forth to the cannon, ready to plug themselves into a battery's crew, if needed.

Then suddenly, the fort itself shook, knocking both brothers to the ground.

Lyman Cameron yelled, "They landed one finally, damn Yankees!"

Ears ringing, neither brother could hear the other, but John guessed what his brother had been saying. He shook his head and yelled back in response. He had been looking right at the 24-inch rifle seconds ago when it happened. "That wasn't a Yankee shell! The 24-inch exploded as it fired! Must have had a defect in the barrel, some fracture that overheated or something!"

They pulled themselves to their feet, but there was nothing to be done. The shattered barrel still smoldered. One two-foot section of it was buried in the earthen ramparts, still giving off twisting tendrils of smoke. There was little left of the gun crew, just pieces of gristle and a charred leg missing the rest of its body.

Minutes later, the mighty Columbiad jammed, and despite the crew's frantic actions, nothing could be done about it. Then one Federal shell passed cleanly through the embrasure, striking a 32-pounder, killing the crew. Additional shells landed inside the fort with regularity now. More and more gunboats had brought additional guns to bear and found the range. The barracks were on fire, and geysers of water burst from the flooded fort grounds over and over again.

But Tilghman's brave crews were finding the range also. Through one of the embrasures, John Cameron saw one of the 32-pounders tear into a gunboat. The shot plunged deep into the vessel, finding the boiler with an explosion of steam and boiling water.

The boat was disabled, and no doubt many sailors had suffered a horrible, scalding death.

But the other gunboats had received only glancing blows and near misses, nothing that disabled them.

One by one, the Confederate guns were being knocked out of commission. The brothers were carrying two wounded gunners away from the carnage of their embrasure when they passed by a grim General Tilghman and Lieutenant Colonel Haynes.

"Are we going to surrender, sir?" Haynes asked, flinching instinctively as a shell struck the earthen mound next to them, showering them with dirt and small rocks.

"Soon," Tilghman admitted. "We have only two guns left and not enough men left to man even that."

"No one can say that we did not do our duty!" Haynes declared angrily.

"Sir!" John Cameron pulled the general down as another shell shrieked overhead. It crashed into the collapsed remnants of Tilghman's quarters, sending shards of wood in all direction.

Lyman Cameron helped them to their feet. "Sir, permission to make a run for it if you intend to surrender."

"Granted," Tilghman answered, "Godspeed to you. I'll wave the white flag in five minutes, so get out now."

* * *

"Tell me more about this battle," Daniel Lockett insisted again.

James Lockett looked irritably at his brother as they rode along in the wagon. Since he had returned from Missouri, Daniel's questions inevitably turned back to life in the Army, and despite his best efforts, no amount of glossing over the facts was acceptable for his younger brother. With the town of Kalamazoo now within sight, he did not feel like going into life as a sharpshooter again, though truth be told, he did find himself missing it. There was an undeniable comradery that existed, and he sorely felt that he had failed in his duty – duty to himself, his friends still out there, and to his country.

"I don't suppose you'll just pipe down and let us go to Doyle's and then back."

"James!" Daniel said impatiently. "You've hardly told me anything since you've returned. Every time you say, 'Wait until Mother is not around' or 'Wait until our brothers are asleep.' I'm still not sure when you'll go back. I know that you came back to help Patrick, but when will you rejoin the sharpshooters?"

James Lockett stared stoically ahead, consciously trying not to bite his lip and doing his best to keep his face impassive, as old Sergeant VanderJagt had taught him. He had not admitted the truth of why he had returned to anyone yet, though he did not know how long that could last.

"Don't know, Daniel. I still haven't thought much about... when I'll go back... to the army."

"But if you don't go back..."

"And no, you can't go either!" Frowning, he looked at the boyish face of his younger brother, "I can see right through you, Daniel. No, you can't sign up. You need to run the farm."

Undeterred that his plot had been so transparent, Daniel quickly responded, "But if you don't go back, you can watch the farm."

"No, Daniel."

"But that's what you want to do. You don't want to fight."

Lockett reined in the horse so suddenly that they jerked forward. "That's where you're wrong, Daniel! You've never been so wrong!" There was a menace in his voice and an emotive conviction that Daniel had never seen in his older brother before, and it startled him. He had seen James angry, but this was different. It took him a moment to realize what it was. It was passion.

"I want to fight," James continued more calmly, reflecting on how true those words were. Though he had never realized it until now, he wanted to be fighting. He couldn't explain it, not to Daniel or even to himself, but he knew his place was to be out fighting the Rebels, not back on a farm in Kalamazoo.

It wasn't a patriotic fervor or boyish romanticism, he realized. It was something else entirely. He had never thought much about his future or destiny; the family had always been too hard-pressed in the current minute to think about that. But at this moment, sitting in a wagon with his brother on the outskirts of Kalamazoo, James Lockett came to the staggering realization.

He had a destiny, and it wasn't to toil in the thick, black dirt day after day. He had to get back out there, and he had to keep Daniel attached to the farm like an anchor.

Finally looking at his brother again, he continued on, "I have to go back, somehow, but it won't be with the sharpshooters, Daniel." For the next hour, Daniel sat in mesmerized silence as his older brother related every detail of what had transpired in Missouri – from the stolen silver to the cowardice at Hallsville to the murder of little Amelia.

* * *

"Ah, James!" Ruth Doyle cried from behind the counter of the general store, "Welcome back!" Waddling over, Josiah Doyle's wife threw her thick arms around him. "Sorry you had to return home under such circumstances. Such a good friend you are to Patrick." Stepping back and admiring the blue wool coat that he still wore, she added. "Still in uniform, I see. When do you return?"

"Not long, ma'am," he answered uncomfortably as Daniel busied himself with hunting for their wares.

"But where is your red scarf today?" a soft feminine voice asked.

Turning in surprise, he found himself face to face with Katherine Moffat. Her teasing blue eyes made him think that he was the object of some joke, but the friendly smile on her thin lips changed his mind.

Unperturbed by his silence and glazed stare, Katherine Moffat boldly stuck out her hand, "So nice to see you again, Mr. Lockett."

"James, please," he managed, taking her small hand with a sudden thump of his heart. Fearing that such a small, smooth hand would be fragile in his calloused grip, he squeezed only lightly and was surprised by the powerful return. She smiled in satisfaction at the look on his face.

With a bemused sigh, Ruth Doyle silently withdrew from the conversation. Katherine Moffat had a reputation for impetuous behavior that rankled some in Kalamazoo, but Ruth Doyle found her spirit quite admirable and well suited to life in West Michigan. Now what Katherine saw in the quiet, ever-serious eldest Lockett brother, Ruth Doyle had no idea. But it would certainly make for good gossip.

"Where is your barrel today?" Katherine prodded with amusement.

"Barrel?"

"Yes, the first two times that we met, you were carrying a barrel."

Lockett tilted his head. "So, you do remember the first time that we saw each other, when I was carrying that cracker barrel from the train?"

"Oh, I do remember," she answered with a small smile. "You wanted to dance with me right there on the sidewalk, even with that barrel in your hands. You could have stepped to the side, but you wanted to make sure that I noticed you that day."

Lockett blushed and cleared his throat. "That's not exactly the way that I remember it."

"Well, it obviously worked since I do remember you."

"Um, yes."

"I was very sad to hear about your friend's wife. I had no idea. Is he bearing up okay?"

Nodding, he said nothing, not at all surprised that word had spread quickly.

"You must be a good friend," she added, "To accompany a sick friend all the way back here."

His gray eyes showed no reaction, but silently he studied her. Was that a peculiar glint in her eyes? Why did he get the feeling that she knew something that he didn't? Was she hinting at something else? Was that twinkle in her eye insinuating something? Or was that just her bantering manner?

He could not tell. "Anyone would have done the same," he finally answered, sweating beneath all the layers of winter clothing.

"We heard the Rebels caught our sharpshooters by surprise in Missouri. Was it bad?"

"It was certainly not good," he answered more evasively than he intended. His eyes drifted off, and he suddenly remembered the backs of Orrin Long and Hiram Walker as they ran from the bushwhackers. He had half a mind to mention that their task was made impossible by the incompetence of their officers, but he didn't say anything. It wouldn't help matters now, and Katherine Moffat could surely care less. She was just making conversation, however discomfiting her style.

"But it sounds like you made up for it the next day."

He gazed quizzically at her. He wasn't sure what she meant and began to wonder who she had been talking to. Her father?

"Thank goodness that you chased the Rebels from Missouri, and the Kalamazoo Sharpshooters are on their way to a new state."

"What?"

"Oh, yes, I suppose you couldn't know that last part. It was only telegraphed here yesterday."

"What?" he repeated. He could tell that she took pride in knowing something that he did not.

The door to the General Store swung open with a blast of cold air.

"Ah, there you are, cousin."

The speaker was a thin young man in an officer's uniform. Noticing the soldier next to her, he added, "Oh, hello there."

"Ainsley," Katherine broke in immediately, "I want you to meet James Lockett of the Kalamazoo Sharpshooters."

Reaching his hand out only after realizing that the lithe lieutenant had already extended his, Lockett cautiously replied, "Sir."

"Ainsley Stuart."

"Lieutenant Ainsley Stuart," Katherine corrected.

"I think I should salute you, sir," Lockett said seriously although their hands were still locked in a handshake.

"That's quite all right, James. I'm actually not official yet. I was only wearing the uniform to show my cousin here."

"You look dashing," she declared.

"Dashing?" he laughed, "You are too kind, cousin. Anyone can see that a gangly, long nosed fellow like myself is anything but dashing."

"I still say you look dashing."

"You're one of those who volunteered with Vincent?" Ainsley Stuart asked Lockett, "How have you found the enemy so far?"

"Tougher than most expected, sir," he answered honestly.

Surprised, Katherine interrupted, "Surely you exaggerate. From what I have heard, it will all be over soon."

Not wanting to start an argument with her, Lockett's mind raced to find a suitable escape. "Ah, well, some might say that, but I would not be one of them."

"But we will whip these Rebels at every turn," she declared in puzzlement.

"There is more blundering about than whipping," he replied before he could stop himself.

Before Katherine could argue, as she was prone to do, Ainsley Stuart broke in, "I agree completely, James. Few of my Northern friends concur of course, but I do not think the Southerners will lose one battle and simply give up like they all assume. I had many friends in Washington, most of them now on the other side. They are smart and courageous, and they absolutely believe in what they are doing. I believe you are right, James. We have our work cut out for us to preserve this Union."

"Now Ainsley..."

"And too many of us are unfamiliar with battle," he continued, looking at his cousin, "Men like yourself are at a premium for the Union, James. You've been in battle and know what it is like now."

"You are more right than you know," Lockett replied softly.

"What are you doing back here anyway? Are you on leave?"

"He came back to help his friend," Katherine inserted.

"Oh, yes, I remember hearing about you now. You're the one who brought all of these sick men home. I imagine you'll be rejoining your friends again soon."

"Actually, my term of enlistment is up now, and it sounds like they are already on the move elsewhere." Lockett was surprised at how smoothly the white lie came out of his mouth.

"Really?" Ainsley Stuart replied with a deliberative scratch of his narrow jaw. He stopped in thought. With a sly smile, he added, "We could surely use some experienced men. Have you ever considered a transfer?"

"Transfer?"

"Or perhaps in this case, re-enlisting with a different unit might be the more accurate term?"

With a start, Lockett realized that he had not thought of that simple idea. And it would keep Daniel on the farm…

"Re-enlist with the 12th Michigan, James. We could surely use some experienced men. All of the boys are as inexperienced as I am."

"12th Michigan?"

"Yes, Colonel Quinn is raising a new regiment in Niles."

"I, ah, had not thought of it before," Lockett said slowly, wondering what kind of officer the informal and friendly Ainsley Stuart would make. With a long, thin frame and narrow face, he certainly looked more bookish than rugged, but he knew he shouldn't hold that against a man. Orrin Long looked for all the world like a romantic hero, and he clearly was not. The question was, did this Ainsley Stuart have the courage to face the fire and advance into it, or would he dash away too?

"You don't need to decide now, but if you want to join, I can arrange it. Come see me. I'm staying with Uncle John."

Chapter 13

February 7, 1862

Dear Sister,

Thank you for the kind letter. I received it two days ago when we arrived in St. Louis. We left Sturgeon on the 4th via the North Missouri Railroad. None of us will miss the place. Our mood has brightened considerably since we first heard the news that we were to rejoin the war and let the local militias and Provost Guard worry about the few bushwhackers that remain in Missouri. Finally, we think our sharpshooting will be put to good use. That is, if there is still a war on!

News of the fall of Fort Henry just reached us. It sounds like the rebels scattered without even a good fight and retreated to Fort Donelson. While we sit here on the steamer "Belle Memphis," the war may be ending. First, we steamed down the Mississippi from St. Louis arriving in Cairo, Illinois. A more impressive sight, I have never seen as all these giant paddlewheels splash the muddy waters of the great river. With so many ships and men, I wonder why we do not just sail right on down to New Orleans and get it over with. But alas, after reaching Cairo yesterday, we steamed up the Ohio River to Paducah, Kentucky. At this moment, we are on our way up the Tennessee River to Fort Henry. I am told we should be there by morning.

As you probably know, James and Patrick left with some of the others who were discharged due to illness. The rest of us however have reenlisted for three years like everyone else. Of course, the war will be over long before then.

Give my regards to father and all. I will be home soon.
Your loving brother,
Matthew

February 8, 1862

By now, Luke Bailey had become accustomed to the steady thrum that the steamer made, like the rhythmic breathing of some smoke-belching beast, punctuated with the constant, slapping churn of the paddlewheel against the water. Even the stuttering motion of the wood deck did not seem so strange to him anymore as they frothed the brown water of the Tennessee River and pushed forward.

Their group of four steamers moved together, part of a much larger number. Since the Union Army had shut down traffic on the Mississippi, there was little else for the steamers to do other than ferry General Grant's troops. The steamer captains considered themselves lucky that there was still one paying customer out there.

Even so, there were not enough steamers to move the entire army at once. The first half of Grant's men was already there, but it did not bother Bailey to be part of the second movement. In spite of Matthew Bauer's worries that the war might end before they arrived, Bailey was fairly certain that there would still be at least one big battle before this war ended. Although thoughts of that one big battle would always heighten his anxiety and remembrances of what happened at Hallsville.

Regardless, the steamboats plowed steadily through the rivers.

Despite being the second element, it was not without excitement. Twice, sporadic shots from the trees along the riverbank rang out against the plodding steamers. The second time, three companies of infantry men had lined the starboard side and fired a tremendous volley into the trees. Whether or not they hit anything, it was impossible to say, but there had been no return fire at the time and no more pot shots since.

"We are surrounded by water and thirsty as heck," Matthew Bauer complained from next to him.

"Well, you know what they told us to do, Matthew."

"I know," Bauer said, bending over to pick up the bucket with the rope attached to it.

"Just be careful not to lean too far over. You heard what happened to that Iowan on the transport ahead of us. He fell overboard and drowned as we went over him."

"None of us will ever forget. And how do you know he was an Iowan?"

"Aren't they all Iowans on the boat in front of us?"

"Dunno. From Illinois maybe?

"In any case, just be careful when you throw that bucket over the side."

"It ain't good tasting water, but I guess it is all we got."

"I know. I don't know if it is the water or the fact that all we got to eat are hog jowls and crackers on this boat, but it stinks like you wouldn't believe on that second deck. There's a lot of sick men down there."

"Of course, I know that! You can't miss it, Luke! I slept down there last night, remember? I tried to sleep up here, but the embers from those twin smokestacks kept drifting down onto my blanket. I have three charred holes in it now. So it was either sleep next to the slop buckets and sewer or burn to death while I slept!"

The men milled about where they could on the overcrowded deck, still conscious of the steamer pilot's warning about keeping an even number of men on either side of the boat. It seemed ridiculous that a boat the size of the *Belle Memphis* could capsize if all of the men rushed to one rail to see something. Impossible, yet something about the coal-eyed look of the pilot had convinced the men not to test it. Some of the men who couldn't swim, like Sam Moss, went out of their way to enforce the policy.

While the men grumbled, gambled, and guzzled illicit liquor hidden in their canteens, Luke Bailey looked out across the rail to where the *Belle Memphis's* sister ship, *Meteor*, churned behind them. He tipped his hat to a *Meteor* soldier staring back at him. With his wide brimmed slouch hat, the man was clearly another Western soldier, and Bailey tried to pass the time guessing where the man was from. Illinois? Iowa? Wisconsin?

It was warm, like spring despite what the calendar said, and the *Belle* reeked of sweating men packed too close together. Even the sinking of the sun into a brilliant pinkish orange glow did little to reduce the heat.

But once it became completely dark, Bailey was sure that the chill of the night would descend on them, just as it had for the past two nights.

It felt like they had slowed their pace over the past couple of hours, and a rumor started that the delay was caused by the wholesale capitulation of Confederate forces. The pounding of Fort Henry had finally convinced the Rebs of the futility of their task. Of course, a few hours later the officers dispelled that notion. The war wasn't over.

Wordlessly, Lieutenant Simon joined Luke Bailey at the rail. For a full five minutes they watched the sun sink lower and lower in companionable silence until Bailey asked, "Officer of the Guard again tonight, Lieutenant?"

"Of course," Simon smiled cheerfully, although to Luke it seemed like nothing to smile about. It seemed to him that the duty should rotate at least once to Lieutenant Long or maybe even Captain Vincent, yet every night it always seemed to be Lieutenant Simon, occasionally Sergeant VanderJagt. Still, if the same thought ever crossed Walter Simon's mind, he gave no hint of it.

Bailey knew Walter Simon well enough now to know that the lieutenant was no fool, and any fool could tell that Captain Vincent and his nephew took advantage of their positions, or at least were able to bully the junior officer into additional work. Yet Walter Simon never said an ill word against either. Even when he had helped James Lockett find an exit, Walter Simon had said nothing about Long's actions despite knowing the truth.

Bailey still did not know what that 'truth' was, but he did know that there was more to the story and that Lieutenant Simon knew what had happened. Between that and Simon's general treatment from the other two officers, his position seemed to have all of the responsibility and work without any benefits. At least as a private, he didn't have to worry about responsibility or dealing with Vincent or Long directly, Bailey reflected.

A fish jumped out of the water and came down with a loud

splash, causing his head to suddenly jerk upwards. With a frown he realized how petty his thoughts had become, and he reminded himself of the bigger picture, the greater cause at hand – putting an end to slavery.

"You okay, Luke?" Simon smiled, his scarred cheek wrinkling in a grotesque manner and giving the officer a ghoulish appearance. Realizing that Bailey's eyes were on the still pinkish scar tissue, he stopped smiling. "Pretty horrible, isn't it?"

"Sorry, sir. No, not at all. I didn't mean to stare."

"But you were. It's okay. I'd stare at it myself if it wasn't a physical impossibility."

"But it's not what you think, sir. It doesn't look bad."

"Luke," Simon laughed out loud, "Come now!"

Behind them the grumbling murmur of the sharpshooters changed tone and volume. Men who had been sitting playing cards, writing letters, or reading in the last light of the day suddenly stood up and gathered around the commotion.

"That's the worst part of this," Simon opined as he started to push his way through the crowd, "Too much idle time leads to squabbles."

The wall of human resistance slowly melted away from Lieutenant Simon as the soldiers realized that an officer was trying to push his way into the commotion. At the center of it, Hiram Walker loomed over another man who was trying to struggle to his feet, his nose trickling blood. Yanking the man up by the hair, Hiram Walker lowered another meaty fist into the side of the man's head, dropping him to his knees.

Across the planks of the deck, Lieutenant Simon noticed strewn playing cards. "Corporal Walker!" he yelled, the words drawing attention only after Hiram Walker fired one last punch that put his victim flat on his back. "That's enough!" Simon yelled, irritated that Walker was not heeding him, "Come to attention, now!"

"Or what?" Hiram Walker sneered, turning now to face the much smaller officer.

Even from two arm lengths away, Walter Simon could smell the heavy stench of liquor on the man's breath.

Combined with the man's overall dirty and unkempt appearance, greasy tangled beard, and wild eyes, Hiram Walker looked more animal than human. He was what most men knew as a bad drunk. But Walter Simon was unaccustomed to dealing with men such as Hiram Walker. "Or I'll have you arrested for insubordination," the lieutenant declared, his voice sounding chirpish next to Hiram Walker's deep, gurgling bass.

"Insubordination?" Walker guffawed. He stopped suddenly. "I'll show you insubordination." With surprising speed and dexterity for his inebriated state, he yanked free his long hunting knife from its sheath and lunged forward, the tip of the knife pointing directly at the middle of Simon's chest.

Stunned beyond belief, the officer froze and watched the silver point of the sharpened knife plunge toward his heart. He blinked, and his face twisted into one of confusion when at the last moment, the progress of the knife stopped instantly, as if it hit an invisible brick wall. Taking his focus off the knife point, Simon's eyes followed up Hiram Walker's arm. Like everyone else, he was surprised to see the two strong hands of Luke Bailey clenched like a vise around Walker's thick forearm.

Hiram Walker frowned, equally surprised at the intrusion and at the powerful grip of the preacher's son. For a moment, neither man made another move. Then Hiram Walker's grizzled face contorted, and he took a step to the side to improve his leverage against Bailey, but he stepped on a whiskey bottle lolling about on the deck and lost his balance. Bailey released his grip, letting Walker fall square on his back. The knife clattered from Walker's hand upon impact, and there was silence on the deck.

Finding his voice again, Simon shouted orders to the men behind Hiram Walker. "Grab that man! He's under arrest!" And dutifully the three Wisconsin boys from company A grabbed the man who had cheated and then pummeled their comrade.

Simon's scarred face gave Luke Bailey a look of muted thanks. Bailey simply nodded and stepped back, satisfied that the others had control of Hiram Walker.

"Clear the way!" Simon shouted forcefully to the crowd, as

they marched Hiram Walker off to Captain Vincent.

* * *

"Patrick, no!" Lockett cried, aghast.

This was not what he had expected when he shared his news with McManus, and he realized now that he had not thought all the way through the reaction.

"You don't have to re-enlist too, Patrick. Why would you do that?"

"Why would I *not* do that?" McManus scowled angrily at his friend.

"Because… because…" Lockett hesitated, unsure how to ultimately answer that question without offending or driving his friend into deeper despair about Martha's death.

"I told you in Missouri. You don't make my choices for me, James! I'm my own man!"

"Of course, you are. Of course, I know that."

"You don't owe Martha any promises anymore. You never really did, but even if you had, she's gone now, James! There is nothing to owe – all this foolishness about making sure that I get back in one piece."

"I know, I know," Lockett answered trying to assuage his friend's visible anger. "It's just… but…" He stopped.

"It's what?"

"I'm the one who needs to keep Daniel on the farm, not you. That's not your responsibility."

McManus's eyes narrowed, but he held his tongue. He didn't believe that was the only reason for James to re-enlist, and even if it was, he still saw the plan as flawed. Farming never suited Daniel, and it was only a matter of time until the younger brother shrugged off the burden.

"You've already done your bit, Patrick."

McManus spat irately to the side. "That's what I think of that! What have we done, James? Chase simple people from their homes? Steal the goods from their general stores in the name of the Union? Run at the first shots at Hallsville? We've done nothing! This war won't end with a bunch of 'nothing' being accomplished."

His disgust was palpable.

Lockett could only nod. Patrick had put words to much of what he himself had been feeling.

"You made a promise to Martha once, James. Now, I'm…"

Lockett cut him off with a sudden wave of his hand, "Stop!" He knew where Patrick was headed. "Don't make promises you can't keep! You, of all people, already told me that once!"

"Fine!" McManus replied with his face still flushed with emotion. "But I'm enlisting in the 12th Michigan with you."

Lockett nodded, knowing he'd been beat.

And, McManus vowed silently, you may not want me to make the promise aloud, James, but I'll make it to myself. You watched my back like a hawk in Missouri. Now, I will watch your back until the day I die…

Given how James had oddly developed a talent for finding trouble, McManus knew that it would be a hard promise to keep.

Chapter 14

February 9, 1862

It was early morning with the sky just beginning to lighten when Luke Bailey joined Lieutenant Simon at the ship's rail. Most of the men were just beginning to stir, some complaining about sore backs, most just generally grumbling.

"Coffee?" Bailey asked him, offering a tin cup to the lieutenant.

"Thank you, yes. How did you manage that?" Simon queried, hungrily taking the steaming cup. He took a long drink and felt the warmth course down his throat and into his stomach, taking some of the morning chill off his tired body.

"The pipes that run up through the second deck. If you place the coffee on top of them for a few minutes, it warms it up just as well as if it was over a campfire."

"You're adapting rather well to life on a steamer," Simon chuckled, taking another gulp.

"You look tired, Lieutenant."

"I feel tired, Luke." There was a brief pause before Simon added, "I didn't get a chance to..."

"No need, sir. It was just a reaction. If I had thought about it, I probably would have froze up. I just saw what was happening and something in me reacted."

"Good thing too."

"Definitely a good thing, sir," Bailey smiled.

"Luke," Simon hesitated, "I don't know quite how to say this, but you need to keep your eyes open."

"Sir?"

"Last night, Captain Vincent and Lieutenant Long, they – God knows why – but they decided to give Hiram Walker one more chance."

"What!" Bailey fairly yelled, drawing startled looks from those still stirring.

"Believe me," Simon said, lowering his voice, "No one is more angry about it than I am, but Orrin convinced the captain not to court-martial Walker. Something Walker said to him before we started spooked Orrin. I don't know what, but whatever it was, it was enough to make him fight like Hell to keep Hiram Walker out of trouble."

"But he tried to kill you last night!"

"Don't I know it?" His scarred cheek puckered into a sardonic grin, and there was an almost humorous tone of acceptance in his voice, "But there's little more that I can do about it now."

"This is absurd. This is galling," he fumed.

"There is one piece of good news, Luke."

"What could that possibly be?" Bailey answered in a voice that made it obvious he was thinking about something else.

"You're the new corporal."

"Huh? What do you mean, sir?"

"Corporal Bailey."

"Are you crazy... sir?"

"Not at all," Simon said, "You're the perfect choice. Even Captain Vincent agrees. Obviously, Hiram couldn't go completely unpunished, so Captain Vincent took his stripe away. Rather than open it up to election again and give Walker or his friends the chance to bribe or bully his way in again, the captain just appointed you the new corporal."

"But I can't do that. I can't be the corporal."

"Of course you can. Of all the men in the company, you're the most natural leader. The men, excepting Walker's cronies, respect you. They've been looking to you for spiritual leadership for quite a while now. They might as well look to you on the battlefield too. Besides, we're talking about corporal, not captain. It's not like it will be up to you to lead us into battle."

"But..." the words lost themselves in Luke Bailey's mouth as he suddenly remembered the paralyzing fear of Hallsville.

Later that afternoon, Luke Bailey tried to distract himself from the distressing thought of his promotion. As the bright sun warmed him, he was beginning to wonder if Matthew was right, maybe spring did come earlier to Tennessee than Michigan. It sure didn't feel like any February in Kalamazoo.

They had disembarked an hour ago at the blackened remnants of Fort Henry. Matthew and a number of the others had left the earthen fort with a pass to sight their rifles, and Bailey knew that he should do the same. Of all the men, he needed the practice the most, but he held back and satisfied himself with cleaning the Dimick. Though the idea of pointing it at another man still seemed unnatural, at least the chore of cleaning and oiling the rifle had become second nature.

A cool shadow across his body blocked the sunlight, and he looked up to see the brutish features of Hiram Walker and the threatening scowl of Bart Randle.

"I've got a score to settle with you, preacher boy," Walker said belligerently, "Because of you, I lost my stripe and the extra pay that goes with it."

Surprised by the poise he felt, Bailey rose to his feet and stood straight and tall, looking down at the barrel-chested Hiram Walker. In an even voice, he answered, "Because of me, you're still with the company and not locked in chains for murder in front of a hundred witnesses." Without a pause, he added, "You should thank me."

The words brought on silence and a confused look from Walker but only for a brief moment. A second later, the scowl was back. "Don't try foolin' me, preacher boy. You cost me my stripe, and I'm not gonna forget it. And if you think I'll take an order from you..." He slowly withdrew the large hunting knife from its sheath. Its shining blade had obviously just been sharpened.

"You'll what, *private*?" a voice barked from behind them, emphasizing the last word. Randle and Walker turned to face Sergeant VanderJagt's equally fierce glare. When nothing was said, the Dutchman prodded further, "You'll what, private? I want to make sure I hear ya correctly."

The toughness of Walker's scowl seemed to pale in comparison to the furrowed lines in old VanderJagt's weathered skin.

"Nothing," Walker finally muttered through clenched teeth, barely audible. Without another word, he and Randle turned and departed. VanderJagt let them go, but his eyes never left them.

"Fun, ain't it?"

"Fun?"

"Keep your rifle nearby when you sleep and a hand on your hunting knife, son."

"I don't have a hunting knife."

"No knife?" VanderJagt said with a pause, "Then you really do have problems." He laughed in an odd way and left Bailey standing there, dumbfounded.

February 10, 1862

There were a few light flurries blowing around Kalamazoo despite the fact that the sun was shining through a break in the gray sky. Long, dagger-like icicles dangled off the steep rooftop of the Moffat house, but inside the warm fires and thick rugs made it comfortable.

Katherine Moffat looked at the three blue uniformed young men in the parlor. The color of the uniforms seemed to be the only thing that they shared in common. Her cousin Ainsley looked so thin and frail in his uniform. In spite of the tailor's efforts, it still hung on his naturally gaunt frame like a half askew drapery. And even with the gold trim and markings of an officer, he looked so much younger than James Lockett and Patrick McManus. She knew that they were the same age, Ainsley had told her such, but it was hard to believe that when they were all directly before her.

The two farm boys looked so much older with the weathered etchings around their eyes that spoke of the grimness and ardor that they had long since been accustomed to. She focused on James Lockett's cautious nervousness. While he could talk light and airy like Ainsley, there was a wariness in his eyes that could not be missed, and Katherine half wondered if the tall, wiry farmer was hiding something.

But her suspicions were fleeting. It was much more

interesting to concentrate on the awkward discomfort that James displayed when he was around her. It had been unmistakable ever since she entered the parlor, which she found flattering and amusing.

Lockett realized that Katherine Moffat was looking at his feet, and for an instant, he was certain that he had tramped mud onto the expensive rugs in the Moffat parlor. He had no doubt that the plush red beneath his boot sole cost more than the farm could make in an entire year. With a grimace, he could feel himself blushing, and he looked away, out into the foyer and the broad staircase leading to the second floor. The carved wood railing of the staircase mesmerized him. He had never seen such detail put into a house, never even considered it. From the engraved diamond pattern in the nine foot archways above the doors to the curved legs of the furniture, there seemed nothing in the house that did not speak of elegance… and money. This was how royalty lived, he imagined.

Even the brass of the oil lamp appeared unnaturally polished as the sunlight from the rose-colored parlor window danced off it.

Without thinking, he began to nervously twist the toe of his boot into the thick red carpet again. In all his life, he had never spent much time thinking about wealth. He was satisfied when they put food on the table, but such was the lifestyle of the Moffats that it made him think about things that he had never considered before.

He wondered if Patrick was thinking the same thing, but before he could contemplate it much longer, Katherine's voice interrupted him. "I'm sorry that father and mother could not be here to give you a proper goodbye, Ainsley."

Even as she said it, Katherine winced inwardly. There was that word again, *proper*. How she hated that word. It was her mother's word, yet more and more she found it slipping into her own speech.

"Nonsense," Ainsley replied, "This is marvelous. I understand that Uncle John had business to take care of in Detroit, and that Aunt Louisa wanted to see Detroit again.

Besides, no one knew that I would be needed at the regiment so soon."

Lockett said nothing. He was glad that neither of Katherine's parents was here. He had a pretty good idea that if Katherine's mother had been here, his soiled boots would never have seen the inside of the Moffat's parlor. And though being this close to Katherine Moffat made him more uncomfortable than any Missouri Plains wind had, he still felt a type of elation just being in the same room with her.

All the while, however, he chided himself for his foolish thoughts. Patrick was right. He was just a farmer, and he could never have a future with someone like Katherine Moffat.

"Well, James, do I look the part?" Ainsley asked cheerily. His hand rested on the hilt of the family sword that he was so proud of. He had already related the entire history of the sword to James and Patrick, how it had been specially made to fight the British in the Revolution and then used again thirty years later in 1812.

It was an exquisite creation, there was no doubt. Streaming, meandering vines of bronze and silver formed a protective cocoon around the swordsman's hand. It was impressive looking, but Lockett found himself wondering if it would actually protect one's hand in battle. Who had made the sword – a craftsman or a sculptor?

Ainsley drew the blade from the scabbard, making a sound like a phantom being awoken. The freshly oiled blade gleamed in the light.

"Looks fit for a prince, sir," McManus admired, "Needs some sharpening though, I think."

Again, Lockett couldn't help but wonder about his new officer. Was Ainsley Stuart a cowardly son of privilege like Orrin Long?

"Yes," Ainsley agreed with McManus's assessment, "But there should be plenty of time to correct that. She is a jewel, is she not? Our family jewel, I suppose."

"Yes, sir, Lieutenant," Lockett answered.

Ainsley frowned at him. "James," he said with some consternation.

"I know, sir." Lockett answered stubbornly, knowing what was coming next.

"I understand your point about proper deference when we are in front of the men, but please call me by my Christian name when possible, James."

"It's not about deference, sir," McManus spoke up. Though he liked the young lieutenant and appreciated his efforts to curb the arrogance that some officers felt, it seemed plain as day to him that Ainsley Stuart had little idea of what he was getting himself into. "It's about discipline, sir. Don't worry about whether the men like you or not. It's about whether or not they'll follow you. You're going to ask them to do things that don't make much sense, but they have to do it anyway, without thinking."

Katherine bristled at the gentle rebuke. Regardless of whether it was well-intended or not, it sounded to her like a reprimand. Despite her first instinct though, she held her tongue and waited for Ainsley to reply, but to her dismay, Ainsley's response left much to be desired.

"Well said, Patrick," Ainsley answered, nodding appreciatively, "But I would still prefer to go by my Christian name when possible. There are no other soldiers around right now."

McManus looked at Lockett with a serious look and then broke out into a short laugh. "Alright, Ainsley, though it does sound a bit peculiar in my mouth. Maybe Mr. Stuart?"

"Ainsley," the officer chuckled, "Nobody calls me Mr. Stuart. That sounds like my father. Though I guess people usually refer to him as 'Senator Stuart'."

"Senator?" Lockett asked, looking away from Katherine's profile suddenly, "Your father is Senator Stuart?"

"Of course. You didn't know?"

"I... I never made the connection," Lockett stammered.

"You didn't know that?" McManus laughed, "What a block-headed farmer you are!" He laughed deeply, drowning out the chuckles of Ainsley and Katherine.

Lockett turned red-faced. There was no greater name in all of West Michigan than Senator Charles Stuart. "So that's why you said you lived in Washington D.C."

Ainsley nodded. "Lived there too long, although I always came back to Kalamazoo to spend the summers with Uncle John and Aunt Louisa. Washington gets unbearably hot in the summer."

February 12, 1862

Again, the morning sun warmed Luke Bailey and the rest of the Western Sharpshooters. In rows of four, they tromped towards Fort Donelson as part of Colonel Jacob Lauman's brigade, along with the 2nd, 7th, and 14th Iowa, plus the 25th and 52nd Indiana.

Throughout the easy fifteen mile march down the Dover Road to Fort Donelson, the excited chatter of messmates could be heard up and down the column. Then they were stopping again for a rest. It was the second break already, and the rows of men fell out and lounged on a grassy pasture or leaned up against trees.

"When are these Ai-o-way boys going to find their marching feet, *Corporal*?" Sam Moss said jocularly to Bailey.

Sam and Matthew found particular glee in referring to him as corporal now, he had discovered.

"When I heard that it was fifteen miles away, I was a little worried myself," Pete O'Shea said, "With all the riding we've done on the train and boat, I wasn't sure that my feet were ready for this again, but these green beans are in worse shape than I ever thought I could be."

"Yeah," Sam Moss agreed, facing in the direction of a couple of Iowans, resting nearby, "You boys sure march pretty, but you can hardly leave the Fort before you need a rest."

One Iowan made a face, but they said nothing in reply to his barb.

Sergeant VanderJagt walked heavily over to them and sat himself down.

"Tired, sarge?" O'Shea asked.

"Don't worry yourself, boy. There's no man in this regiment who cain' outmarch me. I only wish we would stop these infernal rest breaks. Of course, take yer rest now, because there might be a point in time where there is no rest to be found."

"I agree with the first part," Matthew Bauer chipped in, "The battle will be over before we get there."

"Ha," VanderJagt snorted, "Wouldn't worry about that, Bauer. They won't start without us. You don't rush a fortified position like Donelson without a second thought or two. No sane man would at least, and I do believe our General C.F. Smith is a sane man. Old, but sane."

"He is a mite old. I just hope he can lead us in battle. I don't want to stop to let our old general catch up."

"Ha," VanderJagt snorted again, "You obviously don't know much about General Smith. You needn't worry about him. He's an old regular. There's no better man in the Army. Seen him in action before. He was just a captain, and I still hadn't shaved yet, almost like yourself, Bauer, but he led our advance across the Salt Lagoon and then later when we took Federation Hill at Monterrey. Them Mexicans know him too, and it ain't because he's so dad-gum tall. Once those guns start roaring, he becomes the damndest man I ever did see."

"I heard that he was an instructor at West Point, and that General Grant was one of his students," Bailey remarked.

"And that tells you a bit of the measure of the man too," VanderJagt added. "Ain't an ordinary general who would take that without being ruffled. His student is now his superior? Ain't so sure about that makin' sense, but that's the Army for ya."

"Dunno 'bout any of that," Sam Moss reflected, "But I guess we will see when we get to Fort Donelson. That is, unless the battle is over by then. Mebbe them gunboats will chase'em out again before we get there, like they did at Fort Henry."

"In that case, we have more than one reason to hurry," O'Shea replied, laying back and closing his eyes.

"What's the other reason?"

"Well, we best hurry because we took nothing with us but these army blankets, haversacks, and three days rations.

Course, as hot as it is, I noticed some of them boys have already ditched the blankets. Spring sure does come early down here."

"Don't forget the 40 rounds of cartridges we carry."

"That's all a soldier needs."

"I still like to eat too."

"Well, it does sound to me like we mean business this time. Three days rations and no tents? This will be no siege. This will be real action, and quick too."

"Hurray for that," Matthew Bauer concluded.

It was a little before dark when Lauman's Brigade arrived within a mile of the fort, joining the rest of General Smith's 2nd Division. Next to them, General W.H.L. Wallace's Division hovered over the eastern approach. To the south of all of them, General McClernand's troops guarded the Confederate positions south of the little town of Dover which was inside the Rebel fortifications. It was difficult for Luke Bailey to imagine that their numbers were so great that they could line up shoulder to shoulder and form a four mile ring around the enemy, but he had heard that was nearly the case.

As the sky grew even darker, the Union army formed a line of battle and stacked their arms for the night. This only served to push the excitement level higher for the anxious troops. It was plainly obvious to even the most inexperienced new soldier that the next day would bring a battle, and judging by the fact that they were already sleeping in line of battle formation, morning would still be fresh when they attacked the fort.

There were no fires in General Smith's lines, since they were too close to the fort and the batteries of Confederate cannon. He wondered if the Rebels would surrender before the battle truly began, just like at Fort Henry.

This was a much different prospect than what he had seen in Missouri. The enormity of the task and sheer numbers of men was on a totally different scale. What would tomorrow hold?

He had seen the remnants of the fortifications at the earthen Fort Henry. It was said that Fort Donelson was a far superior position, and that was why the Confederates had abandoned Fort Henry. If that was the case, how many good Western and Southern boys would die tomorrow?

Would the unseen, uncaring bullet pick him out of the crowd tomorrow? Or would it find Matthew, or Sam? Feeling himself suddenly desperate to read his Bible, he clenched the worn Good Book in his hand, knowing that there was no light to read it tonight.

Each man had wrapped himself in his blanket and formed a long, rolled line – if they had a blanket. Many had discarded them on the way here, sure that spring had arrived as they sweated in the wool uniforms on the march. Now those who did so regretted the decision. It was not bitterly cold, but there was still enough of a chill to be uncomfortable, and there was something about the sudden change that suggested it was only going to get colder.

February 13, 1862

The Kalamazoo Sharpshooters and the rest of Birge's Western Sharpshooters were roused before first light. Forming their lines at the front of the Lauman's Brigade, they waited. Five minutes dragged into an hour, then two, and impatiently, the men waited in their lines.

"Are we going to stand here all day?" Bauer muttered, "Let's get going."

"I guess General Smith is just making sure that everything is set before we start," Bailey answered, but his voice was questioning too.

Finally, Colonel Birge returned from his discussions with the general and faced his Western Sharpshooters. With their motley collection of hats and poor attention to detail in dress and posture, they looked like the dregs of the army. The Iowans in Lauman's Brigade marched with practiced precision, and their uniforms were still new and unadorned by individual touches. Rather than the slouch hats preferred by the Western Sharpshooters, the Iowans wore the short billed caps, or kepis.

But Colonel Birge knew what this motley group was

capable of. Though Company J from Kalamazoo was suspect, he had seen the rest of them overrun the bushwhackers at Mount Zion Church in Missouri. Birge was confident that they would prove their worth again, this time on a much larger scale. He ordered four companies of sharpshooters to the front in a skirmish line, and they stepped forward. Lauman's entire brigade would be right behind them.

Luke Bailey and the rest of the Kalamazoo Sharpshooters formed their loose, staggered skirmish formation with companies A, E, and H. In groups of two, they placed themselves in front of Lauman's Brigade, like the tentacles of an elongated blue beast. Their job was to locate the enemy line and drive in the pickets. As skirmishers, they would fight more like individuals than as a grouped regiment. They would work in pairs, one covering while the other reloaded. They would advance in short sprints, crouch behind whatever cover was available, fire at their own rate, and fight their own personal battles with the Rebel sentries.

'Injun style' is what Matthew called it.

"Redemption, boys," Sergeant VanderJagt repeated three times in a determined voice. There was no audible reply made, but a number of heads nodded. This was the chance for the Kalamazoo Sharpshooters to redeem themselves. They marched toward a small, wooded ravine, anxious to butt heads with the Rebel pickets.

With the only sound being their canteens and cartridge boxes jangling against their sides, the skirmishers separated themselves from the main body and began their task of locating the enemy positions.

Paired together, Luke Bailey and Matthew Bauer both stepped off with hearts pounding, but similarities ended there. The excitement was all that Bauer could think of while Bailey touched the Bible in his pocket for reassurance. In spite of his best internal commands, it did little to still his anxiety.

Crack!!!

The first sound of a shot shattered the morning air. After a momentary pause, there was a series of rifle reports and the sharpshooters to their left began to reply.

Scanning the woods in front of him, Bailey could see nothing except the brown and gray of trees and dead leaves. Suddenly two puffs of smoke appeared from the trees, and he heard the air above him whine with its first passing shot. Next to him, Matthew Bauer raised his rifle and fired at one of the puffs of smoke.

Dumbfounded, Bailey wasn't sure what had happened, and he wondered what his friend was aiming at. He still couldn't see anything in the woods. Then one of the grayish brown tree forms moved, and he realized that he had been looking directly at an enemy soldier. The color of their butternut uniforms blended in almost perfectly with the background!

He raised his rifle and fired at the moving form. Slowly, he lowered the rifle and felt a perverse disappointment when the butternut form did not fall.

The lurching motion of firing and reloading slowed the skirmishers' progress, but the advance was unhalting. They would shoot, kneel to reload, and move forward ten yards before starting the process again. Gradually the distance between the Federal skirmishers and the Confederate sentries closed, shrinking from rifle range to musket range. The closer the sharpshooters got, the greater the fire coming out of the trees. White-gray bursts of smoke seemed to sprout all along the leafless branches.

Gus Jeltema jumped back in startlement as something slapped against the base of his Dimick while he reloaded. Curiously, he studied the solitary ball of buckshot that was buried in the wood.

"Buck and ball," VanderJagt observed with a passing glance as he moved forward and fired.

The air was becoming increasingly thick as the Confederate muskets added their buck and ball to the fray. One large musket ball with three small rounds of buckshot, 'buck and ball' was notoriously inaccurate at any distance and far inferior to the long-range accuracy of the Dimicks. But as the sharpshooters crept closer and closer, the Rebel buckshot became a greater and greater threat.

Bailey saw two more clouds of smoke appear from the

woods and heard the air above him slashed with flying lead. All he wanted to do was turn and run! Disappear! This skirmishing was no type of fighting for a coward such as he! There was no sense of security from the massed battle line. Skirmishers fought as every man for himself, or at least every pair. This was the type of fighting for hardened men such as George VanderJagt or spirited adventurers like Matthew. What was he doing here?

Still, the three hundred men of the skirmish line pressed forward. And judging by the slackening rate of fire, the enemy pickets were slowly departing the trees and falling back.

Bailey repeated a quick prayer for strength, but it did no good. He still wanted to run.

Yet, he did not turn and run. Matthew needed a partner, and Luke couldn't abandon him. So dutifully, he fired, reloaded, and advanced just like the rest of the skirmishers. Fire, reload, advance…

The sharpshooters lost sight of each other momentarily as they entered the tree line where a thin skein of smoke hovered from the departed Confederate musketry. There was no breeze today, Bailey realized. It was perfectly still, which made the sudden cracks of the muskets sound even more startling.

From deeper inside the wooded ravine, the Rebels began firing again, and the two sides traded shots along these rough lines for fifteen minutes. No orders had been given. It seemed that each sharpshooter had already decided that the rate of fire needed to decrease before they could slide into the ravine and attempt the short uphill climb on the other side. But slowly the Dimicks started to take their toll.

Eventually, Bailey looked down into the ravine and saw the first few sharpshooters starting to push forward. The Confederate fire from the other side of the ravine shifted their aim and brought additional fire down into the ravine, but that did not slow the blue coats. If anything, it seemed to encourage more blue to join the advance. Turning to the front, he saw fleeting glimpses of butternut forms scampering off. Before he knew it, Bailey found himself sliding down the steepest section of the ravine on his rear end before popping up to his feet to leap over the standing water at the bottom. He paused to take aim but saw nothing, so he followed after a few of the others who were already near the top.

Realizing that he had never reloaded after his last shot, he halted and grabbed a paper cartridge from his pouch, tearing it open with his teeth as he had practiced so many times now. He mimicked Matthew's impatient voice of instructions as he poured the powder down the barrel, pressing the Minié ball into the barrel and using the ramrod to stuff it all down.

"C'mon, Luke!" Bauer said excitedly, "We got'em on the run!"

There was no respite for the Rebels. Those who had not raced back to the refuge of their own lines were taking increasing fire. The forest resounded with the crack of the Dimicks and the peculiar zing sound that the bullets made in the air, as well as the sound of Minié balls splintering tree branches.

Pete O'Shea and a few others had already climbed the far side of the ravine. With some of the others, they broke into full runs to chase the last remaining Rebels. It was the best Bailey could do to keep up with Matthew who followed on their heels.

But there was no forest here. The trees were nothing but stumps, recently cut down. A barren stretch of broken ground led to a long slope capped by entrenched Confederate rifle pits. Blocking the long slope was an elaborate abatis – sharpened sticks pointing out from all angles, cluttered with thorns. There could be no full dash up the slope; maneuvering through all of the obstacles would take time, time during which they would be sitting ducks for the Confederate rifle pits. The serpentine abatis covered the entire upper slope up to the fort's rifle pits.

"Gawl!" Sam Moss exclaimed, as he joined Bailey at the edge of the woods, "Lookey there!"

"What is all that?" Bailey asked, equally taken aback.

"We'll never get through there!" Sam Moss exclaimed, "Even a rabbit couldn't make it through all that."

Suddenly, a small volley of musketry sent a shower of branches down onto their heads. A number of Confederate heads immediately disappeared behind the safety of their rifle pits as twenty sharpshooters retaliated.

Behind them, Bailey could hear sound and turned to see additional sharpshooter companies coming up behind them.

"This way!" VanderJagt ordered, tugging on his sleeve as he ran by, "We're going to try to get around them." With the rest of the Kalamazoo Sharpshooters behind them, he followed VanderJagt who was chasing Lieutenant Simon who followed the Wisconsinites of company A.

Ahead, he could see the Dover-Fort Henry Road and a number of sharpshooters ducking behind tree stumps and other available cover, however insignificant it was.

Thwackk!

Just below his kneecap, a ball struck a tree stump, and he became aware that they were taking fire from the rifle pits again.

Suddenly, the earth shook with a thunderous BOOM-BOOM-BOOM. The trio sounded like perfectly spaced rumbles of thunder. It took a moment to realize that he had heard his first cannon, fired in a sequence of three.

Blocking the entrance to Fort Donelson via the Dover-Fort Henry Road was a Confederate battery of twelve cannon.

"Keep those guns quiet!" Lieutenant Simon yelled, motioning the rest of the company to find positions where they could keep up fire on the artillery.

VanderJagt pulled the madly waving Lieutenant Simon lower, behind a tree stump, just as a number of musket balls whizzed by overhead, probably saving the young officer's life.

They were two and three hundred yards away, and the sharpshooters began to let their Dimicks do their deadly work. They kept up an incessant fire from behind tree stumps and whatever cover they could find. One by one, the butternut forms fell around their big guns. Some were dragged off. A couple were left on the ground where they laid motionless.

But it took time, and each of the cannon eventually responded.

"Down, boys!" VanderJagt hollered just as one of the artillery crews tightened their lanyard. A split second later, there was the sound of thunder and an enormous cloud of smoke. Even more disconcerting was the sound of multiple thuds into the tree stump to his front and a shrieking overhead whine that shattered the treetops of the ravine behind them, sending a cascade of branches to the ground.

"Canister," VanderJagt remarked to Bailey as he got to one knee and began to reload his Dimick.

"Canister?"

"A tin can filled with a whole mess of lead balls," he answered, popping a percussion cap in place.

Bailey nodded dumbly and jerked to action, realizing that his rifle was loaded. He hurriedly took aim at one of the gunners, the one carrying the long ramrod for the cannon.

"Stay low and keep up the fire!" VanderJagt yelled two times, once over each shoulder. Amazingly in spite of the din, Bailey thought that most of the men heard him.

Dutifully, Lieutenant Simon echoed VanderJagt's order further down the line.

Bailey busied himself with reloading, checking over his own shoulder to see that Matthew was doing the same from behind the perilously thin stump of an immature tree. It provided virtually no protection.

The pattern continued, and eventually, Bailey found himself wondering where Captain Vincent and Lieutenant Long were. In the mad dash, they must have been separated because he did not see them. In fact, half of those around him were Wisconsinites, having gotten mixed together in the hurried actions at the ravine and afterwards.

The cracks of the riflemen and the booming cannon went back and forth, but eventually, the Confederate artillerymen ceded to the obvious. They had no cover and were getting picked off one by one.

Finally, the artillery went silent.

A few of the sharpshooters gave a small cheer as the last of the gunners abandoned his piece. The guns were in no danger of falling into enemy hands, protected by the Confederate rifle pits as they were, but they simply could not be manned in the face of the accurate long-range fire of the sharpshooters.

Behind the sharpshooters, out of rifle range of the

Confederate rifle pits, the main body of General Smith's Division demonstrated, their regimental banners waving gently in the slight breeze, teasing, trying to provoke the Confederates into some reaction or counterattack, but there was none.

Slowly, the late morning and early afternoon evolved into a stalemate. The sharpshooters could keep the Rebels away from the cannon, but the abatis and long slope up to the rifle pits deterred any assaults from the main Union body.

Both sides waited for the other to make the next move.

* * *

"What do you think is going on down yonder?" Pete O'Shea asked Luke Bailey later in the day as they crouched behind a fallen tree on the edge of the hollow.

"Well," Bailey began, only to be interrupted by the crack of a rifle about ten yards away. He looked over and saw VanderJagt begin to reload, seemingly unconcerned as to whether or not he had hit the Confederate head in the rifle pits that had foolishly poked itself into view. "Well," he began again, "I suppose you're talking about all that cannonading south of here?"

The rolling sound of the cannon battle had continued for so long and with such evenness that he no longer took notice. Oddly, it was not even background noise. Somehow, he had put the sound out of his head and concentrated on keeping his own head down and finding targets for his Dimick.

"Of course, he means the cannon," Bauer interjected. "It's been going on forever. What do you think is happening?"

"How should I know, Matthew? This is the first battle I've been in too. Maybe Wallace's Division is making a charge on the center?"

"Sounds like a lot of cannon for a charge," Bauer replied skeptically.

"Maybe he's softening them up first?"

"Wish I knew what was happening."

"Why?" Bailey laughed, "You can't do anything about it. Best pay attention to keeping your head on your shoulders."

"I wonder if we're going to attack these rifle pits today. It's getting kind of late."

"I don't fancy that," Pete O'Shea shuddered.

"I don't see anything happening today, Matthew. General Smith has made some demonstrations, but he can't be more ready to try to cross all that than we are." He paused reflectively. "Right? I hope?"

"We can carry it."

"Don't look so easy to me, Matthew," Sam Moss opined from nearby, eyeing the jagged abatis again.

"And that's without anyone shooting at you. As soon as we form a line and advance, those rifle pits are going to come alive," O'Shea agreed.

"At least we can keep those big guns quiet."

Bailey nodded in agreement. He had never seen canister rip through a packed line of battle, but having seen what it did to the treetops behind them…

These cannon had to be kept quiet.

Lieutenant Simon came up behind them from the deeper part of the hollow. A chilling rain had begun minutes ago. As the rain came down harder, and the temperature dropped ever closer to freezing, the only solace for them was that their counterparts across the abatis were enduring the same miserable weather. Of course, they were probably not as foolish as to ditch their blankets on the march here…

Despite the deteriorating conditions, the only look on Lieutenant Simon's face was that of excited pride. "Hello, boys!" he said cheerfully, dropping to his knees in the mud.

"Lieutenant," they all answered.

"Good news, sir?" Bailey asked, noticing the excited and pleased look that the lieutenant wore.

"No, nothing new, Luke. It is rather exhilarating though, isn't it? The way we drove them in today."

Surprised that Walter Simon, and not Matthew, was showing giddiness, he blinked. "I think the Rebels feel much safer behind those pits, sir."

"True," Simon replied, still unabashed, "But it was a good showing for us today – a start towards removing our stain."

"Yes, sir!" Bauer agreed enthusiastically, emboldened by the lieutenant's confident words. "When are we going to take a crack at their lines, sir?"

"Not sure, Matthew. Rest assured though that General Smith knows the best time. It won't be today though. We're to pull back after dusk. No picket duty for us tonight, thank God. I hardly slept last night, and I wouldn't want to make it two nights in a row."

"In that case, I want to claim that same piece of rotten wood again tonight," Bauer said, "It made a nice pillow."

"Wish this rain would hold up though," Sam Moss inserted, plucking his dampened uniform off his freezing skin. The rim of his hat dripped with water and any shape the poor excuse had retained earlier was definitely gone now.

The first evidence of the rain turning to snow appeared just before darkness fell. By the time the Kalamazoo Sharpshooters returned through the ravine, back to where they had started, the snow had become heavy enough to stick on the wet ground.

As they exchanged places with Company C, the Illinoisans told them about W.H.L. Wallace's failed assault in the middle, which was the sound they had been hearing all day. The volleys of rifle and cannon fire killed many, but it was word of the fires that were started by the battle which burned the wounded where they lie that shook Luke Bailey most of all. Worse yet, any of those wounded who had survived the fire now had to deal with the freezing snow in the middle of the no-man's land.

Chapter 15

February 14, 1862

The Kalamazoo Sharpshooters stood at attention in the exact same spot as the previous day, but today, they needed to stomp their feet to warm up which turned the two inches of snow into a muddy slush.

It was still dark, just before the first light of day, and Luke Bailey was chilled all the way through, like the rest of the sharpshooters. Even tucking his head inside the blanket like a cocooned animal brought no relief from the blasts of cold air that had tormented him all night. Thank God, he had not been so foolish as to discard the blanket on the way here! He could hardly imagine how those who did survived the cutting wind last night. When he had awakened from the intermittent sleep in the morning, there had been an inch of wet, icy snow coating his blanket.

The coffee that Matthew cooked over a small twig fire had brought some relief. At least now he could stand at attention without violently shivering.

"Who do you suppose that is?" someone asked.

He looked in their direction and studied the two generals in the light of the nearby cook fire. One was obviously their own General C.F. Smith. Unusually tall at six foot and three inches, with ramrod posture and a flowing white, twisted moustache, General Smith was impossible to miss. Bailey looked at the other general who was much younger than Smith with smooth skin and trim dark brown hair combed over the side. A long goatee covered the length of his neck like a veil, without which, he would have looked quite young.

"General Wallace?" he suggested.

"General Grant," VanderJagt corrected.

"Are you sure? He looks younger than I thought."

Although he believed the old sergeant, the question was

never actually answered as Captain Vincent and then Colonel Birge addressed them. They were to go back to the same area as the day before and keep the Rebel gunners away from their cannon. To a man, this sounded like exactly what sharpshooters were supposed to do, and despite the cold, most were glad that they were here instead of chasing bushwhackers in Missouri.

With the generals listening curiously, Colonel Birge dispatched them.

"Canteens full?" Birge reminded, "Biscuits for all day?"

Bailey consciously patted his haversack, feeling the stiff piece of hardtack.

"All right," Birge finished, "Hunt your holes, boys."

Silently, the sharpshooters left camp and found individual positions from which they could harass the Rebels and keep the cannon quiet. Many men found positions behind trees and stumps; a rare few carried small shovels with them and scraped better positions behind barriers; some even climbed trees and waited.

And waited.

It was after 3 o'clock in the afternoon when the first Union gunboat engaged the Fort Donelson shore batteries, just under a mile due east of the sharpshooters. The air suddenly became alive with the pounding of large guns as the gunboats traded blows with the Confederates.

From his vantage point high in a tree, Matthew Bauer strained to see what was happening beyond him. In spite of the cannon, the sound of musketry had not yet been heard in volley that day. There had been some attempts by the Confederates to use the artillery battery blocking the Dover-Fort Henry Road, especially after sighting the battle flags of various Union regiments demonstrating out of musket range.

And more than once, it looked to Bauer that a full scale assault on the Rebel positions was due at any moment. It must have appeared the same to some Confederates as they foolishly tried to rush to their cannon, only to fall again under the well-aimed fire of the sharpshooters. Bauer had to admit that he much preferred fighting like this to maneuvering as a whole body. The sharpshooters were truly independent, each man taking care of himself and acting under his own orders. To this point, there had been no shoulder-to-shoulder charges into the enemy fire. He wondered if that would remain the case or if they would have to form up and follow General Smith's main body into the abatis when the time came.

Wedged in the convenient crook of a tall tree, he found himself almost too comfortable with one limb supporting his back like a chair. Better yet, the main trunk of the tree protected him from any fire that could be directed at him from the rifle pits. The only problem was that reloading was awkward and cumbersome, but given the rest of the benefits, he felt sure this was the best position on the battlefield, despite Luke's early requests that he come down before he fell out of the tree and killed himself.

Down the road, he could see the new battle flag of one of the Iowa regiments in Lauman's Brigade. Unfurled in anger for the first time, it bore no resemblance to the tattered Rebel flag that waved behind the breastworks, a recipient of numerous Minié balls.

Meanwhile the gun battle started between the shore batteries and the gunboats. Determined not to be bullied into submission by the gunboats like Fort Henry had, the Fort Donelson shore batteries were putting up a determined fight.

Matthew Bauer watched four black ironclads close on the fort. Each one bore on steadily despite the increasing fire from the shore batteries. At eight hundred yards, he thought they would stop, but they did not.

* * *

Inside Fort Donelson, the Cameron brothers watched the Union gunboats in the distance, slowly churning towards the fort.

The brothers were both silent, and both knew that they were thinking the same thing – they had seen this once before. Without realizing it, each brother clenched his fists tightly, and slowly, a bitter bile of fear crept higher and higher in their throats. Though this was Fort Donelson, their thoughts were back at Fort Henry and the pounding explosions that had erupted around and within that river fort.

While they waited for the artillery duel to fully commence, they could not help but relive it all. From the way the earth shook beneath their feet to the smell of the powder and to the massive explosions and subsequent showers of dirt, it would all be starting again soon.

"Fort Donelson is a much better position than Fort Henry," John Cameron stated, consciously trying to keep the shakiness out of his voice. He felt an older brother's urge to reassure his younger brother at this moment, though he had to admit that he said it as much for himself as for Lyman.

"It is. It is," Lyman Cameron answered, a bit too quickly due to the trepidation that he also felt.

Fort Donelson was a heavily bastioned series of earthworks that followed the contours of the high bluff overlooking the river. Its sixty acres had been dug out and engineered to repel such an attack, and that is what they would do. At least, that is what each brother silently told himself, but they could not help but remember how one-sided Fort Henry's duel eventually became.

Fort Donelson had roughly the same number of guns as Fort Henry, including one of the massive Columbiads and ten 32-pounders, but they were dug in better than Fort Henry's and well protected. The rest of the cannon were closer to the water. About twenty feet above the river, there were also a ten-inch smoothbore and eight 32-pounders.

Higher up, about fifty feet above the river, was the frightful Columbiad and a few other pieces.

"This height difference will help," John Cameron said, repeating what he had heard previously from one of the gunners. "From this height, we'll have the ability to plunge fire down through their decks. It will make our shots more effective."

"Makes sense," Lyman Cameron agreed, but he was not his usual exuberant self as he watched the black vessels approach in the distance.

One boat approached along the west bank of the river, two along the east bank, one in the middle, and three more about a half mile to the rear.

At 3:30, the Confederate batteries opened fire, and ten minutes later, the gunboats began returning fire.

"Should we head for the bombproof?" John asked as the first shots fell. He pointed towards the shelter where soldiers not involved with manning the guns could go. It was connected to the batteries by a deep, covered trench.

"We survived Fort Henry without one. Might as well stay here and watch."

"True, though I don't fancy seeing it all over again. But I guess we did survive that... and the dash out through the swamp."

Even now, he was still surprised by the pace they had maintained after abandoning Fort Henry, even in their fatigued state. And it was a good thing that they had kept such an aggressive tempo, catching up to the rear guard of the infantry who had abandoned the fort on Tilghman's orders earlier that morning, just as the Union cavalry had nipped at their heels. Without that, both brothers knew that they would have surely been scooped up and made prisoners of war.

After a few barrages from the gunboats, both brothers began to reconsider their decision not to use the bombproof.

None of the shore batteries had scored a hit on the boats, and the near misses did nothing to slow the navy's progress. On the other end, the Yankee boats, after missing wildly at first, got closer and closer. Eventually, they found the range, pounding batteries and their fortifications again and again.

At first, the gun crews had been showered with dirt and debris from their fortifications, then there were direct hits on the embrasures, tearing gaps into the defenses, although miraculously, not a single gunner was down yet.

One shot exploded just at the edge of the opening for one of the cannon. Shrapnel whirled through the opening, clanging on the gun barrel, and yet, still no one was down to John Cameron's amazement.

The Cameron brothers had seen the damage that the gunboats could do. They carried larger and heavier pieces than were practical to drag across the land, and the size of their explosions were noticeably more spectacular and violent.

For those who had only seen the army's cannon before, awe-striking as they were, this was completely different.

The lopsided affair continued for what seemed an eternity as the gunboats crept closer. Next to the brothers, a leading Confederate officer turned towards his staff, one of whom was a preacher, and he exclaimed, "Parson, for God's sake pray! Nothing but God Almighty can save the fort!"

800 yards away, the gunboats pounded them.

Then 600 yards away…

The brothers could sense the inevitable happening again. If all of the batteries were disabled, they would be defenseless. There would be no choice but to surrender the fort and the 17,000 men. It would be a disastrous blow to the Confederacy.

400 yards away…

A heavy projectile exploded against the embankment protecting one of the 32-pounders. The resulting landslide buried alive one of the gun crew. The other gunners looked on in horror, conflicted on whether they should pause to dig him out or continue with their unceasing efforts to return fire.

But the shrinking distance also gave the Confederate cannon new accuracy and hope. From the reduced range, the 32-pounders seemed to perform better. One shot smashed the heavy bow anchor from one gunboat. On another, the bow cannon was either hit or exploded on its own.

All of the ironclads were being repeatedly hit now, though it did not seem to slow them.

The gunboat that lost its anchor was then hit again as a shot tore through the small pilothouse, causing it to drift from its line. Within minutes, it had collided with another, causing the second boat to pull back.

And yet the first vessel was as stubborn as ever. John Cameron counted over 30 shots striking it, including two that he was sure had hit below the waterline. It moved with an extreme sluggishness, like a drunk fighter who refused to go down in spite of a multitude of punches.

Another ironclad took a shot in the rudder, severing its tiller lines, and it began floating helplessly downstream, turning round slowly like a piece of driftwood in an eddy.

Finally, at 5 p.m., the ironclad with the smashed pilot house and stubborn, punch-drunk wallow began to pull back and the others followed her.

It had been an hour and a half gun battle. The neat forms of the Confederate embrasures had been thoroughly torn by the gunboat assault, but they had held.

To the Cameron brothers' surprise, they had won.

* * *

Dear James,

I hope this letter finds you well. Sam Moss and the others wanted to pass along their regards. Much has changed since you and Patrick left. As I write this, my hand shakes from the cold, and there is little light to work by so please pardon any errors. We have closed the second day of our siege of Fort Donelson. Though the sharpshooters have performed gallantly and redeemed any mistakes from Missouri, the Secesh still hold onto their fort, and after whipping the gunboats, they are quite full of themselves, shouting down jeers from their breastworks.

The fortifications are an impressive sight, and I do not relish the thought of having to take them. Apparently, General Smith is of like mind, because he has only probed their position thus far. There have only been two killed and fourteen wounded out of the entire division.

At this rate, it looks like we are to starve them out, but that seems a poor choice. Many of us shiver. We have no tents, and some of the boys discarded the blankets on the march here, and we brought only three days of rations. The sleet is beginning again. I am camped in the mud beneath a wagon to find a dry spot to write you. It is only the terrible cold that keeps me awake long enough to write you this letter.

I do not know what tomorrow will bring, but it cannot bring more of the same. The men can only take so much of this. I have no need to tell you, but disease has already taken more boys than battle, and these kinds of conditions are one reason for it. I am sure General Smith is planning out a new strategy. The boys think very highly of him. He spent the day right up in the front with the rest of the boys, trading grim jokes with even the lowliest private.

I'd best be finishing. Either the writing or the cold is making my hand cramp. Keep up in your prayers, my friend.

Luke

Luke Bailey blew out the light of the hooded oil lamp that he had badgered one of the quartermasters into borrowing. Laying his head down, he wrapped his wet blanket around him and tried futilely to sleep.

As he shivered miserably in his makeshift shelter, he said a small prayer for those on picket duty tonight. Though it sounded selfish to his ears, he was very glad that he was not a sentry tonight. As humble as the underside of the wagon was, it was a full mile better than nothing at all.

The night wore on, yet he found himself no closer to sleep. He rubbed his aching neck and wiped his red nose on his sleeve, but it was not his physical discomfort that robbed him of sleep. Not really. It was his mind. No effort seemed capable of shaking the sense of foreboding that he felt.

Though he knew no reason why, he could sense that tomorrow would be more than a day of sniping. It would be a day of something he had never seen before. It would be a full scale battle, and Lauman's Brigade would have to charge up that long slope of obstacles and climb over the enemy rifle pits. And beyond all that, there was still the Fort itself.

He tried to trick himself into thinking that the breastworks were not that tall and imposing, but he couldn't do it. He had seen them up close for the last two days.

Charging those works seemed an impossibility, far beyond all human bravery and gallantry…

Chapter 16

February 15, 1862

The Kalamazoo Sharpshooters walked through the gray light of the predawn, descending down into the ravine as they had the previous two days. Nearby, other clumps of sharpshooters walked stiffly with their rifles, trying to shake some life into their bones. One man cursed as he slipped and fell on the slick ground.

"You kept that rifle covered last night, didn't you, Luke?" Sergeant VanderJagt asked. Each of the first two nights, the old soldier had gone around the company making sure that the men were protecting their rifles from the dampness of the night by wrapping a dry strip of cloth around it. With a zealotry Luke Bailey had seen only with the most devout members of the church, George VanderJagt harangued each man, lecturing on the importance of keeping the rifle in prime working order.

"Of course, I kept her clean," he replied with a yawn.

"Her?" Matthew Bauer laughed, "You've become so familiar with my father's Dimick that it is now a 'her'? You've only really used it for two days." He shook his head with amusement.

"They've been quite the couple of days," Gus Jeltema said, slapping Luke on the back. "We are soldiers now, eh?"

For two days now they had kept those cannon silent. For two days, they had forced the Rebel infantry in the rifle pits to take extra caution in keeping their heads below the lip of the rifle pits.

"Humpphh," VanderJagt grunted, "Fire a couple of random shots, and you boys think you are soldiers? You'll not be soldiers until we mount those parapets before us."

Though they were still deep in the ravine, and the abatis was shrouded in darkness, each man saw the imposing defenses in his mind's eye. The obstacles beckoned them, challenging them.

Bailey spoke eventually, "I have a feeling that we'll test them today."

Most of the others looked at him with some skepticism, a few with foreboding. Sniping seemed more likely than an assault, but as if on cue, the sound of sporadic picket fire from the south reached them. No one thought much of it. There had been various shots in the night since they had arrived. But then something else entirely different reached their ears in the early morning gloom, the sound of volley fire.

"Hummphh," VanderJagt grunted.

"I didn't realize we had an early morning assault planned," Jeltema remarked.

"We don't, or we wouldn't be walking back to our holes like the last couple of days."

"The Rebels are attacking?"

Well south of them, the firing picked up in intensity, alternating between sporadic bursts and volleys. Cannon suddenly roared out, and it was obvious to all of them that this was the beginning of something major taking place to the south of them.

By ten o'clock, the firing south of the sharpshooters was still hammering away at such a pace that they knew the outcome must still be in doubt.

Bailey tried not to think about it too much. It seemed pointless to wonder and worry about it, but it was hard not to. He tried to concentrate on finding targets in the Confederate breastworks here on the northern end of the siege line, but the Confederates were far more careful today. He had yet to see a single decent target.

"Why don't we do something?" Matthew Bauer asked abruptly from behind the fallen tree that other sharpshooters had hauled into place overnight along with some others to create better protection.

"Do what?" Pete O'Shea replied from the hole that had been scratched out behind a stump.

"I don't know. Go join the battle down there."

"Humphh," VanderJagt grunted from twenty yards away, "I think y'all should leave the generaling to the generals."

"I hate it when that Texas accent gets into your voice," Sam Moss complained without malice, "I think I accidentally fell asleep sometimes and ended up inside their lines." He laid back with his eyes closed, unseen behind a separate set of fallen trees, brush, and rocks that obscured him.

O'Shea laughed. "We know you're asleep half the time. Some time, we might just leave you behind so that you *do* wake up next to some Johnny Reb."

The sharpshooters sprinkled throughout the area gave a chuckle.

Behind them, the sound of trampled brush interrupted them and Lieutenant Orrin Long emerged, his face flushed to a bright red.

"Sir," Lieutenant Simon greeted, saluting but not rising from his hole.

Without missing a beat, Orrin Long frowned. His normally clean, shiny face was flecked with dirt. His skin was also reddened, chafed from the cold, and his trim brown moustache was matted with something other than sleet.

Lieutenant Long certainly did not look himself today, Bailey thought to himself.

Yet despite appearances, the unmistakable tone of arrogance was still in his voice. "You will rise when you salute me, Lieutenant. Just because you fancy yourself a sharpshooter, and one of the boys, that is no reason for lack of protocol."

Without complaining, Simon rose to his feet, exposing himself in front of the Confederate breastworks. "Yes, sir," he replied politely, saluting again.

Even though the junior lieutenant displayed no anger at the situation, the sharpshooters around the area tightened their jaws, some not bothering to hide their scowls of disdain.

Suddenly, there was a solitary crack from the Confederate breastworks.

Simon's head jerked violently, and he crumbled to the ground.

Luke Bailey was the closest to him. Instinctively, he reached to catch the falling officer, but he was too far away. Immediately, he scampered on his hands and knees over to him.

"Sir! Sir!" he cried urgently.

But even before he reached him, he stared in horror at the officer, his friend. Simon's eyes bulged and stared unmoving up at the sky, and a ghastly amount of dark, red blood poured out of the side of his skull.

"Sir!" Bailey croaked just as he reached him, placing a hand on each of the officer's shoulders, but there was no movement, no life.

Lieutenant Simon was dead.

The other sharpshooters made no sounds in the sudden silence, not a single sound.

Bailey hung his head and closed his eyes from above Simon's body. "No, no, no!" he cried in an anguished whisper. He found that he was panting, almost out of breath.

There was a growing, menacing murmuring from the other soldiers.

"I..." Orrin Long began, but clamped his mouth shut, unaware of the ugly looks he was receiving. Briefly, he stared at the body, at all the blood. He felt his knees getting weak, so he yanked his eyes away and up to the earthworks beyond them.

Fearing the growing swoon that he felt, Orrin Long was only vaguely aware that one of the soldiers had started to say something, only to be cut off by Sergeant VanderJagt.

But the realization that there might be some insubordination steadied him. Angrily, he snarled at the men. "Put your eyes back on the breastworks. What I came here to say was that General Smith is going forward finally. He's going to take these works, and we are to keep that battery silent." With that, he stomped off, back through the ravine to the rear.

"Yes, *sir*," VanderJagt said, sarcastically emphasizing the last word.

It was actually the Confederates who alerted the sharpshooters that General Smith's battle line was nearing.

With a flurry of activity, the butternut artillerymen hastened to their defenses. The gunners were dashing to the cannon and frantically trying to load them.

Immediately, the sharpshooters opened with a sharp fire. From their hidden positions, they sent a hail of well-aimed Minié balls into the Rebel artillery. Even the shots that missed could prove deadly as they ricocheted off the cannon barrels. With grim satisfaction, they prevented the Rebel gunners from firing a shot.

Finished reloading, Luke Bailey raised the rifle again and slowly picked out another target. Squeezing the trigger, he withdrew the rifle without bothering to watch the outcome and began reloading, his eyes drifting to where Lieutenant Simon's body was. He just could not help it.

It was unreal, like a horrid nightmare! It just could not have happened! Not like that!

It was only when the wave of blue soldiers from General Smith's vanguard swept past him, a hundred yards to his left, that Luke Bailey was able to momentarily put aside the pulsating thought.

General Smith's vanguard was the Iowans of Lauman's Brigade, and they marched forward towards the long slope and waiting abatis. What the Iowans lacked in marching precision was more than made up for by the steadiness of their agonizingly slow advance. The Iowans were in musket range now, and the Confederate breastworks came alive.

The Southerners unleashed a storm such that Luke Bailey had never seen before, or even imagined possible. Volley after volley poured down on the Iowans. The subsequent long veil of smoke obscured the Rebel faces and weapons, although above one of the powder clouds he could see a Rebel banner waving defiantly.

From their elevated positions, the Confederates fired shot after shot so that the air was alive with the twittering, zip-zip-zip of flying lead.

Pausing to look to his left as he reloaded, Bailey watched the blue line pause and then start up the slope. Riding in front of the advance, in perfect alignment with the colors of the 2nd

Iowa, General C.F. Smith sat fully erect in his saddle, calmly moving forward.

He faced directly to the front, occasionally glancing from side to side to check the alignment of the battle line, but never flinching. The air around the general was filled with whipping lead as the Confederates concentrated their fire on the towering horseman. With his battle dress regulation perfect down to the gold braid, his erect stature, and his flowing white moustache, General Smith was the perfect target.

But to Bailey's utter disbelief, despite the unending fire from the breastworks, not a shot hit General Smith!

The drifting white smoke from the Rebels' incessant firing had fully obscured the breastworks now, but Luke Bailey knew that the smoke was not the reason for their inaccuracy. It had to be God's protection!

Next to Bailey, Matthew Bauer shared the same shock at what he was watching. Something caused him to look behind them, and whether it was the smoke screen or the elevated position that the Rebels shot from, he could tell what was happening. The Confederate fire was going too high.

The Rebels were not adjusting their aim for their elevation, and many of the shots zipped narrowly, but harmlessly, over General Smith and most of the Iowans, into the forest behind them.

Even so, to both sharpshooters, victory seemed impossible. From the safety of their hidden positions, they could see the first blue coated forms sprawled on the field. And though the line moved on with agonizing slowness, always closing up to fill any gaps created, they hadn't even reached the abatis yet!

The continual blasting of the Confederate rifles and muskets was overwhelming.

On sound alone, both were terrified, even though they knew the fire was being directed on the advancing Iowans and not on the hiding sharpshooters. It was a tremendous, reverberating, deafening crash of hundreds of rifles and muskets, over and over again!

But the sight of the old general with the flowing white moustache, tall in his saddle and unconcerned, inspired Luke

Bailey like no sermon his father had ever given. General Smith was as calm and confident as any man he had ever seen. The air around the leader was clearly boiling with enemy fire, yet he was utterly unconcerned!

He had to follow this man, Bailey knew. There was something entrancing about it all. He had to lend his weight to the advance, if only to save their general! They had to go forward through the abatis and take those bristling breastworks!

Leaping to his feet, Luke Bailey chased after the advancing blue line as they washed by. Unbeknownst to him, many sharpshooters followed his lead.

They reached the abatis, and the fire reached a new crescendo. More men fell, and the assault wavered. Seeing their hesitation, General Smith turned and put his cap on the point of his sword. "No flinching now, my lads!" he yelled above the fray, holding the cap aloft on the gleaming sword. "Here, this is the way! Come on!" His horse picked its way through the jagged maze of tree branches and obstacles, zigzagging back and forth to find openings. All the while, General Smith held his hat aloft on the tip of his sword.

Lauman's Brigade swarmed after him, determined to keep up. Formations lost all cohesion as the men picked their way through tiny openings; a few climbed over the obstacles and more still tore the barricades apart.

Up the ascent General Smith slowly rode.

Bailey climbed between the protruding, sharpened points of the sticks on one of the fence-like obstacles and then pulled another aside with the help of some Iowans, certain that others would follow behind him through the gap in the defenses.

He ran to his right where there was another opening and followed the others upward. Before his very eyes, those in front of him were whipped with fire, and their shattered bodies were twisted and flung down in all sorts of grotesque angles.

He was alone!

Another fence of jagged sticks barred his way, and he tugged futilely on it, trying to drag it through the cold mud so that others could follow. A musket ball buried itself in the wood, but he struggled on.

And then Sam Moss and Pete O'Shea were at his shoulder. Wordlessly, the three of them pulled the obstacle aside, dragging it like a heavy gate through the muck. Two dozen other men surged through the gap just as they did. The rush knocked him down, but he jumped back to his feet and followed the surge forward.

The front ranks of this surge fell as the Confederates in the rifle pits spouted flame, smoke, and lead. But Bailey and the rest of the Union soldiers pressed on, stepping over their fallen comrades.

Their eyes watered from the hazy white smoke, and they could taste the bitter gunpowder on their tongues, but they stumbled over shredded blue bodies and kept moving forward.

Then suddenly, they were clear of the abatis, and men launched themselves into the Confederate rifle pits. There was no order anymore. Companies were intermingled with other companies; regiments were mixed with other regiments. But it didn't matter. Every man from the densest private to the highest officer knew what had to be done. They were here to capture these rifle pits!

With the obstacle behind them, the Union soldiers were filled with a mindless desperation, exhilaration, and energy. Bloodlust! They fought like maddened brigands, hardly thinking, just reacting to whatever was in front of them.

Behind the first jumbled mass of men hitting the rifle pits, a company of the 2nd Iowa had somehow maintained their cohesion. Surging past General Smith finally, they fired for the first time, unleashing a murderous volley point blank into the breastworks. Without pausing to reload, they leapt into the rifle pits to engage any survivors.

But the only Confederate survivors were already running back, abandoning the rifle pits and praying that there was safety behind the walls of Fort Donelson itself.

All along the entrenchments, Lauman's men were gaining the upper hand. The rifle pits were falling!

Minutes later, the four regiments – the 25th Indiana, 2nd, 7th, and 14th Iowa – planted their regimental flags in the defensive works as the retreating Confederates raced for the safety of the fort.

But the battle was long from over. Turning to the right, Bailey and the others saw a counterattack forming. Five Confederate regimental flags and their men emerged from Fort Donelson itself.

The sight halted him in his tracks. There was a certain unfairness to it all, he thought incongruously. They had done what seemed impossible and taken the Confederate rifle pits, but would reserves arrive in time to help them hold it?

Desperately, the tired men of Lauman's Brigade looked behind them. Where was the support? They would need the rest of the division to make their way through the now undefended abatis and join them in the rifle pits. They would need help, or these hard-fought gains would be for naught.

Looking over his shoulder, he could see additional Union units of infantry and artillery, but they seemed too far down the abatis.

"Don't just stand there, boy!" George VanderJagt yelled in his ear, "We got more fightin' to do!"

Obediently, Bailey turned around and fired into the growing mass of butternut, bent on retaking their defenses.

It was total chaos. Some of the Federal soldiers sought cover from which to fire behind, others elected to stand shoulder to shoulder in small groups and fire into the enemy that rushed them from two sides.

The spearhead of the Rebel counterattack fired a ragged volley, and Bailey felt a body sag into his legs. Looking down, he did not recognize the face, but the ghoulish sound of a Rebel yell snapped his attention back to the front. The others near Bailey fired into the mass without visible effect.

Unwilling to simply wait for the charging Rebels to reach him, Sergeant VanderJagt charged forward by himself with a primal growl. Watching him for a half-second, the other Union soldiers followed and charged after him.

The Rebel spearhead and the small cadre of Yankees collided with the sound of steel, wood, and bone. Just in front of Bailey, VanderJagt drove his bayonet through the stomach of one Rebel. A butternut figure with wild hair clubbed one

Yankee down and then turned his attention on VanderJagt.

Seeing it a split second before impact, the old sergeant tried to dodge the blow, nearly succeeding. But the glancing blow knocked him down and the wild-haired Rebel raised his rifle butt to bring it down on VanderJagt's head. Without a bayonet on his Dimick, Bailey lunged forward with his rifle. The muzzle only served to knock the man off balance, but Bailey's momentum carried him fully into the Rebel, and they went down in a tumble.

In a mass of limbs within a world of raging yells and gunfire, he struggled with the man, hardly knowing which way was up. His sheer size pinned much of the man down, but he found himself half aware of the man struggling to pull out a knife. Acting on survival instinct alone, he reached desperately for the man's hand, slicing his forearm as he grabbed the man's wrist in a viselike lock.

He could smell the man's breath near his face and for an instant their eyes locked, each red-rimmed and desperate. They rolled around, clinging to each other, but somehow the man slid from Bailey's grasp and struggled to his knees. He was about to plunge the knife into him when he suddenly arched upward. Wide-eyed he stared at the Yankee and then pitched forward.

Bailey gaped at the bright red bullet wound in the man's back. It was utter chaos. He had no idea who had just saved his life.

"C'mon, boy!" VanderJagt yelled, grabbing him by a sleeve and pulling him back.

Slowly, the blue coats were falling back to the rifle pits again, and for a second, he feared all the effort would be lost. But before the Rebels could take advantage of the weakening Yankees, Union reinforcements arrived through the abatis and clambered into the rifle pits.

Joined by Cook's Brigade and even some artillery, Lauman's Brigade fought back. Two Parrott cannons had been physically dragged up the slope by the determined Yankee artillerymen, and they fired with an echoing roar.

Canister!

The tin can packed with lead balls and sawdust burst out of

the cannon's mouth, spraying its contents into the gray line of advancing men.

"Reload, Double Canister!" the order was instantly given.

But the shot had already had its intended effect, and Hansom's Kentuckians halted their charge and fell back in disarray towards Fort Donelson.

"Seen Matthew?" Bailey yelled to VanderJagt as he reloaded his Dimick with surprising familiarity.

Grinning at the naturalness of the preacher boy's actions, VanderJagt fired his own rifle. "No," he yelled back, "But that don't mean a whole hell of a lot. When we saw you follow the charge, a right bunch of us jumped up behind ya. I didn't bother to watch who'all came along."

"You were following *me*?" Bailey yelled above the din as he fired at a puff of white smoke.

"We didn't know yer such a hell-bent leader, preacher boy!" VanderJagt laughed with a kind of perverse pleasure amid all the carnage.

Bailey could think of no reply, and he rammed a new ball down his scalding hot barrel.

"Don't worry 'bout, Matthew," VanderJagt declared seriously, "He may have a mouth like the Miss-a-sip, but he can take care of himself."

Bailey nodded, knowing that only a few of the men around them were from their own regiment, much less other Kalamazoo Sharpshooters.

With the air thick with white smoke, the two sides slammed away at each for another hour, but eventually, the Rebels recognized the futility of trying to drive them out. Grudgingly, the Mississippians, Kentuckians, and Tennesseans withdrew to an inner line in front of the fort, and an uneasy peace came over the battlefield.

As night fell and the bitter cold dropped on them again, Lauman's Brigade bivouacked on the ground they had gained. Ever the leader, General Smith shared the bitter night and difficult conditions with them.

Exhausted, Luke Bailey bound up the wound in his forearm and closed his eyes. He fell asleep immediately, even before fatigue parties had been selected to collect the wounded that lay scattered across the abatis and inside the works.

* * *

Truth be told, both Cameron brothers felt lucky to be alive. Even the always confident Lyman Cameron was stunned by the ferocity and violence that he had witnessed.

Until now, they had only seen skirmishes and survived bombardments. They had not experienced the massive clash of infantry on infantry or the harrowing charge into the enemy's rifles.

At six o'clock this morning, the defenders of Fort Donelson had launched their attack on the Yankees at the southern end of the entrenchments, but hopes for surprise were quickly dashed. The Union men were already awake and in battle formation. Worse, some had even thrown together simple earthworks.

Regardless, the brothers and the rest of General Pillow's and General Buckner's men had pressed forward with courageous abandon. Considering that most of them carried only antiquated muskets and shotguns, not new heavy rifles like the Yankees, getting in close was their only chance.

Swathes of men had fallen on both sides, but by noon they had slowly at first, and then with increasing momentum, pushed the Yankees back, so far back that it seemed they would be able to secure the Charlotte Road.

It had taken nearly every bit of strength that the defenders of Fort Donelson had had, only 450 men had been left to guard the entrenchments on the right flank, but they had succeeded…

And then, just when it seemed that victory was in their grasp, General Buckner and his men had been recalled. Apparently, the Yankees had attacked that right flank guarded by the abatis and 450 men, and Buckner was sent to shore up the defense.

To both brothers, it made no sense. If the point had been to punch a hole in the Yankee defense so that the defenders could escape, why go back? They were nearly there!

The gall of it all sat poorly with the brothers and all of their comrades, but now there was a larger problem.

They were trapped again inside Fort Donelson, and with the Yankees in control of the entrenchments on the right, there was no hope of holding out.

Glumly, Lyman looked up when his older brother returned from searching for some food. Lyman knew that there was still plenty of food in the fort, so he was surprised that John was empty-handed.

"Grab your gun and ammunition," John Cameron instructed his younger brother.

"What? Why? Where were you?"

"The rumor is that the Yankees have left the road closest to the river undefended."

"But I thought General Pillow and General Buckner were surrendering?"

"They are, but General Forrest and his cavalry are determined to cut their way out if they have to, and I'm all for that. I don't want to rot in a Union prison camp."

"That makes two of us."

"So be quick about it. Forrest's cavalry and a few other units that were within earshot are leaving in a few minutes."

February 16, 1862

Neither light nor warmth had broken the cold early morning hours when Luke Bailey awoke with a start. He felt a tug on his sleeve and smelled the pungent odor of tobacco. Good tobacco.

"Wakey wakey, boy," George VanderJagt said with a good-naturedness that was unusual for him.

"What? What's happening?" Bailey asked, somewhat amazed at how instantly awake he had become. His eyes flashed around, expecting a whirl of activity, another Rebel counterattack, but there was little going on, just a few men stirring. Most slept rolled back to back where their exhausted bodies had worn out.

"Time to get back with our own regiment," VanderJagt stated, taking another puff on the long drooping pipe that dangled from his mouth.

Taking a sniff, Bailey said, "That smells like real tobacco, not the stuff you've been using for the last few months."

"Exactly right, my boy," he smiled, removing the pipe from his mouth momentarily, "Good num'er of these Southern boys had the good stuff. I grabbed it while the fatigue parties helped the wounded."

"You took it off a dead Rebel?"

"Well, now, he wasn't gonna to use it anymore, was he?" VanderJagt said without indignation.

"I suppose not," Bailey agreed, deciding to drop the issue. He arched his stiff back with a soft moan.

"C'mon," VanderJagt said, "Y'all is too young to be creaky already, and we need to join up with the others."

A couple hundred yards away, most of the sharpshooters slept in their own haphazard pile. Some were beginning to rise, but none seemed as completely awake as VanderJagt. Bailey knew that he had fallen asleep before the older man, and that he had only woken because of him. It would not have surprised him if someone told him that the old sergeant never slept, because he couldn't ever remember seeing the man do more than doze.

Bailey wandered over and sat down next to the square frame of Pete O'Shea, who shoved something in his pocket at the last moment just as he recognized Bailey in the dim light. Bailey didn't see exactly what it was, but he had a pretty good idea that it was more booty from Confederate dead. After a second, he could smell exactly what it was, liquor.

"A little early for that, isn't it, Pete?" he chided, staring out across the darkness at the unseen Fort Donelson.

"Er, probably," O'Shea said hesitatingly, "It's not what you think though. I was just... testing it, you know... it's real Tennessee whiskey, and I need to shake this chill."

"It is still the Lord's Day."

"Is it?" O'Shea asked with genuine surprise and thought about it for a few seconds. "By gum, you're right. It is Sunday. I had completely forgotten."

"Don't know if I much like the idea of fighting on the

Lord's Day. You think General Grant and General Smith will make this a day of rest?"

"Well, I'm sure they're both God-fearing men, but I doubt it, Luke," O'Shea said, glad that the subject had turned away from himself, "Besides, we have the damn Rebels exactly where we want them."

"How's that?"

"Well, we're right on top of Fort Donelson now."

"Is that good?"

"Better than good, Luke. We hold this line, and there is no protection for their shore batteries. After we force the shore batteries to leave, Admiral Foote's gunboats can come back, and together we pound the fort with cannon. Pound it into dust. This is all but over."

Bailey sat, thinking. After a moment's reflection, he nodded and smiled in the pre-dawn darkness. He had been expecting another day of hard fighting, maybe even assaulting the fort itself. But what Pete O'Shea said made a lot of sense to him. The Confederates were completely trapped and nearly defenseless.

More of the sharpshooters and other Union regiments were beginning to roll out of their frozen blankets. Their faces were tired and worn from battle with both the Confederates and the conditions, but steeled by their success, spirits were high.

"Luke!" He heard his name called and turned to see Matthew Bauer standing behind him, an anxious look on his face.

"Matthew!" he answered cheerfully, "Good to see that you're in one piece. Sergeant VanderJagt told me not to worry about you." He looked past Matthew, down into the abatis. The wounded had been removed overnight, but the dead still lay where they had been struck down… And beyond the abatis, back where they started, there was still Lieutenant Simon's body to deal with.

The ghastly remembrance sapped all of the exuberance that had been building. To be killed crossing the abatis was one thing, to be killed because of the pretentious arrogance of Lieutenant Long was something else.

He shook his head to try to clear the dark thoughts, forcing himself to focus his eyes on the slope leading up to the abatis and entrenchments.

From the position they now stood on, the Rebels had fired down on them. Even from here, he could see the underbrush and saplings shriveled from the hail. His eyes latched onto a cartridge box and canteen dangling by their straps on part of the abatis, the owner crumbled below it. The light was still too dim to see such minute detail, but for some reason, he was sure that the canteen had a hole in it from a musket ball. All across the slope, he could start making out anything and everything: a wide brimmed hat, a blue regulation kepi, a shredded knapsack, its writing papers blown into the abatis' entanglements, a broken musket, and bodies – too many bodies.

Behind him, there was the sound of commotion, and he heard the others give a quick cheer.

"What?"

With a look of wonderment, he watched a Rebel enter their camp. He carried a soiled white rag on a pole above his head and was accompanied by a lieutenant and corporal from the 14th Iowa.

The sharpshooters stood open-mouthed.

The Confederates had surrendered. Fort Donelson had fallen.

-III-
... Shiloh

Chapter 17

February 23, 1862

The laughter of men young and old drifted across the camp and into nearby Niles, Michigan. As James Lockett sat cross-legged in front of the wedge tent he shared with McManus and two other recruits, he could not help but think how similar the laughter sounded to the throaty boasting of the Kalamazoo Sharpshooters. Much like before, he found himself surrounded by patriotic Michigan men, certain that their weight would force the South into submission and bring about a quick end to this war.

But that was where the similarities stopped. The former horse fields that they marched upon were clustered with an entire regiment of nine companies instead of just one small company. And unlike the sharpshooters, whose amateur officers paid only token attention to the finer points of battalion movement, the 12th Michigan spent an inordinate amount of time marching. Colonel Quinn and every officer on down took an active part in the training, and the difference was obvious to Lockett.

The supplies were also a dramatic departure from his previous experience. Whereas the sharpshooters had to struggle for tents and uniforms, the 12th Michigan found itself amply supplied.

Yet despite their ample supply, Lockett and McManus stubbornly kept their old uniforms. Faded and worn, they looked a little different than the crisp blue coats of the others. And despite the sour taste that had been left in their mouths from their time with the Kalamazoo Sharpshooters, both kept the red kerchief that had been given to them by the women of Kalamazoo County. Neither could explain why they wanted to keep the now dirtied symbol, but they did, along with their

Dimick rifles rather than taking the government issued British-made Enfield rifles.

"James, what are you doing?" Ainsley Stuart asked, approaching from the side.

The Senator's son still looked out of place with his ill-fitting uniform draped across his gaunt body, but he had proven to be a diligent officer to this point. Lockett was gratified to see that Ainsley required no special attention or treatment, unlike Orrin Long and Charles Vincent.

On the whole, the entire officer corps of the regiment seemed a marked improvement to him.

"I was just thinking," Lockett finally answered.

"I see. Well, I've arranged for some leave for us."

"You have?" Lockett replied with a puzzled look. "Whatever for?" There was not much to do in Niles, and he didn't have any kin in the area to visit.

"Uncle John and family will be in Niles tonight… and Katherine specifically asked that I get you leave."

Lockett felt himself blush slightly. The prospect of seeing Katherine again was exciting; the notion that Katherine had specifically asked for him was even more so.

February 25, 1862

Dear Father,

These are the most curious times. It is nine days since our glorious victory at Fort Donelson. Garrison duty gives the men too much time for temptation. Such dens of iniquity thrive with it. There is gambling and liquor. I see how true now the wise statement about idle hands is.

I thought we were leaving that behind yesterday. We marched 18 miles to a place called Metal Landing on the Tennessee River. The rumor was that the war was over, and we were heading home. It set off such a search for souvenirs that you would not believe. Broken sabers, Confederate buckles. Why, Sam Moss put a 12-pound cannon ball in his haversack! It felt like a hundred pounds by the time we reached the Landing. You should have seen the look on his face when the orders were countermanded upon reaching the Landing. We had to march all the way back the next day!

Will write more soon.

Your obedient son,

Luke

* * *

There wasn't much to Niles, Michigan, other than its attractive train station.

In fact, as Lockett followed Ainsley into the small hotel next to the railroad depot, he wondered if there would be anything in Niles at all were it not that the train to Chicago passed through town.

He rubbed the new chevrons on his shoulder and wondered what Katherine would say about them. He had been named sergeant today, and he was surprised at how much pride he took in that. Experience counted for something, and all along he had been applying the learnings that he had unintentionally picked up from Sergeant VanderJagt. He would have to thank the old sergeant if he ever saw him again.

Upon entering the hotel, it was Lockett who saw Big John Moffat first. His name implied that he was a large, physically imposing man, but he was not. In size, he was of average height and girth. Still, there was a reason that everyone called him Big John, and that was the force of his presence and determination. As Lockett looked at the man with his tall stove pipe hat and finely tailored suit, which was so new that the material still seemed to gleam, there was no mistaking that Big John Moffat was someone of importance. Even his walk or strut seemed to indicate that he was from a class above Lockett.

"Ah, punctual as usual, nephew," Moffat's loud voice could be heard by all. "You caught us just on our way to investigate the fare of this little berg." Moffat grasped Ainsley's hand in a vigorous handshake, and Mrs. Moffat stood by her husband's side, warily eyeing Lockett.

"Ma'am," Lockett said, tipping his cap, feeling very

uncomfortable with her scrutiny.

Realizing for the first time that Ainsley had a companion, Big John Moffat smiled. “Sergeant, is it?” he acknowledged but did not bother to shake hands, “There is a saloon across the way for you while we feed our skinny lieutenant.”

“Yes, sir,” Lockett answered dutifully.

“But...” Ainsley began.

“I’m afraid the offerings in Niles will not be as elegant as the last time we dined, nephew, but that was our nation’s capital.”

“But...”

“Ah, yes,” Moffat interrupted again, “Your cousin is not feeling well and has retired for the night. It will just be the three of us this evening.”

“But...”

“I’ll be over there if you should need me, sir,” Lockett said, pointing to the saloon. There was no disappointment in his voice, nor was there any hint of emotion. If anything, he felt relief. The idea of sitting through a meal with the Moffats was daunting, particularly given the watchful eye of Mrs. Moffat.

Giving Lockett one last look, Ainsley shrugged and followed his uncle.

Lockett sat at the far table in the small saloon. It was mostly empty, just two other souls, up at the bar. Stagecoach men who made the run to Grand Rapids by the look of it, he guessed from their dusty appearance.

He sat quietly, wondering how long the Moffats would eat dinner. With a silent sigh, he realized that he had received a dose of cold reality that he should have expected. The Moffats were so far above him that they did not, and could not, notice him. Though he knew it was for the better, it did nothing to lift his spirits. He had been looking forward to seeing Katherine again. He should have tempered his expectations, he chided himself.

“May I join you?” a familiar feminine voice asked him.

He looked up in astonishment at the smiling face of Katherine Moffat. She teased him with a cat-like grin of amusement. The elegant lines of her face and neck looked terribly out of place in the roughhewn saloon. He could not help but think that she looked like an angel.

"Katherine," he stammered, scrambling to his feet, "I mean Miss Moffat..."

She sat down, leaving him standing, and after a confused moment, he took a seat also. "I thought you were not feeling well."

"I just told mother that because I knew she would be difficult about having you eat with us."

He blinked in confusion, unsure what to say.

"And I so wanted to see you again."

"I… I did too," Lockett managed.

"And so I concocted my little plan," she continued, amused by the effect she was having on him. "How is Ainsley doing? Is he adjusting to army life?"

"He's doing fine. He will be an excellent officer. I'm a sergeant now by the way." He turned to proudly show her the new chevrons on his shoulder.

"That's nice," she acknowledged with less enthusiasm than Lockett hoped. "How much longer will you be training? You're going to miss the war."

"Miss the war? What do you mean?"

"Yes, I've heard that since we have now captured Fort Donelson, we are just one good victory away from ending this rebellion. Then the war will be over."

"One victory away?" He had heard similar talk in camp, but he usually just attributed that to the normal puffery and bold talk of young men who spoke first before thinking. He didn't realize that such talk had pervaded up to Katherine's segment of society.

"You don't sound like you agree, but I suppose I heard this type of pessimism from you before, back in the store when you first met Ainsley, you know?"

"Yes, I remember," Lockett answered, trying to keep the crossness out of his voice. "I'm not sure where you hear these sorts of things, but…"

She cut him off before he could finish. “It’s common knowledge, James. Why, even if it wasn’t, I get information straight from the war.”

He didn’t know what that meant, so he ignored it as he tried to persuade her in a more soothing voice than he would have used with anyone else. “There’s more to it than that, Katherine. I’ve seen some of this war. I fear that there is still much blood that will be shed. Fort Donelson was certainly a great victory, but I can’t see the South giving up so easily.”

“Well, you’re wrong,” she replied with total certainty. “Why, the letter that I got just two days ago spoke of how close the end was. They’ll move up the Tennessee River in a few days, attack the Rebels, and then the war will be over.”

“Letter? What letter?” Lockett asked, struggling to keep the annoyance out of his tone.

“From my fiancée, of course.”

“Your what!” Lockett answered sharply before he could hold himself back. He felt like he had just been kicked in the gut.

“Well, he’s not really my fiancée yet, soon though, I’m sure.”

“You have a fiancée?” Lockett replied in a mystified voice.

“Well, almost, I said. You didn’t know? You know him. You left together.”

“We did? Who?”

Lockett felt his throat tighten even before she answered. He had a terrible feeling that he knew the answer.

And then there was her response, the final indignity to it all. He had never felt so low.

“Orrin Long.”

Chapter 18

March 18, 1862

Savannah, Tennessee was a pleasant little riverfront town, Luke Bailey thought to himself. The sharpshooters had arrived with the rest of Lauman's Brigade, and indeed, General Smith himself on the 12th.

It was a strange atmosphere, he mused, even more strange when compared with the grimness and uncertainty of their time in Missouri. They had re-boarded the steamers on the Tennessee River on March 10, but not before a visit from the governor of Iowa. Governor Kirkwood told the troops with total certainty that the "backbone of the rebellion was broken," and that the war was nearly over. In fact, he declared that they would all be home by the Fourth of July.

Only a very few were prone to disagree. From the generals to the lowliest private, everyone was sure that the end was at hand. One more victory, and it would all be over.

Even with the occasional ghostly bushwhacker's shot from the shoreline, much of the passage on the four steamers had an almost circuslike affair. One steamer, *Meteor*, which was the largest of the Mississippi River packets, had carried numerous wives of the officers, and its upper deck was packed with horses and mules.

Another steamer, *Argyle*, had at one point gotten its large paddlewheel entangled with a tree. The calamitous sound caused the men on board to believe that they were under attack, and so many rushed to one side of the boat that for a moment it seemed like they might capsize.

Luke Bailey shared these and other stories with his latest friend.

Upon arriving in Savannah, he had immediately spied the crisply whitewashed church, and after poking his head in, he had discovered the amiable Reverend Tucker.

And each day since, Bailey had taken the time to meet up with the ever-smiling preacher… and his comely daughter.

It turned out that the reverend was a former soldier himself, back during the Mexican War, and he was interested in all of the goings-on.

At the moment, the three of them walked alongside the path beside the river. They were discussing a number of things. One was the news in the two week old newspaper from Chicago that had reached camp today, particularly the article about Fort Donelson and General U.S. Grant's new nickname. The newspaper had dubbed that the U.S. stood for 'Unconditional Surrender,' since that was the only type of Confederate surrender that Grant had been willing to accept at Fort Donelson.

Another subject was Luke Bailey's surprise at the Union troops' warm welcome in town, especially after the reticence or even hostility in Missouri. He had seen how some of Savannah's citizens had actually enlisted with the 46th Ohio while they were here. Reverend Tucker politely explained that a number of other citizens had previously left to join Confederate units as well, but he left it at that.

The final topic was the fact that they would leave Savannah tomorrow and set up a new camp a little further down the river at a place called Pittsburg Landing, about eight miles south of Savannah. General Sherman and his men were already there, the first of Grant's many divisions that would arrive at the site.

"All of your little white tents will be gone tomorrow?" the daughter, Anna, asked pleasantly. "It will be quite strange that you will all be gone so quickly. The white tents sprung up like a field of mushrooms one night, and then just like that, you will all be gone again."

When she smiled, there was a dimple in one of her cheeks. Between that and her engaging brown eyes, he found her completely enchanting.

"Well, nearly all," Bailey answered, "Most of us will leave, but General Smith will be staying behind a few days while he recovers."

Reverend Tucker nodded in agreement. "Yes, I was just at

the Cherry House yesterday where he has made his headquarters. That fall that he had a few days ago was worse than the old war horse wants to let on."

"Hard to believe that he could ride unscathed through all that fire at Fort Donelson, and then while he is here, he is laid low by such an accident. He was just trying to exit that steamer the *John J Roe* and get in a little boat to be rowed ashore, and then he slipped, putting such gouges in his shins that they had to carry him to the house."

"It was dark out," Anna Tucker offered sympathetically. "I'm sure that he will recover with some time."

"As long as they don't get infected," the reverend stated in an even voice, "I've seen stranger things happen and with an infection… well, that can be the end of it for even the strongest man."

Bailey looked at the preacher.

"I'm sure he'll be fine though," the preacher hastened, "I'm sure by the time the next battle arrives, he'll be in the thick of it."

Bailey nodded. "He'll have time to heal. The Rebels are all down in Corinth waiting for us, but we won't go until General Buell arrives. I've heard that General Grant was given orders by his superior, General Halleck, not to bring on any engagement until General Buell and his men arrive."

"General Buell?" Anna asked.

"Ah, yes, he is marching overland from Nashville. Once he joins us, then we will have double the strength. Then, I'm sure that we will march on Corinth."

"And then?"

"Then? And then the war will be over, I suppose. Do you know Corinth, sir?"

"The one in the Bible or the Mississippi railroad junction?" the silver haired preacher grinned.

"The one in Mississippi," Bailey chuckled.

"Of course. It is not all that far from Pittsburg Landing. About 23 miles, maybe three hours by horse."

"Or two and a half for my father," Anna joked, "He likes to

ride so fast."

They all chuckled. "True," he answered, "Although truth be told, the speed for the ride from Pittsburg Landing to Corinth is always dependent on the weather. There are only two roads that can be taken, and both can turn into a mire like you wouldn't believe with just one decent rainstorm."

* * *

James and Lyman Cameron stared with a sort of gallows humor at what was in front of them.

After escaping from Fort Donelson with General Forrest and his men, without even a shot fired miraculously, they had made their way to Corinth, Mississippi, as had the other various and remote pieces of General Albert S. Johnston's far-flung Army of the Mississippi.

Morale was low, and everything they saw only made the situation more bleak. At the moment, they had paused in front of the local blacksmith's shop where the smithy was turning out pikes due to a shortage of firearms.

"We ain't gonna beat the Yankees with those," Lyman Cameron remarked.

His brother could only nod in agreement. "I hope those are for the locals or something. I know we are low on weapons, but I didn't think that low."

"It's not just the numbers of guns but the quality if you ask me. You know, I went past the camp of the 2nd Tennessee yesterday, I noticed that an entire company was drilling with nothing but old flintlocks."

"I'm impressed that at least someone was drilling," John answered wryly, "Given how inexperienced nearly every man and officer is in this army, we could all use a good bit more drill."

"I suppose," Lyman answered, ignoring his brother's comment about drill. He always hated drilling and didn't see why his brother put such stock in it.

"At least the usage of those old flintlocks will save on the shortage of percussion caps that we have," John quipped,

"Flintlocks. I bet those weapons are older than our grandpappy."

"I did hear that the 20th Tennessee got new British Enfield rifles. Those guns must have made it through on some blockade runner."

They left the blacksmith and headed back towards camp, passing another regiment on the way. This regiment fit perfectly with how their lieutenant had described most of the new troops yesterday, "More like a mob with more enthusiasm than discipline, more capacity than knowledge, and more valor than instruction."

Daily, their numbers grew as individual units came in day after day. Soon they would be at 40,000, but that seemed to create more problems than anything else. Everything was a confused mess. Their own lieutenant had been 'drafted' into emergency duty with the quartermaster to help sort out things. Besides the lack of food, and the even more substantial lack of clothing and boots, the ammunition situation was a mess. Besides the confounding blunders of musket balls getting sent to regiments with rifles, and vice versa, it seemed that even the ones who had rifles could not get the right caliber, such was the diverse mix of weapons from one group to another.

The brothers' commander had made a true mistake when he mentioned in passing how their lieutenant was a particularly organized individual, in front of the quartermaster's assistant no less. Now they were down one good officer.

They halted to let a troop of soldiers cut from left to right. At least, they both assumed that they were fellow soldiers. Not one had a uniform or even a matching piece of clothing, and they all carried spades instead of rifles or muskets. The man at the front of the small column at least wore a uniform, which was the only clue.

"They say that the generals want four miles of breastworks dug around Corinth. Four miles!" Lyman exclaimed.

"I'm not enthused by digging," John grinned to take the edge off what he thought might sound like complaining, "I think I'd rather go through another gunboat bombardment than dig four miles of trench."

"You and me both," his brother agreed, "Although I dare say that your bride back in Missouri would prefer you dig rather than go through that shelling again."

John Cameron nodded, and the easy smile fell from his face. He had not heard from her or anyone in weeks, which was no surprise given how they had pulled up stakes from multiple places now. Still, it would have been nice to hear that she and the baby were all right.

Last he heard, the Yankees who had taken over their little town were gone now. For all he knew, those Yankees might have even been part of the army that attacked Fort Donelson. It was good riddance for sure, and definitely better for his wife and the Munroes. It had to be better without the Yankees watching their every move or trying to impoverish them like when they took all the wares from his father-in-law's store. The last letter from his wife had been very disturbing.

Of course, not all of them were devils, he supposed. There were still the two strange Yankees who had let them go that night in the barn.

In any case, there was a whole horde of Yankees not too far away from what he had heard, and four miles of trenches or not, he couldn't see how they would defend Corinth any better than Fort Donelson.

Chapter 19

March 20, 1862

The three steamers that carried the 12th Michigan plodded down the wide Mississippi waterway, and excitement ran high as many of the Michiganders saw the famed river for the first time. They did not know exactly where they were heading, but everyone guessed it was someplace in Tennessee.

Lockett heard the rumors just like everyone else. He wondered if the Kalamazoo Sharpshooters were there, but any thoughts of a reunion quickly brought back remembrances of Orrin Long, little Amelia, and most recently, the shock of Katherine Moffat's parting words.

He had not told Patrick or Ainsley about Katherine's surprise meeting with him in the saloon. He supposed that Ainsley must surely have known her connection to Orrin Long, and he wondered if Ainsley had not said anything because he was oblivious to Lockett's unusual behavior around her? Or maybe that was how all men behaved around her, so Ainsley thought nothing of it? Regardless, he felt a little soreness towards Ainsley for not warning him. Surely, he must have been in the vicinity for one of the numerous times that Patrick had teased him about the attention that Katherine gave him.

He would have to say something eventually to Ainsley, but it was too embarrassing and painful. Still, he suspected that Patrick already knew that something had happened that night. Patrick could read his thoughts quite often, had for many years now, and they both knew that.

To distract himself, Lockett pulled out the newspaper that he bought before they shoved off.

The newspapers in St. Louis had been full of stories about making one final push in Mississippi or Tennessee. They trumpeted that victory would surely bring about peace, despite the Confederate success in Virginia.

Lockett was not so sure, but he did know that this time he was leaving with a better equipped, better led group of Michigan men.

March 26, 1862

Pittsburg Landing was a patchwork quilt of cleared fields and large swathes of heavily thicketed woods, of a pleasant pond with a peach orchard, and of meandering country roads that connected it all while largely avoiding the multiple twisting little creeks that led into the Tennessee River.

The fields themselves were now covered with white tent after white tent. Like a field of giant mushrooms was how Anna Tucker of Savannah had described it once, Luke Bailey thought to himself as he walked with Matthew Bauer to the next field and set of tents. If she thought there were a lot of tents in Savannah, he could hardly imagine what she would have thought of all these tents. It was many times greater than the relatively few tents that she had seen in her little town.

Luke Bailey's tent was in Cloud's field, like the rest of General Smith's division, which was temporarily under the command of General Hurlbut while General Smith recovered back in Savannah.

General Sherman, whose men were the first to encamp here, was southwest of their camp over near the Review Field and around the Shiloh Church grounds.

General McClernand's division was due north of Sherman, but Luke Bailey and Matthew Bauer were on their way to the newest encampment, which was located between theirs and General Sherman's.

General Prentiss's division and his newly arrived men were over near Barnes Field and Sarah Bell's cotton field, on the southern end of the ever-growing Union encampment.

The sun was starting to sink and put a close to what had been quite a pleasant day. But it wasn't just the weather that lifted their spirits.

Earlier that day, Patrick McManus had shown up in their camp, completely out of the blue. After resounding rounds of backslaps and embraces from dozens of Kalamazoo Sharpshooters, they had learned that Patrick wasn't coming back to the sharpshooters, rather he had joined the 12th Michigan and was in General Prentiss's division, part of Peabody's Brigade.

As if that wasn't enough, Patrick had privately told the two of them to follow him back to the 12th's camp, and that he had a surprise.

Peabody's encampment was row after row of fresh, white, round teepee-like tents, which were larger than the sharpshooters' A-shaped wedge tents. Each company was assigned six of the large Sibley tents, which could hold just over a dozen men each. The remainder were sprinkled around the camp in the familiar wedge tents.

"I guess new regiments get new tents," Bauer remarked, "Now, what is this surprise? Surely, not how grand your tents are, Patrick?"

"You'll see," McManus replied playfully.

Neither Bauer nor Bailey could guess what it was until they saw Lockett's tall frame at the far end of the row.

"How in the world did you convince him to re-join?" Bauer queried, not bothering to disguise his astonishment.

"More like the other way around, Matthew," McManus answered.

"Really?"

The three of them strode up to Lockett who waited for them with a giant smile.

"When Patrick said he had a surprise for us, this was not what I expected," Bailey said warmly, giving Lockett a brotherly hug, followed by Bauer who did the same.

"Good to see you in one piece after Fort Donelson," Lockett greeted.

"We have a lot to catch up on," Bailey agreed.

"What is this?" Bauer asked, pointing towards the chevron stripes on Lockett's sleeve. "A sergeant?"

"And I see Luke is now a corporal," McManus interjected.

"That's strange enough," Bauer grinned, "But James leaves

the army and when he comes back, he's the one who is promoted?"

Lockett shrugged while McManus answered, "James is like a taller, younger version of old VanderJagt."

"I learned a lot from him," Lockett admitted.

"I can't wait to tell him," Bailey enthused.

"Well, I guess you can let him know, but don't tell the others," Lockett said slowly.

"Yes, why all the secrecy?" Bauer asked.

"You're not under charges or anything," Bailey chipped in.

"Still, I'm not sure how Captain Vincent or Orrin Long will react to seeing me. It's best that I just stay anonymous for now, I'd say. Maybe you could quietly tell Lieutenant Simon though. I'd like to thank him again in person."

Bailey and Bauer looked sidewise at each other. Softly, Bailey answered, "He died at Fort Donelson, James."

"Worse 'n that," Bauer muttered with a soft but vengeful tone.

"We'll tell you all about it… it will burn you up like it does us."

Lockett had no idea what they meant by that, but he had a profound sense of loss at not being able to thank Lieutenant Simon for saving his life, even if the lieutenant's plan had cost Lockett his reputation.

Secretly, that was the other reason that Lockett did not want to show his face in camp. He knew his reputation was tarnished forever there. Since he had not been able to defend himself or explain anything, he was sure that nearly all of the men thought him a murderer and a scoundrel. That was how people would think of him at home, once they all returned from the war, but he tried not to think about it. There was too much in the present to worry about. The future would have to wait.

Of course, if it was like everyone at Pittsburg Landing thought, the future was not too far off. One more good fight, and the war would be over.

March 28, 1862

"This place wouldn't be half-bad if it just wouldn't rain so much," McManus observed to Lockett. The sky was lightening, and the patter of rain on the tent was fading, but it was the mud that annoyed McManus and the others the most.

Their boots were always caked in it, and it was difficult to keep their uniforms clean. Worse, General Prentiss was a stickler for clean uniforms. More than one of them had their names taken at General Prentiss's direction during their last review. While they stood shoulder to shoulder at attention, in the light rain, the general had cast a critical eye over each of them. The unfortunate had their names taken for extra duties, including the digging of a new latrine.

Lockett yawned deeply. His eyes were red-rimmed.

"What's going on with you?" McManus asked.

"Didn't sleep well again," he paused and looked around to make sure that there was no one else around. "Nightmares. I keep having the nightmare since we got here."

"Nightmares?" McManus asked.

"It's always the same, about Amelia."

"The girl in Missouri?"

Lockett had not spoken of the day since they had left Missouri, not once, so McManus was surprised to hear it.

"I see her and the blood. So much blood, Patrick! And Orrin Long's leering face, so joyful at it all! The bastard! I didn't have this problem as often back home or even on the steamers, not at all, but now that we are here, the dream keeps coming back night after night, even multiple times last night. I couldn't get it out of my head. I hardly slept."

"Have you seen Orrin since we got here? Why, if I saw him, I'd..."

Lockett cut him off. "Don't say it, and for God's sake stay away from him. I don't need you getting wrapped up in this. One of us is bad enough. Nothing that is done now can change the past."

"Well, I still say that I'd..."

"Enough!" Lockett snapped angrily.

"All right," McManus relented, but only grudgingly.

"Let's talk about something else, anything else."

Were it not for the lack of sleep, life was rather pleasant at Pittsburg Landing, he thought to distract himself.

There was drilling that happened naturally, and of all sorts. For example, much of General Prentiss's drill involved close order marching – right wheel, left wheel, and so on.

He had noticed that the 25th Missouri, also in Peabody's Brigade, added their own style to drill by including a marksmanship contest using a large tree for the target practice. He wished that they had included the 12th Michigan in this. With their Dimick rifles, he felt pretty confident that he and Patrick would do the 12th proudly, particularly Patrick.

"Well, I was saying that this place wasn't half bad except for the rain," McManus started again, following Lockett's instruction to talk about something else.

"It does seem to rain a lot," Lockett agreed with his friend as they walked along the Corinth-Pittsburg Road, past McClernand's camp.

Colonel Raith's brigade of German-Americans was at it again, Lockett thought to himself. He had seen them the day before also.

Raith's men went through a rigid and detailed program of bayonet practice. Lockett had never seen anything like it. The wicked blades stabbed straw sacks or parried imaginary thrusts before viciously burying the gleaming two foot long spikes into the sacks. Cursing sergeants would halt the exercise periodically to correct technique with shocking emphasis on instruction, adding additional invectives in German to promote a heightened level of viciousness in the assault on the hapless straw sacks. One sergeant in particular insisted that each man give a blood-curdling scream with each plunge of the bayonet.

Today, General McClernand himself sat on his horse and complimented them on their work.

"If there is ever a bayonet charge, I want them on our side, even if they are Germans," McManus commented, tilting his head in approval.

Most of the army was done with their martial duties for the

day, however. In a couple of hours, they would start to prepare for the evening meal, but most of the men contented themselves by playing cards. Euchre, sledge, and poker were the most common.

Those who liked to read would do so under the shade of a tree, unless it was raining which would drive them into the tent. Lockett himself would often occupy himself by returning to the journal that he had started in Missouri.

McManus preferred the various contests between companies. There were running contests, jumping contests, wrestling contests, and even a frog jumping contest. McManus found that he preferred the wrestling contests after learning that he was not as fleet of foot as he thought.

Tomorrow morning, they would turn out for another review. This time, General Grant, who had arrived a couple of days ago, would review the men of Prentiss's Division. Most men did not mind the reviews as much as their grumbles would sometimes suggest. It was an opportunity for them to see the generals as well.

But at the moment, Lockett and McManus headed north towards the Landing, where the sutlers were located. Lockett would content himself just to look at their various wares: fruits, jams, butter, old newspapers, and even the occasional rotgut. All of it would be terribly over-priced. At one point, both of the friends would have been too flinty to spend any money with the traveling sutlers who followed the army. But since Martha's death, Lockett noticed that McManus no longer had such reticence when it came to spending money. He was sure to buy something while they were there.

April 2, 1862 (Wednesday)

Lyman Cameron looked around his encampment, just outside of Corinth. If General Albert S. Johnston, commander of the Confederate forces, had given the order yesterday to prepare to move out towards the enemy waiting at Pittsburg Landing, it was not clear to the younger Cameron brother. It did not look any more organized than the day before.

He hated to admit it, but maybe if they had more regular Army officers instead of citizen officers there would be more urgency or clear direction on what to do now.

Since the brothers had made their escape from Fort Donelson with Colonel Forrest and his cavalry, they had become good friends with a number of Forrest's men, and because of that, both brothers had heard the important message that Forrest's returning scouts had shared with General Johnston – Union General Buell was making rapid progress from Nashville. It would not be long before he linked up with General Grant.

Lyman Cameron knew enough to know that they would have to march soon and attack the Yankees, before the Yankees doubled their strength, but it just did not look like it yet.

April 3, 1862 (Thursday)

The Cameron brothers marched with the rest of General Hardee's Corps. The plan was simple; the execution of it was proving to be far from that.

It was a little over twenty miles to the Yankees and about five miles short of that was a place called Mickey's. They were supposed to march to Mickey's today and attack on Friday.

The Confederate Army of Mississippi was organized into four corps. 1st Corps was led by General Polk, 2nd Corps by General Bragg, 3rd Corps by General Hardee, and General Breckinridge led a reserve corps.

From the two narrow country roads that connected Corinth to Pittsburg Landing, Hardee and then Polk would march along the Ridge Road and Bragg along the Monterey Road.

But plans for a quick march and Friday attack had been dashed from the start. Before Hardee and his men even left the town of Corinth, the roads had been accidentally blocked by General Polk's wagons and men. It took hours to untangle the mess and reorganize Hardee's men. By the time the long line of Hardee's troops snaked out of Corinth, it was already afternoon.

They did make it halfway to Mickey's before bivouacking for the night in a light rain. Even so, little did they know that they were already far in advance and doing better than any of the other corps.

* * *

"What do you think?" Ainsley Stuart asked Lockett as they watched a knot of men jeer the two outsiders who wandered into camp. In the distance, a major from General Sherman's staff departed, having given the two men his blessing.

Lockett shook his head slowly and said dubiously, "The major said they could go through camp unmolested."

"They say that they are just farmers looking for their lost cows, James."

Lockett snorted. "For starters, if they did lose their cattle here, amongst all of these men, they'll have no luck. Those cows are surely butchered already and roasting over someone's spit. Fresh beef? Here?"

"It does seem unlikely," Stuart agreed.

"There is also something about the one," Lockett pointed at them. "Their clothes say farmer, fair enough, but the one walks too erect, more like a soldier than any farmer I know. We all have a little hump in the shoulders from manhandling a plow for so many hours."

"So, you are saying that you think they are spies?"

"Maybe... Possibly... Probably," he decided eventually.

"To do what? Figure out how many men we have here?"

"Well, if they are going to walk through the entire camp looking for these cows, they will have a pretty good idea by the time they are done."

In the distance, there was the sound of rifle fire. It wasn't unusual. Whether it was drilling, pickets clearing their guns to check for damp powder or just pickets taking the occasional shot at wildlife in the thickets, it was a regular sound around here.

They had heard that a couple of days ago there had been a

small cavalry skirmish just beyond the picket lines, but that did not seem unusual to them either.

April 4, 1862 (Friday)

The Cameron brothers and the rest of Hardee's men reached Mickey's farmhouse in the late morning. They knew that they were the first of what must be a long line of men that had snaked out of Corinth, but by mid-afternoon they wondered where everyone else was. The two country roads both led here, but there were no signs of Polk's or Bragg's men.

It had rained throughout the night, and they knew firsthand that the roads were becoming muddier, but the mud had slowed them too. It didn't explain why they had arrived so much sooner than the others.

The brothers and a half dozen others sat under a tree not too far from the farmhouse. Drips of water splashed down onto their broad floppy hats, but it was better than sitting in the open as the rain came and went throughout the day.

"I'm hungry," Lyman Cameron said wistfully to his brother.

"Well, you shouldn't have eaten your rations already," his brother answered, even though his were nearly depleted as well. "They told us to cook five days' worth."

"Yes, and as you know, we only had time to cook two days' worth before we had to fall in for the march, and then stand around like fools for hours while they untangled the wagon trains in Corinth before we even began."

John Cameron nodded amiably. "I'm sure that if the captain had known how long it was going to take for them to sort that out, he would have let us fall out to finish cooking the rations. Two days is better than nothing though. I was talking with those boys over in the 22nd Alabama. Their rations didn't arrive until it was time to march, so they cooked nothing, just put the food in the wagon to cook later, but then the wagon overturned in the mud, ruined all of it. They got nothing."

"Which is what I got now," Lyman grumbled.

"You have two days' worth in your belly," John pointed

out.

"I know, I know. I shouldn't have eaten it all already. I just get so hungry. You know that I'm not the only one who has eaten it all already."

"I know you're not," John said tipping his hat more over his eyes. "Take a nap. You'll forget how hungry you are."

As he said that, a rider trotted up to the house from the south. General Johnston had obviously been waiting on him because he opened the door and stepped outside bareheaded before the rider had even dismounted.

The rider's back was to the Cameron brothers. They couldn't hear what he said, but the general's response could easily be heard well beyond them.

"Bragg is only at Monterey! That is only halfway here!" the general exploded. The tall, broad-shouldered general with the thick moustache swung around. The old Army veteran was a man of action, and he seemed ready to go address this himself when he noticed another rider coming, this one making haste, mud flying from its hooves… but coming from the north.

"General Hardee sends his regards, sir," the second messenger began. "Clanton's 1st Alabama cavalry attacked one of the Yankee picket posts with the intent of getting a few prisoners, as ordered. Unfortunately, a regiment of Yankee infantry was drilling well beyond the camp, and the two collided. In the resulting skirmish a battalion of Yankee cavalry joined in and proceeded to push Clanton back a mile, prompting General Hardee to deploy a brigade of infantry and artillery. When the Yankee cavalry crested the rise, the artillery made short work of them. The Yankees have since pulled back."

General Johnston nodded grimly, "I want any prisoners brought back here for interrogation."

The messenger saluted and rode off with the return message, leaving General Johnston to ponder the most important question. His plan depended wholly on surprise. They could deal General Grant a heavy blow, but only if they could surprise him.

Did he still have the element of surprise? Would he? It was obvious that the soonest that they could attack was Saturday and given the performance of his army's ponderous march to this point, even that was in question.

Were the Yankees still unaware that the Confederate Army had left Corinth?

* * *

Lockett walked amiably with Ainsley Stuart to the southwestern edge of the Union camp, where General Sherman's troops were encamped. He didn't know why, but he was in a particularly good mood today. There was no reason for it, but he was bright and cheerful despite the gray clouds and intermittent rain. Ainsley, on the other hand, who always seemed to be ever so chipper, seemed consumed by his own thoughts today.

They were headed to the camp of the 72nd Ohio to meet up with one of Ainsley's friends from Washington D.C., another Congressman's son.

They had drilled all morning in the rain, and his uniform still clung to him like a second skin. The damp wool itched, but it did not detract from his unusually good mood.

"This will be the first time I've seen any of Sherman's men," Lockett noted, trying to start up a conversation with the strangely muted Stuart. The officer gave no reaction, so he continued, "The newspapers in St. Louis called him insane, you know."

Stuart nodded but said nothing. At least, he was listening, Lockett thought to himself. "Why are you so quiet today, sir?"

"Ainsley," Stuart corrected him. There was no one around.

"Sorry. Ainsley, I mean."

"Mail, James. That is the reason for my disposition today."

"Bad news from home?" Lockett asked worriedly. He couldn't help but think of Martha McManus and situations like that.

"No, nothing bad, just confusing. I got a letter from Katherine."

Lockett's stride hesitated ever so slightly.

"She told me to tell you that she was sorry? She said she didn't mean to surprise you in Niles. Did you, did you see her that night in Niles?"

Lockett had told McManus a few days ago about the encounter and her shocking news about Orrin Long, but he had intentionally not told Stuart.

"I noticed that Patrick stopped making comments about her to you. Did you see her, James? Did something happen?"

"Yes, I saw Katherine that night while you were eating dinner," Lockett said slowly, "She was waiting for me in the saloon. The headache was all part of her plan. She..." he hesitated, but then plunged ahead, "She knew that your Uncle and Aunt would not allow me to eat dinner with them, so she pretended to be ill and then surprised me in the saloon." He grimaced, 'surprised' was the right word.

"That does sound like Katherine," Stuart said with a face, "She is a bit headstrong, but why didn't you tell me any of this?"

"I'm sorry, I just..."

"It wouldn't have angered me, James. While you may be right, and my Uncle and Aunt may think less of you because you are a farmer and not a founder, I don't."

"That's not why," Lockett replied quickly. Stuart looked expectantly at him, so he continued. "It was because of something that Katherine said, and frankly, I thought you would have warned me about it beforehand."

"What's that?" Stuart said with total puzzlement.

"It was about Orrin Long. Why didn't you warn me?"

"Warn you about what?"

"You know who Orrin Long is?"

"Of course, our social circles have crossed from time to time."

"He's Katherine's fiancée, or about to be."

"He's what?"

"I just wished you warned me, that's all."

"I… I had no idea, James. I knew that he had some interest

in her, but I had no idea that it was so serious. She told you that?"

Lockett nodded glumly.

"I don't know what to say. I guess you know him and all from your time in the sharpshooters."

"More than I care to say," Lockett blurted out with a sudden fierceness.

"He's a fine officer, I assume. My superior in this military affair to me, I'm sure…"

"Hell, no!" Lockett snapped, causing Stuart to blink at the strident reaction. "If you think that, then you don't know a damn thing about the man, or about yourself. He's not fit to carry a pail of your spit, Ainsley."

Stuart was taken aback by the emotion showed. That was not the James Lockett that he had come to know. "There is more to this than Katherine, isn't there?"

The entire tale of what transpired in Missouri suddenly came spilling out, from their first encounter at the farmhouse to the Munroes and to the death of little Amelia. Once Lockett started to unburden himself, there was no stopping. Breathless by the end from talking so much, he felt a strange sense of exhaustion and relief.

"I know it is hard to believe," Lockett concluded, looking at Ainsley's blanched, open-mouthed face.

Gathering his composure, Ainsley Stuart placed a thin, reassuring hand on Lockett's shoulder. "James, I believe you, my friend."

He had no idea how much those words meant to James Lockett.

An hour later, rain pelted the already soaked sides of the tent near the small, simple wooden structure of Shiloh Church. The constant pattering played on without let up. "I don't envy Colonel Buckland and those men chasing the bushwhackers," Lieutenant William Peterson commented to Ainsley Stuart.

Ainsley's Ohio friend was a determined looking young man, whose receding hairline made him appear older than he was. Only Peterson's voice gave away that he was a much younger man.

"At this rate," Stuart replied, "The Rebels don't need guns. They just need to get enough of us out running around in the rain. Pretty soon, everyone will be sick. They can just sit back in Corinth and wait for the sick roll to grow."

William Peterson laughed.

"It's been a few hours, and this rain isn't letting up," Stuart continued, "We should probably head back to camp, a pity to stay dry this whole time only to soak ourselves on the way back."

The sound of sodden troops reached their ears, and just as Peterson was about to make note of it, the tent flap whipped up to reveal a drenched and muddied young lieutenant. The man stood in the opening with sheets of rain whipping against his cherubic face.

"William!" the breathless lieutenant rushed, then he noticed that there were others in the tent.

"Look what the cat dragged in! It's okay, Stephen," William Peterson said, rising to his feet, "This is my friend Lieutenant Ainsley Stuart of the 12th Michigan and his sergeant, James Lockett."

As if an afterthought, Stephen nodded and then addressed Lieutenant Peterson in an excited voice, "I think you need to get your company ready, Will."

"Why?"

"I just came back with Colonel Buckland from that patrol to investigate the shots."

"Yes?"

"It wasn't bushwhackers. When we reached the picket posts, all of the pickets were missing, not a sign of them! That seemed like too much for a few bushwhackers, so we chased after whoever it was when we ran into some rebel cavalry. Good thing it was raining so hard, because neither side could see each other real well, and they certainly had us at a disadvantage being only two companies of us..."

"But why do I need to get my company together? I wouldn't think that rebel cavalry is cause for concern,

Stephen."

"Wait, Will, I'm not finished. The 5th Ohio Calvary fortunately came to our rescue and scattered the Rebs, chasing them back. I thought it was all over when a few minutes later our cavalry came racing back to us!"

"What? Why did they do that?"

"Said they saw a long line of Confederate infantry and artillery. Colonel Buckland is informing General Sherman right now. I think the Rebels are here!"

Stuart looked at Lockett. "I guess we better get back to our posts, rain or no rain now."

Saying goodbyes and putting on their hats, they began to walk back through the downpour. Their path took them right past the tent of General William Tecumseh Sherman. Even in the pounding rain, they could hear the voice of the general chiding Colonel Buckland and his "green Buckeyes" for exaggerating nothing more than enemy reconnaissance.

As they passed the open tent flap, Lockett looked over his shoulder at the disheveled general with auburn red hair sticking out in multiple directions.

"What are you looking at, sergeant?" a goateed major at the tent's entrance snarled at him, hurrying them on their way.

The entire way back, Lockett heard echoes of General Sherman's mocking tone to Colonel Buckland, "Rebel infantry? Hah! That's the problem with you volunteers! You green Buckeyes! One little bushwhacking party becomes an entire column of Johnston's infantry! There's nothing out there, Colonel! Nothing!"

April 5, 1862 (Saturday)

Thankfully, the arrival of morning brought a break in the terrible weather. Water still dripped heavily from the trees, but the temperature was going back up as the sky brightened, and best of all, the stiff northern wind had stopped.

Sergeant Milton Bosworth of the 53rd Ohio looked at the ground but the buckshot sized hail that lashed the tent overnight had already melted into the ground.

"That was some storm last night," he remarked.

He was a burly, thick-shouldered man of average height, who moved with an oxen-like heavy-footed, ponderous gait. But what stood out most about Milton Bosworth was his personality, not his physical appearance.

Garrulous and talkative to the extreme, every stranger was like a life-long friend, and even the most obvious reticence shown by the stranger did nothing to deter his exuberance or tongue. There was always a story to tell, an opinion to be shared, or a joke to be made. Perhaps that irrevocably outgoing personality explained why the men of the company had elected him sergeant.

He had no experience, like the rest of the volunteers of the 53rd Ohio. Their colonel had experience, albeit with the navy oddly. Colonel Jesse Appler's experience on the sloop of war, *Hornet*, was a long way from the muddy fields of Tennessee, and at times, his men found his ways strange and even backward. Many times, they had silently whispered when out of his earshot that Appler seemed uncomfortable in the woods or leading soldiers.

Bosworth wished that he had joined the 77th Ohio, like his cousin, Captain Mason. Colonel Hildebrand of the 77th seemed much more normal and predictable than Colonel Appler. Regardless, when his cousin had suggested this morning that they break the monotony and take a quick walk out beyond the picket line, he readily agreed, as did fellow 53rd Ohioan, Private Tracey.

Bosworth removed his tarpot style hat and ran grimy fingers through his brown hair before snugly replacing the hat on his head where his thick brown hair curled at his ears and neck so that it wrapped itself around the edges of the hat. He resumed the walk with his two companions with an awkward, almost lurching gait that seemed commensurate with his girth. He slipped clumsily in the mud but caught himself by grabbing the tree before he went down.

"Indeed, that was quite a storm, cousin," Captain Mason replied. He was a man of few words, or at least fewer words than Bosworth, which most people were.

"The Heavens just plain opened up and dumped down on us," Bosworth continued. "Thank God, we were in our tents by then. By golly, good thing we were not on the march with all that. That would have been a cold and miserable slog, not to mention the hail pelting down."

Captain Mason nodded, but before he could reply further, Bosworth added, "Picket post will be up ahead here."

Mason nodded again.

"I see Jonesy up there," Bosworth remarked even as Tracey started to open his mouth. "Ahoy, Jonesy!" he shouted humorously.

Some of the men of the 53rd Ohio had taken to using nautical language, or at least what they considered nautical language, on account of Colonel Appler, although they were careful to do it only when he was not around. They rightly guessed that Appler would take affront to it and consider it some sort of mockery, which it was.

Like most of the men, Sergeant Bosworth was rankled by the colonel. He wasn't really sure what it was like on the deck of a warship, but he imagined it wasn't very similar to being in charge of an infantry regiment.

"Private Jones," Captain Mason greeted one of the pickets. Even though Bosworth was vociferous, he knew enough to let the officer address the pickets first. "We're taking a walk up beyond for a bit."

Jones nodded wordlessly.

Bosworth added, "That means don't take no shots at us when we come back, you durn fool."

Jones wrinkled his nose but said nothing.

"What's that mean?" Bosworth asked before anyone else.

Jones looked cautiously at the officer. "Go ahead," Mason encouraged, "Speak freely."

"Well, sir, just after yesterday and all… well, is that such a good idea? To go out beyond our lines and all?"

"Yesterday?" Bosworth answered with a smirk before the officer could, "What? With the bushwhackers?"

"Well, yes, sergeant. It sounded like more than

bushwhackers to me…"

Bosworth interrupted him before he could finish. "Oh, it does? You're an expert now, Jonesy? Just a few months ago you were the cooper's apprentice, but now you're a military expert? Nonsense. It's just the usual probe by their cavalry or even some nasty little bushwhackers running about. Nothing more."

"If you say so, sergeant, but they swept up all seven pickets yesterday. We've been on our toes all morning, don't want that to happen to us."

"As you should," Captain Mason said hastily, trying to get the words in before Bosworth for once, "Stay alert, Private."

"Be on your toes, just don't have itchy trigger fingers," Bosworth interjected, oblivious to whether or not the officer had more to say. "I'll whistle when we get back, Jonesy. Just don't fire blindly."

The trio had only walked five minutes beyond the picket line, with Bosworth chattering the entire time and mostly uncaring if anyone responded, when Captain Mason placed a firm, cautionary hand on Bosworth's shoulder.

"Shhh!"

Bosworth turned and was about to open to his mouth when Mason's grip tightened, "For God's sake, Milton, be quiet for once!" he hissed.

They were at the edge of a long open field, and in the distance, they saw something so strange that it took a moment for their brains to register the obvious. At the opposite end, they saw a large, large mass of men. They were not in line of battle and were completely unaware of the onlookers gaping at them in the tree-shadowed distance.

"Are those Rebels?" Private Tracey finally managed in a soft voice. Some wore unfamiliar butternut light brown uniforms; some wore no discernible uniforms at all. They did not seem to be in the midst of any real activity. They were mostly lounging and loitering in the distant tree line. For a brief second, the sound of a belly laugh wafted across the field to their ears.

There were hundreds of them, maybe a thousand, and not a horse to be seen. “I think that is Rebel infantry,” Bosworth managed in an unnaturally quiet tone. He sounded like he didn’t believe his own words.

“Worse,” Mason corrected, “Look to their right. Artillery. That’s infantry *and* artillery.”

“But we’re only a few minutes from the picket lines!” Tracey exclaimed quietly.

“And not much further than that from camp,” Mason added grimly. He turned towards Bosworth. “Sergeant, I want you to get back to the 77th’s regimental headquarters as quick as you can. Tell them what we’ve seen here. Private Tracey and I are going to stay and keep an eye on them.”

“We are?” Tracey gulped softly.

“Yes. If I need to send a second message back, you’ll take it, but the sergeant needs to take this one. They might not believe a private, but they will take stock of a sergeant’s word.”

He hoped…

“Yes, sir,” Bosworth answered, sliding backwards from the edge of the trees and racing back as fast as his heavy feet could take him.

Red-faced and out of breath when he arrived back at the regimental headquarters, Sergeant Milton Bosworth found that Major Fearing was the officer in charge while Colonel Hildebrand was out. He quickly told the officer what they had seen, and that Captain Mason was still out there.

Major Fearing told him that he would take the matter directly to General Sherman himself, and that Bosworth should go back to Captain Mason to assure him.

Fatigued, but determined to get back to Captain Mason as soon as possible, Bosworth headed out, and Major Fearing left directly for General Sherman.

But the news was not taken as well as Major Fearing had assumed.

“God damn it!” General Sherman exploded. “Ohio washerwomen! You see ten men and count them as a hundred!

There is no army out there! I want that sergeant arrested!"

Fearing's mouth fell open, and he looked stunned, as if he had been physically slapped.

"Yes, Major! Arrested! That man is spreading rumor!" Sherman thundered, "Harmful rumor! There is a penalty for spreading a false alarm and trying to stir a panic! I'll not have it!"

Fearing continued to look blankly at the general, drawing even more scorn.

"See to it! I can have majors arrested too, by God!"

* * *

Like the other Confederate infantrymen, John and Lyman Cameron struggled through the mud as they tried to make their way to where the vanguard of Hardee's men waited for the rest of the army.

The brothers had long since abandoned the road itself, where their feet sunk to their ankles in the mire, and had opted for the grassy sections alongside the road. It helped at first, but then after hundreds of men tramped along over it, it too became a slippery and draining path. Each step seemed to require more strength than the previous one as the mud clutched at their ankles and wore out their legs.

John Cameron could only imagine how deep the cannon wheels were sinking into the road. Their beasts of burden and the gunners were surely struggling mightily.

As for him and the infantry, they traveled without the burden of cannon or even food. One could not travel much lighter, and yet despite their best efforts, he knew that even they were behind schedule.

Tired and soaked from the previous night's storms, and even bruised from the hail that pelted them, they trudged along. But of all the miseries, the worst was the hunger. He was so hungry. It was hard to say what made him more tired, the mud or the lack of food. He knew for certain that for Lyman, it was the lack of food. His brother had the appetite of a horse, always had.

And yet, in spite of these hardships and the fact that they were marching towards what would be a massive battle, the spirits of the soldiers were high.

"Good God!" his brother exclaimed as the accompanying 8th Texas Cavalry hooted and hollered when a deer bolted in front of them. "Ain't they ever seen a deer before!"

"So much for the element of surprise," John Cameron agreed, "If the Yankees didn't hear all that, then they must have heard them shooting at the rabbits and squirrels earlier. And we're only supposed to be a couple of miles away from the Yankee camps. Idiots!"

By mid-morning they were deployed in a loose line of battle, ready to attack, but then nothing happened. There was still no sign of General Bragg's or General Polk's Corps, not to mention General Breckinridge's Reserve Corps.

And they couldn't attack the Yankees with only a quarter of their strength.

* * *

It was late morning when Colonel Hildebrand himself found the trio of Bosworth, Mason, and Tracey still keeping a wary eye on the Rebels.

Trying to stay tactful and respectful of his superior, General Sherman, Colonel Hildebrand dodged most of their questions, all the while still trying to reassure them, even though they all found it strange and a little alarming that the regimental commander himself had come to see this with his own eyes. For many minutes, he kept a watchful eye with them.

Many of the Confederates had fallen further back into the shadows of the forest, although there was still plenty to observe.

"Could be a brigade… Could just be a large regiment," Hildebrand observed. "Perhaps a reconnaissance in force, perhaps more? Hard to say."

"Do you want me to take any other messages back, sir?" Sergeant Bosworth asked.

"Best not, sergeant. We need to let General Sherman simmer down a bit first, seeing as how he wants to arrest you."

Captain Mason looked at the colonel, expecting some sort of wry smile to indicate that it was a joke, but there was none.

"What!" Bosworth yelped, although he remembered to keep his voice down.

"Don't worry, sergeant. I have no intention of arresting you."

"I hope Colonel Appler sees it that way too," Bosworth muttered.

"I'll check some other picket posts and then go report to General Sherman myself," Colonel Hildebrand added. "If I see more of the same, I'll hopefully be able to convince General Sherman of your veracity. In the meantime, you best return to the 53rd Ohio, sergeant. I believe Colonel Appler was planning on drills in one of the open fields beyond camp, and he'll surely be looking for his sergeants."

* * *

John and Lyman Cameron waited in the wet grass. It was well past lunch, although there was very little food for any bellies. Eventually, one cracker barrel was rolled out, clearly insufficient for all of the men. Making matters worse, half of the hardtack had been turned to mush, and the other half was weevil infested, which did not deter any man in the least.

Hardee's men were ready for battle, but as for the others, only a few lead elements had straggled in.

The brothers watched General Albert S. Johnston and General P.G.T. Beauregard from a distance. In spite of it all, there was something reassuring about the presence of General Johnston. Tall, muscular, and manly, he was the very picture of a leader, plus all of the men knew the Kentuckian's reputation as a fighter earned in the Mexican War, the Black Hawk War, and the Mormon Rebellion.

He seemed to be taking the delays in stride, at least until the most recent messenger returned.

"This is perfectly puerile!" the general exploded. He turned to his aides. "Get our horses!" Within a minute, he and his staff hurried down the road, determined to untangle whatever had snared his army of amateurs and citizens.

"I guess we're not attacking today," Lyman commented to his brother with a shrug.

"It would have been nice to surprise old Billy Yank," his brother nodded, "But I gander that ain't goin' be so."

* * *

It was late in the afternoon, near time for dinner, and Lockett, Ainsley Stuart, and his friend Lieutenant Peterson stood in the field between the encampments of their two divisions. To the right of them were the tents of Sherman's Division and to the left were the tents of Prentiss's Division. All three of the young, blue-coated soldiers faced the quiet woods to the south. They did not see anything in the trees, but the news of the day unsettled them.

"I didn't see any Confederates this afternoon, Ainsley," Lockett said doubtfully, "Are you sure?"

"For certain, James. They were there. I guess you were too busy keeping the men in line like a good sergeant," Stuart grinned, "But they were there. There were definitely Confederate horsemen watching us from a safe distance, at least for part of the time."

"It seems hard to believe. We were barely beyond the picket line. That's pretty bold, so close to camp. What if another brigade was a little further out from us? What if our cavalry happened upon them in their coming and going? These bushwhackers could have been cut off easily."

"I don't think it was bushwhackers, James. They were regular Confederate cavalry."

"Either way, your sergeant is right," Lieutenant Peterson opined, "They would have been easily cut off. I suppose after yesterday that I should not be surprised. They scooped up all seven of the 7th Ohio's pickets yesterday, every single one. They are getting bold."

"Well, I wasn't the only one to see them today," Stuart added, "Captain Donnelly, Peabody's own adjutant saw them too. He was telling the 25th Missouri to get ready for a fight and also said that Peabody would talk to General Prentiss."

Lockett nodded appreciatively. He liked their brigade leader. Colonel Peabody seemed like a good, honest man and had a reputation for dealing fairly with all. Of course, that didn't mean that General Prentiss would see it the same way. Lockett knew that he still harbored some negative feelings against the wooden faced general from their time in Missouri, and he had a feeling that General Prentiss's reaction would be the same as General Sherman's was yesterday.

Peterson noted the dubious look on Lockett's face, "Things aren't much better in Sherman's division," he said discouragingly, "I already told you about how they wanted to arrest that sergeant this morning for 'causing a panic', but in the afternoon Colonel Appler's 53rd Ohio observed horsemen about a half mile away. He sent a company of his infantry to chase them away only to find themselves fired on by some Confederate infantry. When Appler sent one of his lieutenants to report it to Sherman, Sherman told him, 'Tell Colonel Appler to take his damned regiment back to Ohio. There is no force of enemy nearer than Corinth'."

"I wonder what General Grant thinks about all of this," Stuart wondered aloud.

"Same here," Lockett agreed.

They all knew that on the day before Grant's horse slipped in the mud, crashing to the ground, rolling over the general's ankle so severely that his boot had to be cut off. He was now scarcely mobile on crutches and was upriver in little Savannah to recuperate, leaving General Sherman in charge of the immediate area.

Lieutenant Peterson snorted derisively at Stuart's question. "I don't think General Grant knows. I have it from a good source that Sherman sent a message to Grant just an hour ago that said all is quiet here, and that there are only two regiments of infantry and one battery of artillery a few miles out, about

1200 men."

"Just two regiments, eh?" Lockett said skeptically.

"How many men are said to be in Johnston's Confederate Army in Corinth?" Stuart asked cautiously.

"About 40,000," Peterson answered.

"So, is it 1,200 or 40,000 out there?" Lockett asked rhetorically.

"Surely, it can't be the 40,000, James. They must still be in Corinth, right?"

* * *

The Confederate general listened politely.

His jacket was partially unbuttoned, as if his broad shoulders and thick chest prevented it from being any other way. The steady firmness of his brow never wavered, and the full moustache never curled in either disagreement or agreement as he listened to his subordinate outline his fears.

Then the large man, General Albert S. Johnston, commander of the Confederate Army, stood up. He towered over his Richmond chosen second-in-command, General P.G.T. Beauregard.

While General Johnston looked like a rugged leader and man of action, Beauregard was a swarthy skinned Louisianan who looked like a clever, cunning fox – a man certain that his raw intellect was far superior to any man's, including General Johnston's.

Beauregard had just spent the last twenty minutes trying to convince Johnston of the obvious, but a flicker of doubt never clouded the larger man's face. Beauregard tried one last time, in as blunt and simple of terms as possible, "We no longer have the element of surprise, sir. They will be entrenched to the eyes."

He was prepared to go through the logic again, but General Johnston just stood there, as confident as ever that they were about to destroy Grant's horde of Yankees.

Johnston gave a small smile of confidence, "No, my friend," he started, even though Beauregard was far from a friend, "We will attack, and we will surprise them, and we will trap Grant's army against the creeks."

"But General, the attack was to have been launched at dawn yesterday, or even earlier this week to be truthful!" Beauregard was right, the muddy roads and raw recruits of the Confederate Army had made for an agonizingly slow pace and a mockery of their plans. They would not be ready for the attack until dawn the next day, Sunday.

"Grant is still unaware." Johnston spoke with such calm confidence that Beauregard half-believed him even though he knew the man could not be right. Surely by now, the Yankees realized the threat.

"But if Buell's Army has already arrived…" Beauregard continued, trying a new line of persuasion.

"They have not arrived, General Beauregard. Don Carlos would not push his men so hard, would he? We both know Don Carlos Buell. He will have his men on the march but not that fast. Even so, this is why we must attack now, before he can join Grant."

Beauregard knew Johnston had a point. It was better to fight when the odds were even, rather than when outnumbered two to one. But the element of surprise must be gone. If the Union Army was entrenched behind earthworks, an attack would be foolhardy.

"We will attack at dawn tomorrow, and we will surprise them," Johnston said with finality. "We will hit Grant and hit him hard."

Beauregard frowned at the lost debate. He nodded grimly, "In the struggle tomorrow we shall be fighting men of our own blood, Western men, who understand the use of firearms. The struggle will be a desperate one."

Truer words were never spoken.

Chapter 20

As darkness fell across the Union camps, many of the men of the 12th Michigan were nervous. While the regimental bands played their instruments as usual, many of the men fidgeted with a foreboding sense set deep in their bones.

The 12th's pickets had already come back reporting that they could hear movement in the distance, something they had never heard before. Lieutenant Colonel Grimes immediately left to inform General Prentiss, but Lockett and many others already knew what the response would be.

As the light gave way completely to the dark, many of the men in Lockett's company still stirred. Their anxiety was further heightened by the fact that their sergeant did not even bother to try to sleep. What they did not know was that while Lockett was concerned about the enemy, it was his own private nightmare of the little girl in Missouri that kept him awake tonight. He had dozed earlier in the day, only for the searing image to reappear in his mind, even more vivid than before. It was like some harbinger that something similarly violent was about to take place.

So instead of attempting to sleep, he sat quietly next to his friend, McManus, around the fire, nodding to McManus's comments which were focused on the events of the last few days. Were all of their leaders so daft? How could it be that they didn't sense this danger? Was there not one among the leaders who understood?

It seemed that the answer was none, but that was not so. Their own Colonel Peabody had decided on his own to send out scouts from the 25th Missouri to see what they could find.

While most of the Union army slept, Peabody's scouts crept forward to confirm what Colonel Peabody was already convinced of – the Confederates were here.

* * *

The Cameron brothers waited quietly. There was a slender, pale moon tonight, but the dense forest blocked out what light there was, leaving them in a stygian silence.

Hours had passed since the Union bands in the distance had ceased their nightly serenade. It was bizarre to be so close to the enemy's camps that they could hear the tunes so well. The music was familiar to all. Their own bands had played much of the same music back in their camps in Corinth, particularly the favorite, *Home Sweet Home*. It was tempting to sing along, but not a man did. They knew how close they were to the enemy.

Impossible as it seemed, the Yankees were unaware of their presence. Surprise was still on their side… Unless it was a devious Yankee trap, and the blue bellies were waiting behind entrenchments that they had built up over the days, and the music was just a lure to bring the Confederates in.

To distract themselves from such gloomy thoughts, many of the men reflected on General Johnston's written message to the troops, "The eyes and the hopes of eight millions of people rest upon you."

It was a message that many needed to hear, although truth be told, many of the new soldiers reflected on General Beauregard's parting words instead. His final order was to shoot low at the enemy's legs to cause wounded men. The wounded would be dragged off the field by their comrades, further reducing the number of Yankees in the fight.

April 6, 1862 (Sunday)

Colonel Peabody's scouts, led by Major Powell of the 25th Missouri, returned after midnight.

It was easy for Lockett to tell that they had discovered something. He didn't need to be within earshot.

There was no hesitation from Colonel Peabody. They all knew of the standing orders not to bring on any engagement until General Buell and his men arrived from Nashville, but

Peabody's mind was already made up.

As Major Powell started to mobilize three companies from the 25th Missouri to follow him back, Lockett, unaware that a number of his men followed behind him at a discreet distance, sidled up to Major Powell.

A private during the Mexican War with a youthful face, he still spoke with the English accent of his homeland. Powell looked up at the taller Lockett and asked, "Can't sleep tonight, sergeant?"

"Not tonight, sir," Lockett answered, "Permission to join your patrol?"

"All of you?"

Lockett gave a blank look and turned around, surprised to see so many of his company behind him with Lieutenant Ainsley Stuart sleepily emerging from his tent.

"Permission granted, sergeant. The more, the merrier I 'pose in this case. We leave in five minutes."

"I was standing right there when Colonel Peabody gave Major Powell the final orders," Ainsley Stuart said to Lockett as they began to march off in the darkness along the farm road that led to the Corinth-Pittsburg Landing Road.

It was around 3 o'clock in the morning, and there was something unsettling about marching off in the darkness of the hour. They were near the rear of the column of 250 men that stumbled through the wagon ruts. As dark as it was, particularly with the trees blocking out what little moonlight there was, he could only see a few men ahead of him, nowhere close to the front of the column.

What waited for them in the darkness? He wanted to believe that there wasn't much out there ahead of this little patrol, but in the pit of his stomach, he knew something major was going to happen tonight. Somehow, he just knew.

"I believe the colonel's exact words were, 'Find the enemy. Drive in the guard and open up on the reserve, develop the force, hold the ground as long as possible, then fall back,'" Ainsley Stuart continued.

"So let me get this straight, sir," McManus said in a hushed voice, "We're marching off here in the darkness because we think the whole Rebel army is out there – not just some bushwhackers, and our job is to pick a fight with them?"

Stuart paused before answering in a reflective voice, "I suppose that is one interpretation of those orders. I hadn't thought about it that way."

"It's better than sleeping comfortably in our tents and waiting for them to come at us," McManus grunted.

"There's probably not much out there," another 12th Michigan man chipped in with a hopeful tone, "Just a few bushwhackers in for a big surprise."

Before anyone could answer, Major Powell appeared beside them in the darkness, "Quiet!" he demanded in a low, angry voice, "What do you think this is, a bloody excursion for night air? No talking!"

"Yes, sir," they all answered in muted voices.

"Chrissakes, Lieutenant, you're an officer," Powell muttered before heading back towards the front of the patrol.

Quietly, they marched southwest of their camps. Just beyond the edge of the Rhea Field, they paused briefly as Powell spoke with the captain of the 77th Ohio who commanded the pickets.

It was slow going. After more than an hour of marching, Lockett was sure that they had covered less than two miles. In fact, they had covered less than one mile. Only the sound of rustling uniforms and the occasional jangle of a cartridge box and canteen broke the stillness of the night. Unconsciously, Lockett stroked the smooth octagonal barrel of his Dimick. McManus fussed with the cartridge box, and another 12th Michigan man sniffled and wiped his running nose on his sleeve.

In the eastern skyline there was the first hint of light in the damp, misty morning.

Suddenly, each man snapped erect and alert at the crack of two muskets, and then a third.

"Skirmish line! Skirmish line!" Major Powell ordered hurriedly, and the men reacted as best they could in a state of confusion in the darkness, stumbling and tripping but forming a thin staggered line.

In the dim light and mist, Lockett could barely make out the shadowy form of two mounted sentinels beyond them. They appeared almost wraith like, not truly mortal, as they glided in and out of sight amongst the distant trees.

The men from the 25th Missouri at the front of the column had been able to deploy quicker than the others, and they returned fire for Powell's patrol. The first heavy slugs slashed the branches near the horsemen but without effect.

A few more skirmishers added to the fire, and then in what were really seconds, not minutes, the horsemen disappeared from sight, and all was strangely quiet again, so quiet that Lockett could hear his own heavy breathing, even though he had not taken a shot and done nothing more than hurry into a skirmish position.

The Rebel videttes had disappeared, and Powell's patrol continued to move forward cautiously, still in their staggered skirmish line and no longer in column. Something was out there, and advancing in a line as skirmishers, and not in column, was the best way to feel it out without blundering into a trap.

They followed the general direction of the road as it cut through Fraley Field.

As they made their way cautiously across, there was a sudden small volley from the darkness ahead of them. Seven weapons flashed and then went silent again. Lockett thought he could hear the sound of those seven men dashing away through the field from the approaching Federals.

Not a man was down, and they paused only briefly before resuming their path.

There was a second small volley from further back in the field, and this time, some of the men from the 25th Missouri returned fire blindly into where they thought the shots had come from. Lockett doubted that either side had hit anything. After another pause, they continued forward.

The sky had lightened just enough in the murky darkness to tell that there was tree line beyond them. It was hard to tell, but it was maybe 300 yards away, then 200 yards away as they continued their approach.

Without warning, there was a tremendous roar from the trees beyond them. The battalion sized volley was thunderous compared to the previous exchanges. The elongated line of flashes halted the Union men in their tracks, but it did not seem that anyone was down, and there were no screams of agony heard in the echoes.

Lockett thought he saw the shape of a fence twenty yards ahead of them. Tapping McManus on the shoulder, they hurriedly made their way to it and crouched behind a fence post as they returned fire. Many of the other men from the patrol did the same, and for minutes the two sides fired away at each in the gloom with little effect other than making a lot of noise.

Behind Lockett, Ainsley Stuart peered into the middle of the patrol's small skirmish line, searching for Major Powell's silhouette. Taking his family sword out of its scabbard and pulling out the pistol with his other hand, he felt odd, even with the darkness hiding his gaunt and awkward frame. There was something very unnatural about this, and he felt it keenly. Slowly, he reassured himself that the dark of the early morning would hide any alarm on his face, and he quietly recited Colonel Peabody's orders, "Drive in the guard and open up on the reserve." They were in the process of doing just that.

The two sides fired away at each other for what seemed like an hour in the darkness. Stuart's ears became deadened to the crack of rifles and the occasional zing of a bullet, but it was the thump of a musket ball meeting flesh that caught his attention.

With a puzzled look, he looked to his left where the peculiar sound came from and saw a pair of boots and a form lying in the grass. His eyes followed the boots up to the trousers and uniform. Although it was still too dark to see a face, he knew exactly who it was from the full stomach that strained the uniform.

"Ezra Lampkin," McManus said matter-of-factly as he rammed another Minié ball into his Dimick. "He's gone."

Stuart cleared his throat and shouted encouragingly, "Keep

up the fire, boys!" Aware that a few men were gawking at the company's first casualty, he shouted encouragement to them with a voice that none of them had heard before from his skinny body. "Hot and steady, boys! Hot and steady!"

Lockett took aim at what he guessed was a Rebel, although it might have been a tree. As if in answer to his question, a flash appeared from the spot, and he instantly answered it. Although he was sure the shot had been true, and with his Dimick it was well within his range, he could not tell if the silhouette was still there or not. As he took another paper cartridge from his box and tore the end off with his teeth, he wondered how long they would go on like this.

The black of night was slowly turning to a dark blue, and in the growing strands of light he lost count of how many times he had fired.

The change in the rate of fire from the Confederates was imperceptible at first, but slowly, it seemed that the line of flashes from the trees was elongating. More and more Rebels were joining the line that fired on them.

Then off to their left, they saw what looked like thousands of soldiers emerging from the trees. They paused at the end of the field to address their lines and organize, oblivious to ongoing fire in the middle of the field.

"Oh, my God!" one of the men next to Lockett gasped.

Lockett's eyes flashed from one end of the line to the other. The line stretched as far as could be seen. He didn't even want to know what was hidden beyond sight in the trees to the right. It was obvious to every man in the patrol.

This was Johnston's army! The Confederates really were here and not in Corinth!

Stunned, Lockett realized that they had bumped headlong into a massive Confederate assault. No army could organize so many so quickly. The only way that so many men could be in a line of battle already was that they had *already* been marching. The Confederates had planned a surprise attack for this morning!

Were it not for their patrol, the entire Army of the Tennessee would have been caught in their tents!

"Steady!" Lockett said more out of instinct than anything else. But holding his ground was the last thing on his mind. He could feel some of the men creeping backwards. He had not wanted to retreat at Hallsville, but this was different!

This time, he wanted to run – run far and fast. Against this battle line, there was no hope for victory. No bravery could save the day.

"It's the entire Rebel Army!" one soldier uttered in a shocked voice.

"Aye," another agreed.

"Orderly withdrawal!" Stuart echoed the order as the entire patrol began to pull back.

"Orderly!" Lockett snapped, watching one man take off in a dead run.

They retreated back down the road, past the fork, past the Seay cotton field. Most of the men in the company had only one thought, to pull back as fast as possible, but Lockett bit his lower lip, knowing that they were not far from their camps as it was. Had the sounds of fighting been enough to rouse Prentiss and the other generals from their stupor? Where were the others? Had the patrol given the Army enough time to form a defense behind them?

They were met just beyond the crossroads by Colonel Moore who had organized five companies of his 21st Missouri and convinced one company of Wisconsin men who had rushed to aid what they thought were their pickets under attack.

Immediately, Colonel Moore belittled Major Powell and the men of his patrol for retreating.

Seeing this, some of the men from the 21st Missouri did the same. The initial warnings of caution from Powell's men quickly turned to anger, and they pointed at the number of wounded comrades that they had dragged back with them.

"God-damned fools!" McManus growled angrily as Lockett stepped between him and one particularly mouthy Missourian. "That's not even a brigade; that's not even a full regiment. 400 men against 40,000?"

Tight-lipped, Lockett said nothing as he shoved McManus

away from the newcomers. Even as he heard Colonel Moore agree to send back a request to bring up the rest of his regiment, Lockett could only shake his head in despair. Moore's entire regiment was only 800 men. They could do nothing except get slaughtered by the thousands now advancing on them!

Colonel Moore ordered Powell and all the men not actually carrying wounded to join up with him, and they marched off in a column of four. Lockett spoke quietly to Ainsley about making sure that their little group of 12th Michigan men were at the back of this column, but one of the captains of the 21st Missouri insisted that they be in the middle of the column, suspecting that they would run off at the first chance if they were in the rear of the march.

They returned to the Seay cotton field and just as they started to cross it, the Confederates poured a heavy fire into them. Many were killed in that first volley, and Colonel Moore himself fell with his right leg shattered by a musket ball. As he was pulled from the field, the lieutenant colonel of the 21st Missouri assumed command, and he deployed the men on a slight rise in the field facing the Confederates to the west.

To their credit, they held that ground in a sharp fire fight for twenty minutes, but finding that the growing mass of Confederates was turning his flank, he pulled them back into the woods, even as a motley group of three Wisconsin companies joined them.

"Ainsley!" Major Powell called, motioning him over, "Get back to camp and tell Colonel Peabody yourself that we are being driven back. We won't be able to hold this lot. We are facing an entire division or more."

"Yes, sir!" Stuart answered, and he took off in a gangly ramble down the road back to their camp which was barely a half mile away. Awkwardly, he held his scabbard to the side of his leg while he ran.

With sweat streaming down his face, Stuart dashed breathlessly into camp, immediately spotting the massive 240 pound frame of Colonel Peabody.

"Sir, sir!" he cried, dramatically bounding in front of the

colonel and saluting, "Major Powell reports that the patrol is being driven back. It's a division attack, sir!"

"Division?" Peabody said skeptically. He gave a sidewise glance, and Ainsley noticed the Philadelphia journalist who had been in camp the past few days. The man looked oddly out of place in his brown suit and bowler hat.

"Sir, I've seen them," he began again only to be interrupted by a tremendous volley of musketry that sounded like a thunder crack from hell.

The sound of such violent musketry quickly changed Colonel Peabody's tune. No longer skeptical, he ordered the long roll sounded, and like ants from their mounds, men piled out of their tents and left their morning cook fires burning.

How any of them could have been sleeping through all this, Ainsley would never understand.

But with a speed born of desperation and shock from being roused by an imminent threat, Peabody's Brigade began to form up.

As Ainsley Stuart stood there dumbfounded in the middle of the camp, he heard galloping hooves. The rider was General Benjamin M. Prentiss, and he looked down at him with a draconian glare before he spotted Colonel Peabody about to mount his horse.

With a slew of curses, General Prentiss addressed Peabody, but it was only the final words that Ainsley Stuart would remember.

"... a direct flouting of my authority, Peabody! You are held personally responsible for bringing on this engagement!"

"General," Peabody interrupted and saluted from his steed, "I did not bring it on. It is coming without my assistance, but if I brought on this fight, then I am to lead the van!" He yanked on the horse's reins and chased after his men forming up to block the country road that was just beyond their own tents.

The thunderous volley that Stuart heard in camp was the work of Woods' Mississippians. The musket and Minié balls slammed into Moore's and Powell's men with devastating effect. Lockett looked around at the cries of agony on either side of him. Some men were returning fire; others were dazed into sluggish inaction; many were dead already.

It was a slaughter with only one possible outcome at these odds. There was no chance of victory, but they had to stand and fight. They had to give Grant and Sherman time.

They had to slow the enemy for the sake of the rest of the army!

Grudgingly, they gave ground, firing as they slowly shuffled back. Lockett raised his rifle and fired into the approaching mass of butternut still shrouded in the white smoke of their volley. Missing the enemy seemed impossible against such a massive advancing wall of men – slowing the wall seemed equally unlikely.

"Close the gaps," a captain ordered, bleeding heavily from a shoulder wound. Obediently, the defenders crowded together to erase the gaps caused by fallen men. Then new gaps would appear as the musketry whistled through the branches, snapping bone and wood alike.

The captain began to wave his sword with his good arm and was about to give another order when he was struck down by a musket ball. Seemingly oblivious to the loss, most of the men continued to fire as fast as they could load, but that rate of fire became slower with each round.

Taking another paper cartridge from a cartridge box that he had taken off a dead comrade, Lockett began to reload as he inched back with the rest of the men. He bit into the end of the cartridge and tore off the end. This time, he did not bother to spit the few grains of black powder out of his mouth. He had no moisture left with which to spit.

With McManus on one side, he fired and fired again. So many times that he lost count, but always, they were forced to give ground. He knew they were giving as good as they could, but their line continued to shrivel while the long lines of Confederates only grew. Ponderously, the Confederates would move forward, always threatening to overlap the outgunned defenders on both flanks.

It was shortly after 7 a.m. now, and Lockett was vaguely

aware that the sounds of battle were spreading. As he reloaded yet again, he thought he heard fire from their distant right where Sherman's men were camped. For a moment, he wondered how Ainsley's friend Lieutenant Peterson was faring.

He finished reloading and aimed his Dimick into the advancing wall, but his shot harmlessly flew into the upper branches of the trees as he was jostled by the soldier behind him, crowding forward for his own shot. Without a word or face of disgust, Lockett ignored him and dropped the butt of the gun to the ground and began the process all over again. The burning hot barrel stung his hands, but he hardly noticed. Finished, he pinched on another percussion cap and raised the Dimick, firing into the oncoming line of Rebels.

Ainsley Stuart watched Peabody's Brigade form up. Miller's Brigade guarded their left flank. Two brigades and a battery of artillery were still too little. He had seen enough to know that.

And what of Major Powell's patrol? James? Patrick? Anxiously, he chewed on his lower lip. Those were his men up there, ahead somewhere – bearing the brunt of the fulminating attack.

As if in a daze, he started to walk through Peabody's line into the forest up ahead. He could see no men, but the sounds of battle were coming through loud and clear – echoing, threatening.

"Sir!" an anxious voice cried out to him as it was obvious to all that the rail thin officer was about to disappear into the cacophony raging in the trees ahead. Stuart turned to see another lieutenant chasing after him.

"Where are you going?" the fresh-faced young man said to him.

"To rejoin my men."

"Sir, I wouldn't do that. You're as likely to run into the Rebels as you are to meet up with your men now."

"But those are my men."

"Sir," the young man said, "I would consider it an honor if

you would fight with us, sir. There is nothing else you can do for your men up there."

Stuart hesitated, pondering the truth in the man's words. With a sorrowful face, he nodded and walked back to Peabody's line with the man. It was only then that Ainsley recognized the young lieutenant as a fellow officer from the 12th Michigan.

With a nervous silence, Peabody's line waited for the appearance of the Confederates. Suddenly, the firing in front of them stopped and a few minutes later, a few blue forms raced out of the woods, like animals escaping a forest blaze.

"Hold you-r fi-re!" The order rang down the line as the remnants of Moore's men raced through the line.

They were no longer full of bluster, Stuart thought savagely.

Some of the men stopped to join up with Peabody's line, but many continued to flee from the onslaught without breaking stride.

Lockett and McManus were among the survivors fleeing towards the next line of blue.

"Johnny Reb send you running?" jeered one of the Wisconsin men in Peabody's line as Lockett and a few others rushed towards them.

Lockett had half a mind to grab McManus by the collar to prevent him from going after the soldier, but he needn't have worried. McManus was far too tired for that.

With a sense of the inevitable, they waited with the Wisconsin men to confront the Rebels for what seemed like the hundredth time already, and it was only 7:30 in the morning. One of Peabody's men next to him gasped, and Lockett eyed the now familiar sight of mismatched butternut that stretched the edges of his vision.

"Steady, stea-dy," the order rang up and down the line.

Slowly, the massive Confederate line advanced towards them. A shrill, ghoulish yell rose up from the Rebel ranks – a reverberating, sepulchral call...

Chapter 21

Six months of memory passed through James Lockett's mind as the massive Confederate volley tore into the blue line of defenders. Minié and musket balls whipsawed through the air, snapping branches, slamming into trees with audible thuds, shrieking as they raced overhead, and some knifing deep into men's bodies. Yet, Lockett somehow heard none of it while his mind raced from Kalamazoo to Missouri to Kalamazoo to here…

It had all started with the unexpected conversation with Martha McManus, his promise to keep Patrick safe, his promise to himself to keep his brother, Daniel, from the fray. And then there was the shock of what he had seen from his own side in Missouri… So many memories raced into and out of his mind in that second – a lifetime in a split second…

He felt the breeze of a Minié ball whip near his ear.

The memories disappeared from his consciousness at that moment, and he snapped alert again.

He had not been hit, but the man behind him had, smashing a gruesome hole into his face. The body collapsed into Lockett's knees, knocking him to the ground.

"James!" he heard a concerned cry from next to him.

Blinking, Lockett pulled his legs free from the man's lifeless body and rose to his feet. "I'm okay, Patrick!"

The Peabody line survived that first devastating volley. With a mixture of pride and surprise, Lockett saw that the line had held intact. There were many holes in the line, but they were still fighting.

Fighting for their very lives, but they had not run.

The men kept up their fire, and the two sides traded blow for blow. They were holding the Rebels for now, although Lockett could see through the trees that some Rebels were moving to the right, heading for the unprotected flank.

Behind his men, Colonel Peabody rode, rallying them with his presence and voice.

For nearly half an hour, Minié balls and musket balls filled the air with a familiar zip and zing. Each man seemed to be fighting an individual war against a faceless butternut clad enemy, firing as fast as he could reload. Lockett looked behind him as Peabody rode by again, and he found himself stirred by the presence of the large man. Though suffering from four wounds, Colonel Peabody seemed unaffected.

A musket ball whizzed by close overhead, and Lockett wondered how many more could possibly be deflected by this invisible shield that seemed to protect him. For a moment, he wondered again if God intended for him to die here, in this wooded thicket in Tennessee – so far from home, yet so close to friends like Patrick, Ainsley, Luke, and Matthew.

Even as his mind wandered, he mechanically continued firing and reloading.

But the wanderings of his mind were halted by a cry of despair behind him. With a quick glance over his shoulder, he saw Colonel Peabody on the ground, shot in the head. The line began to break as a few men decided they could take no more, and they fled through the trees. Seconds later, a cry came up from the far right as the Confederates overlapped the line and began to turn the flank. There was momentary panic as it seemed that some of the Rebels had gotten in behind them!

Suddenly, the entire line gave way, and panicked men began to stream backwards towards their own tents. It was pandemonium and every man ran for himself!

Bending down to grab another two cartridge boxes from the dead around him, Lockett raced after McManus. They sprinted through their camp in Barnes Field. There seemed to be Rebels everywhere. Firing! Taking prisoners!

They rounded one neat row of tents and were surprised by two muddy Confederates emerging from one of the tents, each with food in his hand.

McManus knocked one into the other, as they streaked past. Lockett dodged the falling Rebels and hurdled the still burning cook fire in one clean jump. He did not look back at the equally stunned Rebels who now sat in the mud, but with their prized food safely held high.

Other bluecoats joined them, and they fled beyond their camp, beyond where there seemed to be any Rebels. Lockett paused momentarily behind one of the quartermaster's wagons to catch his breath and fire at the pursuing Rebels.

The Confederates were charging en masse now, swooping in on the disorganized and shattered Federals, taking dozens of prisoners. Some made the mad dash across their old camp, but many suffered the greatest indignity of all, shot in the back as they ran. It was chaos all across the encampment.

The remnants of Peabody's and Miller's brigades paused to fire at their pursuers, as Lockett had done, before continuing the retreat through the field. From behind wagons, tents, a pile of hay, and trees, they sporadically spat back at the enemy, but it was like throwing peas at the side of a barn. Their efforts had no visible impact on slowing down the Rebels.

They ran until they reached the low, wooded section beyond their camp. Pausing there to reload, Lockett looked with astonishment at the number of strewn bodies across their old camp. But it was not the sight of the dead and dying that shocked him. It was the sight of the Confederate advance grinding to a halt!

The Rebels were plundering the camp. More intent on food and booty than on pursuing the shattered Federals, the Confederate advance had stopped!

"I don't believe it," McManus mumbled.

Lockett noticed more than ever that the butternut wave was not homogeneous. In fact, the enemy appeared almost like a ragtag mob. Some had full uniforms of butternut, some wore only coats with civilian trousers, some had no uniform at all. Nearly all of them, however, paused their attack to scrounge around the captured Yankee camp. Coffee that had been left on cook fires was now devoured. The fresh bread that had been the luxury of the camp was now being scarfed down by men from Mississippi, Alabama, and Tennessee. Soldiers ducked into tents and came out with watches, tin plates, anything that could be stuffed into a haversack.

"Think they'll take your writin' book?" McManus joked.

Lockett shrugged. "I hid it under my bedroll as usual, but I suppose so. Looks like they intend on taking everything else." He gave a bewildered stare.

A few Confederate officers struggled to regain discipline. Some were able to convince their men to collect prisoners instead of booty, but most were unsuccessful.

Even so, the Confederates had another problem now. The Rebels were ill prepared to deal with so many prisoners. Like the temptation to loot, the number of prisoners accomplished what Peabody's Brigade had not been able to do, slow the Confederate assault.

For a shockingly long hour, the Rebels were held at bay with nothing more than an occasional pot shot to disrupt them.

* * *

Sergeant Milton Bosworth worriedly watched his Colonel Appler in the camp. Bosworth had awoken in the dark of the early morning. At first, he had thought that the sounds of gunfire were just exchanges between nervous pickets, but then the intensity picked up to a level he had never heard before.

After a man from the 25th Missouri with a wounded arm had wandered into the Ohioans camp, babbling that they were about to be attacked, a messenger had been sent to General Sherman, but Bosworth already knew how that would be received. So far, he had avoided being arrested, thanks to his cousin, Captain Mason, and Colonel Hildebrand, but he had no confidence in General Sherman.

As the morning sky started to brighten, Bosworth only felt his unease grow. Around 7 a.m., there was confused chatter around their cook fires that their own pickets were engaging Rebel skirmishers, but nothing seemed confirmed.

To his surprise, Bosworth saw General Sherman and his staff ride into camp, dismounting at the 53rd Ohio's tents. A minute later, from the thick brush of the small creek that ran in front of their camp, Confederate skirmishers emerged like wraiths.

Bosworth did not see them at first. His eyes were on his lieutenant who ran towards General Sherman, yelling at the top of his lungs. It took a moment for the words to register in Bosworth's brain.

"General, look to your right!"

General Sherman twisted and looked in the direction. Just as he did, a spray of musketry from the Confederate skirmishers lashed the area. Sherman's orderly fell dead, and Sherman himself looked in shock at his own hand, which had received a ball of buckshot.

"My God, we are attacked!" Sherman declared in astonishment.

Even as Sherman and his staff tried to gather their wits, Colonel Hildebrand and a patchwork of Ohioans were already trying to organize a defense.

Muddy Southerners began to emerge from the rain-soaked bog next to camp. Neither side was fully sure of the situation and where friend or foe was located, but that did not stop the hastening fire which was seemingly going in all directions at once.

The Confederates themselves were equally surprised to find themselves already amidst a Union encampment.

Bosworth joined the rest of the 53rd Ohio trying to take up a position behind a stream in two hundred yards of open ground, separated from the 57th Ohio and 77th Ohio.

Colonel Appler belligerently ordered his men to face to the left, which left Bosworth aghast since he had already seen the Rebels emerge from the other direction. Finally recognizing the mistake, Appler then re-positioned the men in the proper direction.

But he seemed confused by the men in that direction, unsure if they were Rebels or fellow Ohioans. As the Rebels began to rummage through the tents, he decided that they were Rebels after all and gave the order to open fire. The blast of fire caused the Rebels to pull back momentarily. They worked to organize their disjointed gaggles of men and then advanced on the Ohioans again, but their gathering numbers were still small and the Ohioans were in good position to repel them.

But to Bosworth's shock, he heard Colonel Appler then bellow, "Retreat! Retreat, save yourselves!"

Many of the men followed Appler's example. Only the men on the right held their positions and prepared for the next Rebel assault.

Bewildered, Bosworth spun in a full circle. Realizing that there were few men remaining around him and that another mass of muddy Confederates was pushing its way through the thickets and bog, he took off in a plodding sprint after the bulk of the 53rd Ohio.

* * *

John and Lyman Cameron cursed the swampy thickets for the thousandth time. They were all a muddy mess. Even their fastidious leader, Irish-born General Patrick Cleburne was coated in mud after being thrown from his horse earlier in the dark.

All through the darkened early morning hours they had struggled through these bogs. To their right, they had heard varying degrees of gunfire for a couple of hours now. As for themselves, they had fired a few times at the shadows ahead of them, but their officers had restrained them since they were unsure if they were firing on friend or foe.

To be honest, John Cameron was fairly certain that at least one of the times they had fired on their own men. In the dark and incredibly dense thickets, it was impossible to maintain cohesion and order. He knew that they were supposed to be the left flank of the attack, but it was beyond reason that they really knew where they were anymore.

Their brigade was supposed to be men from Arkansas, Mississippi and Tennessee, but somehow there were many Louisianans among them now, and he had no idea where they came from or where they were supposed to be.

As they slogged towards the Union army, he could only

imagine what horrible defenses awaited them. The sound of gunfire had been going on for hours. Even if by some miracle the Yankees had not figured out days ago that they were coming, they would surely be ready now – waiting for them as the light grew and the mist began to lift.

In front of them, particularly to their front left, the sound of intense shooting suddenly erupted.

Both Cameron brothers had supposed that they were now the lead elements but apparently not.

He and the rest of the men in the bog struggled forward, spurred on by the sounds that grew and grew. After fifteen minutes the first of the wounded started to come back. One of the men said he was from the 2nd Tennessee, which was in their own brigade. He described a hot fight up near a simple wooden church. The Yankees had put together a stiff defense in the woods and behind some logs. The man insisted that it wasn't an organized entrenchment but that the fighting was heavy.

Finally, they emerged from the thicket, and there was an opening beyond them. The volume of the sound doubled, and the air was thick with clouds of smoke, but below the hovering white skein, they could see muddy, butternut clad bodies coating the ground.

The brothers and those with them crept forward into a ravine where some surviving Tennesseans took shelter. In fact, General Cleburne was there as well.

"Boys, don't be discouraged. This is not the first charge that was repulsed. Fix bayonets and give them steel," he encouraged.

John and Lyman Cameron looked at each other. They both had bayonets, but neither had actually expected to ever use one. They were both more confident of their shooting eye than in the steel.

But the words had only limited effect, and it took more cajoling and organizing to get the men ready for the next attack. In the meantime, the Mississippians of the brigade tried to carry on without them, but of the 425 Mississippians who started, 300 ended up dead or wounded near the little church or in the grounds of the Ohioans' camp.

One of the men told the brothers that these were the camps of the Union General Sherman, but that meant nothing to the brothers as they stared agape at the carnage.

They tried again and again to dislodge the men in blue and were further aided when Confederate artillery began to arrive, but it was bloody going. While one whole section of the Federals collapsed, the rest of the Yankees held firm and both sides continued to pour reinforcements into the area.

By 9:30, six separate Confederate brigades plus artillery assaulted the area. Eventually with artillery support, the 20th Louisiana and 9th Texas pushed back the Federals. Many of the 20th Louisiana were German, and their wild German yells echoed against the more common Rebel yells as they finally succeeded in securing the Union camp.

Chapter 22

Matthew Bauer, Luke Bailey, and the rest of Birge's Western Sharpshooters began to march down the River Road towards the peach orchard with the rest of Lauman's Brigade. Up in front of them was Colonel Williams. Behind them there was the young, fresh-faced General McArthur and his brigade from W.H.L. Wallace's division.

Marching in the rear of Lauman's column, Bauer looked over his shoulder at the 50th Illinois in McArthur's brigade. "Look at those funny hats," he said.

"Scotsmen," Bailey replied.

"I like the little ball on top," another soldier laughed.

The conversation continued down such an idle path as a guard against their nervousness. They had heard the sounds of intense fighting all morning, and now they were marching closer to the ever booming and cracking sounds. The steady stream of refugees from Prentiss's division did little to cheer them. While some were genuinely wounded, many were just badly scared, so scared that the normal jeers had no effect on any of them. The shirkers continued to run for the Landing as if the devil himself was on their tail.

At the head of the column, an officer of the 3rd Iowa announced that any man seen deserting his post would be shot. His regiment gave a resounding cheer.

"Those were Prentiss's men. You think James and Patrick are okay?" Bauer asked Bailey. He had been searching the faces of the shirkers as they passed by, each and every face. He didn't expect to find James or Patrick.

They passed a pond and a blossoming peach orchard. Williams' brigade had taken up a position at the opposite end of the old cotton field. The sharpshooters and the rest of Lauman's brigade filed in beside them, forming a right angle on Williams' left.

It was nine o'clock now, and they waited as the sounds of battle neared. Surely, the Rebels couldn't have pushed this far already, Bailey thought to himself.

* * *

Lockett, McManus, and a few other remnants of Peabody's Brigade fell back out of the wooded ridge beyond camp after giving token resistance. Despite their sniping, the Confederates had gathered some semblance of organization again and were pushing forward.

Scarcely better than individuals, the Union men retreated again, obliquely away from the Eastern Corinth Road, heading north. It was as if they were retracing their steps back to the Landing.

"I'm getting damn tired of retreating," one of the men grumbled. There was blood on his leg (someone else's), on his shoulder (his), and two gouges in his forehead from flying pieces of tree. The musket ball had grazed him, passing cleanly through the muscle at the edge of his shoulder. If it had been any closer, it would have mangled the joint. Still, it was a struggle to reload his weapon, much less raise it and aim, but the stubborn man was not about to skedaddle.

"At least you can say we were the last to retreat," McManus replied as a couple of stray Confederate shots zinged by overhead.

"I'd say those who got captured get that honor," the man grimaced through clenched teeth.

They passed through the edges of Davis field, and they saw another line of Union blue forming up, waiting for the Confederates to appear. As they crossed through the far right of this line, McManus recognized the battle flag of the 33rd Indiana in Lauman's Brigade.

Lockett shouted to one of the Hoosier officers who watched them intently. "The Rebs are right behind us, sir."

The officer nodded and pointed behind the line. "The rest of your brigade is reforming behind us."

"Yes, sir."

"That was Lauman's Brigade," McManus interjected, looking at Lockett, "I recognized their colors."

"Wonder where the sharpshooters are?" Lockett answered, spinning around and scanning the line while he walked backwards, but he could not tell where their friends were.

As they reached the thin wagon cut in the dense thicket, they heard a familiar voice cheer them.

"James!" Ainsley Stuart yelled, bounding up to greet them. One hand held the scabbard to his leg, and in the other he surprisingly carried a rifle now.

"Ainsley!" Lockett exclaimed in a grateful, but tired voice.

The sounds of battle sprang up again behind them as the Confederates engaged Lauman's and Williams's Brigades.

"I should have known you would be on the horse's tail," Stuart grinned madly.

"Where've you been, Lieutenant?" McManus asked, "Don't tell me you missed all the fun?" He thirstily emptied the canteen that Stuart offered.

"Never fear, Private McManus. I've had plenty of fun."

"There will be more where that came from," Lockett said, "How about some ammunition?" Three empty cartridge boxes dangled around his neck.

"Back here," Stuart pointed, "I ended up helping Hickenlooper's battery get away. How about you?"

"Hickenlooper?" Lockett said with some surprise. Even though they had held that ground so long, the end had come so swiftly that he assumed the Confederates took the cannon. "They made it away?"

Stuart nodded. "They're formed up over there with the rest of us from Prentiss's Division."

"And how many is that?"

"About 500."

Lockett and McManus stopped what they were doing and looked aghast at him.

"500? Out of the whole division?"

"What about the 12th?"

"Some of it is here. It's hard to say, Patrick. We're all so scattered. There could be more of them scattered anywhere from here to the River to the Landing. So scattered... Why, it must be some sort of miracle that brought us back together."

"Yeah, a real work of divine intervention," McManus grumbled, "More like we are just trying to follow orders best we can."

They refilled their empty cartridge boxes amidst the crash of weaponry behind them. The Rebels had now run into Lauman's line from the sound of it.

"Glad to see at least you put away that silly sword and picked up a rifle, sir," Lockett said, tapping the battered rifle that Ainsley held.

"The sword wasn't much use," Stuart admitted, "But it's not silly. It's a sign of honor."

"So, we're to stop the Rebels here, sir?" McManus interrupted, "Along this wagon cut?"

"Yes, we will stop them here on this sunken road."

Lockett looked skeptically at the twin tracks of the wagon trail in the tall grass. It ran eastward from the Corinth-Pittsburg Landing Road to the Hamburg-Savannah Road. Well worn over the years and washed out by numerous rains, it was like a shallow trench, twenty inches below everything. Surrounded by hickory and oak trees that had budded but not fully leafed, there was some protection while not completely obscuring their vision. "I suppose it is as good a place as any we've had to this point."

* * *

Luke Bailey watched the 13th Ohio battery unlimber their six guns as the sharpshooters waited. They had seen the last remnants of Prentiss's division come through the field and forest, and everyone along the line knew what would be just behind those retreating soldiers.

The men of Lauman's Brigade had seen battle before at Fort Donelson. The boom of cannon, the crack of musketry, and the zing of Minié balls were nothing new to Lauman's brigade, but Bailey found himself wondering how the untested

Ohioans manning the cannon felt. Even though he had seen battle and felt the tremor in his legs at Fort Donelson, today felt completely different. What he was seeing was previously unthinkable. What would it be like to have seen nothing of battle but what was happening today?

Rebels began to appear at the edge of the woods across the field, just behind the Hamburg-Purdy Road. Surprisingly, there was only tentative musketry exchanged. Being at the right angle joint between Lauman's and Williams' brigades, the sharpshooters were well-placed to retaliate with their long range Dimick rifles.

Matthew Bauer took aim at a distant Confederate holding their flag aloft and fired. With a flash of satisfaction, he saw the flag fall from the man's hands as he fell. The moment was fleeting, however, as another Rebel instantly rushed to pick it up.

Bauer hurried to reload and then took his time finding a target again. He had come to the conclusion that shooting an ordinary soldier was a poor use of his skills. Instead, he patiently scanned the field for an officer or flag-bearer. Spotting a soldier waving a sword, he fired and was disappointed as the man retreated unharmed back into the trees.

Southwest of them, Confederate cannon opened up, and Bauer suddenly felt very vulnerable. While the Union cannon roared in reply, he could not tell where the Union cannon were aiming, if indeed they were aiming at all. In contrast, the Confederates were clearly attempting to silence the Union batteries. Chunks of earth were torn up as the shells exploded near the Ohioans.

Then instantly, he was blinded by an enormous flash. The very air seemed to explode, and a blast like a tornado knocked him to the ground where the earth still shook from the tremendous explosion. It seemed minutes before the soft ground of the cotton field quelled its reverberations, longer still before the gritty dirt and debris ceased raining from above.

A lucky Confederate shell had found a Union caisson, and the subsequent explosion, fueled by the ammunition, obliterated any trace of the caisson, the six pull horses, or the eight artillerymen. The cannon, 20 yards in front of the caisson, had been tossed like a toy and flipped upside down.

But worst of all, the explosion unhinged the rest of the 13th Ohio artillery. Immediately, they abandoned their remaining cannon and fled the field in a panic.

Bauer felt a firm hand pull him up from the ground. It was George VanderJagt, and he barked something at him, but Bauer couldn't hear a thing, just an unstoppable ringing in his ears.

Despite the pounding of his head and the incessant ringing, one thought still came to the forefront of his mind – they had no more artillery support, and it was obvious where the Confederate artillery would focus their attention next.

Despite the lack of artillery support, Lauman's Brigade and the rest of General Hurlbut's troops held their position. The sharpshooters sniped from long distance at the Confederate infantry in the distant woods, but mostly, they flattened themselves as best as possible from the continuing barrage of Confederate cannon.

There was little they could do to protect themselves, but as Colonel Lauman and Colonel Birge conversed behind the burrowing sharpshooters, the two officers appeared as calm and unconcerned as if they were chatting aimlessly on an ordinary spring day. But finally, fearing a Confederate infantry assault, General Hurlbut pulled his two brigades back. Bauer and the rest of the sharpshooters agreeably fell back across the cotton field and ended up lining the fence around the Peach Orchard.

"That's a fair amount of open ground for them to cover now," VanderJagt yelled in Matthew Bauer's ear.

Bauer looked at him blankly. The ringing had partially stopped, but the words were incomprehensible to him at the moment. He looked around and noticed immediately that he did not see Captain Vincent and that the company looked smaller.

"Where is everyone?" he asked, "Did we get separated on the withdrawal?"

"We are a little out of place," the grizzled sergeant replied, noting that they were tucked between companies of Colonel Pugh's regiment of Illinoisans, "But I think yer referrin' to our shirkers."

"Shirkers?"

"By now, at the pace they were running, Hiram Walker and his friends are probably back at the Landing."

Bauer bit his tongue to hold back a flow of un-Christian curses.

The battle had tapered off for the moment, and yelling was no longer necessary.

"They're gathering themselves for a charge," VanderJagt observed matter-of-factly.

* * *

Lockett felt a peculiar rumbling in his stomach and looked up to the sun high above, marking it as not even noon. But any ideas of food were erased by the crashing sound of cannon. As he looked down the line, he could see three batteries of cannon and knew there was more Union artillery north of their position.

Men flattened themselves to the sunken road, but the shallow trail provided only the bare minimum of protection from the Confederate shells. The earth trembled and shook, like an angry beast awakening from a slumber.

Federal cannon returned fire, and Lockett put his arms over his head and closed his eyes. The shriek of each shell seemed to be crying something, and he prayed that none of them would screech his name.

A shell exploded into the trees directly behind them with a splintering echo. A second later, he heard a large branch crash to the ground. Another explosive shell sheared off a tall tree fifteen feet from the ground, like a demonic scythe had cut through it in one swipe.

"I think I'd rather face muskets with my sword than this," Ainsley Stuart yelled in his ear, "I hate the idea of being blown to bits by some unseen cannon shell."

A shell shrieked overhead and shook the earth, showering

them with dirt.

"Don't be jinxing us now," Lockett hollered back over the din.

Another shell landed among a clump of men 40 yards to their north, leaving lifeless, bloody blue clumps of meat. Lockett shut his eyes tightly.

"I'm sure I'll get my wish though," Stuart yelled back, "There will be a charge behind this bombardment for certain."

McManus wriggled closer to them, raising his voice, "What's the debate here? Anything is better than laying here throughout all this."

Eventually, the shrieking shells stopped, and the only sound was the Union batteries. Soon they stopped too, realizing that the Rebels had quieted. The trio looked at each other.

"Ready?" Lockett said after a pause to Stuart, tapping the percussion cap on Stuart's rifle.

They peered into the thicket ahead of them. Lockett guessed that he could only really see forty or fifty yards into it, so thick it was with brush, tangles, vines, and trees. And even then, he doubted he could get a clean shot through the mess greater than twenty or thirty yards.

From the thicket came the ghoulish yell of defiance that had become all too familiar. All along the sunken road, men from Iowa, Wisconsin, Illinois, and Michigan packed in, shoulder to shoulder, along a short section of fence rail, behind trees, or crouched on a knee and waited.

The sudden eerie stillness and silence unsettled all of them after the long, loud bombardment that had preceded this.

"Here they come!" came up a cry.

Lockett could see movement of some sort all along the front. With an agonizing slowness, the movement came closer and closer. Finally, he could make out the actual forms of Rebels struggling through the tough thicket. They were fifty yards away now, and he could clearly see that they were having trouble maintaining their formation in the tangles and brush. But with either a sort of arrogance or unflappable determination, they paused from time to time to reform, either oblivious or unconcerned about the Union defenses ahead.

"Wait, steady!" the unknown major from Iowa said from behind the trio as he paced up and down the line.

The Confederates closed to almost one hundred paces, and Lockett fought to concentrate on his aim and ignore the fact of how close they were. They held their fire, waiting.

"Fire!" came the order.

What seemed like a mile long blaze of flame erupted from the Union line. With a chorus of snapping wood and cries, the Confederate line shuddered and buckled.

Lockett went about the familiar process of reloading. He had scarcely fished out the paper cartridge when the Union batteries added to the mayhem. With thunderous booms, they fired loads of canister into the Rebel line. Like a giant shotgun, the lead balls shredded tree and man alike.

A few Confederates returned fire, plucking some Iowans off the fence rail, but most of the Rebels began to retreat back into the thicket. Their painstaking efforts to maintain some sort of formation were no longer adhered to, and they fell back, each man at his own speed. Their lines had been torn with gaping holes.

"They'll think twice about doing that again," an Iowan next to them said gruffly, as he finished reloading. He rested his rifle on the top fence rail, making it easier for him to shoot with one arm. Blood dripped down the sleeve of his other arm. Given the amount of blood soaking the sleeve, Lockett decided that the man had been wounded long ago, not in the most recent charge.

As the first wave fell back, Lockett felt some relief as he looked along their long line. For the first time today, he thought they might have a defense organized well enough so that the Confederates couldn't simply overlap them and force them back. With most of W.H.L. Wallace's brigade on the right and Hurlbut on the left, they might have enough to stop the Rebels. Finally, the Rebels were facing more than piecemeal opponents.

"Here they come again!" the cry went up a few minutes later, and they again saw movement in the thicket.

This time there was no waiting for a massive volley. Musketry and cannon immediately reacted to the movement, and the attack was again beaten off, this time before the Rebels had even come close.

* * *

From behind the fence railing in the Peach Orchard, Luke Bailey and the rest of the sharpshooters watched the stunning sight of three Confederate brigades in line of battle emerge from the woods. Their flags waved brilliantly in the breeze of the sunny day.

He scanned the long line of unfamiliar uniforms. Some wore the usual butternut like those at Fort Donelson had. Others seemed to be wearing no uniform at all, and a few wore bright uniforms that were more appropriate for a great costume ball with their bright red and blue knee-high leggings and fez-like caps.

Though their uniforms were different, the Confederates all moved with the singleness of one great, giant machine. Lurching forward, the Rebels began to move towards the sharpshooters and the rest of General Hurlbut's men.

Almost physically feeling the weight of the impending assault, Bailey suddenly thought of General Smith back in Pittsburg Landing with his bad leg. They could sure use him now. General Hurlbut seemed fine, but all of the men knew what they had in the reliable, old general.

"Oh, God, please save us," Bailey could not help but pray as he gaped at the enemy moving toward their thin line.

Plumes of white appeared from the Confederate artillery supporting the attack. For some reason, Bailey had long ago stopped noticing the booming echo of cannon as they traded shot for shot.

But now, the fire intensified, and it was impossible to ignore.

Shells shrieked overhead and burst with thunderous bangs behind him. One shell tore a gash in the earth, another ripped a peach tree from its roots, another obliterated a rider on his horse. One moment, the man was riding madly to the front, a messenger no doubt, and the next moment, rider and horse seemed to disappear in the heavy smoke. Only when the smoke began to lift, did Luke see the horse twitching on its back. The rider was nowhere to be seen.

Bailey stared around them with a sense of wonder. The peaceful, new blossoms from the peach trees fell like fresh snow amid the hail. The petals coated everything with a surreal white blanket. The barrage continued for fifteen minutes. By the end of it, his smoke irritated eyes would have sworn that it had snowed in the little peach orchard. Numerous blossoms floated in the air like gentle snow flurries.

Tearing his eyes away from the incongruous distraction, he noticed that the slow-moving Rebel assault was within range. Some of the sharpshooters had already begun to fire. Union artillery shells fell among the Rebels, throwing up mounds of earth, and small gaps were already beginning to appear, but more Rebels filled in.

The Federal soldiers packed behind the fence railing put up a heavy fire. He couldn't imagine advancing into such a continuous wall of flame. Even if the shots were utterly inaccurate, the mere vision of such firepower had to be a deterrent.

Yet, the Rebels traded shot for shot. Shoulder to shoulder in the open field, the Rebel brigades returned the fire coming from the Peach Orchard.

Matthew Bauer crouched next to his friend behind the fence railing and scanned the area. He could see the Secesh officers urging their men forward and concentrated on a rotund, gray-coated officer grabbing the regimental banner from the hands of the color sergeant, waving it dramatically as he stomped forward, daring his men to follow their flag.

With a squeeze of the trigger, Bauer spun the officer around in a circle. The brief advance halted in confusion and disarray.

All along the Peach Orchard fence, men reloaded and fired as fast as they could.

The Confederate resolve began to waver in the face of the

murderous fire. As if to spur them to a decision, the Federal artillery belched rounds of double canister, and the hundreds of lead balls mercilessly cut men down where they stood. Their spirit faltering, the Rebels began to inch back, firing as they went. A few could not take it anymore and broke for the safety of the woods. But most slowly, and stubbornly, walked backwards in the face of the fire, as if to say that the blue coats may have won this round, but they were not broken and would try again.

Gradually as the Rebels removed themselves, the cotton field revealed the crumpled forms of so many men… hundreds and hundreds…

Without a sigh of relief or remorse, Matthew Bauer lowered his rifle until the butt rested on the ground, and he closed his eyes.

* * *

Lockett and the rest of the patchwork Prentiss men watched another Confederate wave move through the thick underbrush, their lines again completely tangled, and in disarray, each man tried to maneuver through the thicket. Next to him, the bloody-sleeved Iowan rested his rifle on the fence rail for support, and McManus similarly took aim.

Holding their fire until about 25 yards this time, the Union line erupted again in a wall of flame, decimating the Rebels who were stumbling through the woods. Cannon roared from near point-blank range, ripping giant holes in what remained of the disarrayed Rebel lines.

Smoke shrouded their position and blurred vision, but it was ignored as each man now hurriedly reloaded and fired again into the smoke filled forests. Confederate retaliation was mild as their line broke again and retreated in the face of such horrific fire.

The forest was quiet for a moment except for the echoing howls of the wounded and cries for help. Lockett saw two lone figures rise to their feet. Each was wounded and dragging a leg, but one was far worse off. Using his comrade as a crutch, the mangled Confederate tried to limp out of the thicket, dragging his leg and shattered arm behind him. Without thinking, Lockett raised his rifle and took aim. Then he felt a hand on his barrel, pushing his aim down.

"Leave them be, James," Ainsley Stuart said in a calm, but forceful voice, "We won't be troubled by them again today."

"Yes," he gulped, realizing that he had been about to kill a man – a man with a family and life probably not unlike his own. Suddenly, he felt a terrible distaste for this war, for what it was doing to them all. They had become animals and butchers.

"You ought to have killed one of them," the Iowan groused next to them. "It's either kill them, or they kill us. He ain't gonna be back today, but there is sure gonna be more battles after today."

Lockett swallowed hard. He felt like telling the man that this had to be the battle to end all battles. How could anyone go on after this? And besides, they were being pushed back towards the river by the Rebels. If this didn't stop, there would be no army anymore. But he stayed silent. In his head, an urgent voice told him the Iowan had a point.

Still, the fields were littered with enough dead, dying, and maimed to fill the whole country.

But with a dark realization, the urgent voice in his head won out… No amount of distaste could end the war now. Like it or not, the war was real now and would continue. There would be more death, more killing! The sooner this war ended the better, but he knew they were all powerless to stop it now.

Through the thicket, the Southerners came again, having regrouped and again they were cut down by unforgiving fire. Again, and then again over the next hour and a half, the same groups of battered Rebels tried to reach the Union position on the sunken road, and each time they were driven off with heavy losses.

Though each Rebel charge knocked more blue-coated men off the fence rail, Lockett couldn't imagine that the Southerners had enough men to continue at this rate. But each time, they came back again…

With an unspoken sense of dread in the Peach Orchard, Luke Bailey watched the Confederate battle line emerge from the woods again. This time, he counted four brigade flags, and it looked like a fifth one down to the east.

"They're attacking the length of the flank this time," VanderJagt remarked, not bothering to duck as artillery bursts landed in front and behind them again.

"How can you tell? Doesn't look any different to me than the other two times," Matthew Bauer yelled above the din, uncorking a shot from long range. His face had been blackened from the day's fighting, and his hair was matted to his forehead with sweat. He did not look young anymore.

The Rebel ranks moved closer and closer, and the two sides traded shots. With thick white smoke beginning to shroud the Union line again, Bauer searched for another officer and spotted a man on horseback actively rallying his troops, making himself as conspicuous as possible. He fired and began to reload. As he replaced the ramrod, he looked up, surprised to see the rider still there. Again, he fired at the man.

And again, he looked up to see the rider still there. This time, the Confederate was getting close enough so that Matthew could see that the rider seemed to be waving a tin cup in the air to urge his men forward.

Nearby, Pete O'Shea recoiled and stumbled backward. With a stunned look on his face, he stared down at the spreading crimson on his chest. He dropped to his knees, unseen by anyone else, and died with none of his friends aware of what had happened.

Seconds later, a Rebel shell found the zigzagging split rail fence and tore out an entire length of railing, spraying men down around it.

The fighting was as hot and furious as they had seen. Lead flew thick through the air, and the ground shook with the stomping of thousands of men and the impact of cannon shells. Smoke blocked vision and a million things seemed to be happening at once, all accompanied by the deafening sounds of gunfire and wounded men crying out for help, but Bauer was only half aware of it. Again, he fired at the rider, knowing that his aim was good enough to hit the man, even from this distance.

"By God!" VanderJagt hollered from two spots down, "There's General Johnston himself!" He pointed at the large man on horseback waving the tin cup.

Finally, the Federal line began to buckle under the onslaught. The Confederates did not slow this time, and the Federals could sense that there was no stopping them. All around there were blue coated casualties. Sensing that the Yankees were close to breaking, the Rebel officers redoubled their efforts, convinced that this charge would succeed where all others failed.

With a startling realization that the troops to the left of them had given way, Lauman's Brigade and the rest of Hurlbut's line were ordered back. Nothing could stop the Confederates now. They owned the entire left flank.

For the remaining Federals along the sunken road, they were on their own now…

As they retreated, Luke Bailey remembered the pond behind the Peach Orchard and licked his blackened, parched lips, but the sight of the pond sickened him.

Face down at the edge of the pond, some even floating out in the middle of it, were a number of dead bodies, and even dead horses, their blood turning the pond red in color. Wounded men, desperate for one last drink had expired on the very edge of the water hole.

Grabbing him by the arm, even as the preacher's son was vomiting, George VanderJagt pulled him along to the new line of defense that they were setting up to block the River Road just beyond the bloody pond.

"C'mon, son," VanderJagt yelled amid the roar of cannon and continual musketry, "I've already lost Gussie. I'll not lose you too."

Chapter 23

Ainsley Stuart returned with more ammunition for their little cadre in the middle of the Federal line on the sunken road.

"This can't still be the same day," Lockett sighed, leaning forward with his eyes closed and head resting on the lowest rail of the fence.

"Aye," McManus replied, "It's the same day, and darkness is nowhere near yet."

"How can these Johnnies keep coming?" lamented one of the Iowans.

"They can keep coming," another Iowan answered, "Because they know it's only another mile until they drive us back into the river, and then all of Grant's army will have to surrender."

"I'm not spending any time in a dirty Secesh prison!"

"Then we better hold them here as long as we can," the Iowan continued, "Because Buell's Army of the Ohio must be nearly here. If we can hold on for reinforcement..."

With the sounds of battle still crashing to their left, they had no idea that their protection over there had been driven back through the peach orchard.

It was just after 2:30 when Lockett and the others stirred again and watched another Confederate line of infantry bash its way through the thicket. Just as before, the air was full of lead and smoke. The zing and zip of Minié balls cut through the air with such regularity and frequency that it seemed that they were in the middle of a hornet's nest with millions of maddened insects diving through the air.

Zip, zip, zip. Lockett heard the shots whiz by, just overhead. With a start, he jumped back as one shot smacked into the wood railing and deflected just past his ear with a zing.

The smoke was beginning to build again. But no longer was it merely fueled by rifle and cannon. Now, parts of the damp thicket itself were on fire, and through the smoke, the Confederates marched. With the gray pall behind them, they seemed like a force of demons cast out of Hell and bent on destruction. And despite the frenzied Yankee fire and terrible losses they were suffering, the Southerners continued towards the sunken road, firing as they went.

From his position on one knee behind the fence railing, Lockett worked the ramrod down his fouled Dimick. The spent black powder from so much use clogged the barrel and made it difficult to ram the Minié ball all the way down. During the periodic lulls between Rebel charges, the men lining the sunken road would try to clean their weapons. Without any hot water nearby to remove the clinging clumps of powder, the soldiers used the next best thing, urine.

Despite his efforts to clean it during periodic lulls, no gun could handle such a rate of fire without fouling, and Lockett set it aside for now and picked up the rifle of an Iowan who had fallen. Anxiously, he pulled the trigger and fired into the Rebels who were now only thirty paces from the sunken road.

Ainsley Stuart worked his pistol free and emptied it into those struggling through the thick brush.

Though they were close to the sunken road, it was too much for the Confederates, too many of them had fallen, too few were left to capture the Yankee position. The few Confederates left standing made their way back through the thicket as fast as they could.

Gasping for air as if he had just run a long race, Lockett collapsed alongside his weary comrades. The Confederates had gotten close that time, too close. He wondered how much more they could possibly take.

To their front, a wounded Confederate gave a horrifying scream as the fire in the thicket engulfed him. After his yelling resounded along the front for what seemed an eternity, it stopped abruptly.

* * *

From behind the latest Confederate attack, John and Lyman Cameron watched in helpless exhaustion. Cleburne's Brigade had tried multiple times to take the sunken road hidden in the dense thicket and failed.

John Cameron considered the area impossible to take. It was a slippery field and thicket of blood. He called it the slaughtering forest, but the more common description that had quickly taken root with the Confederates was that the area was the 'Hornet's Nest'.

It was an apt description also, John Cameron had to admit, and in dismay, he watched Gibson's Brigade attempt to take it. It was Gibson's third attempt, and for a moment, it seemed that they had progressed further than ever.

But at thirty yards from the road, an enormously long row of fire devastated his line. With the Yankees holding nothing but empty rifles, Gibson's remaining men tried to surge forward. Their bayonets were already on their muskets. This was their chance, but the thickness of the undergrowth slowed them significantly and had broken their lines so badly that some men in the rear ended up firing on those in the front.

Again, the charge failed, and they fell back. A few men dropped to the ground either from weariness or plain stubbornness and joined some of the 16th Louisiana who remained in hidden positions to snipe away at the Hornet's Nest.

The Cameron brothers admired their bravery and stamina, but while the sniping might take down a few Yankees, both brothers knew that sniping alone would not take the contested ground.

* * *

Another wave of Confederates struggled through the brush, as determined as ever to break the Union center.

"How many charges is this?" an Iowan asked with some weariness, as the firing resumed.

"I stopped counting after five," McManus answered, "Maybe eight or nine now."

The firing gathered intensity, and the defenders clung stubbornly to their line. Their numbers were dwindling now, and they were rapidly running low on ammunition, yet they hung fast.

Hickenlooper's battery, now out of canister, had begun firing the less effective solid shell into the advancing Confederates. Yet, the Rebels continued forward. Remorselessly, they stepped on and over the bodies of dead comrades, firing as they went.

Lockett's face was so blackened from powder now that he looked like a miner. His lips were caked black, and his hands were callused and burned from so much firing that he could scarcely feel anything. With red eyes no longer capable of watering, he squinted through the smoke and fired into the fog that had developed from the fighting again.

"Boys, I'm out of..." the bloody-sleeved Iowan began and then spun around, collapsing to the ground at Lockett's feet.

"No!" Lockett cried, crawling over on his knees to the small man. He didn't even know the man's name, but he had grown an amazing attachment to the man over the previous hours.

"Get back in line, sergeant!" the patrolling major said from behind.

Lockett snapped his head around with a burning glare at the officer but saw that the major too was bleeding from an arm wound. With a deep breath, he answered, "Yes, sir."

And again, they drove off the attackers.

* * *

Luke Bailey and the other sharpshooters stood shoulder to shoulder in Wicker Field, firing at the Confederate battle line as they approached. He fought with VanderJagt on one side and Matthew Bauer on the other. With a painful inevitability, they gradually gave ground, hustling back to form another defensive position with a reserve regiment. They held momentarily before being forced to do it all over again.

Wallace's and Prentiss's last reserves appeared from the woods on the right, but even the crossfire wasn't enough to stop the Confederate wave. Despite their losses, the Rebels could sense victory was at hand. They had finally broken the stubborn Yankee defense line that had held all afternoon. The Yankees could be swept up piece by piece.

The sharpshooters fell back through their camps in Cloud Field.

Suddenly, Luke Bailey felt a powerful burning sensation from the side of his head. His vision of the approaching Rebel flags blurred then blackened. Oddly, he was still aware of falling to his knees and hitting the ground. He could hear his own voice talking to him in calm tones but knew that he was not trying to speak. Then all was black.

Chapter 24

The barrage of cannon fire was like nothing anyone had ever experienced. Despite the continual bombardment of some sort throughout the day, this new hammering was different. Instead of a few batteries trading fire with Hickenlooper and the other Union cannon, this felt like all of the Rebel cannon west of Virginia had gathered together for one massive bombardment, all centered on the sunken road.

In fact, this was virtually true. After repeated attempts to crack the Union center, Confederate General Ruggles had gathered every piece of artillery on the field for a massive bombardment of the area that the Confederates were calling the 'Hornet's Nest.'

It would have come as no surprise to Lockett and the others to learn that Ruggles had gathered more cannon for this bombardment than had ever been gathered before in the history of North America. It had taken an ungodly time and human cost, but the Rebels had finally realized that the Union position was too strong for the brave but foolhardy charges. Now, the Rebel artillery was going to pound the position into submission.

The earth-shaking thunder roared continuously without let up. It seemed that as soon as one cannon fired, another was lit off, and again, and then again. As Lockett, McManus, and the other survivors braced themselves and scratched deeper into their meager cover, it seemed that an infinite number of guns pounded away at them. Spouts of flame and dirt sprung up around them like well springs.

They lost track of time as the cannon fired over and over, driving off the few Union cannon that were still functional.

"I don't think we'll be able to stop them this time," McManus yelled into Lockett's ear. He wore a pained expression as another shell slammed in behind them.

"We don't have enough ammunition as it is now," Lockett

shouted back in agreement, "Unless Ainsley gets back here with more. We'll have to give ground."

"I doubt he'll try to come back through all this," McManus yelled back skeptically as the earth spouted again. "He'd be a fool to try."

"He'll try," Lockett frowned. He looked over to where the Iowan's body still laid. They had no time to do anything for him. The best they could do was cover his face with Ainsley's handkerchief.

Minute after minute went by. Shell after shell. Debris from the explosions constantly rained around them.

Finally, through the spikes of flame and dirt, he saw the familiar outline of Ainsley Stuart running towards them. With his hand again clamped to the bouncing scabbard at his side, he ran half bent over, his head tucked into his bony shoulders like a turtle trying to protect itself.

Other than the rifle the young officer carried in his left hand, he appeared empty-handed.

Another shell screamed by overhead, and Lockett buried his head in the ground, knowing this one was close. When he looked up through the smoke and falling dirt, he did not see anyone.

"Ainsley!" he yelled, jumping to his feet. He spotted a body on the ground near where the shell had landed.

Oblivious to the other shells crashing down, he sprinted to his friend's side, sliding to a stop and covering Ainsley's body with his own as another shell sent deadly shrapnel flying in all directions.

"Ainsley," he croaked, looking at Stuart's contorted face.

With a sickened feeling, he saw no foot where Ainsley's boot had once been. The top of his boot deteriorated into a blackened stump where dark, red blood began to flow.

McManus skidded up next to them. He whipped off one of his leather suspenders and immediately pulled it as tight as physically possible across Ainsley Stuart's stick-like thigh. Knowing that bleeding to death was Ainsley's worst enemy now, Lockett whipped off his uniform jacket and tied it around the stump and raised the leg in what he feared was a futile effort to staunch the bleeding.

"No ammunition!" Stuart choked out the words.

"We have to get him out of here, back to a surgeon!" Lockett shouted above the crashing shells. Though he could not hear him as another shell exploded, McManus nodded in agreement.

"McClernand and Sherman gave away!" Ainsley struggled, gripping Lockett fiercely by the front of his shirt "I had to get back to warn you!" His face contorted in pain.

The words did not register in Lockett's brain. All he could think of was getting Ainsley back to the surgeons.

"Hang on, Ainsley! We're getting you out of here!"

They began to lift him when Ainsley spastically spat out the words, "The sword, James! Don't leave the sword!"

Seeing the scabbard that had been cut from his body nearby, Lockett ran over and grabbed it. "I have it, Ainsley! I won't lose it, I promise!"

With a cry of agony from him, they lifted Ainsley Stuart.

McManus had his Dimick slung over his shoulder. With one hand on Ainsley's belt and another under his shoulder, he took one side. On the other side of the fallen officer, Lockett's one hand held the sword, the other grabbed Ainsley's light body by the belt, his bleeding leg propped high on Lockett's shoulder between his arm and neck. The warm blood instantly began to coat Lockett's neck and ooze down the rest of his torso. Together, they hoisted the slender officer and took off as fast as they could through the carnage.

The news of McClernand's and Sherman's retreats caused them to fear the sight of Rebels appearing from the west, but what they saw first were Rebels from the east.

"Hurlbut must have given way too!" McManus huffed. "We're about to be surrounded!"

Behind them, they heard the Union line open fire as it had so many times that day. The Rebels were making another charge at the sunken road, but that was the least of their worries now.

Lockett's eyes flashed from the Rebels on the right to

movement on the left, spotting more Confederates emerging there too. Rebels on both sides! Ahead of them was an ever-closing gap that led to safety. *The hornet's nest that they had manned so long was surrounded!*

Bullets whizzed in, some aimed and some stray, smacking into trees and earth, as the Confederates pushed forward, firing on the run to stop anyone from escaping their trap.

"Leave me!" Stuart moaned, stirring from his near unconscious state.

Without wasting their breath on a reply, they ran faster with their load, but it did not seem enough. The gap to safety seemed a hundred miles away.

"Faster!" Lockett gasped. The opening was closing, and there seemed to be more and more Confederates nipping at their heels, angling to block their escape.

It was like a nightmare. From all sides, the forest seemed to crawl with Rebels and that terrible Rebel yell. The cries chased the three boys from Kalamazoo, and with each step their feet became heavier and heavier.

Lockett could see light at the edge the forest, and he prayed that the meadow that lay beyond them was still Union held, or at least, a no man's land.

More shots zinged through the air, one of them tugging at McManus's jacket. Ahead of them, one speedy Confederate had managed to make it to the opening before them. He leveled his rifle, expecting the Yankees to surrender, but with lungs bursting and legs and shoulders burning, Lockett and McManus continued directly at him.

As they closed to twenty yards away, Lockett began a desperate, throbbing yell. It was not unlike the rebel yell they had heard all day, but his scream spoke more of blood thirst and complete desperation. All he could see was the opening and the sight of the lone man blocking their path. Knowing that nothing was going to stop them, he continued to yell as they hurtled toward the Rebel.

With a stunned look on his face, the Confederate looked down at his rifle after it misfired, the hammer falling on a dud percussion cap. He began to turn the rifle around like a club, but it was too late. Without breaking stride, McManus lowered a shoulder and ran clean over the man.

They burst out into the meadow like drowning men surfacing for air. Running for all they were worth with their load, they churned across the meadow. Ainsley's blood had drenched Lockett's undershirt, turning the entire right side dark red. It was sickly smelling and warm, but at least Ainsley continued to moan with each step, Lockett thought to himself.

Ahead, they could see Union blue hidden behind the tree line.

They had run the gauntlet and survived, he thought wildly!

Completely winded, they collapsed to their knees just in front of a fresh-faced, clean-shaven captain beneath an unfamiliar regimental banner.

Spotting the officer's sword in Lockett's hand, he mistook Lockett for an officer. "Sir? Are you all right, sir?"

"The Lieut'ant… needs to see… the surgeon… right away…" Lockett gasped out of breath, pointing to Ainsley.

"Of course, sir," the captain said, and four men came forward, sliding a blanket under Ainsley to use as a stretcher.

"And you better… get ready… to hold… this position," Lockett continued between panting breaths, not realizing that the captain had confused him for an officer, "The Rebels are… right behind us…"

"Yes, sir," the captain responded, worriedly looking into the meadow, "The colonel should be back soon. He's still trying to find us some ammunition."

McManus looked around and noticed that their arrival had caused half of the regiment to gather around curiously and gawk at the wild men who had burst from the meadow and wooded hollow beyond.

"Get ammunition?" Lockett questioned sharply.

"Yes, sir," the captain answered, now wondering what rank this imperious, coatless officer held, thinking Lockett must surely be more than a captain to take such an aggressive tone with him.

"Yes, sir," one of the lieutenants added for Lockett's

benefit, "We just arrived, just got off the boat less than an hour ago."

"Hell," one unseen man in the crowd crowed, "We only mustered in last week. This was our first night sleeping on the ground."

My God! Lockett thought, realizing how close they must be to the Landing. The Confederate army is about to burst from the hollow, and we have to stop them with completely green soldiers who have no ammunition!

"Captain," Lockett growled angrily, his frustration from a day's fighting flowing over, giving his voice strength and venom that he did not think that he had. "The Rebels are about to come through that meadow, and we have to stop them! Here! Right God-damned here!"

"But we have no ammunition, sir," the captain said meekly.

"You have bayonets, don't you?" Lockett snarled before he knew what he was saying, "We haven't bled this much today to surrender now!"

"Bayonets!" Lockett heard someone order, and it was echoed down the line.

"Here they come!" cried another voice, spotting the loose butternut skirmish line emerge from the hollow.

The gaggle of soldiers from the fresh regiment was already dispersing into a ragged row.

Lockett clenched the Stuart family sword tightly and glared at the Rebel menace now coming through the meadow. His face was black with powder burns and powder residue. His shirt was drenched in dark red blood. His hair was heavy with sweat and matted to his head. Before James Lockett knew what he was doing, he took two steps to his front and bellowed in a voice that was not his, "Regiment! Show'em your steeeeeel!"

A booming, tremendous "Huzzah!" rose up and echoed across the meadow, and then the regiment broke double time from the woods. With bayonets flashing in the sinking sunlight, they charged across the field.

Stunned, the Confederates in the meadow stopped their progress and began to fire into the haphazardly organized charge.

The fire slowed the men of the new regiment at first, but not Lockett. With Ainsley Stuart's sword held high over his head and his blood-drenched shirt acting as some sort of banner, Lockett was a fearsome sight as he charged to the front. With his legs burning and his mind trapped in blood lust, he did not bother to look behind him to see who was following him. He would attack by himself if he had to now.

Seeing his disregard for the fire, the regiment gathered new momentum and fell upon the Confederates with a clashing of steel and the crack of swung rifles.

Many of the Confederates retreated against this unexpected counterattack, but some remained in the field and battled hand to hand.

Lockett slashed wildly at a butternut coated man, cutting across the man's arm as he attempted to swing his rifle.

All around him, there was a blurring frenzy of swinging rifles and lunging bayonets. So much happened, so fast, it was hard to distinguish color – friend or foe in the melee.

With a cry, he launched himself at a Rebel who was focused on charging another man in blue. With a slash across the back, the man fell, and Lockett ducked instinctively as another Rebel swung his rifle at him, grazing the top of his head. Though his mind was foggy, his instinct knew enough to lash out with the sword as he struggled to maintain his balance, and he felt the tip of the sword penetrate the soft flesh of the man's belly.

Lockett righted himself and was ready to fight on when his foot hit a blood slickened patch of grass. With a flash of astonishment, he felt himself crashing onto his back, noticing just before impact that there was a Rebel officer looming above him, sword raised, ready to drop it on him. Lockett started to futilely roll to his side to avoid the blow when the Rebel's face shriveled in pain and confusion.

Removing his bayonet from the Confederate officer's side, McManus gathered Lockett by the arm.

The Rebels were falling back into the forest, awestruck by the ferocity of the Yankee counterattack. Wisely, Lockett and the regiment did not pursue. Without a foe to fight in the meadow, they gradually made their way back to the tree line having stunned the Confederates and given them second thoughts about advancing.

Wearily, Lockett returned to the tree line. With a mixture of satisfaction and concern, he noticed that Ainsley had been taken away. Beyond them in a gathering of officers, the captain from the regiment motioned towards Lockett, and an extremely irate colonel approached.

"How dare you lead my men on a suicidal charge!" the colonel bellowed, waving a finger at Lockett. "Who are you? I'll have you written up for this, sir! I don't give a damn what rank you are! You killed two of my boys!"

Before Lockett could answer, another colonel on horseback with thick, curly silver hair and an equally gray beard approached. This second colonel reined in his snorting black steed. "Well done, sir!" the second colonel exclaimed, bending down and reaching out for Lockett's hand, "It would be an honor to shake the hand of the man who led such a brave charge! That was exactly the kind of tactic we needed to give us time to form a new defense line!"

The second colonel clearly knew what he was interrupting as he snuck a quick peek at the regimental commander, but the other colonel missed the wry look.

"And who are you?" the first colonel snapped, not recognizing the man or the natural gravitas that he possessed.

"Colonel Webster, General Grant's chief of staff," came the answer in a foreboding voice.

"I see," the first colonel replied slowly in a soft and now acquiescent voice.

"Now, as I'm sure you were just saying, Colonel," Webster continued, "You were about to tell Mr..."

"Lockett, sir," Lockett filled in for him.

"Thank you. Mr. Lockett, here, about how critical and wise that charge was in stopping the Rebel advance."

"Yes, sir. Exactly, sir," the first colonel answered, swallowing his pride.

"Well done, Mr. Lockett," Webster finished, righting

himself in the saddle and pointing to Ainsley's blood all along Lockett's shirt, "I believe you should have that wound looked at immediately."

"It's not mine, sir, but thank you," Lockett answered but at the same time there was a series of thunderous artillery booms, and he wondered if Colonel Webster had even heard him.

"I'd be obliged if you come see me later tonight, Mr. Lockett."

"Yes, sir. Of course, sir."

Colonel Webster rode off.

The regimental colonel then watched Grant's Chief of Staff go and then turned wordlessly on his heel, pointedly ignoring Lockett.

For a moment, Lockett stood alone and puzzled by all of the events.

"They thought you were an officer," McManus chuckled softly, tapping the Stuart family sword and noting that without a coat, Lockett wore no insignia of rank.

Lockett's mind still whirled from the charge and what had just happened. He shook his head to clear it.

"What?" McManus asked, "That Reb musket butt scramble your brains?"

Lockett looked at the darkening sky and listened to the ebbing sound of battle. The day was finally dying out.

"No," he said slowly, "I'm all right… I suppose... Let's go find where they took Ainsley."

Chapter 25

Lockett and McManus leaned back wearily against a tree. The sun had gone down, but the place still rang with the boom of artillery as the two Federal gunboats on the Tennessee River pounded where they guessed the Confederate positions to be, what had been the tents and camps of the Union army at the beginning of the day.

But it wasn't the sound of the cannon that kept their exhausted bodies awake as they leaned back against the tree. They still hadn't found Ainsley Stuart. The sheer number of wounded was shocking. They had walked through endless areas of wounded men. Lying in haphazard clusters near confiscated cabins or large white tents, the moans of the dying were still upon their ears. They would never forget the sights or the smells.

There had been a literal pile of limbs outside the surgeon's tent, six feet high! It was like nothing they had ever imagined. They stared aghast at it for a second before McManus started vomiting in shock. Seconds later, Lockett did likewise. Shakily, they each placed an arm on the other's shoulder to steady each other as they moved on through the disordered rows and clusters of wounded.

Some of the wounded at least had blankets beneath them, but most were simply laid on the ground. Lockett did not know how many they had seen, or even how many clusters they had seen, but he knew that Ainsley was in one of them… somewhere.

The smell of death and dying was still strong in his nostrils, mixing with the heavy smell of gun smoke that he guessed he would never lose now. He tried to concentrate his thoughts elsewhere, but he kept drifting back to the images of the gut shot, the amputees, and the dead.

There were more wounded to search, but neither

Michigander felt up to the task at the moment. They had learned that Ainsley might not even be at Pittsburg Landing anymore. From asking around, they had learned that many of the wounded had already been taken back to Savannah by steamer.

They had also learned about more than just the wounded. They had seen with their own eyes the number of frightened shirkers milling about the Landing. It wasn't hard for them to believe that throughout the day the number of terrified men swelled into the thousands.

They had heard about entire regiments breaking and running away like the 53rd Ohio, and of other regiments making courageous and desperate stands against overwhelming odds all across the battlefield. But every time, these piecemeal defenses had collapsed under the weight of the Confederate juggernaut.

McManus had also heard about how they had fought the entire day without General Lew Wallace's division. Those sorely needed men got "lost" on their six mile march from their camp at Crump's Landing, arriving from that northern point only after darkness had fallen.

Most frightening of all, they had seen how close their last line of defense was to the river. *There was no more ground to give.* They were literally two stone throws away from the dark waters of the Tennessee. There was nowhere else to fall back. This was it.

Both of them knew this army had been beaten today. It seemed that they would be driven back into the river the next morning except for one thing… They had also seen deliverance firsthand. It was the arrival of reinforcements. General Buell's Army of the Ohio was arriving, stepping off steamer after steamer. Each trip brought more fresh troops to the battered Union lines.

"I s'pose I should go see Colonel Webster now," Lockett said in a tired voice with his arms crossed as he shivered without a coat.

"I'll wait here," McManus replied, "Then we'll go look for

Ainsley again."

Lockett waited inside Colonel Webster's tent.

"I'll be with you in a moment, Mr. Lockett," Colonel Webster said without looking up from the papers that covered a second line of desks in his tent.

A first set of tables stood between Lockett and the colonel, and Lockett couldn't help but notice the large map of the area. In dark writing, he read the words "Last Line" next to the jagged dashes that were perilously close to the river. Frowning slightly, he didn't need a map to tell him that. That was perfectly clear to him already.

Colonel Webster scratched out his scrawl on his writing desk as Lockett's eyes scanned the tent. It was different from the glimpses he had seen of Captain Vincent's tent so long ago. Colonel Webster's tent was practical and obviously a place of work. Lit by two lanterns, he could clearly see that the aging, but distinguished looking, colonel had been busy organizing a defense.

Finally turning around and looking up with a calm face, Colonel Webster said, "Thank you for coming, Mr. Lockett. My, that is even more blood on your shirt than I remember."

"Not my blood, sir. This is my lieutenant's blood, sir." His voice was hoarse and harder to hear than usual. Whether it was from all of the gun smoke throughout the day, or the periods of yelling to be heard over the sounds of the battlefield, he wasn't sure, but his voice rasped painfully against his throat with each word.

Webster nodded sympathetically, "You've seen a great deal today, I am sure, Mr. Lockett. What regiment are you with?"

"12th Michigan, sir. Peabody's Brigade."

Webster's face betrayed no emotion, but his voice did. "You *have* seen a lot today, Mr. Lockett."

"Yes, sir. We were with Major Powell first, his patrol in the middle of the night, and then…" The croak of his painful voice trailed off.

Colonel Webster eyed the sword that Lockett still clutched

with one hand. "I take it that the sword was your lieutenant's."

"It is, sir," Lockett answered with some surprise that Webster had guessed as much.

"I didn't think you were an officer," Webster continued, looking down at Lockett's pants and simple, mud-covered leather brogans.

"Sir, I never told anyone that I was an officer..."

"You just let them assume you were."

"Well, I suppose, sir. But it didn't really occur to me until later that this is what they thought. I just wanted to stop the Rebels right there. I'm just a sergeant, sir."

"Indeed. In either case, they followed you." Webster cracked a small, tired smile. "Good thing they didn't recognize your trousers as an enlisted man's like I did."

Lockett blinked in surprise.

"That charge was exactly what was needed at the time, Sergeant Lockett. It broke the Rebels' momentum, gave them a reason to think a little bit about doing it again, which was exactly what we needed. Time. It makes no difference to me, Sergeant Lockett, who led the damn charge, only that it was made. It was the right decision at the right time."

"Yes, sir," he answered with some confusion.

"We have too many officers who got their positions because of who they know, not what they know. Too many officers who are not leaders of men. *You* are obviously a leader of men, Lockett." Webster stopped and looked him over from head to toe. The young sergeant had a muted confidence with a quiet steely-eyed look, Webster thought to himself. Even so, the young sergeant appeared to be a generally unassuming man, not unlike General Grant himself. "This army needs men like you, Lockett. In two minutes, you convinced a group of strangers to follow you in a bayonet charge without ammunition. You led without looking back to see if they were there. That's the kind of leader General Grant wants."

Lockett blinked again, unaccustomed to such praise and unsure what it all meant. "Sir, I don't mean to contradict you, but I'm just a farmer."

"So was General Grant," Webster shot back, "And not a very good one at that. Why, before the rebellion started, he even tried his hand as an ordinary shopkeeper in Galena, Illinois but look at him now. You're his type of man, Lockett."

Webster paused with a peculiar smile on his face, "How would you like to be Lieutenant Lockett instead of Sergeant Lockett? Sam Grant doesn't care where you came from if you can lead and fight like that."

Lockett's eyes widened. "Lieutenant? You can do that?" he managed.

"Hell, I can do damn well anything I please, as long as General Grant agrees, and I'm sure he'll agree to this."

A lieutenant! Lockett thought to himself.

"This battle is not over yet, Lockett. With Buell's men and that laggard Lew Wallace finally here, we can turn the tables on the Rebels tomorrow. What I need you for is some of these bits and pieces. We have a number of broken units that could be put together as reserves, and I could use a few officers to lead them. What do you say, Lockett, like to help lead one of these fragments? Are you up to the challenge?"

"Yes, sir."

"Excellent." Webster scratched out some orders at his writing desk. "Give this to the quartermaster for a new lieutenant's uniform and report back here before dawn to Lieutenant Colonel Calliford."

"Yes, sir," Lockett saluted. He was about to leave when the tent flap opened and a short, bearded man with observant eyes and a rumpled general's uniform limped painfully into the light.

"General Grant," Webster said, rising to his feet and saluting.

"Colonel," Grant returned, curiously eye-balling Lockett and the dried blood that covered his clothes while Lockett stood at attention.

"This is the Lieutenant Lockett who led that charge I mentioned earlier. He was just on his way out."

"Well done, *Lieutenant*," General Grant said with a knowing smile.

"Thank you, sir," Lockett responded.

General Grant returned his salute and dismissed him.

Lockett wore the new lieutenant's uniform with a new scabbard belt for the Stuart family sword and carried two rubber gum blankets under his arm that he had coerced the quartermaster into giving him. Colonel Webster's signature went a long way he had discovered.

Still stunned by the dramatic turn of events, he slowly walked from the quartermasters. He was exhausted yet elated. He was an officer? He was an officer!

In the lightless night, he had more than once tripped over a man, alive but tired. Men were sprawled wherever they could behind the lines. Lockett observed the steamers bringing regiment after regiment. They jostled their way through the shirkers who crowded the landing, threatening those they needed to in order to clear a path and stay off the boats.

Even further away from the Landing, Lockett noticed more troops tromping in the dark, stepping many times on men asleep on the ground in the darkness. Colonel Webster had not been exaggerating, Lockett concluded. There were thousands of newcomers who had joined them and more coming.

In the dark, with his mind completely somewhere else, he did not see the man crossing his path, and they bumped into each other, although neither man fell. The other man snapped around and glared at Lockett, "How dare you..." he began before his angry face melted into one of disbelief and then anger again. He leaned in close in the dark to make sure that his eyes did not deceive him. "You! What are you doing here, Private Lockett?"

Lockett immediately recognized the voice and felt himself straighten up. A scowl burned across his face. With a clenched jaw, he looked squarely into the eyes of Lieutenant Orrin Long.

"I asked you a question, Private Lockett," Orrin Long sputtered.

Lockett did not answer and instead studied his old nemesis's uniform. Was he another cowardly shirker milling about the Landing?

"Where are the sharpshooters?" Lockett asked with an edge to his voice instead of answering Long's question.

"We were separated. I don't know," Orrin Long replied hurriedly, bending closer again in the dark to examine Lockett's new uniform.

"An officer?" Long said aghast, "Impersonating an officer! You can be shot for that! Why, you should be hung just for returning to the Army at all!"

Something inside of Lockett snapped at that moment, and he reached out with both hands and grabbed Orrin Long by the neck. His hands dug into the soft flesh around the man's windpipe. Orrin Long's arrogant eyes bulged, and he gasped for air.

"You coward!" Lockett snarled menacingly, "You abandoned your men again, just like at Hallsville! I know you must have! And you threaten me, you murderer?" Lockett squeezed even tighter. He could see the whites of Orrin Long's eyes bulge out further. "I should kill you now!" he said through his fury.

Orrin Long struggled futilely for breath, his hands clawing weakly at Lockett's wrists.

"You make me sick!" With a final squeeze, he released his grip and threw Long into the mud. Without another word, Lockett gathered the gum blankets off the ground and turned on his heel, heading off into the black night. Orrin Long sat on the ground gasping, wordlessly rubbing his bruised neck.

Lockett had barely composed himself by the time he found McManus sitting under the same tree.

McManus took Lockett's proffered hand up and leaned in closely in the dark to study his friend and the new uniform that he wore.

"They made you an officer. Is that a lieutenant's uniform?"

Lockett stood in front of his old friend, suddenly at a loss for words.

"Daniel is ne'er going to believe this," McManus remarked, clapping him on the shoulder. "C'mon, I found another batch of wounded. Maybe Ainsley is there."

They made their way through the rows of wounded lying in a field beyond a weather worn cabin and billowing white surgical tent. Illuminated from the inside by lanterns, Lockett could see the ghastly silhouettes of a surgeon sawing something. The delirious cries of pain echoed in the night air, and he quickly lowered his eyes. If it wasn't for the need to find Ainsley, he would have surely turned around and fled in the other direction. That sight and the sounds were worse than facing a Confederate battle line.

Slowly, the two of them walked through the chaotic clusters of men lying on the bare ground. It was difficult to make out faces in the dark and walking was treacherous with randomly laid men sprawled around. More than once, he had lightly stepped on an errant limb, although depressingly, cries of pain came infrequently from the man's lips.

The darkness hid the contorted, dirty, sweat-caked faces of the dying and the dead.

There were men everywhere – without arms and legs, men with head wounds, and others with chest wounds. The smell of blood and death hung heavy on the air. It was impossible to believe that they were in an open air pasture and not trapped inside with the odors, such was the strength of the smells.

After what seemed like an eternity, McManus grabbed him, pulling him to where he had found Ainsley Stuart.

Ainsley was lucky. He still laid on the same blanket that the men from the regiment had transported him on. Dried blood from his wound covered the bottom quarter of the blanket. He was still alive, but only just barely. Unconscious and unresponsive, the only clue that Ainsley had been attended to was that a bandage had replaced Lockett's coat around Ainsley's stump. Between a slit in the bandages, they could make out the medicinal plaster that coated the end of the limb.

They knelt close to their friend. His shallow breathing gave them little reason for optimism.

"He's still out," a weak, hoarse voice told them.

Glancing over, Lockett saw a one-armed lieutenant

watching them. The man twisted weakly on his blanket next to Ainsley. He was small and scrawny, and despite the weakened voice, there was still a chirp of energy from the man.

"The Reb shell did most of the doc's work," the man croaked hoarsely, "There wasn't much more for him that they could do."

"Thank you," Lockett said softly, not knowing what else to say.

"He hasn't been awake since I came to, Lieutenant..."

"Lockett," he answered, "How about you, sir? Anything I can do for you?"

"Nothing that can be done," the man laughed bitterly, "John Wesley Powell, at your..." he coughed roughly, "...service." Lieutenant Powell rubbed his scrawny jaw with his remaining hand and added, "On second thought, some water would be greatly appreciated."

McManus was already uncorking his canteen before the man had even finished the sentence and helped hold the container while the man drained the remaining half of the canteen, spilling a good section of it across his chin. When he finished, he looked up with a tired smile, "Didn't realize how thirsty I was."

Lockett nodded and focused his attention back on Ainsley.

"I'll keep an eye on your lieutenant as best I can," John Wesley Powell added.

"I would appreciate that," Lockett answered, "I'll be here a bit longer, but soon I suppose I'll have some more Rebels to attend to."

McManus held out his hand and felt the first droplets of rain. "God save all," he whispered dejectedly, "On top of all else..."

Lockett spread out one of the rubber gum blankets across Ainsley. "How about some protection from the rain?" he asked, already spreading the second gum blanket across John Wesley Powell.

"Thank you mightily, sir," Powell said as the clouds opened up and torrents of rain descended on Pittsburg Landing.

Lockett eyed the pasture and the wounded helplessly

soaking in the rainstorm.

John Wesley Powell spoke up one last time for the night. In a weak voice, he said, "I'm from Illinois, Lieutenant Lockett. Where do boys who stick together like you three come from?"

Lockett pulled his hat lower over his eyes. "We're Michigan boys."

* * *

Matthew Bauer and the rest of the sharpshooters wandered in the trees just east of Chambers field, far north of where their camp had been the night before. Despite their sacrifices, they had failed to hold the Confederates and had been pushed north with the rest of Hurlbut's and McArthur's men throughout the day.

While their losses were not as heavy as some, like the utter destruction of Prentiss's Division, the sharpshooters were at half of the strength they had left Kalamazoo with. Disease, losses at Hallsville, and especially today's battles had taken a heavy toll on the company.

Pete O'Shea, Gus Jeltema, and many others were now gone, and they had carried Luke back to the surgeon, his head creased by a Rebel Minié ball. A dozen or so Kalamazoo Sharpshooters were also missing, due mainly to desertion, Orrin Long among them. The captain's nephew had disappeared after the Peach Orchard, and no one had seen him since.

As Matthew Bauer shivered in the pouring rain, he listened to the gunboats keep up their continual fire. He found it impossible to sleep despite the exhaustion that racked his body. His fatigued mind drifted in and out, always with thoughts that came back to wondering about James and Patrick. Had they escaped? He heard that a few of Prentiss's men had shot their way out of the trap. Were James and Patrick among them, or were they like the Dobbins twins, prisoners? Or were they lying like so many others, face down in the muddy fields?

The rain kept on, and he knew he should get some sleep because there would be more fighting tomorrow. Lew

Wallace's men had finally arrived and filled in on the right. The fresh troops probably meant a counterattack in the morning.

But sleep would not come. Like many others on both sides, Matthew Bauer spent a sleepless night wandering among the trees and heavy raindrops.

* * *

In the cloudy, moonless gloom of well past midnight, John and Lyman Cameron huddled in the captured Yankee tent. Like all but the pickets, they had trudged back with the others from the front line to the Yankee encampment that they had captured in the morning.

They knew that they had won a great victory. The sheer distance that they had pushed back the Yankees made that clear in their minds, even as they pondered the incredible cost that it had come with. There were few familiar faces left in General Cleburne's battered command. They hoped it was just because they were hopelessly intermixed with other Confederate brigades, but in their hearts, both brothers knew that they would never see many of those familiar faces again.

They were utterly exhausted, but sleep would not come.

John said it was because of the rain. Shortly after midnight a drenching downpour had commenced. Even though they were under a tent, there were so many holes in the canvas from the morning's gunfight that the tent offered scant protection against the deluge.

Lyman said that the reason for their sleeplessness was not the rain but because of the Yankee gunboats. Their massive guns had been firing since dusk. It was blind fire, from the river over the trees, into the areas well beyond, but the incessant sound of those big guns was enough to keep them awake, according to Lyman.

In truth, he wasn't sure if it was the sound alone. Even though the shots were fired blindly and randomly, the sound and size of their explosions were so much more than a normal artillery piece. On occasion, the shells found some poor, luckless souls. Earlier, one had landed square on the tent where some Alabamians huddled. One moment they were there, then the next there was nothing but a shallow, smoking crater.

Even the dead were not spared the naval wrath. On their hike back to the tents, the brothers had come across a swath of land that was littered with corpses, some even in neat rows. One of those rows had been obliterated by a gunboat shell. None of the living were harmed, but the shell sent a shower of body parts from the dead in all directions.

But at least the main battle was over, both brothers thought wearily to themselves. Come morning, they would finish off the defeated Yankees. That was the only comfort to the terrible losses that they had incurred.

The sound of horses stirred them from their thoughts, and upon poking their heads out of the tent, they were surprised to learn that General Cleburne himself was in the tent across from them.

A lantern from inside the tent came on, illuminating General Cleburne. The normally dapper young Irishman was muddy, wet, and worn out. If the general looked like that, both brothers could hardly imagine how bad they themselves must have looked. The only thing positive about their appearance was that at least they had gorged themselves on the food that the Yankees had left behind, which helped with their hollow-eyed stares.

"Forrest, that you?" General Cleburne asked, coming to the front of the tent. He accidentally touched the brim of the tent opening, causing a pool of water that had collected in the overhang to dump down on his head. "I'd curse, but I'm too tired to," he grimaced, wiping the water from his face.

Forrest ignored that and asked instead, "Where's headquarters, Cleburne? I need to get there right away."

"I'm not sure where the hell this tent is, never mind where headquarters is, Forrest. Now, what is all this about?"

"I've been sending scouts along the river to keep tabs on the Yankees and the Landing. They're reinforcing, heavily. Buell must have arrived!"

"That is the same thing that that Yankee General Prentiss that we captured claimed to Beauregard. He said that Buell had arrived, and they'd turn the tables on us in the morning. Beauregard laughed it off, of course. He said it was pure bluster and then went on a diatribe to Prentiss about how the North will never conquer the Confederacy."

"Never mind Beauregard. What did General Johnston say?"

"You didn't hear?" Cleburne asked with surprise, looking more alert now, "Johnston is dead. Shot when he went up to the front line to lead a charge this afternoon. Shot in the back of the knee, and it bled down into his boot. When he fell from the saddle, they couldn't find the wound at first. Bled to death." Cleburne shook his head miserably.

"Beauregard is in charge?" Forrest asked with some concern, but he knew the answer if Johnston was gone.

Another gunboat shell landed four hundred yards away with a momentary flash of light that startled his horse, but the consummate horseman steadied his mount and put his attention back on Cleburne. "Look, I need to find headquarters. If the enemy comes on us in the morning, we'll be whipped like hell."

"I'd try that direction," Cleburne pointed to the east. "That is where they were a few hours ago."

And Forrest rode off to warn them.

Chapter 26

April 7, 1862 (Monday)

Again, the crack-crack of skirmishing rifles resounded, but this time it was different for Matthew Bauer and the rest of the sharpshooters who made up the skirmishing line in front of Lauman's Brigade. Today was a new day, and with the remaining units of Sherman's and McClernand's divisions on either side, they found themselves in the vanguard of the first organized Union counterattack of the battle.

Beyond Sherman, Lew Wallace's fresh division anchored the right flank and also marched on the small creek of Tilghman's Branch.

To the east, Buell's Army of the Ohio began to march through the ground that the Confederates had abandoned during the night.

Startled Confederate pickets fired solitary shots before fleeing in the face of the crushing force. The battle that they thought they had won had suddenly turned against them. Even in the early morning light, the Rebels could tell the size of the behemoth bearing down upon them.

North of the sharpshooters, the sound of Union musketry drew closer at first, and then farther away, as Wallace's fresh men drove the Confederates from Jones field and outdistanced the tired survivors of April 6.

Behind the sharpshooters, the battle line of blue tried to ignore the stiffness in their bones and the heaviness of their drenched uniforms. The sun was just over the horizon. A new day, a new battle, a new outcome.

But they were tired, and the advance was slow and ponderous. Still, the sheer size of their firepower began to overwhelm the outnumbered Rebels, and slowly, ever so slowly, Lauman's Brigade neared the creek.

Then with a blink of amazement and dejection, Bauer saw a

Rebel line of battle counterattack to their right, ready to re-cross the Tilghman Branch and drive Lew Wallace's and Sherman's men back.

George VanderJagt stood next to him and watched in surprise also but without dejection. Rather, there seemed a serious look of approval on his face. "We have the brave fools this time," the old soldier commented, pulling on his dirty beard.

"What?" Bauer asked.

"Today, we'r'll better organized. They cain't collapse a line with that charge. We'll enfilade them."

"What?"

"We'll turn and catch'em in a crossfire, boy."

A minute later, Lauman's Brigade received the order just as VanderJagt predicted. Before he knew it, Bauer was looking down the length of the Confederate line. He took aim at the Confederate flank with the rest of the Yankee soldiers. Just as they had received at Hallsville, now they were getting the opportunity to enfilade the enemy flank. The edges of the enemy line crumbled. More and more Rebels looked to their right in surprise to see fallen comrades and advancing Yankees.

Bravely, the Confederate attack continued. Whether through courage or ignorance, the Confederates disregarded the mounting losses on their right side and continued to plow directly into Wallace's and Sherman's line where they were already receiving brutal fire.

Bauer was beginning to wonder what it would take to stop these Rebels. Perhaps, James had been right after all, these Rebels would fight with an unstoppable vengeance to protect their homes. But finally, the Rebel line began to shudder to a disjointed stop. Human endurance could no longer face such fire, and with a stubborn reluctance, the Southerners began to fall back, firing as they went. Pride refused to allow most to hurry back, and many paid a price for that pride.

The Union advance continued, and they resumed their heavy-footed march through the trees. Holding position in the line was difficult because one had to step around trees and other obstacles, but the line always moved forward. It was surprisingly difficult to keep up at times.

Again, they stepped over and on the bodies of fallen Rebels. Before yesterday, Bauer would have tried to avoid stepping on the bodies, both Yankee and Rebel alike, but now it was too common. If a body happened to be laying in his stride, he would step on it, just as he would a fallen tree.

Sometimes the body would stir ever so slightly but not usually. This time, however, the body did more than stir.

With only a quick glance down, Bauer noticed the shabbily dressed Rebel in simple trousers held up by worn suspenders. The man, who had been playing possum, yelped and leapt up to his feet, starting to take off but not sure in which direction to head.

All of the commotion caused Matthew Bauer to trip, but he got up immediately.

The Rebel seemed to dance in place, unsure what to do now. Bauer stared at the man while the sporadic sounds of battle echoed ahead of them as the battle lines clashed again.

The Rebel held his muddied hands in front of him as Bauer pointed the rifle at him. "Awl-right, Yank," his frightened voice cried, and Bauer noticed beneath the dirt and grime that the Rebel was a boy even younger than himself.

"You there!" one of Lauman's officers shouted, trotting back, "What are you doing back here?"

"I have a Rebel prisoner, sir," Bauer said in a slightly stunned voice.

"I see. Well, take him back. There's a detachment of Sherman's Buckeyes taking back other prisoners. Why don't you catch up to them and then hurry back."

"Yes, sir," he answered, motioning the Rebel back through the woods with his rifle.

* * *

Lieutenant James Lockett marched forward with his small, motley company under the command of Captain McGee, a Chicagoan whose previous company had been mostly captured north of the sunken road. With four other remnant companies, they made up part of the reserve for Buell's advancing division.

They were Hawkeyes, Hoosiers, Buckeyes, Minnesotans, Wisconsinites, and Michiganders. For once, he did not observe any boastful rhetoric among the men. This group was too tired from the long night and too dejected from the previous day. Despite their varied backgrounds, they did have one thing in common, they all had tasted bitter, bitter defeat one way or the other yesterday. Some like Sergeant Milton Bosworth of the 53rd Ohio had tasted it in particularly harsh fashion.

"We had them in that field," Bosworth had related to him earlier in the morning, "More'n half of them was already down on that field when our colonel cried out, 'Retreat! Retreat, save yourselves!' We had them, Lieutenant Lockett! There was no need to retreat!"

When Bosworth had said that to him, Lockett sensed that Lockett himself was now under the sergeant's scrutiny. Left unsaid was Milton Bosworth's true question, was this officer like the colonel of the 53rd?

They marched four abreast past the Dill Branch and lingered within sight of Lauman's old camp in Cloud Field. McManus made eye contact with Lockett but said nothing. They knew exactly what the other was thinking. How had the sharpshooters fared yesterday? Luke? Matthew? VanderJagt and the rest?

Well ahead of them, out of eyesight, there was firing where Hazen's Brigade led the march through the ground that the Confederates had withdrawn from during the night. The firing continued for another hour, but the motley reserves held their place. Some rested their weary bodies, laying down in the mud, or sitting on fallen trees. And they waited… and waited. For some, it was an uneasy time, and they were not anxious to rejoin the battle that they had run from a day earlier. But for many, they wanted a chance for redemption after yesterday's failures. They didn't want to be known as men who had skedaddled.

Patrick McManus sat silently, listening to the echoing gunfire, staring off in the general direction of the dense thicket around the sunken road.

Lockett conferred with Lieutenant Colonel Calliford, and as McManus watched the exchange, he was surprised at how normal it seemed to have James as an officer.

"If they're just gonna hold us in reserve all day..." Milton Bosworth groused.

"You'll what?" McManus said with a smirk. The sergeant from Ohio was a non-stop talker. That much he had learned already.

"I don't know... but I'll be mad as a hornet."

"We'll be in reserve all day," another 53rd Ohioan chipped in, "They think we're a bunch of yella-tailed cowards after yesterday."

"That's why we need another chance!" Bosworth replied stubbornly.

"We're not all 53rd Ohio here," one of the men remarked edgily, "And they don't raise no cowards in Wisconsin."

Milton Bosworth jumped to his feet, only to be grabbed around the collar by Lockett, which was probably fortunate for Bosworth since the Wisconsin man was massive and obviously eager to take out his frustration on someone.

"No one calls me a coward," Bosworth replied, still straining against Lockett's grasp but not very hard. Bosworth was not a small man either. With his squat neck, broad back, and hunched shoulders, he could easily have pulled free.

"I left half my friends on the field yesterday! You think I'm worried about you, Buckeye?" the Wisconsin man snapped.

"Shut your trap, both of you," Lockett said evenly. The only two names he knew were Patrick's and Milton Bosworth, and at this point, he had no intent of learning more. To Bosworth, he added, "You're a sergeant, so act like it. Get the men together. We're moving out."

On the double quick, they marched through Cloud Field and then Wicker Field, where the smell of gunpowder still hung over the new corpses from this morning's fights.

The sense of déjà vu chilled Lockett. It seemed impossible, but they were headed back through the woods to the sunken road. As they hastened to join up with Hazen's and Smith's brigades, the sound of Confederate cannon filled the air. Nearby, another Union brigade attacked south across the cotton field near the peach orchard.

Though the roles were reversed, the outcome was still the same as Confederate muskets and cannon shattered the charge and sent the Yankees backwards.

But unaware that the charge had been foiled, Hazen's and Smith's Federals moved forward in two lines, coincidentally sweeping into the area where the Confederates were moving in for a counterattack, protected by a company of Louisiana artillery.

Lockett and the rest of the reserves rushed to catch up to the main body. In the tangle of the thick woods, they accidentally veered south and suddenly found themselves in the front, instead of the rear.

With a moment of confusion, they broke from the woods and found themselves face to face with the Confederate artillery.

The Rebels were faced to the northeast, ready to defend against an attack from the main body. They had no idea that they were now squarely in the sights of Calliford's reserves.

Lieutenant Colonel Calliford trotted up to the lead company, curious what the hold up was.

"We seem to be the van, sir," Lockett said drily.

"So we are, Lockett," Calliford replied, "We best get out of column and into line of battle then."

Astonished that the Confederates had yet to realize their presence, the four companies of reserves spread out in a small line of battle. With a simple nod from Calliford, they surged forward into Davis's wheat field, toward the unsuspecting cannon. Lockett wished that he still had his rifle, but he had left it behind when they carried Ainsley away yesterday. Now, all he had was a borrowed Army revolver from John Wesley Powell and Ainsley Stuart's sword.

Startled at the sudden appearance, the Louisiana battery began to wheel their weapons around to meet the new threat.

"Fire!" The order came, and the Yankees emptied their

weapons as they advanced. The hail of Minié balls cut down a number of Louisianans around their cannon.

"Reload and advance! Independent fire! Independent fire!"

Some of the men stopped to reload, but most hurried forward, not bothering to load again. They had decided that it was better to be in amongst the cannon rather than in front of them.

Even so, the Louisianans were still able to wheel some cannon around, and one spouted a deadly hail of canister, disintegrated the entire left side of the Union charge, killing Captain McGee.

"Capture the guns!" someone cried out.

Other than capturing a regiment's colors, the capture of cannon was the biggest prize of all. And they were there for the taking, right in front of them! These men who had tasted nothing but defeat the day before launched themselves forward like madmen.

Another blast of canister shredded three Minnesotans as it fired just yards away from them, but it was too little, too late as the Union troops swarmed over the Louisiana battery.

In the blur of motion, smoke, and sound, Lockett was vaguely aware of the Union soldier next to him dropping to his knees. Looking up to see the cause, he spied a cannoneer with a smoking pistol, Lockett raised his revolver and fired one for the first time in his life. The recoil snapped his wrist upward and the shot flew wide and high.

The cannoneer hurriedly bent his revolver in half and tried to quickly reload.

Lockett did not hesitate. He ran forward in a full sprint, worthlessly firing the revolver as he went. None of the shots hit the Rebel, and with the Stuart family sword in his left hand, he dove madly on top of the man just before he could finish reloading.

All around him, the field had turned into another wild melee of hand-to-hand fighting. Shots went off at point blank range and rifle butts clashed with long bowie knives. But Lockett did not hear or notice any of it at that moment as he struggled with the artillery man in the mud. Feeling the Rebel go limp after he had smashed the butt of the pistol into the man's temple, he struggled to his knees and looked up.

Milton Bosworth was about to drop the butt of his rifle down onto a man's head, and McManus too was fighting like a wild man. Holding his Dimick extended like a club, he looked for another target. At his feet already were two fancifully dressed Louisianans.

Lockett raised his pistol again and realized it was empty.

He had lost track of time when he heard a new cry and from the corner of his eye, he saw two Rebel infantry regiments rushing forward to assist the overwhelmed artillery. Shots began to whip in among them, thudding against flesh, zinging away from cannon barrels. Worse yet, Lockett knew they were exposed. There was no reserve coming to help them hold this position. They were supposed to be the reserve after all!

Even if they could finish capturing the guns, they would never be able to hold them. With no choice, Lieutenant Colonel Calliford gave the order to fall back.

Milton Bosworth fired once more and then looked at Lockett. The words of his flapping mouth were drowned out in the sounds of battle, but Lockett knew well enough what was said. They were retreating again.

* * *

On the right flank, Grant's army had progressed. By mid-afternoon, they were again in control of McClernand's old camp and nearly in possession of Sherman's.

It took Matthew Bauer most of the day to catch up to the sharpshooters, but it was not the distance that slowed his rendezvous. It was the wounded. As he made his way across the fields of battle, fallen Rebels and Federals alike littered the ground. Some were dead, but many were wounded and primarily unattended. He had stopped to help the first two, eventually leaving his canteen with the second, but the sheer number was overwhelming.

He saw men on the ground, collapsed behind fence rows,

behind trees, anywhere that an eye could see.

Bauer found himself ashamed by the naïveté of his early boastful words. They had left Kalamazoo so certain of their ability to end the war, never realizing how insignificant they were. On this one pasture alone, there were more dead than there had ever been Kalamazoo Sharpshooters – three times over.

James had been right. This was no great adventure full of glory and victory. It was a test of stamina. Who could take more bitterness? Who could ignore the destruction around them and continue on with a blind eye?

How many men had the sharpshooters lost? Was Luke among them now? Had George VanderJagt, Sam Moss, or any of the other sharpshooters he had grown so close to been killed today? And what of James and Patrick?

His feet grudgingly obeyed his mind. He was tired, more tired than he had ever imagined possible. The physical was bad enough, but it was the mental and emotional exhaustion that caused his shakes and made his feet feel numb as he stumbled through the woods. Eventually, he had to pause and place both hands on the trunk of a large tree to steady himself.

He couldn't help but notice that this oak, so far behind the lines of fighting, was spared the nicks and gouges from the Minié and musket balls that so many other oaks bore across this blood-soaked part of Tennessee. He clutched the tree with extra intensity. This tree was firm; some of the others across the battlefield had been whittled by half their width from the numerous shots as various soldiers had hid behind them for protection.

He hunched his shoulders at the remembrances and tried to hold back the retching.

When they had left Kalamazoo, he expected some to die, but nothing like what he had seen over the past twenty-four hours. The scale was appalling and unimaginable. Entire towns, many towns, had had their entire male population wiped out. Even the towns who had menfolk survive would never be the same.

There had been all manners of deaths. Some were killed with hardly a mark or never uttering a sound. Others had shrieked like demons in agony, and others yet turned into such offal that they didn't seem human anymore.

It took many minutes to gather himself. To go back to the sharpshooters and experience more was insanity, but at the same time, the forest and its immediate, solitary quiet was unsettling, like something was lying in wait for him.

He needed to get back to the others, and he forced himself forward, resuming his stealthy walk through the woods.

He wasn't sure how long he moved like a wraith through the trees. His senses were warped now, but he could tell that there had been a small fight in this stretch of the woods – a few gouges in the trees and some blackened wadding from paper cartridges on the ground, although no bodies.

He noticed these things, but he did not slow. All was still quiet for a few more minutes when he heard something in the woods up ahead of him.

It was a slight rustle. Perhaps a small animal? That seemed unlikely now. The sounds of fighting had driven all of the animals from the forest.

He knew that the Confederates had long since departed from this stretch of woods, so he thought about calling out.

But he held back. Could it be some sort of deserter? Those vultures could be desperate, unhinged men, he reminded himself. They were probably murdering the wounded where they lay so that they could empty the unfortunates' pockets.

The noise had stopped as he slowed. While it probably was not a small animal, perhaps it was a literal vulture that had flown down to investigate one of the plentiful meals?

Whatever it was had moved on, and he had just started to quicken his pace when it started again, this time with the huff of exertion.

The forest was thick here, like in many parts of Pittsburg Landing. He could only see about thirty feet in front of him. Moving with very conscious stealth now, he slowly picked his way through the brush.

To his surprise, he had come upon a Rebel trying to drag a

body through the woods. He was clearly tired and had both arms wrapped around the torso of the body. The body was covered in blood and the head lolled limply as it was dragged over a tree root. The body's heels made two shallow furrows in the mud as he was dragged along.

Though Bauer had not made a sound, the Rebel dragging the body suddenly looked up, right at him. His hand darted into the belt of the body that he dragged, yanking free a pistol that was tucked in the dead man's belt.

Bauer instinctively raised his rifle also, and both men pointed their guns at the other, fingers on the triggers.

But each held back, more on instinct than recognition.

They looked each other in the face, each muddied, powder burned, and blackened so that they were hardly recognizable. Their weapons did not waver, but neither did they fire.

"I know you," Bauer managed as the familiarity of the face dawned on him. He then looked down at the face of the bloody Rebel body, recognizing him also. "Ivy's brother-in-law?"

"He's dead," Lyman Cameron answered bitterly. "Killed by you Yankees."

Bauer nodded, though his mind was slow to register the words.

They stood there for a long, quiet moment, weapons still aimed at the other.

"What are you doing?" Bauer finally asked.

"Taking him home for a proper burial. I ain't gonna leave him here in the woods for the wolves and the vultures. He'll be buried where his family can find him someday."

Bauer stared blankly at the younger Cameron brother before answering, "You'll never make it. You're a mile or so behind the lines now, not to mention on the wrong side of the line."

"I'll make it."

"You don't have the strength left to carry him that far. I can see that."

"Not much choice," Lyman Cameron snapped, brandishing the pistol for emphasis. "And I ain't gonna be a prisoner rottin' in a Yankee jail either!"

Again, there was a long pause with the weapons pointed at the other. Finally, Bauer lowered his rifle to Lyman Cameron's surprise.

"Leave him," Bauer said gently.

"I tol't you..."

But Bauer waved his empty hand, "I'll see that he's buried, and somehow, I'll let Ivy know where."

Lyman Cameron stared in shock at him, "And me?"

"You just go and Godspeed to you. Hope you make it, but it seems unlikely, even without your brother's body, but at least there is a chance for you then. There's been enough killing."

"Enough for ten lifetimes," Lyman Cameron agreed, lowering the pistol. "Except, this war ain't over. You know that, right, Yankee?"

"I know," Bauer answered wearily, "I know. I just can't do more. I can't. Not today."

"You're jus' gonna let me walk away from here, and you promise a proper burial for John?"

"I do."

"If it weren't for what I saw in Missouri, I wouldn't believe you... But... I do believe you."

Lyman Cameron tucked the pistol into his waist and dropped to a knee. One hand snatched the hat from his head, and he placed the other on his brother's bloody chest. Closing his eyes, he muttered an inaudible prayer.

Then he stood up and gave a final nod to Bauer, and with that, Lyman Cameron left.

Matthew Bauer sat heavily on the ground next to the body of John Cameron, acutely aware of the promise he made.

He had no regrets.

Chapter 27

Lockett and the rest of the reserve company waited for the next set of orders. They were "his" company now. Captain McGee was dead, but Lockett spent no time reflecting on that. Instead, his eyes were glued to the sunken road that lay ahead of them. They were at a different section of it than he had defended the day before, but he knew exactly where he was.

The bodies of dead Federals still lay where they had fallen. He guessed that these had been cut down the day before. His eyes skirted down the narrow trail, curving around the bend to where he guessed that he, Patrick, and Ainsley had so steadfastly fought the day before. He contemplated wandering down there but shook the thought from his head.

They were in reserve of Crittenden's division now with a number of other piecemeal units. And this was *his* company now, his responsibility. He needed to focus on his duty.

He looked over at Patrick and was not surprised to see his old friend similarly subdued, listening to Milton Bosworth chatter on. The Buckeye did not seem the least bit fazed that Patrick was only paying him scant attention.

Ahead of them, they could still hear skirmishing as Crittenden's men assessed how stiff the Rebel resistance was across the Purdy Road.

Not far beyond that road was the field where they had camped with Peabody's Brigade. It seemed so long ago now. Even retreating across that road and through the field seemed like ages ago.

I am so, so tired, he thought wearily.

It was nearly two o'clock when Lieutenant Colonel Calliford received word to move the rag-tag group forward to reinforce Crittenden.

"We'll be making an assault for certain," one of the Iowans commented to no one in particular as they moved off through the thicket. They aimed for the Corinth Road, which would take them south to Crittenden's line, but the short cut did not materialize as they struggled through the tough thicket that was littered with dead Rebels.

Lockett was shocked at the carnage his defense of the sunken road had wrought. He knew they had withstood at least ten separate charges, and he had seen the dead Federals near the sunken road, but he was still not prepared for the wretched sight of hundreds upon hundreds of dead Confederates, lying at every conceivable angle in the thicket.

All ordinary conversation stopped as they marched through.

Ahead, he struggled not to step on one of the dead as they passed through a particular line of fallen Southerners who must have been cut down in one devastating volley, like scythed grain. They were neatly in line next to each other, a grotesque patchwork carpet.

"Good God!" Milton Bosworth mumbled.

Lockett could not help but look at some of the unseeing faces that stared back at him. What courage drove men to continue over and over again, over the very top of so many of their comrades?

So many men... Twisted, contorted, trapped, as if the thicket itself had reached out and snared them.

Minutes later, they paused upon exiting the thicket. Ostensibly, this was to reorganize since so many men had become separated in the dense woods, but to Lockett and many others, it was needed just to collect their composure.

He leaned against a tree with a vacant stare as he looked at the area they had just come through. McManus stood next to him, and for many minutes neither said a word.

Eventually, McManus broke the spell. "What are you thinking about, James?" he asked in a hushed voice.

Usually, McManus knew exactly what he was thinking, Lockett reflected. He gave the red head a wry look. His answer would be confounding. He was sure of that.

Finally, he answered, "Honestly, I was thinking about Ivy Munroe."

"Ivy Munroe? The girl from Missouri that Matthew was

sweet on?"

Lockett nodded sadly. "Something she said just kept going in my head as I looked at those faces, all those dead Rebs in there."

"What was that?"

"It was when Matthew and I were watching her family in the barn that first night. She scolded us, said that we weren't any different from them – that we were the same. And looking at those bodies in there, it's even more true now than it was the day she said it – *'you ain't no different than us'*."

"You ain't no different than us," McManus repeated, "You ain't no different than us."

* * *

Finally, they reached the Purdy Road and fell in line with the rest of Crittenden's men.

The Rebels had formed at the edge of the woods that blocked Peabody's old camp from view. If the Yankees wanted it back, they would have to cross the open space of Barnes Field.

Confederate artillery began to shell the trees where Crittenden's men were forming up. To many who looked across that open expanse, it looked like ten miles.

How many times could he face death like this and still be breathing in the next hour, Lockett wondered more out of curiosity than anxiety. He felt strangely alone, like he wasn't even here, even as a shower of twigs fell down on him from a shrieking shell blasting through the treetops. It was like he was watching himself from somewhere above.

"That was our camp just yonder," McManus explained to Milton Bosworth.

Bosworth nodded aggressively. "For once in this battle, I want to capture something, move forward and not back."

"We have them on the wrong foot now," Lockett observed. His brow knit itself in determination and an intense, gray-eyed mask came over his face. "We take this field, and they will be in full retreat then."

"You sure?"

"I guarantee it, sergeant. You men, we lost at every turn yesterday!"

His small, mismatched company was listening intently to him now.

"We've been pushed and pushed. Not one of us here knows what it is like to capture ground and hold it." The uncomfortable reminder caused a few to nod. "God as my witness, we'll not withdraw this time! We will take this field and our camp back!"

His little company gave a resounding, "Huzzah!" Then, from somewhere down the line, another deep, guttural "Huzzah!" sounded, and then another, and another, far beyond where his voice could possibly have carried. His insignificant little company was not the only one ready to advance!

Minutes later, the order came, and the entire line started forward, disjointed at first, and then with each man shoulder to shoulder with the next.

Milton Bosworth gave a loud whoop and raised his rifle in the air with a clenched fist.

In front and behind them, shells burst, sending dirt into the air, but Lockett did not notice. His eyes were anchored across the field, as if that could calm the nauseating fear that tried to grow inside of him.

"One final push will break them!" A galloping colonel yelled as he rode behind the advancing line.

The shriek of another shell, close over head, made many men duck on instinct, but Lockett continued forward, as if unimpressed by the near miss. His men struggled but succeeded in keeping up with him.

Confederate musket shots cracked through the air. Some zinged by overhead; some ploughed into the muddy ground in front of them; some thudded sickeningly into the blue line.

One company of Federals stopped to return fire and reload, but Lockett and his men continued forward, holding their fire until they were closer, oblivious to it all – the eye-watering smoke, the sickening smell of powder and flesh, the deafening and unceasing roar of the guns. These men were all too familiar with it now.

They were halfway across the field, and he watched impotently as a Rebel artillery man adjusted his aim. The Rebel finished ramming home a load of canister shot, just as a Union shell exploded behind him, showering him with dirt and smoke and causing the gunner to drop to his knees, but it was not enough. A different Rebel ran forward and pulled the chord attached to the lanyard, igniting the touchhole of the gun.

Like a giant shotgun, the cannon sprayed death around Lockett. Some lead balls flew overhead, many hit the soft ground in front of the advancing line. Some of those deadly balls buried themselves in the soft mud, but many bounced up, still capable of shattering a man's leg or tearing into his lower torso.

But most of the canister ripped directly into the line. The Iowan to his right dropped to his knees immediately, howling and holding his face with both hands before falling abruptly silent.

Instinctively, Lockett grabbed the man's rifle as he marched by. He felt naked with only Ainsley's sword in hand.

The Federal rifle fire began to intensify as fewer and fewer men held back. The thickly packed Union troops began to have an effect, and he started to notice small gaps appearing in the thin Rebel line. No longer were the butternut clad Rebels one long line of men, shoulder to shoulder. Their ranks had been thinned considerably.

In the middle of the defense, another Rebel gunner began to reload his cannon as Lockett and the others drew even closer. They were less than fifty yards away, and the Union artillery had stopped for fear of hitting their own.

Musket balls zipped around him from the artillery's supporting infantry.

The Rebel gunner withdrew his ramrod from the cannon's giant muzzle, and Lockett could see that they were seconds away from firing another devastating blast of canister. A few

Federal rifle shots winged off the thick cannon barrel, and Lockett sheathed the Stuart family sword and readied the dead Iowan's rifle on his shoulder.

Peering down the long barrel of the Enfield rifle, he could see the large black hole of the cannon's muzzle aimed directly at him and for a moment there was nothing in the world besides him and the cannon. There was no sound as he watched the Rebel place the lanyard in the Napoleon cannon's touchhole.

The gunner stepped back, ready to touch off the shot.

Lockett pulled the trigger, his Minié ball spinning through the air, racing against the cannoneer's arm as he stretched the triggering cord taunt. Time seemed to stand still as Lockett looked down the length of the rifle and watched certain death await him.

But the instant before the man could pull the lanyard free and fire the Napoleon, Lockett's shot hit square in the man's chest. Like a mule kick, the man collapsed inward, arms flapping and the cord slipping from his grasp.

The Federal line rushed forward on the Southerners.

Rebel reinforcements emerged from the woods behind the cannon, but not to fire. They came to pull their cannon away from the advancing Yankees, to remove them to safer ground. They stiffened their defense and met the Yankee charge, trying to give the gunners enough time to get away with their Napoleons and Howitzers.

The Confederate infantry succeeded in giving them time to hastily withdraw their cannon, but the battle had been won. The retreat was on.

The battle swirled for a few minutes more, but the outcome was never in doubt. Barnes Field was theirs.

Epilogue

Three hours later, James Lockett and Patrick McManus walked into their old camp with the rest of Crittenden's men.

Across Pittsburg Landing, the Confederate line had given way – on the right, in the middle, and on the left. The Confederates were now in full retreat back to Corinth. The sound of rear-guard action could still be heard, but for Lockett and most of the Yankees and Rebels, the battle of Shiloh was over.

As they made their way back to what had been Peabody's camp and then a Confederate camp for Breckinridge's men the next night, Lockett searched for his old tent.

Milton Bosworth and Patrick McManus watched curiously as he stepped around the face down body of a Rebel and peered into his tent. It was still standing despite being ripped and torn with bullets.

His bedroll was gone, but he could see his journal and pencil exactly where he had left them, as if he had just returned from his patrol with Major Powell. Gathering them up, he said nothing as he rubbed the leather bound book, his mind flashing from one event to another.

They had survived. Somehow, God in Heaven, they had survived!

With a silent whisper, he thanked God for his protection, and in his next breath asked that the war end, but in his heart, he knew the end was not near.

Peering in from the opening of the tent with his finger poking one of the bullet holes, Milton Bosworth cleared his throat, "Ah, Lieutenant, sir? Are you all right?"

"Fine, Milton," Lockett answered, "I just wanted to see if my journal was still here."

"Gonna do some writin' about all this here?" When Lockett said nothing, Milton Bosworth added, "It'll make a fine story, sir."

"Milton," Lockett said with a pause, looking up at Patrick McManus standing behind the Ohioan, "*I fear this story is only beginning...*"

Historical Background

Lockett's Innocence is a work of historical fiction, emphasis on historical, because as the saying goes, sometimes truth is stranger than fiction. While the central characters of James, Patrick, Ainsley, Luke, and Matthew are fictional, the attitudes, events, and paths of the various regiments are based on historical fact and timelines.

At all times, I did try to maintain historical accuracy. Following are some brief historical footnotes that I made in exploring the history. In the rare case where I did take literary license, you will find it here.

Section I - The Boys From Kalamazoo

While the Kalamazoo Sharpshooters are fictional (based loosely on actual units with fanciful names at the start of the war like the Coldwater Cadets, Jackson Grays, and Michigan Hussars), Birge's Western Sharpshooters did exist. Their path and experiences are what the Kalamazoo Sharpshooters followed and experienced.

Truly a combination of farm boys from various states, (primarily Illinois, Wisconsin, and Michigan), Colonel Birge's men fought bushwhackers in Missouri, silenced the cannon at Fort Donelson, and found themselves on the bloody fields of Shiloh. Though their name changed later in the war to the 14th Missouri and then the 66th Illinois, most still referred to them by their original name, the Western Sharpshooters.

The state of Michigan was aflame with the early fervor surrounding the Civil War. When President Lincoln asked for volunteers, Michigan was among the first to answer the call. By the opening battle of the war, the first battle of Bull Run, only one Western state managed to send a regiment to Washington D.C. in time. Michigan's quick answer to the call led President Lincoln to proclaim his famous, “Thank God for Michigan!”

Fueled by anti-slavery hotbeds and Underground Railroad stops, Michigan soon found itself with more volunteers than needed for President Lincoln’s quota. Many Michigan men found themselves helping other states fill their quotas and serving in their regiments.

As might have been expected, the experiences of the civilian soldiers at the start of the war began inauspiciously. The Western Sharpshooters’ time in the Benton Barracks in St. Louis gave them an introduction to the army, but what most of them recalled was the general disorder of trying to get weapons, uniforms, and having to spend time making their own bullets.

Missouri itself was at times a raw introduction to a section of the country and sentiment that most had not seen firsthand. Missouri had been engulfed with internecine warfare long before the arrival of the Western Sharpshooters. The political and vigilante maneuverings of the “Wide Awakes” in St. Louis was of particular importance as their possession of the Federal Armory was a serious blow to Confederate fortunes in Missouri and the West in general.

But eventually the Western Sharpshooters left St. Louis and began their often fruitless task of taking on bushwhackers and trying to maintain uneasy relations with the local population.

One company of Western Sharpshooters did suffer a stinging defeat at Hallsville, but Colonel Birge’s men redeemed themselves with a resounding victory the following day at Mount Zion. This devastated bushwhacker activities in that part of Missouri.

While Matthew’s and Luke’s encounter with bushwhackers and the escape via railroad handcar sounds like fiction, it is actually based on the accounts of one of the Michigan boys of Company D in the Western Sharpshooters.

Section II - Separate Paths To...

Section II begins with James and Patrick returning to Kalamazoo, and the reader meets Katherine Moffat and Ainsley Stuart. To be clear, while the Moffats were one of the founders of Kalamazoo, and Senator Charles Stuart was one of the most popular and well-known individuals in the state, there was no Katherine Moffat or Ainsley Stuart. Nor are they based on anyone. They are simply fictional characters.

And while the boys from Kalamazoo end up taking different paths to Shiloh, there are two significant historical events that occur first, witnessed from the Confederate side by the Cameron brothers and from the Union side through Luke and Matthew.

The first historical event is the capture of Fort Henry along the banks of the Tennessee River. One of a number of forts constructed in Tennessee to protect the state from invasion, Fort Henry was not well located, to put it mildly.

The site was selected perhaps more for its expediency than any true topographical advantage. Seventeen guns were mounted inside the fortified position, eleven directed towards the river and six towards the landward side, which was further protected by 12,000 yards of trenches and rifle pits.

The fort was on low terrain and commanded by higher ground on both sides of the river. Worse yet, its low-lying nature made it prone to the waters of the river itself. At one point, the fort was inundated with two feet of water.

Despite these drawbacks, the Confederacy attempted to defend it against Union gunboats on the morning of February 6, 1862; however, as the Cameron brothers witnessed, it was a brave but doomed attempt. By 2 p.m., the Confederates waved a flag of truce and shortly after 3 p.m., General Grant and an assortment of Union navy and army men had taken control of the still smoldering fort.

Next up for the Union was the more daunting task of taking Fort Donelson, but the easy capture of Fort Henry gave the Union a dangerous overconfidence. Unwilling to wait for any reinforcements, General Grant began the short march from Fort Henry to Fort Donelson. In their urgency to attack before the Confederacy could regroup, the overland march was conducted with orders that each regiment (roughly a thousand men per regiment) would have only four wagons for supplies, a wildly insufficient amount of support.

This was further exacerbated by the initial warm weather causing many of the men to discard their blankets and heavier articles of clothing only to find a half day later that the weather took a sudden turn towards bitter cold and snow.

Adding to the challenge, Fort Donelson was no Fort Henry. Located on a ridgeline above the river, Fort Donelson covered about 60 acres, and its walls and parapets jogged back-and-forth along the contours of a ridge. These were further protected by significant rifle pits, entrenchments, and abatis.

Difficult conditions aside, the Union spirits were still high, and many expected a short, nearly bloodless victory again, like they had done at Fort Henry. There was a certainty that Admiral Foote and his gunboats would dominate again and force the fort into submission.

On February 14, the gunboats churned slowly towards the fort. Initially, things looked grim within the fort.

The quote within the story of, "Parson, for God's sake pray! Nothing but God Almighty can save the fort," is an actual quote from Confederate Nathan Bedford Forrest. And it did seem as if the fort would eventually be pounded into submission, but a tactical mistake may have saved them from that fate. While the gunboats and their heavy guns had the advantage from a distance, the boats eventually strayed too close to the fort, coming within more effective range for the many Confederate 32-pound cannon. The ironclads were repeatedly struck. Two of the gunboats collided while the *St. Louis* had her pilothouse wrecked by a well aimed shot, and the *Carondolet* was struck 35 times, including below the waterline. By 5 p.m., the gunboats were forced to withdraw, leaving General Grant with a new problem since he had really made no plans to take the fort except by gunboat.

He comforted himself with the certainty that he had time to

devise something since he was sure that the Confederates would not go on the attack…

But overnight, Confederate General Floyd had come to the conclusion that they needed to break out of the Yankee encirclement. While both armies suffered from the cold overnight, the Union did not notice the preparations going on inside the fort. The Confederates left just a single regiment to protect the fort from the Union's left flank, and at first light in the morning, the Confederates launched their assault on the unsuspecting Federal's extreme right flank.

By noon, they had pushed the Union so far back that Grant's men had lost control of the coveted Charlotte Road. The road to escape was open, and yet valuable Confederate troops were ordered back to the fort to protect it from the attack that Union General Smith was successfully launching at the opposite end of Fort Donelson.

Amazingly, the charge of General C.F. Smith is true to life. Time and time again in researching the capture of Fort Donelson, I found account after account describing their astonishment and exhilaration in seeing their General Smith proud and erect in his saddle, leading the charge through the abatis as if protected by God himself. For whatever divine reason, despite drawing much of the Rebel fire, General Smith was never hit during his audacious assault.

As night fell across the area, the Union army was clearly in a place to finish Fort Donelson in the morning. That night, Confederate General Floyd met with his generals, and it was decided that they would surrender Fort Donelson (although not until Floyd himself had made an escape).

Luckily for the Cameron brothers, Confederate Nathan Bedford Forrest did not agree, saying, "I did not come here for the purpose of surrendering my command, and I will not do it if they follow me out."

Taking his men and a few others, they found one remaining open road and made their escape.

This was a particularly important fact for the story since the reader really needed the Cameron brothers to get to Corinth so that they could see the difficult march from Corinth to Shiloh.

Despite Forrest's escape, Fort Donelson was a terrible loss for the Confederacy. About 2,000 of their soldiers were killed or wounded, and 12,000 to 15,000 valuable soldiers were captured. General Grant's losses were about 2,600 killed or wounded.

With the fall of Fort Donelson, Union spirits in the West hit astronomical heights…

Section III - ...Shiloh

Section III opens with the Sharpshooters arriving with Lauman's Brigade in Savannah, Tennessee, where interestingly some of the locals joined the 46th Ohio.

As depicted in the story, confidence was sky high and nearly everyone thought the war was near its end. The quote to the troops from Iowa's Governor Kirkwood is included within the story, but other telling ones abound also.

General Grant wrote to his wife, declaring that there would be one more "big fight" and that "it appears to me to be the last in the West."

General Lew Wallace similarly stated that the rebellion "is closing fast."

That level of confidence permeated down to all ranks, and the common soldiers were similarly certain that the war was near its end.

Even the untimely injuries to General Smith and General Grant did nothing to slow the enthusiasm. But their absence from the field at the start of the battle and in the critical days leading up to it create one of the many 'what if…' questions that abound with Shiloh.

Would General Smith, for example, have recognized the many clues and realized that the Confederate Army had left Corinth? It is certainly possible that the experienced veteran (and West Point teacher of Grant, Sherman, and many of the generals on the Confederate side) might have realized that something was afoot. Without that initial element of surprise, the battle of Shiloh would have looked very different.

Unfortunately for the Union, Smith was incapacitated by the injury to his shins. Even with the precaution of resting in Savannah, the injury became infected, and he died in Savannah a few weeks after the battle.

While Confederate General Albert S. Johnston wrestled with how best to defend Corinth, particularly in light of the possibility of Buell linking up with Grant to double the Union strength, there was really little choice. He had to attack before the linkage was made.

But as they say about the best laid plans, the Confederate march from Corinth to Shiloh was an agonizingly slow and disjointed disaster. Between the weather and the army's inexperience at executing a large scale troop movement (and all the logistics that go with that), what should have taken one to two days turned into many days, and it is frankly quite shocking that the element of surprise was maintained.

Hopefully, the reader was able to see through the eyes of James Lockett, Ainsley Stuart, Milton Bosworth, and Luke Bailey to understand the many different opportunities that the Union Army had to recognize what was happening.

As I like to do with the historic people who are in the story, I try to use as many direct quotes as possible. This is including General Sherman's disbelief at what was being reported and his belittling comments to his fellow Ohioans, calling them "washerwomen", "green buckeyes", telling them to go home, and wanting the sergeant arrested who reported seeing the mass of Confederates. He just could not conceive of the Confederates leaving Corinth and attacking. It wasn't until he saw the first Rebels appear from the thicket outside his own tents, having them kill his orderly, and wound him with buckshot in his hand that he realized the reality of the threat.

As for Confederate generals Johnston and Beauregard, I also tried to use as many quotes as possible. For Beauregard, the element of surprise seemed impossible after the numerous delays and the smattering of run-ins with various Union forces.

It is hard to say if General Johnston truly believed that he still had the element of surprise. His words and actions certainly suggest that he did, although one must wonder if that was just a front put up by the man in charge, knowing that he had to attack before Buell arrived – with or without an element of surprise.

Regardless, as Beauregard presciently observed, it would be a difficult day. "In the struggle tomorrow, we shall be fighting men of our own blood, Western men, who understand the use of firearms. The struggle will be a desperate one."

And desperate it was.

In spite of all the warnings, the element of surprise still existed. Were it not for Major Powell's patrol, it would have been a complete surprise.

Despite his superiors' lack of concern and fully knowing that there were standing orders not to bring on any engagement, Colonel Everett Peabody sent Major James Powell and scouts from the 25th Missouri out at midnight to see what they could find. They returned only a couple of hours later, having located some sort of Confederate presence in the dark. Shortly before 3 a.m., Peabody directed Powell to go out again, this time with 3 companies from the 25th Missouri and a detachment from the 12th Michigan.

It remains unclear to this day why the detachment of the 12th Michigan went out with the Missourians. Perhaps they were just awake and available in the middle of the night, like Lockett and his comrades were in the story.

In any case, the 200 men slowly made their way through the dark of night. Their encounters were as described in Section III. First, they came upon Confederate videttes (sentinels on horseback), then skirmishers, and then something much more significant.

In the growing light of the early morning, it became painfully clear to the little patrol that something momentous was happening. It does not take much imagination to imagine the shock of the initial contact, or how galling it would have been when they were castigated by Colonel Moore of the 21st

Missouri for falling back. His overconfidence was quickly shattered. In the first volley that he saw, his leg was seriously wounded, and he was dragged from the field.

With at least some warning now, piecemeal parts of the Union army fought to slow the leviathan moving upon them. Foolish recriminations from General Prentiss to Colonel Peabody for "bringing on the attack" aside, Prentiss and his men did the best they could under the circumstances to slow the Confederate army, but truth be told, the dense thickets and the presence of food (and booty) in the Union camps, did more to slow the advance than anything else.

Through the eyes of the Cameron brothers and then Milton Bosworth, I attempted to give the reader a view of the Confederate attack on Sherman's camps and the disintegration of Colonel Appler and half of his 53rd Ohio.

Writing after the battle and then even after the war, Sherman denied that the division had been surprised, but that was clearly not true. In fact, even Sherman eventually admitted in one letter to his brother that "I confess I did not think Beauregard would abandon his railroad to attack us on our base."

Or perhaps it was more clearly stated by a lieutenant in the 15th Illinois, "Surprise was never more complete."

What perhaps makes this more astounding is that even after the initial fight began with Powell's patrol and then later parts of Peabody's Brigade, much of the Union army still had no idea what was happening. Some went about their normal morning routines thinking that the sounds were mere skirmishing between the pickets or excessive target practice by other Union soldiers or even a deranged regimental colonel who had his soldiers doing live fire drills first thing on a Sunday morning.

For readers who might wonder what happened to some of the primary historical people at Shiloh, here is a quick summary.

Colonel Peabody was killed, shot in the head in those early defensive stands, as covered in Chapter 20.

Major Powell survived the initial onslaught and was heavily engaged throughout the day. He was wounded 11 times before being taken from the field. The last wound proved fatal, and he died that night.

General Prentiss, after leading the spirited defense at the sunken road, was captured when the Hornet's Nest was surrounded and fell. Taken to General Beauregard overnight, he declared to the Louisianan that Buell had arrived and that the Confederates would be trounced the next day. That seems more like bravado than actual knowledge on Prentiss's part, but it did prove true.

But no story about Shiloh could be complete without covering the Hornet's Nest and the Peach Orchard.

The Peach Orchard is one of the most incompatible imageries that one can envision – delicate white and pink blossoms floating through the air like snow flurries at first and then in a near blizzard of blossoms. All stirred up by intense gunfire and artillery explosions from a horrific clash. Gentle blossoms drifting in the air, death all around.

The sharp infantry and artillery fighting flowed back and forth, with both sides taking heavy losses. Taking matters into his own hands, General Albert S. Johnston rode up, curiously waving a tin cup that he had taken from a Union camp, and urged, "Men of Arkansas, you who boast of using cold steel, don't waste your ammunition. Come and show us what you can do with the bayonet."

Rallying, they charged again and forced McArthur's Illinoisans and Lauman's Hoosiers and Kentuckians back. Inevitably, the rest of the line caved, and the Peach Orchard fell. But Johnston's lingering near the front eventually cost him his life. A short while later, he was shot behind the knee, and the blood drained unseen into his tall riding boot. When he collapsed and his aides searched frantically for the wound, it was not found until too late.

Shortly after 3 p.m., General P.G.T. Beauregard took charge of the Confederate Army.

As the Peach Orchard fell, that left only the 'Hornet's Nest' along the sunken road to bar the way. For hours, it had stubbornly resisted one Confederate charge after another, providing Grant's Chief of Staff, Colonel Joseph D. Webster, vital time to create one last line of defense.

For those who have visited the Shiloh battlefield, they will be surprised by how unremarkable the sunken road appears today. It is certainly nothing so dramatic as the sunken road (Bloody Lane) at Antietam for example. In fact, much of it seems hardly 'sunken' at all. Accounts from immediately after the battle and even in memoirs shortly after the war give it varying degrees of depth, ranging from 8 inches to 3 feet. I opted for what seemed the most consistent depth of approximately 1.5 feet, which is similar to the description of Private Charles Morton of the 25th Missouri who described it as, "about fifteen inches or more deep, affording excellent cover and good rest wile firing."

The washed out road doesn't sound like much, but when combined with some fence railing, an extremely dense thicket, and artillery protecting the flanks, the Union turned it into one of the most remarkable pieces of defensive ground in the entire Civil War.

Brigade after brigade attempted to take it – Stewart, Johnson, Anderson, Russell, Gibson, and Cleburne. Each Confederate brigade was battered senseless in their attempts.

Finally, the Confederates opted for a new approach and gathered virtually every cannon that they had on the battlefield. Approximately 60 artillery pieces pounded the Hornet's Nest for 40 minutes. Finally, with that bombardment and the Union pullback on the flanks, the Hornet's Nest fell, but not until they had provided Grant's army with the crucial hours it needed to gather itself and pull in more reinforcements.

As night fell across the horrific and gruesome landscape, now littered with thousands of dead and wounded, the Confederate Army caught its breath and wearily rested, confident that the next morning would yield total victory against their defeated opponent. Beauregard telegraphed Richmond that he had won "a complete victory."

In fairness to the Confederates, it is easy to see why they thought victory was at hand. They had pushed through an enormous amount of ground, captured thousands of Union soldiers, and taken possession of their camps. Any visitor to the battlefield today will absolutely be struck by how far the Confederates advanced and how little land was left behind Grant's Last Line of defense. They really were backed nearly into the river.

However, as the Cameron brothers overheard Forrest's concerned remarks to Cleburne that night. The Union was being significantly reinforced by fresh troops. First of all, General Lew Wallace and his wayward division had now filled in on Grant's right after marching in the wrong direction. Instead of arriving in the late morning of the battle's first day, or worst case early afternoon, they did not arrive from their six mile march until 7 p.m.

Of even greater importance, General Buell and his multiple divisions had arrived. Grant now outnumbered his foe almost two to one, and just as importantly, half of his men were fresh.

By early morning, it was clear that day two of Shiloh would be very different. Grant's fresh troops pressed forward aggressively on both flanks while Sherman's and McClernand's survivors pushed up the middle. Like a boxer being battered from a flurry of punches, the Confederates staggered backwards throughout the morning. Attempted counterattacks bought only brief respites and by the afternoon, the exhausted Confederate Army withdrew, wearily heading back down the same roads to Corinth.

It is here that I would like to note the one small bit of literary license that I took. In Chapter 25, Lockett and McManus find the wounded and unconscious Ainsley Stuart next to the now one-armed John Wesley Powell. Yes, that is the same John Wesley Powell who went on to become the remarkable Western explorer and first to raft the length of the Grand Canyon.

Powell was at Shiloh and wounded on April 6 in the Hornet's Nest, but he was luckier than Ainsley Stuart and many others who suffered in the mud outside makeshift field hospitals that night. Powell was one of the wounded who was evacuated by steamer that day upriver to Savannah, Tennessee.

Two days after the battle, his right arm was amputated, and after a touch and go recovery, he actually recovered enough to rejoin his artillery unit later in the war, before going onto great feats of exploration, one-armed and all.

Powell was not the only significant person who found himself on the horrific battlefield that Shiloh was. Besides Grant and Sherman, other future leaders of note included 20th President of the United States James Garfield and 23rd President Benjamin Harrison. In addition to them, there was the oft-derided General Lew Wallace, who later went on to write the famous novel, *Ben Hur*.

The battle of Shiloh was the bloodiest event in American history up to that point in time. By the end of April 7, more American soldiers had died in that one battle than in all American wars combined!

Historians can only speculate why Generals Sherman and Grant were so oblivious to the looming Confederate threat. Were it not for Colonel Peabody's disregard for orders and sending out Major Powell's patrol, the outcome of the battle and maybe the war would have been quite different. The warning that the patrol gave the Union army, while partially ignored, did save them from waking to find 40,000 Confederates in their camp.

Even with the warning, it was only the stubborn resistance on the sunken road for nearly six hours that saved Grant's army from complete destruction.

As with many Civil War battles, there is a *"what if"* to add to the intrigue or the significance. There are many "what if" questions that people have pondered over the years, such as what if Johnston had not been killed? What if the Confederates had done the rare thing and continued the attack at night? What if Peabody had not sent out Powell's patrol?

But perhaps the most consequential of any of these, is what if the Union had lost this battle? They were certainly close to utter defeat. Grant and Sherman would have been totally discredited and never given charge of an army again. How would future Union fortunes have looked without Grant and Sherman on the scene?

But that is not what happened, and it is only 1862. The war has only just begun, and it is after Shiloh that the Union finally comes to the grim realization that this war will not be won so easily.

James Lockett and his comrades know that with total certainty. There will be many more battles before Lockett can return to Kalamazoo…

ABOUT THE AUTHOR

A Michigan native, T.J. Johnston is the author of the James Lockett Civil War historical fiction series, including *Lockett's Innocence*, *Lockett's Betrayal, Lockett's Crucible,* and *Lockett and the Devil's Path*.

A history lover, a long-time author, and a believer in the importance and gripping tension of accurate history, he has degrees from Hope College and Michigan State University. He currently resides in Texas where he is working on subsequent historical and mystery novels.

www.ingramcontent.com/pod-product-compliance
Lightning Source LLC
Chambersburg PA
CBHW021432240626
47153CB00001B/122

* 9 7 9 8 9 9 1 9 3 8 4 0 2 *